THE PORTAL

A DELPHI GROUP THRILLER

JOHN SNEEDEN

The Portal
Copyright © 2015 by John Sneeden

All rights reserved. No part of this book may be used or reproduced by any means whatsoever without express written permission of the author, except in the case of brief quotations embodied in critical articles and reviews.

This is a work of fiction. Names, characters, businesses, places, events and incidents are either the products of the author's imagination or used in a fictitious manner. Any resemblance to actual persons, living or dead, or actual events is purely coincidental.

Cover design by Damonza
Formatting by Polgarus Studio

ISBN-13: 978-0-9907112-3-0 (Paperback Edition)
ISBN-13: 978-0-9907112-4-7 (ePub Edition)

To my dad, James Sneeden. I miss you.

Be among the first to learn about John's future releases and special discounts by signing up for his newsletter at:

www.johnsneeden.com/?page_id=108

The process is quick and simple. Your email address will not be sold to anyone else, and the newsletter will only be used to inform readers of new releases or special discounts.

"The Nephilim were on the earth in those days, and also afterward, when the sons of God came in to the daughters of man and they bore children to them. These were the mighty men who were of old, the men of renown."
Genesis 6:4

"There were two hundred, total, that descended in the days of Jared upon Ardis, the summit of Mount Hermon."
The Book of Enoch 6:5

CHAPTER ONE

Taipei City, Taiwan

THEY SAY THE most critical battles of espionage are won through attention to detail. David Parsons didn't know who *they* were, but he'd learned the hard way *they* were right. In a subsequent debrief of the evening's events, he would confess to a number of sins, but one in particular proved to be the most egregious. He had violated one of the agency's most fundamental rules when working in the field: never, *never*, drink more alcohol than your target.

And Parsons hadn't just broken that simple maxim, he'd trampled it, spit on it, then beat it with a baseball bat. And when he had, he'd immediately ceded control to one Wu Mei-ling, the woman who was supposed to have been putty in his hands.

The disastrous night began auspiciously at a four-star Indian restaurant in central Taipei. Mei arrived promptly at 7:00 p.m. and was unabashedly ecstatic about the choice. What she may not have realized was that the decision to dine in that particular establishment hadn't been the simple whim of her date. As with all decisions made by the CIA, the choice of restaurant had only been determined after a long and thorough examination of her personal file in Langley, Virginia. Mei's social media posts betrayed a strong penchant for the cuisine of northern India, and Parson's handlers also hoped spicy food might lead to a greater intake of alcohol.

About an hour into the meal, Parsons gestured toward the half-eaten plate of chicken tikka masala in front of Mei. "You're full already?"

She grinned and shrugged. Was the reaction a subtle hint that she was ready to leave? He hoped so.

Parsons didn't think the thirty-four-year-old Chinese national was particularly beautiful, but he did love her smile. He also loved her svelte figure, honed from countless hours at Taipei's most expensive gym.

The CIA had first zeroed in on her father, Wu Shing, almost a year earlier. His profile on the Ministry of Foreign Affairs website indicated he was a low-level diplomat, but as NSA technicians began to peek at his phone records, they discovered something astonishingly contradictory: Shing had a nasty habit of talking to known Chinese defense intelligence experts. His real position, they surmised, was somewhere under the broad umbrella of military technology.

The decision to gather more information on Shing through his daughter Mei hadn't been a particularly difficult one. As agency profilers had perused her social media accounts, they quickly learned that she had a penchant for all things Western, particularly the US art scene. They also learned she had the loosest pair of lips they'd ever seen. Nothing in her life seemed hidden from view. Her Facebook page was littered with the sordid details of her dates. It was also filled with photographs of her frequent attendance at wine tastings, art exhibits, and orchestra performances. One profiler said that calling her an open book was an insult to open books.

The opportunity for first contact had come a month earlier when her name appeared on the guest list of a party given by the American Institute in Taiwan, or AIT. Was her attendance at the gala a hint that she was sympathetic to the West? Did she have her eye on the bigger art scenes of New York and LA? The agency couldn't be sure, but they *were* sure of one thing: they'd never know if they didn't ask.

The job of "wooing Wu," as one low-level Langley technician described it, fell naturally into the hands of Taiwan-based field agent David Parsons. Not only was Parsons a veteran of covert affairs, but he was also markedly handsome. And while the glamorous side of intelligence was often overplayed in espionage films, it certainly didn't hurt when trying to build rapport and gather information.

"Come on." Parsons pushed the bowl toward her with a finger. *Remember, it has to be her decision to leave.* "I know you can do better than that."

"I guess I'm just a little too excited," Mei confessed.

His pulse quickened. Was that the green light he'd been looking for? They had already planned to return to his flat after dinner, but he needed to make sure he didn't push too hard.

He took another sip of champagne and said, "I hope you're not nervous."

She giggled. "I don't know. I just like being with you." Her face reddened. "So yes, I'm probably a little nervous."

"I think you know me pretty well by now." He reached across the table and squeezed her hand. "Which means there's no reason you shouldn't be comfortable around me."

"I just know you come from a rich family, and I'm a simple girl."

Parsons lifted an eyebrow. "Now wait. *I* come from a rich family? What about you? The last time I checked, you were the daughter of a diplomat."

"Yes. But you know that's just a title." She looked over at a couple speaking loudly at the table next to them then turned back to him. "My father is a simple man, and we're a simple family. Remember, I spent most of my life in the country, far away from here." She waved her hand at the restaurant's opulent decor. "This has not always been my life."

He nodded in feigned agreement. Her father was anything but a simple man.

"I do remember that. And it's one of the things I like about you. In America we'd say you're down to earth."

Mei's brow furrowed. "Down to earth?"

"It means you're practical, sensible, easy to talk to." He smiled. "It's a compliment."

As Mei opened her mouth to respond, the server, a tall Indian man with the wispy mustache of a teenager, appeared. Parsons noted a leather check holder tightly clutched in his hand, a not-so-subtle hint that they needed the table. "Can I get you anything else?" the waiter asked.

Parsons did want to leave, but Mei had barely touched her champagne. It was the one piece of the arrangement that concerned him. He was working on his fourth flute, and she'd barely finished her first. He'd have to remedy that back at his flat.

He looked at Mei and raised an eyebrow.

"I'm done," she said.

Parsons looked at the server. "I believe that will be it."

The man bowed slightly then placed the check on the table. "Very well. I'll just leave this with you."

Parsons quickly pulled out a credit card in the name of Peter O'Donnell, placed it in the holder, and handed it back. "Here, you can just take it now. We're in a bit of a hurry."

***

A light drizzle fell as the two stepped into a taxi outside the restaurant. The driver, a heavy smoker of Vietnamese descent, greeted them in broken English as they settled into the back. Parsons leaned forward and gave him the address through the hole in the glass partition.

"I get you there quick," the man assured them with an exaggerated smile.

After barely a glance in the mirror, the cabbie whipped out into the heavy Friday evening traffic. He then directed the car skillfully through the crowded streets of Da'an, the cultural and residential center of Taipei. Despite the weather, Parsons noticed that there were still throngs of stylish female shoppers scurrying in and out of high-end clothing stores and restaurants. *A spot of retail therapy wasn't about to be put on hold because of a little rain*, he thought.

After leaving Da'an and crossing over into Xinyi, the driver slowed the vehicle and pulled up in front of a luxury condominium tower. The rain was coming down harder now, sending torrents of water down the sidewalk. Parsons paid the fare then stepped out and opened his umbrella. After taking Mei's hand, he escorted her into the front lobby.

As they crossed the shiny tiled floor of the atrium, Parsons glanced over at his date. Her eyes widened at the building's opulence, although the gesture seemed a bit contrived.

Still trying to play the role of the country girl.

Mei caught him looking at her and said, "It's beautiful. I feel so out of place."

Parsons had to admit that his current cover was about the best that agency money could buy. It was a time of austerity for most regions, but not Taipei. Despite the communist facade, Chinese hierarchy was impressed with money, and in order to penetrate their world you needed copious amounts of it.

"Sometimes I do too." He put a hand on her waist as they approached a bank of elevators.

A concierge stood just to the right. He bowed and greeted them in flawless English. "Good evening, Mr. O'Donnell."

"Thank you, Han."

A minute later, they exited onto the thirty-fifth floor. As they turned down the hall, Mei slipped her arm through his. He smiled.

"So beautiful," she said, admiring the marble floor in the

corridor. "I think you're too good for me." She poked him gently in the ribs.

"Don't be silly. Do I act like I'm too good for you?" He leaned over and gave her a quick peck on the lips.

Moments later they arrived at his door. Parsons stepped in front of Mei, inserted his key card into the metal slot, and typed in a seven-digit code. After a two-second pause, the light at the top of the panel turned green and a lock clicked loudly.

The interior was dark when they entered. Parsons felt around until he found the dimmer switch on the wall. He pressed it, and the darkness slowly transitioned to a soft glow.

"Welcome," he said, waving her in.

"Oh my, I ..." Mei said as she walked out of the foyer and into the living room.

The flat was decorated in a decidedly contemporary style, with smooth stone walls and a sprinkling of Scandinavian furniture. Beyond the living room was an open kitchen and dining area. Both shared a floor-to-ceiling glass window looking out over suburban Taipei.

Mei walked through the dining room and stood at the window, taking in the view. "I've never seen the city from here."

Parsons joined her at the glass. "Compliments of my father's company."

Mei seemed to stare at a nearby condominium tower before shifting her gaze toward the twinkling lights of downtown Taipei in the distance. Finally, she turned and looked at him. "I'm sorry?"

"The view... it's compliments of my father's company. Do

you like it?"

"Do I like it?" She looked back through the glass. "I think I could really get used to this."

"Well, first things first," Parsons said, crossing into the kitchen. "For now, how about just telling me what you'd like to drink?"

"I'll have whatever you're having."

"Make yourself at home," he said, nodding toward the living room. He plucked two glasses from the hanger under the cabinet then pulled a bottle of chilled sauvignon blanc from the fridge.

While pouring the wine, he watched Mei walk over and sink into the couch, crossing one leg over the other. He lifted an eyebrow then returned his attention to the wine.

"You know, you never tell me much about your father's business," she said. "I don't even know what you do."

Parsons stopped pouring for a moment, pondering his answer. "I will." He finished pouring the wine, picked up both glasses, and left the kitchen. "My father is a very private man." He handed a glass to Mei then set his on the end table. "His export business has been wildly successful and… well, he's humble and doesn't like to advertise the fact that he's done so well. And frankly, I try to respect that."

"No, I understand." As Mei lifted the glass, it slipped awkwardly out of her hand, soaking her dress before she caught it. "Oh my!" she said, standing up and wiping herself with a bare hand. "I'm so clumsy."

"You know, there are better ways to proposition me," Parsons quipped as he stood.

She popped him playfully on the arm. "You're naughty."

He leaned over and gave her a quick kiss. "Let me get you another glass and a towel."

"Thank you. I'm so sorry."

"Don't worry. There's more where that came from."

Parsons took her glass and returned to the kitchen. He uncorked the bottle and filled the glass once again, this time almost to the top.

He paused and tried to formulate a way forward from here. How far should he take the conversation tonight? The psychologists at Langley had warned him against trying to push too far too fast, but if she wanted to talk, why stop her? As he re-corked the bottle, Parsons decided to play it safe. In the spy business, patience was an agent's best friend.

"If you don't have enough wine—"

"I have plenty!" he said. "Be right there."

He was still disturbed that she had been so cautious in her alcohol consumption. Conversely, he was also disappointed in himself that he'd pushed beyond his usual limit. One more glass to make her comfortable, then he'd be done.

After grabbing a towel, Parsons returned to the couch. "Here you are," he said, setting her glass on the table and handing her the towel.

He settled in next to her and drained the remainder of his sauvignon blanc.

"I've never done this before," Mei said as she wiped her dress. "I'm so embarrassed."

"Don't be."

Finally Mei threw the towel onto the table and leaned into

him. "You sure you can forgive me for being so clumsy?"

"I don't know. I may need a little convincing." He cupped her chin and gently pulled her mouth toward his. Their lips pressed together as their arms encircled one another. Parsons felt the warmth of her embrace and began to nibble on her neck. Mei tilted her head back slightly.

Suddenly he stopped and pulled back, rubbing his temple.

"What's wrong?" Mei asked, forming her mouth into a pout. "I'm not making you happy."

Parsons looked around the room. Even though he was seated, it seemed to wobble slightly. He felt like a child who'd been swung around in the air then placed down and asked to stand.

"No, of course you make me happy." He looked at her. The image of her face was fuzzy, so he rubbed his eyes. "I'm not sure what it is. Probably the combination of champagne and wine. Just hit me a little hard."

She tapped the end of his nose. "I warned you not to drink too much."

She was right. He should have stopped drinking a long time ago. Then again, it seemed odd for his body to react this way. He wasn't used to drinking champagne, so maybe the carbonation was the culprit.

"You sure you're okay?" she asked.

He suddenly found it hard to combat the feeling of drifting off. "Sorry..."

Mei pulled him closer, rubbing the back of his head gently. "Just relax."

THE PORTAL

***

After his eyes closed, Mei asked the man she knew as Peter a few questions in the silly voice she'd been practicing for weeks. Hearing no response, she poked his head gently several times. Still nothing. The pill had done its work, and even sooner than she'd expected. The idiot had probably quickened the process by drinking so much.

Satisfied that he was completely out, she propped his body against the back of the couch, slamming his arm roughly against the cushion. It was all she could do not to spit on the American pig.

Mei stood and reached into her purse. She pulled out two latex gloves and a laser pointer. After glancing at the man one more time, she crossed the room and turned off the lights. She then walked quickly over to the window in the dining area, staring at a condo tower one block away. After counting off floors, she turned on the pointer and aimed the red dot at a window with a small statue perched on its sill.

She waited patiently. She knew a surveillance team was hidden there, the same team that had been watching the American for the last three weeks. Seconds later, the curtain moved slightly, and a red light flashed three times.

No one had followed them, and she was free to proceed.

Mei turned off the pointer and returned to the living room, approaching a series of cabinets built into a wall near the front door. She pulled on the latex gloves and opened the cabinet on the far right. She pushed a few books aside and found what she was looking for, a small gray safe. She entered a memorized code on the pad to the right. It contained twenty-one digits, but her entry was flawless. Seconds later, a tiny light to the right of the pad shone green. She turned the handle and opened the door.

Perfect. The customized computer tablet was right where her people had said it would be. She slid it out carefully and returned to the couch.

After powering up the device, she reached into her purse and retrieved a thumb drive. Before proceeding, she glanced over at the American. His eyes were still closed, and his breathing was regular.

"In a few hours, we'll know exactly who you really are," she whispered in Chinese.

Turning back to her work, Mei snapped the thumb drive into a slot on the side of the tablet. Seconds later, a box popped up on the home screen, and a bar began to fill from left to right. The Trojan was loading. About a minute later, the bar had filled completely, and Mei removed the drive. She then shut the tablet down, walked over to the safe, and placed it inside, careful to position it precisely where it had been before.

Once she had moved the books back into place and closed the cabinet door, she returned to the couch and sat down next to the American. She pulled his left arm over her shoulder and snuggled up against him, settling in for the half hour it would take for him to wake up.

CHAPTER TWO

Sandpoint, Idaho

ZANE WATSON'S ARM snapped forward, sending his line looping out over the cold, clear water of the stream. The fly landed so softly that it barely made a disturbance on the surface.

Come on, I know you're there.

The gentle movement of the water carried it a few inches, causing it to spin and twirl invitingly. The operative waited patiently, confident the sheltered cove would yield another strike.

Suddenly he saw a hint of movement as a dark silhouette rose out of the depths. It seemed to hesitate, but seconds later the water swirled violently and the fly disappeared.

He turned the reel firmly, enjoying the light but feisty tugs. Despite its size, the fish made several good runs before finding itself spinning in the confines of an oversized net. Reaching down into the cold water, Zane closed his hand around the slippery body and lifted it gently into the air. He took a moment to admire one of the masterpieces of nature. A smudged pink line ran the length of its body, surrounded by a sea of black dots that looked like they'd been painted there by an artist flicking a wet paintbrush. In terms of beauty, the rainbow trout had no rivals.

Zane had already released four that afternoon, which meant this one was going to take up residence in a pan back at the lodge. His stomach growled at the thought of a plate filled with fried trout, wild rice, and roasted asparagus.

The operative paused and thought back over the last several days. The remote vacation had been just what he'd needed. The lodge and the hundred acres it sat on were owned by CIA field officer Garet Slater, who had inherited it from a wealthy uncle with no kids. Since the two had time off, Slater had invited Zane to join him for a week in the wilderness. They would hike and fish during the day and share war stories over cigars and cognac at night.

Unfortunately those well-laid plans had been dashed when Slater was called back to Langley on the day he was to leave. Instead of fishing and smoking cigars, he would be boarding a white Gulfstream GV at Andrews Air Force Base. National security was calling him to an undisclosed location.

A generous man, Slater had told his friend to go ahead and make use of the lodge. Zane, who desperately needed some downtime, had graciously accepted.

Slater was a special spook in that he was one of the few rank-and-file agency operatives who had knowledge of Zane's employer, The Delphi Group. Among other things, he knew the clandestine organization conducted investigations that the US government could not or would not associate itself with, primarily those involving bizarre events such as scientific advances, the paranormal, or any other category not suitable for transparent budgets.

Created in the wake of the events that took place in Roswell, New Mexico, in 1947, the organization went from being directly under the auspices of the federal government to being privately owned and funded under the black budget of the CIA.

The owner of Delphi was Dr. Alexander Ross. Fittingly, he had become known as the Oracle, the sage of ancient Greece. Like his namesake, Ross had earned the reputation of having an uncanny ability to gather important information. Those skills had been honed over a long career, first as a CIA case officer and later as Director of National Intelligence. His no-nonsense approach, coupled with his natural affinity for clandestine work, made him the perfect leader for an organization like Delphi.

Delphi's headquarters were located on the top floor of a modern, mirrored office building on Wilson Boulevard in Arlington, Virginia. Its employees used a private lift just past the main bank of elevators in the lobby. It hadn't taken long for the secretive nature of the organization to trigger much speculation among employees of the building's other tenants. In fact, it was not uncommon to hear the name Delphi whispered at the Starbucks in the lobby on any given morning.

In addition to the main office in Arlington, Delphi owned four training and deep-cover facilities across the US. They also owned a number of smaller offices and safe houses throughout the world, primarily in Europe and Asia.

The organization deployed approximately two dozen operatives at home and abroad. Zane Watson was designated as senior operative, a post he had held since joining Delphi. Watson was a former Navy SEAL who had been honorably discharged due to a severe knee injury suffered while conducting a snatch-and-grab operation in Yemen. Disappointed at not being able to serve but determined to make the most of what he did have, Watson enrolled in computer science at North Carolina State University. He was able to obtain a full degree in only two-and-a-half years, an accomplishment that would later catch the eyes of the right people. And if that weren't enough, he'd also been able to obtain a pilot's license simultaneously.

The injured knee would later be repaired with advanced surgical techniques developed at Duke University. At that time, the former SEAL had settled into his civilian life as a pilot instructor based out of Raleigh-Durham International airport. It was at RDU that Watson had reconnected with former high school classmate Claire Williams, a flight attendant for a major airline.

The relationship was the proverbial match made in heaven, with the seed having been planted years ago in school. But the time spent apart eventually took its toll and brought the relationship to a halt. Many still predicted the two would get married at some point in the future, but Watson had his doubts. Sometimes when a ship sailed, it never came back.

Watson was single, childless, and enjoying his life as a pilot instructor when approached by Dr. Alexander Ross in the mid-2000s. Ross had heard of the SEAL's reputation, not only as one of the best soldiers ever to rise through the ranks, but also as a man of brilliant intellect. The fact that he'd been able to obtain his college degree in under three years spoke for itself.

It took a number of flights between Reagan National Airport and RDU, but the Oracle was eventually able to bring the former soldier on board by making one major promise, that Watson could continue to live in Raleigh and work as a part-time flight instructor. The future operative had said it was one of the terms he wouldn't negotiate, and Ross was more than happy to oblige.

Realizing it had suddenly grown darker, Zane glanced over his shoulder. The sun had dropped below the mountain ridge behind him, leaving splashes of lavender and fuchsia in its wake. Nightfall was only minutes away.

His stomach now growling insistently, he sloshed through the water and onto the bank. Turning north, he walked along the stream, stopping at a grove of willows where he'd hidden Slater's ATV.

After placing the trout in a bucket, he stripped off his waders and replaced them with hiking boots. As he placed the rod behind the seat, he caught something in his peripheral vision. A red light was blinking in his tackle box.

The phone.

Zane shook his head and let out a sigh. The Oracle had probably left him yet another long-winded diatribe in voice mail. The last operation in Switzerland and France had caused an uproar on both sides of the Atlantic, and Ross couldn't seem to put out the fires on his own. The constant contact had become so annoying that Zane had begun tossing the phone into his tackle box each morning.

Let Carmen help him this time.

But as he turned to walk to the front of the ATV, he stopped. In the recesses of his mind, something bothered him about what he'd just seen. A few seconds later, he realized what it was. His voice mail and text notifications were always green. This light had been red.

He reached into the box and snatched the phone out. After unlocking the screen, he frowned. Slater had asked him to download a mobile application that communicated with the security system of the lodge, and a notification from that application indicated that one or more sensors had been triggered.

"Probably a deer," he muttered.

But as he was about to clear the notification, Zane remembered reading that while a large mammal might occasionally set off one of the sensors, they were calibrated to filter out most wandering animals.

An odd feeling pinched Zane's gut as he scrolled through the phone's icons. After finding the app, he opened it and stared at the additional information displayed on the screen. His brow furrowed immediately.

That can't be possible.

And yet that's exactly what the screen showed: a total of seven sensors had been triggered, two along the main road leading to the lodge and another five in the forested perimeter to the south.

Seven?

He frowned. The data was pregnant with significance. Not only did the numbers concern him, but the triggers from multiple directions were telling as well.

Zane slid the phone into his pocket and reached back into the box. After lifting the false bottom, he retrieved the matte-black Glock 21 hidden underneath. He then pulled out a tactical suppressor and snapped it into place, tucking the weapon into his belt.

As Zane climbed into the front seat of the four-wheeler, one thought was seared into his consciousness.

The lodge was under attack.

CHAPTER THREE

"THIS IS ROSS," said the distorted voice on the other end of the phone.

Zane pressed the device tightly against the side of his head and shouted, "Ross, it's Watson."

He was pleasantly surprised that he'd been able to reach the Oracle. Cell reception was hit-and-miss in northern Idaho, especially in the valley.

"Who?"

"Watson!"

The ATV bounced out of a pothole, nearly throwing the phone out of Zane's hand.

"Watson? I can just barely hear—"

"Ross, I don't have time to explain," Zane said. "I know Garet is out in the field, but—"

"You're breaking up. I can't..." Finally, the Oracle's voice disappeared in a burst of static.

Zane held the phone in front of him. The signal bars showed no reception. He cursed and tossed it into a cup holder on the ATV. He had a satellite phone back at the lodge, but ironically he'd left it there to avoid contact with the Oracle, who was the only man who might be able to help him contact Slater.

In the end, it probably wouldn't matter anyway. It might take hours for the Oracle to run down Slater, hours that the operative didn't have. And even if he'd been able to reach him in short order, he doubted the CIA officer would've had any idea who was encircling the lodge. If he'd had such information, he would've passed it along already.

Another pothole helped refocus Zane on the situation at hand. The dirt road was rising now, with dense firs and birch trees closing in on both sides. The lodge sat on a plateau near the top of the mountain, which would only take another ten or fifteen minutes to reach in the ATV. But riding all the way up wasn't an option. The engine was much too loud. He'd have to approach on foot.

Who was waiting for him just up the mountain? Short of a sensor malfunction, the only logical explanation was a professional hit team. But if that was the case, then who were they after, Slater or himself? Zane knew that there were a number of people who'd love to have his scalp, but he doubted any of them knew where he was. If they did, then Delphi itself was in danger.

A large boulder loomed just ahead on the left. It was the one Zane had been looking for. Just before reaching the rock, he turned the four-wheeler off the road and into a clearing. Once the vehicle was out of sight, he killed the engine.

Wasting no time, Zane quickly hopped out and stepped to

the back. He opened the tackle box and raised the lure trays, exposing several magazines underneath. He snapped one into his Glock, chambering the first round, then put the remaining three in his pocket.

Looking into the box again, he pulled out a sheathed knife, a monocular, and a tactical flashlight. He needed to travel light, but he also needed to be prepared for a number of different eventualities.

Zane stared at his phone. The bars still showed no signal, which meant he'd have no access to the device's GPS software. He turned it off and stuffed it in his pocket. He wouldn't need satellites anyway. He'd spent the first day of vacation walking the mountain, learning every nook and cranny of the area around the lodge. He'd have no trouble finding his way up.

After making one last check of his gun, Zane began his ascent. Darkness had fallen, which prevented him from moving as fast as he'd like.

Ten minutes later, the ground began to level off. He was nearing the plateau. Directly ahead was a line of large firs, which he knew were situated along the clearing on the south side of the lodge. He paused for a moment, listening for any sound. Hearing nothing, he sprinted to the trees, dropping down to his hands and knees when he arrived. He then lay flat and wiggled underneath the limbs until he got to the other side.

He pushed aside a limb. The clearing opened up in front of him. To his left was the dark silhouette of the barn he'd driven the ATV out of earlier in the day. From there the clearing ran slightly uphill to the right, where the lodge was situated. The home was a massive three-story affair, rustic and yet modern. It was mostly dark now, save for two lights that Zane left on at all times.

"Where are you?" Zane muttered to himself.

He knew from the sensors that one or more attackers had approached from the other side of the lodge, along or next to the paved entrance road. He also knew that another group had approached from the direction of the barn to his left. And if his memory served him correctly, there would be a third group directly opposite his position, on the other side of the clearing.

What concerned him most was the likelihood that the attackers were using night vision and thermal imaging equipment. That would give them a distinct tactical advantage. The key would be to position himself behind them, since they were likely focused on the lodge.

Pulling out his monocular, Zane trained it on the barn. It was hard to make out any detail. All he could see was the outline of the structure and the surrounding trees. If someone were hidden there, it would be almost impossible to pick them out.

He bit his lower lip. Since night had just fallen, the attackers were probably waiting for a signal to launch. Should he make a preemptive strike? Or should he simply watch and wait? If the latter, he could always let them do their thing and depart. When you were outnumbered, that was often the smartest thing to do. Live to fight another day, as they say.

But Zane quickly dismissed the thought of just walking away. The men were undoubtedly professionals and wouldn't leave behind any trace evidence. That meant their identity might forever be hidden if they were simply allowed to leave. And if they came up empty in the house, they would surely turn their attention, and their thermal imaging equipment, toward the surrounding forest.

No, despite the potential dangers, Zane knew he needed to take action in order to have any hope of gathering information. More specifically, he needed to apprehend one of the intruders and take them to a remote location using the ATV. He could then question the subject until he could call for a backup team.

So what now? He clenched his jaw as he thought about how to proceed. The first question that came to mind was one he often asked when in this type of situation: What would he do if he were in their place? How would he organize an attack?

One thing he'd want is a sniper positioned to cover the operation from a distance. But where would he place the gunman?

The barn.

He turned and looked at it. Except for a few bushes and rocks scattered across the clearing, it afforded a shooter a clear view of the lodge. Short of climbing a tree, no other place would provide such an advantageous position.

But where specifically? Zane searched his memory of the barn. The gable roof was a nonstarter. Its pitch meant you'd have to sit or lie at an angle. You could also lie inside, but that might limit your view.

Suddenly Zane remembered a stack of two-by-fours on this side of the barn. Garet had told him he was going to use the lumber to build a new cover for his well. Being both level and elevated, the pile was the perfect place to shoot from.

Zane raised his monocular. After moving it around a bit, he finally found his target to the left of the barn. Was anyone there? There seemed to be a slight irregularity to the top of the pile of lumber, but it was too dark to tell exactly what it was.

An idea rose to the surface of his thoughts. It was bold, risky even, but it might just help him find out if someone was hiding in the shadows.

Reaching out, he slid his hand across the dirt. After patting around for a few seconds, he finally closed his fingers around a small rock.

After tucking his gun away, Zane wiggled out from underneath the tree and rose to one knee. He took a deep breath, concentrating on the direction he was going to throw the rock and how far. Getting those two things right was critical.

Drawing back, he launched the stone with as much force as he could muster. As it flew toward the other side of the clearing, he grabbed the monocular and focused it on the stack of two-by-fours.

Seconds passed, but he never heard the rock land. Had it been too small to make a noise?

Zane squinted through the eyepiece, determined not to take his eye off the target.

Just when he was about to give up, he saw a round shadow move on top of the pile. It was a subtle, yet distinct, turn of a head.

The hairs on Zane's neck stood on end.

The sniper had given himself away.

CHAPTER FOUR

IT TOOK ZANE about three minutes to circle through the woods and come up behind the barn. When he arrived, he paused just inside the trees and allowed his eyes to adjust.

He was directly behind the structure, so he moved a couple of trees over in order to see down the right side of the building. He then lowered to one knee and trained his monocular on the woodpile. As he brought everything into focus, the body of a man materialized, lying prone on top of the two-by-fours, his rifle pointed toward the lodge.

Zane looked up. Darkness had now settled over the mountain, so it wouldn't be long before the signal to attack was given.

Knowing time was short, Zane slipped from behind the fir and crept softly forward. He trained the suppressed Glock squarely on the man's head, ready to shoot if it became necessary. If all went according to plan, he wouldn't have to.

He was about halfway there when he heard a soft voice. No others were around, so the man was probably speaking into a headset. Zane took several steps forward and stopped. At first there was only silence, then the man began speaking again. Zane stiffened as he recognized the language.

What are they doing here?

He crept a bit closer. The man was talking faster now, clearly giving some sort of instructions. The attack was either imminent or had already commenced.

Finally, the man grew silent. He then raised his rifle into position, signaling that he was ready to provide cover. It was the moment Zane had been waiting for.

He launched forward, covering the remaining ground with cat-like speed. As he neared the man, his foot hit a rock, sending it skittering loudly against the pile of lumber.

The sniper turned at the sound, but since he was lying on his stomach, he was in no position to defend himself. Zane took one more step and leapt, bringing the butt of the Glock down across the man's head. Both rolled off the stacked lumber, and by the time they came to a stop, the man was out cold.

Had they been heard? Zane waited but couldn't hear anyone approaching. Nor did any sound come through the man's headset.

Without wasting any more time, Zane grabbed the man's ankles and dragged him behind the barn. Pulling out his flashlight, he turned it on and directed the beam at the man's face. He was wearing night vision goggles, which Zane quickly ripped off and tossed aside. Illuminated by the light was the face of a young Asian male. Zane knew from the earlier conversation that he was a Chinese national.

As he pondered why they might be conducting an assault on Slater's lodge, a small snippet of information tried to rise to the top of Zane's thoughts, but he couldn't bring it out. He'd have to worry about it later.

He entered the barn and found a length of rope and a rag then returned to the man and quickly bound his wrists and ankles tightly, stuffing the rag into his mouth.

Remembering the night vision goggles, he picked them up and slid them over his head. Immediately the night transitioned to a milky world of greens, blacks, and whites.

Now on more equal footing, Zane sprinted out to a sapling in the clearing and lowered to one knee. He saw movement just ahead. Two dark silhouettes had exited the woods and were now moving toward the lodge with speed. They were hunched over, waving automatic rifles back and forth.

Since the two men were facing in the other direction, Zane stepped out from behind the sapling and sprinted to a bush about halfway across the clearing, just behind the gunmen. They continued toward the lodge, obviously trusting that the sniper had them covered in the rear.

Zane ran after them, knowing their own steps would mask the sound of his approach. Seconds later, the two men parted. Zane followed the one on the right, who eventually pulled up behind a gazebo and stopped. Stealth was not an option now, so Zane bore down on his target. When he was a few yards away, the man turned. At first he seemed startled, but then he recovered and lifted his rifle.

But he was too late. Zane already had his pistol up, a red dot wiggling on the man's forehead. He squeezed the trigger once. There was a soft spit, and the man writhed spasmodically before crumpling to the ground.

Zane ran past the body without a glance. He knew the man had died instantly. After skirting the gazebo, he saw the other gunman running just ahead and watched as he disappeared into a grove of young cedars planted around the back deck of the lodge. Zane continued to the spot where the man had entered, pausing a few feet inside. The saplings were arranged in neat rows like a Christmas tree farm. Unfortunately they were all about seven feet tall, preventing him from seeing anything beyond the row he was in.

Where is he?

There were no sounds. No signs of movement. It was as if he had disappeared into thin air.

Stepping forward, Zane looked down the next row. Empty. Had he already crossed the deck and entered the house? It didn't seem possible, although he couldn't rule it out.

As he waited, Zane heard shuffling just ahead, near the deck. He crouched and moved forward slowly. Just after he passed the final line of trees, a shadow closed in on him from the left.

He'd been waiting.

The attacker brought his rifle down toward Zane's head, but he lifted an arm instinctively, just enough to avoid being knocked out cold. Instead, he received a glancing blow that sent him tumbling backward.

As Zane hit the ground, the night vision goggles dislodged and his gun tumbled out into the darkness. The attacker pounced ruthlessly, pounding Zane's head with clenched fists.

Zane withstood the wave of punches then reached up, yanked the man's night vision goggles down, and simultaneously pulled the man toward him. Zane then used his own forehead to smash the man's temple. The attacker grunted in pain, and Zane kicked him off.

Zane rose quickly to his feet and got into a defensive crouch. Surprisingly, the man was already up. Turning, he growled, lowered his head, and charged. Zane reached down and loosed his knife from its sheath. Seconds later, the man hit him. As Zane fell backwards, he held the knife in place, allowing momentum to do its work, impaling the man on the blade.

As the man expired, Zane pushed him away and got up on one knee. He listened, but he heard only the buzz of insects. Other than the man's growl, the fight had taken place in relative silence.

After locating his gun, Zane crept to the edge of the deck. Both lights that had been on were now off. The other attackers were inside, using the darkness to their advantage.

Zane turned left and sprinted to the side of the house. As he rounded the deck, he saw a small door leading to the garage. He opened it slightly then peered inside. Slater's Toyota 4-Runner was parked directly in front of him, and the door leading inside was off to the right. As far as he could tell, no one was waiting to ambush him.

Stepping inside, Zane located the electrical panel on the wall to his right. He lifted the cover gently and saw that the main breaker had indeed been turned off. That suited him just fine. He knew the house better than they did.

Skirting the SUV, Zane walked up the steps that led into the house. He opened the door about a foot and slipped into the corridor beyond. On his left was a utility room, its door slightly ajar. Zane used his gun to nudge it all the way open. All clear. After removing his boots, he continued down the hallway and entered the kitchen. He paused and listened. A few seconds later, he heard a slight creak overhead. At least one gunman was on the second floor. In all likelihood, they were all on the upper floors by now.

Zane walked past the kitchen island and squatted in front of the sink. Once there, he dropped down on all fours and felt under the cabinet door until he found the HVAC vent. Sliding his fingers under the edge, he gently pried it off, careful not to let it clang to the floor. He thrust his hand in the space beyond and closed his fingers around three flashbangs hidden there. He pulled them out and stuffed them into his shirt pocket.

Slater, keenly aware that he might someday be targeted, had constructed a number of false vents and compartments throughout the lodge, hiding everything from flashbangs to pistols to knives. There was even a stash of hand grenades in the crawl space, but Zane didn't have time to retrieve them.

He exited the kitchen and turned left down a hall that ran to the front. When he reached the foyer, he stood silently underneath the giant antler chandelier. He could still hear the creak of footsteps above.

A few feet away, the open stairway twisted in a spiral to the second and third floors. The house was designed with a central atrium running all the way to the top. Each floor had a square landing that wrapped around the stairwell, giving access to all rooms on that level. Zane looked up but saw nothing. Most of the lodge's blinds were closed, shrouding the interior in darkness. At least he'd taken his boots off, giving him the advantage of stealth.

Zane took the stairs, his gun raised in front of him. Upon arriving at the second floor, he stepped out onto the landing and listened. Most of the sounds seemed to be coming from the third floor, but he needed to clear the second floor first. The last thing he wanted was to get squeezed between teams.

Knock.

He heard something fall over in a room at the front of the house on the same floor. He turned left and moved in that direction. It was so dark it was like walking in a cave. When he was about halfway down the landing, Zane heard another knock, followed by footsteps that seemed to be getting louder. Whoever was in there was coming out.

He looked around. There was a door immediately to his right.

The bathroom.

Thankfully the door was already open, which allowed him to enter without making any noise. By the time he stepped inside, a plan had already formed in his mind. Without night vision goggles, he needed a way to turn the odds back in his favor, and he thought he knew how to do exactly that. He felt around until his fingers touched the drinking glass next to the sink. Slater's cleaning staff kept the place stocked like a five-star hotel.

The footsteps grew louder.

Zane snatched the glass off the counter then set it on the

landing right outside the door. As soon as he did, someone exited the room at the front. Zane jerked back inside and closed the door.

Had he been seen?

The footsteps continued without pause, so Zane backed up a bit further and raised his Glock with both hands. As he waited, the footsteps stopped. Had the man seen the glass? The tactic's effectiveness was predicated on the assumption that few people ever looked down at their feet.

Suddenly he heard a voice. The man was likely speaking into a headset, letting the team commander know another room had been cleared.

Without warning, the steps resumed again. The man was only a few feet from the bathroom door now.

A second later, Zane heard the clanking of glass. He immediately squeezed off three suppressed shots, the rounds ripping through the thinly constructed door. There was a groan and then a thump as the attacker fell.

Moving with speed, Zane crossed and opened the door. Looking down, he saw the dim outline of not one but two bodies. *Two birds with one glass.* If his sensor count had been right, that meant only one or two gunmen were left.

He heard movement above, then a light drew his eyes downward. A red dot wiggled at his feet, eventually working its way to his chest. Zane dove to his left instinctively. A hail of bullets rained down from the third-floor landing, shredding the banisters and the drywall.

Zane hit the floor and rolled onto his back. He was now able to discern the position of the gunmen by the flash of their weapons. Lifting his Glock, he fired twice. There was a scream then a loud clank as a rifle landed in the foyer below.

The surviving gunman fired several shots. Zane crawled over to a large supporting column and squeezed off two return volleys. He fished one of the flashbangs out of his pocket, pulled the pin, and launched it toward the third floor. As soon as it went off, he fired at the man illuminated by the light. The intruder let out a groan of pain then staggered down the landing and into a room.

When Zane stood, a sharp pain shot up his leg and into his groin. Feeling around, he found a wound just above one of his knees. Apparently he'd been grazed by one of the bullets. The pain was intense, but retreating wasn't an option.

Limping over to the stairs, he ascended slowly. Upon arriving at the top, he tossed his old magazine aside and snapped in a new one.

Zane moved down the landing, keeping tight against the wall to reduce his profile. When he arrived at the doorway, he leaned forward and glanced inside. A bit of ambient light came through the blinds, allowing him to see the entire room.

Where did he go?

Zane stepped inside with pistol raised. It was then that he saw the man, propped up against a dresser. As far as Zane could tell, he wasn't holding his weapon.

That's strange.

Zane approached cautiously, his finger in position to pull the trigger if necessary. He could now see that blood oozed from a wound on the man's chest. He'd need quick medical attention if he were going to survive.

THE PORTAL

As Zane drew near, the man lifted one of his hands and put something in his mouth.

"No!" Zane shouted.

He dove and tried to grab the man's hand, but it was too late. The man's throat was moving, sending the pill on its way.

He probably had less than a minute. Zane pulled the man's night vision goggles off. Staring back at him was an Asian male in his late twenties or early thirties. Zane shook his shoulders. "Who are you?"

He said nothing, so Zane shook him again, this time more roughly. "Who do you work for?"

The man leaned forward as though he were going to speak, but then spit in Zane's face.

Zane ignored the act. "Who did you come here for? Tell me."

The man began to cough. Seconds later, a river of foam spilled from his mouth and his head tilted forward. Zane pushed his head back again, but this time there was only a blank stare.

Whatever secrets the man had held, they were gone.

CHAPTER FIVE

Arlington, Virginia

ADAM CLINE DEFTLY maneuvered the obsidian-colored Jeep Cherokee through the early-evening traffic of Arlington, Virginia. He was doing the best he could to strike a delicate balance between giving his passenger a comfortable ride and still making it to their destination on time. He had only been with Delphi for six months, but one thing he'd learned already was that Dr. Alexander Ross despised tardiness.

He cursed under his breath as another light turned red. After coming to a stop, he glanced into the rearview mirror at his passenger. The man stared out the window, seemingly lost in his thoughts. His long brown hair, which fell to the shoulders of a stylish gray button-down, framed a face that one might expect to find on any number of magazines in a grocery store rack. He was anything but a typical operative, Adam thought.

Strangely, the normally friendly man had scarcely moved or

spoken since climbing in at Reagan National. Was it jet lag? That was certainly possible, although his pose seemed more pensive, as though something were troubling him.

The light turned green, and Adam mashed the accelerator to the floor.

"Don't worry about Ross," said the man in the backseat.

Adam blushed then looked into the rearview mirror again. "Excuse me?"

The man returned his gaze. "The Oracle... don't worry about him. Just get us there in one piece and you'll be fine."

"Sorry." Adam glanced at his watch. It was 6:55. "It's just that Dr. Ross wanted me to have you there by—"

"Seven o'clock. I know. Once I get there, all will be forgotten. Trust me, sometimes I think I know the man better than he knows himself." After a brief pause, he continued. "You're right, he doesn't like people being late. It's in his DNA. But right now there is too much going on to worry about what time I step through those doors. Let's just get there safely."

Ten minutes later, Adam braked and turned right just before a tall mirrored office building. He followed the service road around to the rear and pulled up in front of a red awning that ran from the building to the parking lot.

The passenger pulled the strap of a duffel bag over his shoulder. "You coming in?"

Adam turned around. "No, sir. Dr. Ross wanted me to take your things to the hotel and check you in."

"Sounds good." The man held up an ID card. "By the way, Ross didn't revoke my privileges, did he?"

"No, sir. You should still be good."

Adam watched as the tall operative limped down the sidewalk and into the building.

Zane Watson was home.

***

When the elevator door slid open, Zane realized nothing had changed in the months since he'd last stepped foot in Delphi headquarters. Directly in front of him was a sleekly modern reception desk, with a stone waterfall gurgling soothingly just behind. In the center of the stone was a bronze plate that read Delphi Group.

As he stepped out of the elevator, a smartly dressed woman in her early thirties looked up from a stack of papers on her desk. She had auburn hair that was pulled up and tied in the back and a face that was both pretty and disarming.

She grinned as Zane moved toward her. "Wow, love the new do!" she said with a wry smile. "You know, I can recommend a good stylist right here in Arlington. She's great with long hair like ours."

Zane placed both hands on her desk. "I haven't stepped foot in here for months and the first thing out of your mouth is a sarcastic remark about my locks?"

"Sarcastic? Who's being sarcastic? Would love to talk product sometime!"

Zane shook his head slowly. "How are you, Kristine?"

"I'm doing great, Zane." She stood, came around the desk, and gave him a long hug. "We've missed you." She pulled back a bit and looked down. "How's the leg?"

"Hurts like the devil, but I think I'm going to make it. So you're doing well?"

She nodded. "I'm great."

Zane noticed a little tick in her expression, a hint that there might be a little more there. "You're not still dating that clown from Maryland, are you?"

"Clarke? Ummm, no."

Zane raised an eyebrow. "What did I tell you about that guy?"

"He wasn't that bad."

"Do you want me to go back through all my predictions to see how many came true?"

Kristine held up a hand. "Please, no." She laughed. "Now that you mention it, he was pretty bad."

Zane squeezed her shoulder. "I guess spotting scum is a subset of my professional skills."

"Well, you did have him pegged, that's for sure."

Zane leaned back and glanced down the hall. "Switching gears, where is our fearless leader?"

"Waiting for you in his office. Do you still remember the way, or shall I escort you?"

"Unfortunately, I still remember."

She gave him a little wave. "Let's catch up when you guys are done."

"Will do." He pointed at her. "I want to hear about your product."

She laughed and returned to her seat.

Zane strode past the maze of glass offices. The Oracle liked the openness of glass, claiming it produced happier and more productive employees. Tellingly, he didn't apply the same rules to his own space.

Several technicians waved at Zane as he passed by, unable to break away from phone conversations. He missed being here. He wished he could have arrived earlier and spent some time catching up but knew that wasn't possible now. Whatever the Oracle wanted to talk about was likely going to take up the entire evening.

As he approached a set of oak double doors at the end of the hall, a voice spoke from the speaker to the right. "Come on in, Watson."

There was a quick buzz followed by a series of clicks. Zane turned the handle and entered.

The office would be the envy of any CEO. The exterior wall was composed entirely of tinted floor-to-ceiling glass. The Oracle's massive desk and ergonomically correct chair were situated in front of the glass, allowing Delphi's chief to swivel around and take in the view if he needed inspiration.

A modern-looking conference table filled the right side of the room, and a circle of leather chairs was arranged on the left. Set in the wall behind those chairs was a nondescript door. Zane knew that just beyond, a spiral staircase led to the roof. The Oracle was a connoisseur of fine cigars, and the hidden retreat allowed him to enjoy a smoke in the evening.

As the Oracle rose from his seat, Zane could see the spires of Arlington office buildings behind him, their interior lights just beginning to glow as evening settled over the city. A few miles away was the Potomac River, winding its way east toward the nation's capital.

The Oracle walked around the desk. "I see you can't even make it through vacation without getting shot," he said, pumping the operative's hand. He looked down and said, "Speaking of which, how is the leg?"

"It's seen better days."

The Oracle frowned. "A little bird told me the wound got infected."

"Unfortunately, your little bird was right. I'm so pumped full of antibiotics that I could probably drink a gallon of sewage and survive."

The Oracle waved him over to the leather seats.

Zane rubbed his leg dramatically as they moved toward them. "You know, it's funny, but I never seem to get any comp time or pay no matter what happens to me out in the field. I'd like to speak to HR before I leave."

The Oracle shook his head. "Comp pay? Aren't you the man who owns two personal airplanes? And besides, I *am* HR, so you can just talk to me."

As Zane approached the seating area, a man rose out of one of the chairs. Zane hadn't noticed him before. He was in his early thirties, with dark hair parted on the side. Pulling off a pair of reading glasses, the man stepped forward and extended a hand. "Zane."

"Brett Foster," Zane said, grasping his hand. "Were you hiding over there?"

Brett returned to his seat. "Sorry. I had to get a message out to someone in the field. Figured I'd let you two exchange pleasantries first."

Brett Foster was the chief technology specialist for Delphi.

He had attended MIT in the early 2000s and graduated with honors. After graduation, he'd entered private industry, working for several research and development companies at the famed Research Triangle Park in North Carolina. As fate would have it, one of those companies was a consultant for the CIA, and that was when the brilliant young techie caught the eye of the head administrator of the CIA's Office of Information Technology. His work was so well regarded that his name eventually made it all the way up to the director himself.

Knowing the CIA couldn't pay Foster enough to pull him away from private industry, the director passed his name on to Alexander Ross. Ross was then able to couple the excitement of covert work with a substantial increase in pay to lure him to Delphi.

"We've kept Brett busy lately," the Oracle said after they were all seated.

"Is there ever a time when he isn't?" Zane asked.

"This is a whole new level of busy," the Oracle said.

Brett looked at Zane. "Let's put it this way... I've spent the night here four times this week."

Zane raised an eyebrow. Delphi employees were highly motivated individuals, and long hours were the norm, but spending the night that many times in a week went beyond anything he'd ever heard of before. It made him wonder what was going on.

"I'm impressed," Zane said.

"So, if anybody deserves a pay increase, it's him," the Oracle said.

Zane sat forward and placed his arms on his knees. "I take it the overnighters are related to why I'm here?"

"They are." The Oracle glanced at his watch. "Although that will have to wait until our other guest arrives."

Zane frowned. He hadn't been told that someone else would be joining them. Who was it, and why hadn't the Oracle told him before?

"How about a drink while we wait?" the Oracle asked as he rose from his seat and walked toward a mini-fridge in the corner. "Watson, as it's after seven, ordinarily I'd offer you some alcohol for your leg. But I don't think our guest would be too thrilled to find you holding a glass of Scotch."

Suddenly Zane realized who was coming. No wonder the Oracle had been coy.

"Besides, if you're up for it, we're all going to the Old Ebbitt when this is over." The Oracle stooped and retrieved three bottles of water. After closing the door, he handed a bottle each to Brett and Zane.

Zane opened his and took a sip. "So, who is our illustrious guest?"

The Oracle stared at Zane. "I think you can probably guess."

As if on cue, a loud beep sounded from a device on the Oracle's desk, followed by Kristine's voice. "Dr. Ross, Assistant Director Hathaway is here."

The Oracle walked over to the desk and pressed a button. "Thank you, Kristine. Please send him down." He then pressed another button to disengage the lock.

A few seconds later, the door opened and a tall man with

dark hair entered the room. The assistant director of the CIA was dressed impeccably, as always. His charcoal Italian suit was adorned with a crisp white pocket square, and his laced Oxfords were polished to a mirror-like sheen. Zane had often wondered if the man ironed and starched his boxers.

"Brooks, nice to see you again." The Oracle extended his hand before nodding in the direction of the leather chairs. "I believe you remember Zane and Brett."

"Ah, Zane Watson." Hathaway always spoke with a contrived accent that Zane placed somewhere between British and high intellectual. The man was fake before fake became cool. "What a relief to find you here and not out in Europe, causing an international row."

"I'm just glad that you're still funding those rows," Zane replied.

Hathaway shot him a look before turning to shake Brett's hand.

The Oracle gestured toward the chairs. "Please have a seat."

Hathaway made it no secret that he detested Delphi. He was an agency man and found it unthinkable that any operation should ever be farmed out to a private organization.

As everyone took their seats, the Oracle walked over to a switch near the door and dimmed the lights. As soon as the room darkened, the lights of the surrounding buildings suddenly shone through the window with greater intensity.

The Oracle rejoined the group and sat down. "Zane, Brooks wanted me to bring you up to date on something that has... how shall I say... been passed around like a hot potato." He paused, looking first at Hathaway and then at Zane.

"Without beating around the bush, the whole thing arose in the aftermath of your operation in Switzerland and France."

Zane raised an eyebrow. "What? Other than smoothing things over with our allies, that was put to bed weeks ago."

The Oracle drew in a deep breath. "Unfortunately, it wasn't, not by a long shot. In fact, it looks like we're just starting to peel back the skin of a very big onion."

Zane's brow furrowed. What on earth was he talking about?

The Oracle nodded at Delphi's chief technology specialist. "Brett, please start the slides."

CHAPTER SIX

BRETT LIFTED A controller and pressed a button. There was a dull hum as a projection screen lowered out of the ceiling. Once it was in place, he made a few keystrokes on his laptop, and an image appeared.

Zane frowned. What on earth was he looking at? It appeared to be a scientific diagram, with a series of four concentric circles. The smallest circle was labeled Earth.

The Oracle leaned forward in his chair. "Watson, as you may or may not know, there is a division of NASA that monitors celestial objects using radio waves."

Zane nodded. "The DRA. Division of Radio Astronomy."

Hathaway's eyes widened, clearly in surprise that the operative knew the answer.

"Bravo, Watson. In addition to their work with celestial objects, the DRA also monitors the universe for sounds."

"What sorts of sounds?" Zane asked.

The Oracle paused for a moment, as though considering his answer. "Any sounds, but particularly those they believe might be sent by intelligent beings."

"ET."

The Oracle nodded. "Yes, ET."

Zane's mind flashed back to Delphi's last operation. A group led by Russian billionaire Alexander Mironov and former Roman Catholic priest Vincenzio Marrese had taken over the CERN command center in Prevessin, France. The takeover gave them unfettered control of the Large Hadron Collider, or LHC, the most powerful particle accelerator in the world. Their plan had been to use the collider to open a doorway to the heavens, through which they thought would come an alien visitation. Mironov and Marrese believed these same aliens had visited earth in ancient times, bringing with them the technology that had been used to construct a number of megalithic structures around the globe, including those in Egypt and South America.

A Delphi team led by Zane had thwarted those plans, but at great cost. The collider had been pressed beyond its working limit, triggering explosions that caused extensive damage to several buildings and the collider itself. In addition, Dutch physicist Markus VanGelder was killed by one of the blasts.

But something else had happened that night, a series of events that continued to haunt Zane to this very day. As a battle raged for control of the center, he followed former priest Marrese to the underground tunnels that housed the collider itself. He soon discovered that Marrese was holding captive Philippe Bachand, a pastor from Geneva who had assisted Delphi.

During the subsequent chase, Zane discovered that a

mysterious column of light had appeared while the collider was in use. He had also seen at least three giant creatures, all of whom seemed to have come out of the column of light. In the intervening time since the mission, Zane had noticed that the memory of their appearance had faded. In fact, it had faded so much that he now wondered exactly what he had seen, if anything. Were the giants some sort of alien beings? Or were they figments of his imagination, brought on by smoke inhalation and the effects of anesthetic agents he'd been given earlier that night?

After the event was over, French police and emergency personnel combed the facility, but no reports of anything out of the ordinary ever surfaced. If something had been found, Zane felt sure word would've gotten back to Washington.

The Oracle cleared his throat and continued. "As I mentioned, the events at CERN didn't mark the end of the story. On the night of the operation, the DRA picked up an odd sound coming from the area around Geneva and Prevessin." He used a laser pointer to indicate the area between the innermost circle and the next one out. "It came from the troposphere, the first layer of the atmosphere." He looked at Zane. "Apparently that sound was recorded around the same time that Mironov's team operated the collider."

Zane returned Ross's gaze. "Does NASA believe there is a connection?"

The Oracle nodded. "Officially, they're reluctant to talk, but when you get them alone, there are a few who say a wormhole was beginning to open. Others believe it was some sort of celestial link between our dimension and another one."

"Back to the noise." Zane paused then asked, "Do the NASA scientists believe it was made by the collider itself?"

"No. Again, this sound had a unique signature. CERN has been around for a while, so any noise emanating from the collider would be something they'd have on record." The Oracle nodded at Brett, who pressed a key on his laptop. The next slide appeared, depicting a man with salt-and-pepper hair and a goatee. "The DRA subgroup that monitors these sounds is led by a man named Dr. Stetson Clark. Dr. Clark knew from news reports that the US had been involved in an operation near Geneva, and called his contact in Washington to let him know what they had found. And that's where I'll let Brooks take over."

Hathaway stood and took the laser pointer from Ross. "As you can imagine, the US government takes any and all intergalactic communications seriously—"

"Wait," Zane interrupted. "We're already classifying this as an intergalactic communication? Isn't that a little premature?"

Hathaway glared at the operative. "If you'd wait and listen to what I have to say, then you might change your mind."

The Oracle turned toward Zane. "Let him finish, Watson."

"As I was saying, the US government takes all intergalactic communications seriously, as it also does any reports of UFOs, strange craft, alien beings, and abductions. And it's probably no surprise that we view these things through the lens of national security. That means that all cases are handled by the CIA and its affiliates."

"Which would include Delphi," the Oracle said.

"Correct," Hathaway said. "In any event, while certainly

compelling, the sound that registered that night did not set off any alarms in DC. It was what came in its wake. Something we believe could be one of the most important discoveries in decades."

Zane frowned deeply.

Hathaway then nodded at Brett, who brought up the next slide. Zane leaned forward when the image appeared. It was a detailed map of South America, with a black dot blinking over northern Brazil.

Hathaway looked at Zane. He seemed pleased that he now had the operative's attention. "The director asked Dr. Clark to look into the matter further. We needed to know if this was a simple anomaly or something that warranted further attention.

"A few days later, the director received a call from Clark. They *had* found something significant in one of the reports generated by their monitoring equipment." Hathaway used the laser pointer to indicate the blinking black dot. "Just minutes after the sound was picked up in France, there was another corresponding sound picked up here, in Brazil."

Zane nodded and whispered, "The Amazon basin."

"The sound in Brazil had all of the same intrinsic properties as the one from France," Hathaway continued. "In fact, we believe it was a response... a signal... a communication of some sort."

"Is that near a town or village?" Brett asked.

"Not that we know of," the Oracle said. "You're talking the heart of the rainforest."

"I'm no expert on audio transmissions," Zane said, "but I just find it hard to believe they can't identify either sound."

"We have to rely on what they've told us, Watson," the Oracle said. "They're the—"

Hathaway cut him off. "There is one thing I neglected to tell you. I got a call from Dr. Clark this morning, and he was able to pass along something that has, quite frankly, deepened the mystery." He looked at Zane. "Alexander told you that the signature of the sounds was unique. Actually, that's not entirely true. The DRA team was finally able to make a partial match, a slight overlap with a sound they cataloged several years ago."

The Oracle's brow furrowed. "From where?"

Hathaway nodded at Brett. "I sent Mr. Foster an additional slide late this afternoon."

As Zane watched, the image of a galaxy appeared. He recognized it immediately.

"The sound they found in their database originated in our closest neighbor, the Andromeda Galaxy. It was hard to pinpoint the precise location, but they believe it came from an area of dark matter."

"Good grief," the Oracle muttered.

"Yes, and I'm sorry I didn't tell you, but as I said, I just received the information this morning."

Zane leaned back in his seat. "So what does this mean?"

Hathaway looked at the Oracle, who got up and took the laser pointer back from him. Brett advanced to the next slide. The image that appeared wasn't what Zane expected. It appeared to be an official photo of an Asian woman, much like one on a driver's license or company identification. Zane studied her face. He guessed she was in her early or mid-thirties. She was more pleasant-looking than attractive.

"This is Wu Mei-ling," the Oracle began. "She is the daughter of a low-level Chinese diplomat, at least that's the official version."

"In other words, she's a spook," Zane said, his eyes still fixed on the picture.

"Yes, she is," the Oracle said. "And apparently a good one." Brett advanced to the next slide. Another photograph appeared, this one depicting a man in his forties with brown hair. "This is David Parsons, the agency's senior field officer in Taipei, where Ms. Wu was operating. He had established contact with her and was in the process of recruiting her when disaster struck.

"Apparently Chinese intelligence knew that Parsons worked for the CIA. He was under deep cover, and we still don't know how they were able to determine who he was. Unfortunately, that gave them a leg up."

"This doesn't sound like it's going to end well," Zane said.

"It doesn't. She managed to drug Parsons in his condominium then accessed virtually all of the electronic information stored on his agency-issued tablet."

"So what happened to Parsons? Is he dead?"

Zane could see Hathaway squirming in his seat, clearly uncomfortable that the agency was being placed in a bad light. No wonder he'd let the Oracle take over.

"No. Wu drugged him while they were on the couch, and after he passed out, she planted a Trojan in the tablet. The malware then copied all of the information contained in Parsons's files and transmitted it to a server used by the

Chinese military. Anyway, after planting the Trojan, she stuck around until Parsons woke up. They'd been drinking heavily at a restaurant earlier that evening, so he figured he'd simply succumbed to the alcohol."

Zane shook his head. "In other words, he never realized he'd been compromised."

"Exactly."

"Then how did we find out?"

Hathaway cleared his throat and said, "We discovered it using sophisticated antivirus software developed by the NSA. It didn't pick up the Trojan when it was loaded but was able to place it in quarantine after a full scan was run the following evening. Unfortunately, by then the damage was done."

"And Wu?" Zane asked.

"She disappeared off the face of the earth," the Oracle said. "We were going to play dumb, leave the Trojan in place, and feed the Chinese bad information through Parsons's tablet, but apparently they were able to get everything they wanted and pulled out."

Zane remained silent for moment. Finally, he looked up and said, "This is all quite interesting, but what does it have to do with an audio transmission from the Amazonian rainforest?"

"I'm glad you asked, Watson," the Oracle said. He turned and motioned for Brett to bring up the next slide. It was a picture of Garet Slater, CIA field agent and owner of the Idaho lodge Zane had just visited.

Zane leaned back and rubbed the stubble on his face. "Okay, now I'm even more lost than before."

The Oracle stared at the operative for a moment. It was as though he was waiting for him to put it all together.

Suddenly a few fragments of understanding pierced his thoughts. "So, the information grab in Taipei is what brought the Chinese to the lodge?" Zane asked.

The Oracle nodded slowly. "Correct. Slater had just sent Parsons a correspondence, one that Parsons hadn't even read yet. In that email, Slater said that he would be at the lodge the following week, and he asked Parsons to join him to discuss a new operation."

Zane frowned. "So they were coming after Parsons? They had their information. Why kill him?"

"They weren't after Parsons," Hathaway said. "They were after Slater." He began to pace. "Garet made a big information grab in Taiwan a few years ago, one that did considerable harm to the Chinese military. They have a long memory and saw this as an opportunity to exercise some payback, so they triggered a sleeper cell operating out of Los Angeles."

Zane nodded. "Okay, that makes perfect sense. I'm with you. But I repeat, what on earth does a Chinese hit team operating on American soil have to do with a sound transmitted from the depths of the Brazilian rainforest?"

"A lot," said the Oracle.

CHAPTER SEVEN

THE NEXT SLIDE displayed an email. The print was difficult to decipher, so Brett zoomed in on the image. The Oracle took a long sip of water, giving Zane a chance to read it.

The email was from Garet Slater to David Parsons. Its content seemed innocuous, giving the details of a family vacation. In fact, it was so innocuous that Zane guessed it was likely sprinkled with coded language employed by the agency.

The Oracle used the laser pointer to highlight the sender, receiver, and subject line at the top. "As you can see, this is an e-mail that Garet sent to David. Brett, please move to the next slide." The next image was a typed Word document. "Even though they were using a secure channel, the language was coded because it included details of an upcoming operation. It's a double layer of protection that was meant to prevent the kind of breach that took place in Taipei."

The Oracle hovered the laser dot over the first translated sentence, and Zane's eyes widened. "What Garet was actually doing was letting David know that he was being called off of his work in Taipei in order to lead an operation in Brazil."

"We had to get him out of Taipei anyway, so we figured why not send him to the other side of the world," Hathaway added.

Zane leaned forward. "So, let me guess... they were both going to hunt down the source of the signal."

"Precisely," replied the Oracle. "Parsons served as our station chief in Brazil for seven years. He knows the country like no one else in the agency and has contacts throughout the region, even in the north.

"The operation was to be spearheaded by the agency, with assistance from a Special Operations task force." Brett brought up the next slide. It showed the bodies of the five Chinese agents killed in Idaho. Zane had been there when the photos were taken. Three sustained gunshot wounds. The other two showed no outward sign of injury. Zane had watched one of them take a cyanide pill and discovered later that the sniper at the barn had managed to free a hand and do the same thing. "Which brings us to the Idaho hit team. As you already know from our final report, we were unable to identify any of the bodies."

"I still find it hard to believe we don't know who they are."

Hathaway scowled, apparently perturbed that the agency's work was being questioned. "Watson, their fingerprints didn't show up in any database, and they arrived in a sport utility vehicle that was stripped of any identifying marks, including VIN. The license plate was stolen a couple of years ago in California. At this point our best guess is that they were a sleeper cell that had been tucked away in the greater Los Angeles area, waiting for just such an opportunity."

"But here is the little bow that ties all of these things together," the Oracle said. "Because the Chinese were able to decode the location of the lodge, we can only assume that they are now also aware of the operation that was planned in Brazil."

Zane pointed at the slide. "In looking at the translated code, I see that there are vague references to a possible alien outpost and the search for alien technology. It's possible they took *alien* to mean foreign or hostile. If I were looking at this, the true meaning would be a bit murky."

"Perhaps, although it's equally possible that they have a clear understanding of what's going on," the Oracle pointed out. "We still don't know how much, if any, of this they were able to translate. But we have to run on the assumption that they know everything."

Zane nodded in agreement. "So, you're thinking there is at least a small chance they'll send in their own team?"

"We believe it's possible, yes. Remember, it's also very unlikely that Chinese intelligence officials got any information from their hit team in Idaho."

"Why is that important?" Zane asked.

"Since it's likely they never heard back from their hit team, it's also likely they now believe Garet Slater is still alive. And if he's still alive, then they may be running under the assumption that he's on his way to Brazil."

"Which means they'll see it as a second chance to kill him."

The Oracle nodded. "Precisely."

Hathaway looked at Zane. "Not only did they take it personally, but they probably believe that a successful hit will discourage future attempts to gather intelligence on Chinese soil."

Zane had to admit they had a point. If the Chinese were brazen enough to attempt a hit on American soil, then they certainly wouldn't hesitate to take someone down in the rainforests of Brazil. The only question was how much information they had been able to glean from the coded email.

"Is it really worth sending a team down there anyway?" Zane asked. "Are we really expecting to find something?"

The Oracle and Hathaway exchanged glances. "Watson," the Oracle said, "as crazy as it may sound, we believe that transmission, which some have called a signal, may indicate the presence of some sort of alien outpost. There is even talk of a downed ship." He looked at the operative as though trying to discern his reaction. "Look, do we know for sure there is something down there? No, we don't. We're all a bit skeptical about it, but there is no way the director is going to just drop this. The DRA stands by their declaration that this is some sort of intergalactic communication."

Zane rubbed his chin, something he did reflexively when deep in thought. Even if something had been there before, he doubted it would be there now. If these were highly intelligent beings who had previously been able to cloak their presence on earth, then it was doubtful they'd just wait to be found. On the other hand, he knew they had to go look.

"Garet is a tough cookie and can take care of himself," Zane said, "but if it were me, I'd double the military component of the team."

"Garet isn't going," the Oracle replied, "so he won't need protection."

Zane frowned. "I know he's a target, but you said he was the perfect man for the job."

"The agency isn't even going."

Zane raised an eyebrow. Suddenly everything knit together in his mind, including why he'd been called to Arlington.

"The agency was completely prepared to take on this operation," Hathaway explained. "In fact, as I mentioned earlier, it's part and parcel of what we do. But too much has been exposed. We're going to keep Garet where he is now. To be honest, we're actually going to have him communicate with his superiors through what you might say are semi-secure lines."

Zane nodded slowly. "You're basically going to broadcast that he's not in Brazil and that it's business as usual at the agency."

The Oracle nodded then paced just outside the circle of chairs. "They could've put together another team, but we all decided that it was best handled by a group that as far as we can tell isn't known to the Chinese."

"Delphi."

"Yes," the Oracle said. "Despite all the fireworks in Switzerland and France, we still believe that Delphi operates in complete anonymity. If we're known to any foreign government or organization, then it hasn't shown up in chatter yet."

"Won't the Chinese still be on the lookout for an American

team? Does it really matter who goes? Don't get me wrong, I'm looking forward to the opportunity, it's just—"

"To use the vernacular of our times… the agency is a little freaked out right now," Hathaway said. "This might surprise you, but I agree with everything you just said. I argued that we should press forward and the Chinese be damned. However, I was the minority voice."

Zane wasn't surprised. Hathaway always believed the agency could conduct operations better than any other branch of government, including those under black budgets. He did have to admire the man's willingness to go head-to-head with the Chinese.

"So when do we get started?" the operative asked.

"Almost immediately," the Oracle said. "Our intelligence is scant right now, but we believe the Chinese may already be assembling a team to travel to Brazil. Based on reports from our watchers, we don't think they're down there yet, but we do think that if they're going, they'll be there soon."

"There is one thing that doesn't seem to add up," Zane said as he stood from his leather chair. "Where exactly do they think they're going? Based on what I read in the email, the only thing they know is that we're investigating a strange signal in northern Brazil."

"Brett," the Oracle said, looking at the chief technology specialist.

Brett opened his laptop again and said, "If you'd had more time to read the translation of Garet's email, you'd see that he did give a somewhat precise location." He brought up a final slide. "Here is a map we put together with help from the DRA.

It's a bit more precise than the description in the email but not much. The bottom line is that the Chinese probably know the general area we're focused on."

"So basically we're starting on a level playing field?" Zane asked.

"Pretty much. Although the DRA is trying to pin things down a bit more."

Zane looked at the Oracle. "I guess that means I need to start putting together my team."

Brett and the Oracle exchanged a quick glance before the Oracle looked at Zane. "Your team has already been assembled."

Zane frowned. That's not what he wanted to hear. "Who are you sticking me with?"

"Some familiar faces," the Oracle replied. "And a few surprises."

CHAPTER EIGHT

Washington, DC

ZANE TURNED AWAY from the window of the private room at the Old Ebbitt Grill, a look of surprise spreading across his face. "*Amanda Higgs?*"

The Oracle signaled the waiter to bring more drinks before turning back toward Zane. "Yes, Amanda Higgs."

Brett looked up from his laptop. "He told you to expect a few surprises."

The three had arrived at the famed Washington restaurant twenty minutes earlier. Not surprisingly, it had been filled with an overflow crowd of tourists and regulars. Thankfully, the Oracle had called ahead, which meant that a pretty blond hostess pulled them aside when they entered and lead them to what had become Delphi's unofficial social retreat.

Zane smiled. "Interesting."

"How so?"

"I just remember how adamant you were that she be taken

off the team in Switzerland."

"I've always been one of her biggest fans," the Oracle said. "I'm sure you remember how glowingly I spoke of her prior to your meeting in London. But that was then and this is now." The Oracle drained the last of his brandy and set the snifter on the table. "Besides, I think you'll understand more fully once we've had a chance to discuss the operation in greater detail."

Zane turned and looked out of the window once again. The rain was beating mercilessly on the sidewalk outside. Two women rushed by, their arms locked around each other as they huddled under a shared umbrella.

The waiter reentered the room with their drinks. After taking the fresh snifter of brandy, the Oracle gestured for Zane to take a seat.

"Don't get me wrong," Zane said as he sat down. "I'm a big fan too. I'm just a little surprised that you changed your tune so quickly."

"I think you'll find this is going to be one of the most unique operations we've ever taken on," said the Oracle. "And because of that, I've had to think outside the box."

"Any other surprises?"

The Oracle held Zane's gaze for a moment. "I have some good news and some bad news. First of all, Brooks insisted on having final say in the team's makeup, and I didn't want to push back too hard since they agreed to hand us the reigns."

Zane's mouth twisted into a smirk. That didn't surprise him at all. "That's obviously the bad news. What's the good news?"

"The good news is that after all was said and done, we put

together an outstanding team. In fact, I think you'll be thrilled."

Zane let a line of bloodred Bordeaux run into his mouth then lowered his glass and smiled. "We'll see about that."

"Let's put it this way," the Oracle said. "I was pretty much able to get everyone I wanted. Brooks seemed satisfied with being a part of the process. He didn't really override any of my choices."

Zane raised an eyebrow. "I'm impressed."

The Oracle nodded at Brett. "Let's take him through the team."

Brett turned his laptop around so that the screen faced the other two. He reached over and used the touchpad to initiate a series of slides. After a brief pause, the first image appeared. Zane's eyes narrowed as he studied the details. Four soldiers dressed in camo were standing in a field, M4A1 carbine rifles slung over their shoulders. Behind them was the green swath of a longleaf pine forest.

"Green Berets?" Zane asked, staring at the rifles.

The Oracle nodded. "This is your muscle. Seventh Special Forces Group. Eglin Air Force Base, Florida."

Zane couldn't be more thrilled. Although he was a former Navy SEAL, he had nothing but respect for his US Army counterparts. "Eglin? That makes perfect sense. Western Hemisphere specialists, if I'm remembering correctly. South America, Central America, the Caribbean."

The Oracle took another sip of brandy. "They're still at Eglin but will be leaving for Manaus tomorrow morning," he said, referring to the largest city in north-central Brazil. "We thought about sending more man power—"

"No, four is perfect," Zane said. "The smaller the footprint, the better."

"That was our thinking as well. Counting you, we'll have the equivalent of five Special Ops soldiers on the ground. We realize the Chinese could be there, but due to the vastness of the search area, we think the likelihood of engagement is slim.

"That being said, if you get the slightest whiff of trouble, then our liaison at Eglin tells me he can have as many as fifty boots on the ground within a few hours."

"That quick?" Zane asked.

"He wouldn't say how, and I didn't ask. I've been told we have ships in the area, perhaps off the coast of French Guiana or Brazil. It's possible there are a few detachments on one of those vessels. It's also possible they're deployed somewhere on land."

"If the Green Berets say they will have boots on the ground in a few hours, then they will," Zane said.

The Oracle nodded at Brett. After a new image came up, he continued. "Meet Dr. Katiya Mills, professor of anthropology at NYU."

Zane raised an eyebrow at the attractive woman smiling back at him from the photograph. She had long brown hair that fell to her shoulders, and her lips were colored with bright red lipstick. She was Caucasian, but something about her seemed exotic. Perhaps it was her eyes. He guessed she was late thirties.

"Good grief," he said, as he took another sip of wine. "I love you, Ross."

"Down, boy," replied the Oracle. "As I said, she's a professor of anthropology. And you know what that means, Watson? It means she's familiar with primitive cultures and will be on to your caveman tactics pretty quickly."

Brett chuckled.

"In all seriousness, why an anthropologist?" Zane asked.

"Isn't it obvious? Remember what it is we're looking for down there. I realize you're probably skeptical, but we must be prepared for any eventuality, including first contact."

Zane swiveled his chair toward the Oracle. "If we were going down there to penetrate an indigenous tribe, then I guess I'd understand the need for an anthropologist. But contact with aliens? Isn't that a little bit outside of their purview?"

The Oracle twirled his snifter then set it on the table. "Apparently there are many different divisions of anthropology. As you probably know, its primary focus is the study of human culture, both past and present. What you might not know is that there are some lesser-known branches that deal with less traditional subjects… even alien culture."

"So you're telling me she's an alien anthropologist?"

"I'm not sure that's the precise nomenclature, but it's close enough."

The Oracle nodded at Brett, and seconds later the next slide appeared. This time it was another photograph and associated bio. The man pictured seemed to be approximately the same age as Katiya Mills. He had short dark hair and a face that seemed frozen into a permanent scowl. For some reason, Zane sensed this one was going to be trouble.

"And who is Mr. Sunshine?" Zane asked.

"This is Dr. Maxwell Cameron. He's an associate of Dr. Mills at NYU."

"Another anthropologist?" Zane asked.

The Oracle nodded. "His specialty is linguistics."

"The guy seems to have all the charm of a castrated weasel."

"So glad you're keeping an open mind, Watson. He and Dr. Mills just happen to be two of the leading anthropologists in the country. One would think you'd be thrilled to have them as part of your team."

"Dr. Mills, yes. This one? Not so sure."

"I should also point out something else. You mentioned indigenous people earlier. There is a high likelihood that you'll run across indigenous Brazilians. I understand there are at least three tribes known to live in and around the target area. And if contact is made, you'll want Dr. Cameron there. He speaks approximately a dozen indigenous languages."

While something about the man was unsettling, Zane had to admit it made sense to bring along someone with his skill set.

Seeming to sense the need to move on, Brett brought up a picture that Zane recognized immediately.

"And that brings us to Amanda Higgs," the Oracle said. "In studying to be an archaeologist, she completed quite a bit of coursework in anthropology. Not to mention she seems to have an uncanny knack for solving riddles." He looked at Zane, a gleam in his eye. "As you know, we've already asked her to be an archaeological consultant to Delphi, and I figured this trip might help me understand whether or not we should try to bring her on as a full-time employee."

"Assuming she's interested, I think she'd be a wonderful addition," Zane said.

The Oracle nodded at Brett. "Our chief technology specialist has had a few conversations with her, and he told me that if offered, she'd accept. Long story short, she accepted."

Zane had always believed that Amanda's knowledge of history and ancient artifacts made her a natural fit at Delphi. She didn't have the physical tools or weapons training to work in the field, but those were things she could be taught.

The Oracle cleared his throat as the next photograph appeared. It depicted a dark-skinned man standing on a dock. Zane guessed he was in his late fifties or early sixties, although his weathered skin might make him look older than his years.

"This is Jorge Salvador. Fifty-four years old. Brazilian. He's going to take you down the river and through the jungle. He's been on the agency payroll for the better part of two decades. He works on an as-needed basis. When not helping the agency, he operates a cruise boat that runs out of Manaus."

"His own cruise boat? That's convenient."

"I think you'll like the accommodations," the Oracle said.

Brett brought up a photograph of the vessel. It was a two-story affair that sat low in the water. The hull was a brilliant white, and the name *Izabel* was printed along the side near the bow. Zane had visited the Amazon years ago, and the ship seemed typical of those that ferried tourists up and down the river.

"Nice. It looks like the Cadillac of cruise boats. I guess our friend has done well for himself."

"I hear business is good," the Oracle replied. "I'm sure he'd do quite well even if he weren't working for us."

"Exactly what sort of work did he do for the agency?"

"Much of his file was redacted, but from what I could tell, it seems he spent a lot of time facilitating the movement of CIA operatives in northern Brazil. He's even done some work in Venezuela."

Zane took another sip of Bordeaux then asked, "Does the agency really have a significant interest in that part of the world? It seems like the drug trade would be a bit outside their interests."

"You're right, they aren't concerned with drug trafficking. Their concern is all of the bad guys from around the world who are trying to set up shop down there."

"Terror groups?"

The Oracle nodded. "Yes, the usual suspects. Al Qaeda, ISIL… even Boko Haram has a small presence there."

Zane looked back at the photograph. "I'm assuming he has a crew?"

"There are two additional crewmen. I don't have photographs, but they've been working with the agency as well. Hathaway tells me that no one knows the backwaters of the Amazon better than these three men."

"Speaking of our destination, how big is our target area?"

"As Brett alluded to earlier, the DRA has been working with the Brazilians to pinpoint the precise location of the audio transmission. I'm told they've narrowed it down to a five-square-mile area. Salvador has been working on it as well. You'll get more information in your package."

"How much of a journey are we talking?" Zane asked.

The Oracle looked at Brett. "I'll let Brett take it from here."

"I've been in touch with Jorge Salvador," Brett said, "and we've worked out a tentative itinerary." He paused and pulled up a map of Brazil, zooming in on Manaus. Their route was highlighted in red. "We're going to depart Manaus this Sunday evening. We'll travel west on the Amazon for two days before turning north on a tributary."

"At some point the water will be too shallow to take the boat any farther," the Oracle interjected. "That's where most of you will get off."

"*Most* of us?" Zane asked.

The Oracle nodded. "One of the Brazilians will take the boat back down the river to a small town. Apparently Salvador owns a small dock there. His man will wait there until it's time to go back and pick you up."

Brett used his cursor to drag the remainder of the route into view. "As you can see, we'll traverse the remainder of the route on foot through the jungle. Although it's impossible to know how long it's going to take, we should expect a minimum of two days to reach the target area."

Zane finished the last of his wine and placed it on the table. "If my math is right, that's four or five days to get there. That's *deep* in the jungle." He looked at the Oracle. "When do we leave?"

"You and Brett will board a charter tomorrow."

CHAPTER NINE

People's Liberation Army General Staff Headquarters
Beijing, China

COLONEL ZHENG LEE stood and looked out the glass window of his office. Night was falling over Beijing, and a seemingly endless river of red taillights flowed down the boulevard below him. The workday was mercifully coming to a close.

He glanced at his watch. In five minutes, his driver would pull up to the front of the building. After picking up his wife at their residence, they would be driven to the airport to catch an evening flight to Chengdu. Zheng smiled. This was the first vacation he'd had in almost a year. By this time tomorrow he'd be away from the smog and dirt of Beijing. Not to mention he'd be able to shut his wife up once and for all. She'd been nagging him for months about taking a trip, giving him a litany of other military wives who seemed to travel almost constantly.

Their destination was a mountain villa with his wife's sister and her husband. The women would spend their days in Chengdu shopping. For his part, Zheng planned on taking hikes and spending lots of time on the porch with bottles of Tsingtao.

Zheng heard a buzzing behind him. Turning, he saw his mobile phone sitting on his desk, a light blinking to indicate he had a text.

Probably the driver telling me he's early.

He grabbed the phone and stared at the screen.

It was General Kong's secretary. Zheng was to report to the general immediately.

He frowned, unsure what to think. He didn't report directly to Kong. The general was responsible for China's Special Forces. So why was Zheng being asked to meet with him? Something didn't make sense. Whatever the reason, he knew it couldn't be good.

Zheng cursed under his breath. He'd almost made it out of this wretched place.

He glanced at his watch again. His car would be arriving any minute. He sent the driver a quick text indicating he'd been held up but would text him again when he was on his way down.

After grabbing his coat and turning out the lights, Zheng proceeded down a lengthy corridor to a row of elevators. When the car arrived, he stepped in and pressed 40, the floor of the high command.

As the car began to move, Zheng felt beads of sweat forming on his forehead. It was bad enough to have to go to the fortieth floor. It was even worse to go there for a meeting with Kong. The man was known for his prickly personality and volatile temper.

The elevator dinged loudly, and the doors swished apart. Zheng stepped out and was approached by two guards whose faces were etched with permanent scowls. He'd almost forgotten the protocol for those visiting the fortieth floor. Remembering the drill, Zheng lifted his arms as one of the soldiers waved a paddle over every inch of his body. There were no threatening beeps, so the soldier grunted that he was clear.

Zheng was wondering what to do next, when he heard the click of heels. An attractive woman in her thirties strode toward him. She was dressed in a gray business suit and was speaking into a headset.

So this is where all the good-looking ones work.

"Good evening, Colonel Zheng," said the woman after ending her other conversation. She bowed slightly. "Follow me, please."

As they walked, Zheng asked, "Do you know what the general wants?"

The girl turned and smiled but said nothing. He doubted she even knew but figured it was worth a try.

At the end of the hall, they turned right. A few seconds later, they arrived at Kong's door on the left.

The woman turned her head away from him and spoke into the mic of her headset. A moment later, she turned and said, "The general will see you now."

The woman turned the knob and opened the door, motioning him in. After he entered, she bowed and closed the door behind him.

Kong's office was like his personality, simple and no nonsense. A desk, two bookcases, and two chairs that looked like they'd been purchased at a yard sale. It was exactly as Zheng had pictured it.

"Have a seat," grunted the portly general from behind his desk.

As Zheng sat down, he noticed the incredible view out of the window behind Kong. If not for the gathering darkness, Zheng figured he could see Chengdu from here.

Kong beat the keys of his laptop a moment longer before finally pushing it to the side. The general then sat back and crossed his arms. "Zheng, thank you for coming. Can I get you something to drink?" Zheng opened his mouth to speak, but Kong continued without waiting for an answer. "You are here because of your experience in South America."

Zheng frowned. *What on earth could this be about?* He had worked in Peru for three years in the 1990s, but they were three of the most uneventful years of his career.

"I was only there for—"

"The Americans have found something in Brazil, north of the Amazon." He raised his eyebrows and said, "We don't have all of the details, but we believe it may involve alien technology."

Zheng's eyes widened. "Aliens? As in extraterrestrials?"

"Is there another kind?" Kong asked pointedly.

"Surely we don't believe it's true," Zheng asked. "The Americans are known to chase all sorts of silly things."

Kong drew in a deep breath and said, "Whether it's true or

not doesn't really matter. What matters is the Chairman of the Central Military Commission thinks it's important, and if he thinks it's important, then we think it's important."

Zheng stiffened at the mention of the chairman. "I understand. But how could there be alien technology in the middle of the jungle?"

Kong shrugged. "The chairman believes a craft may have crashed there, something like that. He believes we could find some sort of new metal, new propulsion system… who knows what."

"Interesting."

A phone vibrated on Kong's desk. The general picked it up and stared at the screen. "That is the chairman. He probably wants to make sure everything has been communicated." Kong rose from his seat. "You will now go to see Lieutenant General Huang, who will brief you on the details of your operation."

Zheng stood, a frown forming on his face. "My operation?"

Kong fixed his gaze on the colonel. "You're leading a team to Brazil, Zheng. You're the highest ranking officer with experience in that part of the world."

Zheng felt a rush of panic. He hadn't been out in the field in years, which had suited him just fine. "Do we know the dates?" he asked. "I want to make sure I'm back from my vacation in time."

Kong frowned. "Vacation?" He gave a brief chuckle. "There will be no vacation, Zheng. You can take it when you get back. Your mission begins in two days."

"Two days. I—"

"That will be all, Zheng." Kong nodded toward the door.

Zheng turned slowly, scarcely able to believe the strange

turn of events. It would do no good to argue. If the chairman had appointed him as team lead, then there would be no way out. He grabbed the knob and turned it.

"Oh, and Zheng," Kong said.

Zheng turned back toward the general.

"You should feel honored to lead this operation. You're going to have a special guest."

Zheng's brow furrowed. "Someone I know?"

"You've probably heard of him." He paused for dramatic effect then said, "Ho Chen."

Ho Chen. Where had he heard that name before? Zheng searched the recesses of his mind but was unable to bring anything to the surface.

Seeing his confusion, Kong smiled. "You may know him better by his other name, Jùrén."

Zheng's pulse quickened. *The Giant.* So, all the whispers were true. He *did* exist. The man, if he could even be called that, was said to stand seven-and-a-half feet tall with arms the size of tree trunks. Some believed he was an anomaly of nature, while others believed he was the product of genetic manipulation. Whatever his origin, he was said to be the most powerful man on earth. Those who believed he'd been cooked up in a lab said that he was likely a forerunner to soldiers of the future, massive men who could move as quickly as a leopard. One officer had even told Zheng that Ho could lift the end of a car as easily as others could lift a coffee table.

"I guess he wasn't just a rumor after all," Zheng finally said.

Kong smiled. "I can assure you that Jùrén is quite real, Zheng. In fact, you're going to meet him tomorrow morning."

CHAPTER TEN

Manaus, Brazil

AMANDA HIGGS LET out a long sigh as the cab driver used his nicotine-stained fingers to count out her change for the third time. Could this get any more frustrating? The last twenty-four hours had been a nightmare, and the driver's cigarette smoking and incessant chatter during the ride over had been the straw that broke the proverbial camel's back.

The two-stop journey from Austin to Manaus had been fraught with problems. The first round of trouble came in Houston, when the airline published the wrong terminal for her connecting flight. Then in Miami there was the unexplained hour-long wait on the tarmac. And if that weren't enough, her five-hour flight to Brazil provided the clincher: she spent the entire flight next to a man whose snores could drown out a foghorn.

Then the hotel in Manaus proved to be only slightly better. It was clean and possessed a friendly staff, but a group of

Dutch ecotourists in the suite next to hers had drunk and partied until the wee hours of the morning.

The driver gave a little grunt of satisfaction, drawing Amanda out of her thoughts. After counting for the third time, he'd finally been able to get the money right. He handed her the stack of bills with a meaty paw and said, "It has been pleasure. I always like to practice English! Thank you!"

"No, thank you," Amanda said, handing a few of the bills back as a tip. She couldn't help but like the man. Yes, his cab had been filled with smoke. And yes, he'd talked non-stop since she'd entered the car. But he seemed kind and had managed to get her where she was going.

He pointed toward a boardwalk a block away. "The boats are just ahead. If you want a drink before you leave, try the Café Maria. It's my cousin's place. Tell them Tiago sent you and they might give you discount."

"Thank you again," Amanda said, bending over to give him a little wave.

As the Brazilian made a quick U-turn and headed back toward the city, Amanda let out a little sigh. Her body ached from head to toe, and she felt a migraine coming on, but she was finally here. In a few short minutes, she'd be with people she knew and the nightmare of the last twenty-four hours would be over.

She pulled out the telescoping handles of her luggage and started down the boardwalk. On her right was a line of cafés and bars. Ahead and to the left was a long series of docks that stretched into the distance. She had exchanged a few texts with Zane that morning and knew that the boat would be all the way at the end.

The smell of freshly cooked food assailed her nostrils as she walked. Several men stood in front of their shops, offering wrapped pieces of fish and skewers of cooked meat. She was tempted but resisted and continued on her way.

As she neared the docks, she saw the sign for Café Maria. She hadn't planned on stopping, but she was thirsty. Why not? It might be days before she had anything other than bottled water and MREs.

The covered but open-air restaurant was packed with humanity. There were perhaps a hundred tables, all kept cool by twirling fans that dangled from the high ceiling. Pushing through the crowd, she was surprised to find two empty stools at the bar. She promptly sat down on one then scooted her luggage up as close as possible.

One of the bartenders slid toward her, placed his hand on the bar, and asked something in Portuguese. Amanda did a double take, startled at the man's appearance. He looked exactly like Enrique Iglesias, right down to the boyish locks combed across his forehead.

The man raised an eyebrow and patted his hand gently on the bar. Amanda blushed as she realized she'd been staring at him. "Oh, sorry. An orange juice in a to-go cup, please."

Enrique lifted a thumb to signify he understood. As Amanda looked through her purse for some bills, a man stepped up to the other open stool and bent over the bar.

Another American, she thought as she looked at him out of the corner of her eye. He was wearing a Carolina Hurricanes cap, and a pair of aviator sunglasses hid his eyes. His arms were well muscled and tan, as were the legs that stuck out of beige cargo shorts.

"You know, I'm pretty sure he saw you blushing," the man said.

Startled, she turned toward him. "Excuse me?"

The man sported a week's growth of beard, but his features seemed vaguely familiar.

He gave her a wry smile and said, "I just need you to know I'm a little hurt that you don't recognize me."

And then it hit her. Why hadn't she recognized him immediately? "*Zane?*"

"The one and only. How are you?"

"I'm great!" she said, throwing her arms around him.

After the long hug, he pulled back and rubbed the stubble on his cheek. "Not a bad disguise, eh?"

"You had me fooled." She noticed he didn't have his customary long locks. "Did you cut your hair?"

Zane patted his cap. "No, just tucked away. You look great, by the way."

"Thank you."

The bartender returned with Amanda's orange juice. She fished in her pocket for money, but Zane waved her off. "This one's on me."

"Why thank you."

He then turned to the bartender and ordered something in Portuguese.

"Wow, you speak the language. I'm impressed."

"I know about fifty words, and that was probably a third of them."

"So what did you get?"

"Some frozen pineapple concoction. It's my second one. Figured it would put me in the mood. How was your trip?"

She rolled her eyes. "Don't ask."

Zane laughed. "Uh-oh. I won't, then."

The bartender returned with the drink. Zane thanked him and placed several bills on the counter.

Turning, he grabbed the handles of her luggage. "You ready?"

She held up her orange juice. "As I'll ever be!"

As they walked along the docks, Amanda marveled at the number and variety of boats. Everything from kayaks and motorized canoes to a few large yachts and cruise boats sat moored to the docks. There wasn't an inch of unused space anywhere.

"Is everyone here?" she asked.

"No, we still haven't heard from two members of the team."

Amanda could sense frustration in his voice. "I hope nothing is wrong."

He paused a moment before answering. "I was supposed to speak to our two anthropologists last night and never heard from them."

"Did you call them?"

He nodded. "No answer. I'm sure everything is fine."

Amanda decided to change the subject. "I have to tell you I'm so looking forward to meeting Dr. Mills."

Zane's brow furrowed. "You know her?"

"Of course. Well, I don't *know* her… I know of her. She's a big name in academic circles. One of the biggest—"

"Well, well, look who's here," said a male voice ahead.

Amanda looked up. A man with dark hair stood on one of the docks next a large cruise boat. He held a box, and a huge grin was plastered on his face. She recognized him immediately. "Brett!"

The technology specialist leaned over and set the box down next to some others. "Glad to see you made it all safe and sound."

Amanda ran over and hugged his neck. Pulling back, she said, "I'm safe... not sure about the sound part."

"Well, at least you got here in one piece."

"Amanda, I'd like to introduce you to some members of our team," Zane said.

She turned and noticed that four men were standing on the deck of the boat just a few feet away. There were all dressed the same in multi-pocketed cargo pants and dark gray T-shirts. One of the men was African-American and bald. Another had close-cropped blond hair. The remaining two wore full beards and hair down to their shoulders. The shorter one had wavy red hair and the other dark brown.

Despite their garb and varied appearance, she knew immediately they were all military. The two with longer hair had probably grown it in order to blend in. She had seen pictures of SEALS in Afghanistan who had done the same thing.

Zane gestured toward the African-American soldier. "This is Corporal Desmond Wilson."

He smiled and offered his hand to her. "You can call me

Dez."

"Nice to meet you, Dez," she said.

Zane next indicated the one with the close-cropped blond hair. "This is Corporal Paul Nash."

"Nice to meet you."

"The pleasure is all mine." His eyes roamed a bit much for her taste. *Need to keep my eye on him,* she thought.

"And finally," Zane said, gesturing toward the other two men, "we have Sergeant Landon Tocchet and Sergeant First Class Rod Bennett."

The two men leaned over the rail and shook her hand.

"Nice to meet you, ma'am," Sergeant Bennett said. He tugged on his hair and said, "I apologize for our appearance."

"No worries. I'm sure after a few days in the jungle, you guys won't even want to look at me."

"I sincerely doubt that," Zane said.

Amanda popped him on the arm as the soldiers returned to their duties. She noticed that Nash looked at her as he walked away. He gave her a little smile, but she quickly turned to look at Zane.

Brett lifted a hand to shield his eyes from the early-morning sun. "Still no sign of Dr. Mills?"

Zane frowned. "Not that I saw."

"I checked online, and their flight arrived on time last night."

"Are you sure there's nothing wrong?" Amanda asked. "You seem concerned."

Zane finished the last of his frozen drink and threw it into a nearby bin. "Not necessarily concerned about their safety.

I'm sure they're fine."

Brett looked at Amanda. "Let's just say he's not a big fan of Dr. Mills's colleague."

Zane shot him a glance.

"Dr. Maxwell Cameron?" she asked. "What's wrong—"

"I'm sure nothing is wrong with Dr. Cameron," Zane said. "Just an old soldier's intuition." He patted her on the shoulder. "My big concern is actually you. Pretty girl from Austin trying to survive in the jungle."

She laughed. "Look, I've traveled all over Africa and the Middle East. I've been bitten by nasty bugs, crawled on by spiders, struck at by snakes, and I even survived a dust storm in the middle of the desert. I think I can take care of myself."

"Not bad for an academic," Zane said. "Unfortunately I think we're going to run across some things that will make that look like child's play."

"You sure you aren't the one who's scared?" Amanda shot back with a smile.

Zane winked at her.

"He's right, you know," said someone behind her.

Amanda turned to see a man in his fifties or early sixties standing on the boat. He must have slipped up quietly while they were talking. He had dark hair flecked with gray, a bushy mustache, and a pleasant but weathered face.

The man lifted a cigar and took a slow draw. After blowing a plume of smoke in the air, he said, "The jungle can be a terrifying place for those who visit for the first time. You must give it all the respect it deserves."

Zane gestured toward the man. "Amanda, I'd like you to

meet Jorge Salvador. He's the captain of the *Izabel*."

She extended a hand. "Hi, I'm Amanda Higgs."

"The pleasure is mine," he said with a smile. "I hope I didn't scare you. I've always found it better to let people know just how different the jungle is from what they're accustomed to."

"The good news is that I've been in a few rainforests before, just not here," Amanda said.

Jorge nodded as he took another draw. "That's good. Just remember that we're going deeper than any tour group would ever go." His eyes narrowed. "In fact, we're going deeper into the jungle than most scientists go. And for the unprepared, it can be a frightening experience."

"I can assure you I have the deepest respect for the jungle."

He nodded, although she couldn't tell if he believed her or not. He seemed like a nice guy, but more importantly, he seemed like the kind of guy you'd want watching your back out in the middle of Amazonia. He was the kind of man who knew secrets, the kind that could kill you.

Zane nodded at the boat. "Brett, why don't you introduce Amanda to the crew?"

"I'd be happy to," Brett said, swinging a section of the railing back. "Welcome aboard."

Amanda stepped up onto the craft and wondered how long it would be before she'd step off again.

***

As Brett escorted Amanda onto the boat, Zane heard a man speaking loudly from the boardwalk. "So they expect us to travel on a small—"

"Are you sure this is the right one?" the woman next to him asked.

"Of course I'm sure. The name is right there."

Zane watched as the two stepped onto the dock, pulling wheeled luggage behind them. The woman was wearing a solid-red T-shirt, snugly fitting jeans, and running shoes. Zane immediately recognized Dr. Katiya Mills from her pictures. *The photograph hadn't done her justice,* he mused. The woman was a classic beauty. Her lush brown hair was pulled up into a ponytail, and her smooth, cream-colored skin made her seem even younger than her thirty-seven years. She was even wearing her trademark red lipstick.

Standing next to her was a man who needed no introduction. Maxwell Cameron's shaggy dark hair looked longer than Zane remembered. What did look the same was the permanent sourpuss expression on his face.

As the two approached, they seemed surprised to see Zane and Jorge standing there.

Pushing back from the rail, Zane and Jorge walked down the ramp. The Brazilian extended his hand. "My name is Jorge, and I'll—"

"Cameron Maxwell," the man said, shoving the handles of their luggage at the Brazilian. "Let me just say right up front that Dr. Mills and I won't be staying in a room below deck. You can put our luggage—"

"There are no rooms below the waterline, senhor," Jorge replied.

The woman stepped forward and extended her hand. "I'm

Katiya Mills. You'll have to excuse both Cameron and me if we seem a little tired. It's been a long trip."

"Zane Watson," Zane said. "I've been trying to reach you all morning."

"I know. I'm so sorry. I had the cell turned off, trying to save my battery."

She seems sincere, Zane thought. *The excuse is a little lame though.*

Maxwell looked at Zane. "Well, you told us to be here today, and here we are. No harm, no foul."

Zane thought about reminding him that they were supposed to arrive by noon but decided to bite his tongue. He was determined to keep things as peaceful as possible, even if the guy was a jerk.

"And here you are indeed," he said.

"Allow me to show you to your rooms," Jorge said. He grabbed the handles of Katiya's two suitcases, ignoring the ones Maxwell had thrust toward him.

The linguist muttered something under his breath and followed them up the ramp.

CHAPTER ELEVEN

THE MAN SITTING outside the café took another slow sip of coffee and set the cup down on the table. He picked up the Manaus newspaper and held it in front of him, using it as a shield while he watched the two men on the boat about fifty yards away.

Squinting, he watched their lips move in unison with the voices that crackled through his earbuds. His English was poor, so he found it difficult to follow everything they said. In the end, it didn't matter whether he understood them or not. The entire conversation was being transmitted to a remote location, where it would be translated later that day.

There was a bit of static, so the man adjusted the position of his listening device, which was constructed to look like an MP3 player. It was a design feature that allowed the user to operate only a few yards away from the target. The Americans always boasted of their superior technology, but as far as he knew, they had nothing like this.

Despite the tactical advantage, the man still felt a bit

unsettled operating so close to his targets. He was old school and would've much preferred conducting surveillance the old-fashioned way, from a distant rooftop or from inside a communications van.

Suddenly the man's eyes narrowed. Two more people, a man and a woman, had approached the boat. He recognized them immediately from the photographs he'd studied over the last several days. Both were professors from NYU. If his information was correct, that meant the entire American team had arrived. It also meant they'd likely be departing soon.

His work now complete, the man stowed the listening device and earbuds inside his rucksack. He threw a few bills on the table, stood, and stepped out onto the boardwalk. The crowds were still thick, allowing him to blend in without fear of detection. Everything had gone off without a hitch.

Two minutes later, he arrived at dock fifteen. A Brazilian teenager stood from a bench as he approached. After paying the boy, the man walked until he found the skiff moored where he'd left it that morning.

After climbing in, he untied the rope and pushed away from the post. Once the craft was clear of the other boats, he started the engine. It sputtered to life, sending plumes of acrid smoke into the air. He puttered past the end of the dock and turned west, easing through the no-wake zone.

He smiled as the boat skimmed across the water and the wind beat against his face. The Americans had chosen a small team, perhaps emphasizing mobility over strength. That would be a fatal mistake. Yes, there were current and former US Special Forces soldiers in the group, but most of the others looked soft. American soft.

Now out on the river, he opened the throttle. Seconds later, he passed the *Izabel*. An excited shiver ran through his body as he stared at the people he would soon kill.

CHAPTER TWELVE

Amazon River, Brazil

AFTER A LIGHT dinner of broiled fish and fruit, the group gathered on the bridge of the *Izabel*. Zane and Jorge stood at the front next to Marcos, who was at the helm. The others were seated in folding chairs arranged in a semicircle.

A storm raged outside, rocking the boat slightly as it chugged downriver. Rain pounded the roof so hard that it sounded like the beating of a hundred snare drums, while wind swept across the bow, carrying with it small tree limbs and leaves.

As the rain hit a momentary lull, Zane cleared his throat and said, "First of all, I'd like to thank each and every one of you for coming."

Max Cameron leaned toward Katiya. "What is this, *The Love Boat?*"

Zane looked over at him. "Excuse me?"

"Thank you," Katiya said, digging her elbow into Max's

side. "It's a pleasure to be here."

Zane nodded but let his eyes linger on Max a moment before continuing. "As I was saying, thanks to each and every one of you for coming. We have a long, tough journey ahead, and I need you to pay close attention to what we're going to cover tonight." He nodded at Brett, who typed out a command on his laptop. A satellite map of the Amazon River appeared on a wall to the operative's left. He lifted a laser pointer and hovered the dot over a city. "We have just left Manaus, which is here. Sometime tomorrow we will take this tributary north toward our destination." He moved the red dot along the route. "We'll follow the tributary for another day before finally anchoring somewhere along in here." He hovered the dot over an area near where the tributary disappeared into the green of the jungle. "That means we'll be in the boat for about two days before starting our trek across land."

Amanda raised her hand. "What can we expect once we're off the boat? Are there trails, or are we going to have to cut our way through the jungle?"

Zane noticed Max rolling his eyes and shaking his head. Katiya elbowed him again.

"Jorge, perhaps you can answer that," Zane said.

The Brazilian pulled an unlit cigar from his mouth and said, "There is a path that runs east then north through the jungle. I've traveled it many times. Unfortunately, it's been a while, so I can't guarantee what it will look like now. Any of you who have spent time in the jungle know a place can look completely different even after a year or two."

"Our ultimate goal is to reach an area right along in here." Zane twirled the red dot at an area well north of the tributary. "When we arrive at the perimeter, I may lead a one or two man team into the target zone before we bring all of you in."

Katiya cleared her throat. "Zane, I think it's important that Max and I be a part of any team that might establish first contact, whether with indigenous people, extraterrestrials, or something not yet defined. It's going to be vital that we have people who can communicate if necessary."

Zane nodded. "I appreciate that. Right now, we don't even know what we're going to find once we get there. Safety has to be our first priority, and the area we're going to enter is—"

Max held his hands in the air. "Of course we don't know what to expect. Dr. Mills and I still haven't been given access to map routes or the audio files of the supposed transmission."

"Your maps are right here." Zane jerked a thumb toward the image on the wall. "As for the audio file, I haven't had access to that either. But even if you had it, would you know what you were listening to? Of course not. The bottom line is, we know where the signal came from. What we don't know is what caused it."

Max muttered something and shook his head.

"Have they heard anything since the first broadcast?" Amanda asked.

"No, they haven't. But they are continuing to monitor our atmosphere for additional sounds. If they can shed more light on the target zone, they will."

Landon Tocchet, the Green Beret in charge, raised his hand. "Sir, is there anything we need to be aware of? Hostiles, dangerous animals, that kind of thing?"

Corporal Nash patted his M4 rifle. "Yeah, just tell us what needs to die, and we'll make it happen."

"Yes, there are a few things we all need to be aware of," Zane said. "And with that I'll turn it over to Jorge." He nodded at the Brazilian.

Jorge stepped forward. "Please remember that the most dangerous part of the Amazon is the water—the creeks, streams, and dark pools that seem to be everywhere. It's in those places that you'll find... how you say in English... your worst nightmares: leeches the size of your hand, caiman, electric eel, piranha, and even the anaconda." He looked at Max. "Unless I've given you the green light, please don't enter any body of water. Stay clear and pay close attention to my instructions. We want everyone back alive."

"What about human hostiles?" Tocchet asked.

Jorge crossed his arms and thought for a moment. Finally, he said, "There are tribes in the area, but I wouldn't call them hostile. Most are peaceful and won't bother you unless provoked." He walked over to the image on the wall and moved his finger along the route they would take across land. "Most of the area we'll pass through is either outside or along the edge of tribal communities. So, it is possible that we'll encounter an Indian or an indigenous tribesman. But I wouldn't say it's likely. And even if we do, they shouldn't pose a threat. There are hostile tribes in the jungle, but most are many miles to the west." Zane thought he saw a flicker of something in the Brazilian's eyes. A secret perhaps.

Katiya looked at Zane and caught his attention. "I hate to

beat a dead horse, but that goes back to what I said earlier. Max and I need to be there when you enter each new stretch of jungle. As you probably know, Max can speak over a dozen indigenous languages. In fact, he and I have both worked with tribes around the world, including ones in other parts of the Amazon. We know how they think and how they react to contact with those from the outside world."

"Dr. Mills—"

"Call me Katiya." She gave him a grin.

"Katiya, the two of you do have impressive resumes. That's one of the reasons you were selected for the team. And I agree with much of what you said a moment ago." He paused for a moment then continued. "Let me promise you this… I'll assess the situation when we get there. If I feel comfortable, then we may all go in together. If not, then my first priority has to be getting all of you out alive. We don't believe this mission involves any imminent threat to our national security, so the gathering of information will always be secondary to everyone's safety."

"I appreciate that," she said. "That's all we can ask for. I would just remind you that Max and I are here voluntarily. We knew the danger involved and gladly accepted. We don't want to do anything stupid, but at the same time, risk is an inherent part of this entire operation. There is no way to avoid it. We'll be in a danger zone the minute we step on land."

Dr. Katiya Mills was even more impressive than Zane had expected. He'd always known she was a striking combination of beauty and smarts; a brief perusal of her dossier had told him that. What he hadn't anticipated was her ability to communicate and work through difficult issues. The Oracle had hit a home run in choosing her.

"Fair enough. I give you my word that you'll be at the point of the spear whenever possible."

A gust of wind sent a sheet of rain splattering across the bridge's windshield, and the boat shook in response.

Amanda's brow furrowed. "Do we know anything specific about the area we're targeting?"

Zane and Jorge exchanged a knowing glance. "Actually we do know a little," Zane said. He lifted the laser pointer again, focusing on the same area he'd indicated before. "Brett was able to use advanced software to enhance the satellite image to near-HD quality."

Brett pecked away at his laptop for a moment then looked over at Amanda. "What we found was a topographical anomaly, something that makes this area unique in the Amazon basin, at least as far as we know. To say that it's strange doesn't begin to tell you how bizarre this place is." He turned his laptop around so that Amanda could see the image on the screen. "It's a crater, or at least it resembles one. There are rocky ridges around the perimeter, and as you can see, the rainforest fills the interior."

Katiya scooted her chair around so that she could see better. "Do we know how it formed and what's in there?"

Brett shook his head. "We don't know how it was formed."

Jorge addressed her. "At this point, the only thing we know for sure is that it is some of the deepest, darkest jungle anywhere. But what concerns me is not what we know about it, but what we don't know about it."

THE PORTAL

"Our people are continuing to look at everything they can find," Zane said. "Topo maps, enhanced satellite images... they're even going through books written by naturalists who've spent time in the area." Zane clicked off the laser pointer. "But one thing is certain, we'll know when we get there."

Katiya looked at Brett. "I'd like to get the coordinates from you so that I can do some snooping around tonight."

Brett nodded.

"And with that, we'll call it a night," Zane said. "We'll have more tomorrow, but for now, I need you all to get a good night's rest."

As the group stood, mumbled conversations filled the room.

Zane wondered if there were already some who wished they'd stayed in Manaus.

CHAPTER THIRTEEN

AMANDA LOOKED BOTH ways before tapping lightly on the door. She hoped it wasn't too late for a visit, but she also knew there might not be a better opportunity to speak to Dr. Katiya Mills one-on-one. They had been introduced just prior to the group meeting, but there hadn't been time for anything beyond pleasantries.

As an archaeologist, Amanda was familiar with the field of anthropology. That meant she was also familiar with the giants of the field, including Dr. Katiya Mills. In preparing for the trip, Amanda had reviewed a number of her papers. She found it all fascinating, but it had only served to generate more questions.

She was about to knock again, this time more firmly, when she heard a rustling in the room, followed by the pad of footsteps. There was a clicking, and the door opened about an inch.

Amanda smiled. "Hi. It's me."

Katiya opened the door all the way. She was wearing a terry

cloth robe, and her soft brown hair was pulled into a ponytail. She smiled. "Hello. Amanda, I believe?"

"Yes. When we met earlier, I didn't get a chance to properly introduce myself. I hope I didn't—"

Katiya swept her arm back, inviting her into the room. "You're not bothering me at all. I'm so glad you stopped by." Once Amanda was inside, Katiya gestured toward a folding chair near the window. "Please, have a seat. Sorry my room is not more accommodating."

"Thank you."

Amanda noticed a laptop and stacks of papers strewn across the bed. Katiya pushed the laptop aside and sat back against a pile of pillows.

"Can I offer you a drink?" The anthropologist lifted a bottle of water in the air.

"No, I'm fine. Thanks though."

A gust of wind blew a sheet of rain against the window. Katiya glanced briefly at the glass before turning toward Amanda. "So, I hear you teach at UT Austin?"

"I do. I was a graduate assistant for a couple of years, and now I'm a full-fledged professor. Currently my emphasis is on field work and research papers, which suits me just fine."

"I spent a few months there and loved it."

Amanda gave her a quizzical look. "I didn't know that."

"I was there for maybe two cups of coffee."

"Did you like it?"

"I probably loved it too much." Katiya chuckled. "Austin is that kind of place. What happens on Sixth Street stays on Sixth Street."

A broad smile spread over Amanda's face. "Funny you mentioned Sixth Street. That's often the first thing people ask me about when I tell them I live in Austin."

"It's probably a good thing I was only there for the summer. No telling what kind of trouble I might have gotten into if I had stayed."

"It is a great place to live, particularly if you're young." Amanda watched as the rain gathered in rivulets on the outside of the window. "I haven't had much time to socialize, but I'm okay with that."

Katiya reached over and closed her laptop then pulled one foot toward her. "You know, it's probably none of my business, but if I could pass along one thing, it's this: don't let your twenties pass you by without having a little fun. Unfortunately, that summer in Austin was one of the few times I let my hair down. I wish there had been more of those over the years."

"But look at all you've accomplished. I'd say you've done okay."

"And yet I would've traded it for more time with my friends. More time spent being a twenty-something. Perhaps even more time with someone special."

"You never married?"

Katiya's eyes fixed on a random stack of papers on the bed. "No, and to be honest, I've never even gotten close. When I was about your age, I decided that I was going to be the best anthropologist in the country. I know that sounds a bit cocky, but it was more a search for knowledge than it was a desire for recognition. At least I hope that's true."

A gust of wind howled outside, spraying more rain across the window.

After it died down, Katiya continued. "Some say that I've achieved that goal. But what does that mean exactly? I guess I'm still trying to find out. I don't necessarily regret it, although I'd love to have more balance. You know, I've made a living studying humankind, and now I've discovered I know very little about the humanity around me. It's the irony of ironies." She smiled. "But I'm going to change all of that."

Amanda nodded. "What you say makes perfect sense. It's amazing how similar our thought processes are." She raised an eyebrow. "And maybe you're right. Maybe I do need to socialize more. I'm a Christian, and how else am I going to share my good news if I don't get out into the world and meet new people?"

"Exactly," Katiya agreed. "I'm always curious about the beliefs of others. Perhaps we can—"

Suddenly the door to the room swung open. Amanda jumped at the noise. When she turned, she saw Maxwell Cameron standing there. When he saw her, his frown transitioned quickly to a look of surprise.

"I... I heard voices," he said. "I—"

Katiya seemed strangely unaffected by the intrusion. "Max, have you met Amanda?"

"Ah, yes... we met earlier."

Amanda extended her hand. "Nice to see you again."

"Nice to see you." He shook her hand but kept his eyes on Katiya. "Don't you need some rest? It's getting late."

"We're just going to talk for a few minutes. We're fine."

"But—"

"We're *fine*, Max."

He took a few steps backwards but then stopped. "Okay. Let me know if you need anything."

"Thank you, Max."

"And let me know—"

"I'll see you in the morning, okay?"

Max glowered but backed out of the room, closing the door behind him.

Amanda faced Katiya again. "Sorry, but I have to ask… does he always just barge in like that?"

Katiya let out a long sigh. "You'll have to forgive Max. He and I are close friends, and he cares about me. A lot. I know he's a bit overbearing, but he really does mean well. If it weren't for him, I doubt I'd be where I am today." She poked a few random pages on her bedspread with a finger. "As I'm sure you know, the academic world can be filled with backstabbing and jealousy. And because of that it's good to have a friend who'll watch your back. For me, Max is that friend."

Amanda nodded. She agreed that friends were invaluable, particularly in academia, but it still didn't explain or excuse the man's odd behavior. Couldn't she have found someone a little more stable to run her support network? He seemed a little odd for that role.

Amanda decided it might be a good time to switch gears. "So tell me about alien anthropology. I'm fascinated by the topic."

"Well, can I tell you a dirty little secret?" Katiya's eyes

beamed playfully.

"Of course. I love dirty little secrets."

Katiya leaned forward and whispered, "There really isn't anything to tell." After holding her serious look for a moment, Katiya laughed. "To be honest, I was afraid someone was going to ask me about it, and I guess I should've expected it might be you. I'm exaggerating a bit. We've actually conducted quite a bit of research, but the field is still in its infancy."

Amanda sat upright. "So tell me what you have done."

"Well, for one, I've conducted a lot of interviews. And when I say a lot, I mean *a lot*."

"How many?"

"I lost count a long time ago. If I had to guess, I'd say I'm probably approaching a thousand."

Amanda's eyes widened. "And who have you interviewed? What's it all about?"

"Right now it's the primary way we gather information. We want to talk to anyone who claims to have seen an alien craft or who says they've been abducted." She bit her lower lip. "Let me make a clarification: we don't interview just anyone. The people we sit down with must have an unassailable reputation for character and ethics. In fact, I probably spend almost as much time looking into each person's background as I do conducting the interview itself."

"So, be honest... do you believe these people are telling the truth?"

"Yes, I do," Katiya answered without hesitation. "My assistants and I do a pretty good job of screening out the nut jobs and the people with a reputation for exaggeration. Once we do that, we find we're talking to people who are both truthful and stable." She shrugged. "Obviously, there is the occasional story I'm skeptical of. But I'd say that's the exception and not the rule."

"Have you been able to gather any concrete evidence that we're being visited?"

"Amanda, you're an archaeologist, so you know there is research and then there is *research*. For example, you conduct digs and extract things out of the earth: pottery, vases, weapons, cooking utensils, ancient tablets. Then you document those findings in a tangible way.

"It's different in our field. There's very little physical evidence."

"Okay, but *very little* physical evidence? That implies there is *some*."

Katiya held her thumb and index finger slightly apart. "A tiny little bit, yes. And that's what really gets me excited."

"Well, let's hear it."

Katiya paused for a moment. It seemed like she was sorting through what she could share. Finally, she looked up at Amanda and said, "Okay, here's one. Two years ago we interviewed a man from a small town in Vermont. Great reputation in his community. Owns a chain of highly successful hardware stores in the eastern part of the state. He has a lot to lose if people think he's turned into some sort of flake, and yet he still spoke out.

"Anyway, he claims he was abducted on three separate occasions. Each time, he was placed in sort of a hypnotic state before being levitated and carted out of the house. His story was so compelling that we decided to conduct a second interview with him under hypnosis. It's something we often do with convincing cases. It was during that second interview that we picked up a piece of information that hadn't come out before. During the final abduction, which had taken place only a week before, one of the beings did something unusual. It placed a hand on one of the sliding glass doors at the back of the man's home."

Amanda's brow furrowed. "He remembered that? It seems like an awfully small detail for someone to recall."

"That's the benefit of placing the subject under hypnosis. Recall is amazing in that state. You wouldn't believe the detail we get. On top of that, we ask questions about everything, and I mean everything. Sometimes I think we're more thorough than the police."

"How did the hand on the sliding glass door come up?"

"When I asked him to describe being taken out to the ship, he spoke of the sliding glass door being opened wider to allow him to pass through. I asked if the door opened on its own or whether they touched it. He said they touched it."

Amanda sat up straighter in her chair.

"Immediately after bringing him out of hypnosis, we sent a forensics team out to dust the door. And he was right. There was a print exactly where we thought it would be, about two-and-a-half feet off the ground."

"What did the print look like?"

Katiya exhaled slowly. "I can't lie. It was bizarre. Our forensics expert tells us the ridge design is unlike anything he's ever seen."

"Oh my. I'm surprised I haven't read about this—"

"We haven't told anyone, nor have I included it in any of my research papers... not yet anyway. There are still some things we're looking into that I can't even share with you tonight."

"You haven't told the government?"

Katiya laughed. "The government? Why should we tell them anything? They hide everything they have then ridicule those who produce their own information." After a pause, she said, "But things are changing. I think you're going to hear them admit to a few things soon... very soon."

Amanda was about to say something but stopped when she heard the soft pad of footsteps outside the room. Seconds later she heard a door open and close.

Katiya took a swig of her bottled water. After setting it back on the nightstand, she said, "We've also obtained other evidence, mostly of a sexual nature. A number of abductees, primarily women, complained of having their bodies probed, sexually. They don't remember the details because they eventually lost consciousness."

"They were drugged?"

"That's the likeliest answer, although it's also possible they were placed in a hypnotic state using some advanced form of telepathy. The bottom line is that none of them remember anything of substance after leaving their homes.

"Some of the victims had physical marks that bore witness to the fact that they had been abused, but as you can imagine, those could have come from a number of different sources, even from contact with someone in their family. So we continue to document the details and hope that at some point we'll have our breakthrough, something we can bring to the world." She smiled. "And that's why I'm here."

"That makes sense," Amanda said. After a long silence, she looked at Katiya and smiled. "You know I have to ask this… do you think we're going to find anything?"

"That's a good question. The honest answer is that I don't know." She gestured toward her laptop and the piles of paper. "I didn't share this at the meeting, but I've discovered some pretty interesting things about our target zone. So much that it makes me suspicious that there is something going on out there."

Amanda's eyes widened. "So what did you find?"

Katiya smiled. "Give me another day or two, then we can talk. I'm still trying to put a couple of pieces together."

"You tease."

Katiya smiled. "I promise you'll be the first to know." She glanced at her watch. "Besides, it's getting late. I think we can both use some shut-eye."

Amanda stood. "Can't blame a girl for trying though."

Katiya slid off the bed and stuck her hand out. "I'm so glad you've joined the team, Amanda. I feel like we're kindred spirits."

"It's funny, but I feel the same way."

Katiya stepped across the room and opened the door. "Sleep well."

"You too."

Amanda stepped out into the hall, closing the door behind her. As she started toward her cabin, she heard a thump behind her. She turned, but no one was there. She figured the noise must have come from the door at the end of the hall, which led to the stern. Who would be out there at this hour?

Probably just a stick or a limb hitting the boat, she thought.

Hearing nothing else, she turned and walked toward her cabin.

CHAPTER FOURTEEN

THERE WAS A brief flash of light as the door at the back of the *Izabel* opened. A man draped in a raincoat stepped outside, closing the door behind him. He crossed to the rail, doing his best to ignore the storm that continued to rage along the river.

Thunder grumbled overhead, and a gust of wind sent sheets of rain whipping across the stern. The man cursed under his breath. If the cabin walls weren't so thin, he never would've ventured out into the tempest.

He turned and looked back at the door. It was still shut. *Quit worrying.* No one would come out in this weather. And even if they did, he'd already concocted a story that would explain why he was there.

Confident he wasn't being watched, the man pulled a phone from his pocket, leaning over to shelter it from the rain. He used a thumb to scroll through the contacts list until he found the name he was looking for. A quick tap initiated the call. After two rings, someone picked up but didn't speak. As the wind whipped his coat, the man hunkered down and passed along his first report. He gave them the precise location of the *Izabel* as well as a few pertinent details he'd picked up during the presentation earlier in the evening. His contact seemed pleased but reminded him that all the guidelines were to be followed. If they weren't, then he knew what to expect.

After telling his contact he understood, the man ended the call and placed the phone back in his pocket.

He lingered for a few minutes, thinking about all that had transpired that day. He'd been able to gather a lot of information already, and no one seemed to have noticed anything was amiss. Even the team lead, supposedly a sharp man, didn't seem to suspect a thing.

Suddenly a bolt of lightning flashed less than a mile away. The man realized he'd been outside long enough. Turning, he crossed over to the door, and like a hooded phantom, he slipped back inside.

CHAPTER FIFTEEN

Amazon Rainforest, Brazil

ZANE SHIELDED HIS eyes from the midafternoon sun as he strode down the boat's ramp and onto the sheltered beach. It was the first time he'd set foot on Brazilian soil in almost two days, and it felt good. This was where the real journey would begin.

As others began to stream out onto the small strip of red sand, he looked up. The rain and clouds had finally retreated, and the rainforest was bathed in a soft golden glow. The foliage was teeming with creatures, large and small, searching for food in the wake of the rain. Primates screamed from distant treetops while insects buzzed around a myriad of flowering vines.

Suddenly, he caught a flash of color out of the corner of his eye. He turned and saw a large bird flapping across the river, nesting material dangling from its bill. Seconds later, it disappeared into a large tree on the opposite bank.

The jungle was returning to life.

In a way, the poor weather of the last couple of days had provided a valuable service. Everyone had been forced to stay inside and recharge their batteries after long flights. Zane had spent most of his time going over the route with Jorge. They had discussed areas of potential trouble, including the possibility of flooding. The rains seemed to have fallen over a wide area, but they wouldn't know its effects until they began traversing the jungle on foot.

Zane unscrewed the top of his thermos and took a sip of coffee. He watched the others spread out across the beach, their necks craned as they soaked in the beauty around them. Katiya and Max moved toward a row of flowering vines where insects of various kinds were buzzing with activity. As expected, the linguist had been prickly throughout the trip. He seemed to survive on bottled energy drinks, and Zane wondered how much more obnoxious he would become now that he'd be forced to drink water.

Zane's eyes moved to Katiya. As he watched her crouch to examine a flower, he felt a little surge of warmth. He tried to push it away, but it lingered stubbornly. He would normally attribute such a feeling to physical attraction, but this seemed different. It was a development he'd have to monitor. Maintaining personal discipline while working was something he prided himself on. And while Dr. Katiya Mills was certainly someone who would warrant any man's attention, this was not the time or place. At least, he hoped not.

"I agree one hundred percent," said a male voice from behind him.

Zane turned to find Brett standing at his shoulder. "I'm sorry?"

Brett set his backpack on the ground and nodded toward Katiya. "Uber hot."

Zane shook his head. "Was it that obvious?"

"Don't feel bad. If you hadn't noticed, I might have asked for your man card."

Zane's eyes returned to the group. "How is everyone doing?"

"For the most part, good," Brett said as he took a swig of bottled water. "I think everyone has cabin fever and is just ready to get going."

"I am too." Zane reached up and wiped away the beads of sweat that had already gathered on his forehead. The breeze generated by the boat, as well as the storms, had given them a false sense of cool comfort. After stepping off the boat, that changed immediately. They weren't even under the canopy yet, and the humidity was already suffocating. "My big concern is preparedness."

"How so?"

Zane took another sip of coffee and screwed the cap back on his thermos. "I've had to survive out in the jungle before, and nothing really prepares you for the wave of discomfort that hits you out here. The heat, the clouds of insects, the sudden rains that soak through clothing in seconds. Not to mention all the deadly critters that lie in wait for the uninitiated." He nodded toward the others. "Unfortunately, some are going to have trouble adjusting, and we need to make sure we get them—"

Brett pointed across the clearing. "I think Jorge wants us."

Zane looked up and saw the Brazilian standing at the edge of the forest, motioning them over.

As they approached, Jorge pulled back a few leafy fronds and hacked them off with his machete. "We're in luck. The trail is still here, although the entrance was grown over a bit. That probably means no one has used it in the last few months."

Zane stepped forward and peered into the opening. A path wound through the maze of trunks beyond. "Wow, that's tight."

The Brazilian shrugged. "At times it will be tight, and at other points it will open up a bit."

"No, that's fine." Zane's eyes narrowed as he focused on something a couple of feet away on the trail. He squatted and carefully picked up a leaf, exposing an impression in the soil. "But I'm not so sure no one has been here recently."

Brett squatted next to him. "What is it?"

Zane looked up at Jorge. "Did you step in here?"

The Brazilian shook his head. "No. I was walking along the edge, pulling limbs back and looking for the trail. When I found it, I called you over. Why?"

Zane picked up a stick and pointed at the impression. "Because that's a footprint."

"Maybe it's one of the local tribesmen," Brett said.

"An indigenous tribesman wearing boots?" Zane asked. He used the stick to point out a few faint horizontal marks made by the sole.

Brett nodded then stood and looked back at the beach. "Then why wasn't the sand covered with tracks? I was one of the first down the ramp and didn't see a thing."

"The storm would've washed away any exposed prints," Jorge said.

"He's right," Zane said. He turned and pointed at the vegetation overhanging the trail. "This print was protected by the jungle."

Brett looked farther down the trail. "Is that the only one?"

"I believe so," Zane said, standing. "From this point forward, it looks like the path becomes a mat of compressed vegetation. A professional tracker could probably find more prints. Unfortunately, I'm not that good."

Brett turned to Jorge. "Well, you did say that tour groups occasionally use this route."

The Brazilian's eyes narrowed as he surveyed the ground. "Occasionally, but not very often. Generally they enter the jungle earlier."

"The one thing we do know is that the print is relatively fresh," Zane said. "I seriously doubt anyone would've come through here last night during the storm. And we haven't passed any tour boats since leaving Manaus."

"At this point, I don't think there's reason to get too concerned."

Zane put his hands on his hips and looked at the impression once again. Could that be the boot print of a soldier? He thought so, but then again it could also be the boot print of an ornithologist or a herpetologist. Delphi had a database of prints, but this impression was too light and too faint to show up on a photograph. Besides, as Brett said, there was no need to ascribe any sort of ominous origin to the discovery.

A female voice broke the silence. "Did you guys find something?"

Zane turned, snapping out of his thoughts. Katiya and Max were standing a few feet away. "Ah, yes... yes, we did." He pointed to the opening. "Jorge found the trail."

Katiya looked at the trail. "Great." She turned toward Zane. "You sure everything's okay? You look concerned."

Zane worked his mouth into a smile. "Not at all. It's just a bit narrower than I expected." He nodded down the path. "The good news is that there doesn't appear to be any flooding."

Something seemed to catch Katiya's attention. She squinted, then her eyes widened. "Oh my! Huicungo!"

Zane tried to follow her gaze. The only thing he saw was a line of palms about twenty yards away. The trunks seemed to be covered in sharp spines. "Hui what?"

Katiya led them to the trees. As they neared, she pulled out her phone. "It's a huicungo tree." She stood in front of the nearest one and took a few pictures. "There are billions here in the Amazon basin. Their seeds are used to make black rings."

Brett frowned. "Black rings?"

"Rings... you know, the kind of ring you put on your finger." She stepped closer and took a close-up picture of the spines. "Not only that, but there is a soft substance inside the seeds that is used to make cosmetics."

"Okay, I thought you were an anthropologist," Zane said.

Katiya looked back at him and smiled. "I am. But my first love was biology. I've always had a fascination with the South American rainforest. The beauty, the biodiversity." She held her phone close to the trunk and tapped the screen. "At one point I even thought about making it my life's work."

"Hey, check it out," Brett said, lifting a finger toward the upper portion of the tree. "Monkeys."

Zane looked up. A family of monkeys had apparently been watching in silence until the group's approach. Now they scampered across one of the lower branches. They were moving fast but seemed to be grayish brown with white faces.

"We must have disturbed them," Max said.

"Saimiri... squirrel monkeys!" Katiya exclaimed, holding her phone up to video the experience.

As Zane watched, one of the younger monkeys tossed something toward them.

"Dang apes," a male voice said from behind them.

Zane looked over and saw that Nash had joined them. The corporal lifted his rifle.

"Time to show them who's boss," he said.

Zane opened his mouth to speak, but it was too late. Nash squeezed the trigger, spraying bullets into the foliage above. The monkeys screamed in fear, leaping through the trees with lightning speed and disappearing into the jungle.

"Stop it!" Katiya shouted, running toward him.

"Hey, hey," Zane reached out and pressed the soldier's arm down. "What in the hell do you think you're doing?"

"Jerk," Katiya said. "Those are protected animals."

Nash backed away, glaring at the two of them. "They're dumb apes." He waved a hand at the forest. "We need to let all these beasts know we mean business."

"Do not under any circumstances fire at animals unless

someone's life is in danger," Zane said, fixing his gaze on Nash.

Bennett came running over, undoubtedly drawn by the gunfire. "What's going on?"

Nash jerked his gun toward the huicungo trees. "Those apes started throwing—"

"One of the squirrel monkeys threw us some food, probably a peace offering, and your soldier started firing at him," Katiya said.

Zane gave Nash a stern look then turned to Bennett. "Get your corporal under control, Sergeant."

"It won't happen again, sir." Bennett turned to Nash and said, "Go help Corporal Wilson with the supplies."

Nash hesitated.

"Now, Corporal!" he commanded.

Nash glowered at Katiya briefly then marched off.

Bennett turned to Zane. "I'll make sure that doesn't happen again, sir."

Zane nodded as the sergeant departed after Nash.

Everyone stood in stunned silence for a moment. Finally, Zane said, "Okay, let's gather our things."

As the others moved off, Jorge said, "That one is going to be trouble."

Zane nodded. "I'm hoping it's just operational jitters. I've seen that before, particularly when a soldier is exposed to a new environment. But your point is well taken."

Jorge gazed up at the foliage where the monkeys had disappeared. "I fear the jungle may have just marked us as the enemy."

CHAPTER SIXTEEN

ZANE SURVEYED THE faces gathered around him on the beach. Beads of sweat glistened on foreheads, and several were already sucking on canteens. Their time on the river had probably given them a false sense of comfort. From this point forward, there would be no percolated coffee in the morning and no oscillating fans in the evening. Instead, there would be unrelenting heat during the day and a horde of flies, mosquitoes, and other biting insects at night.

For several in the group, the jungle trek would be the toughest thing they'd ever faced. Until you'd experienced it for yourself, you couldn't begin to imagine how tough it is to live in a place where your very survival is challenged each and every day.

Zane's eyes soon rested on Katiya. Her hair was pulled up in a ponytail, exposing the soft lines of her face. It was hard to imagine she was only a few years away from forty. If anything, she seemed even more beautiful here in the tropical heat.

As she blew her bangs out of her eyes, she seemed to catch

him staring at her. The hint of a smile crossed her face. Did she know what he was thinking? He smiled back then averted his gaze.

"We're finally here," he announced. "This marks the beginning of the most difficult phase of our journey." He nodded at the boat. "The quicker you realize that we're leaving comfort behind, the better off you'll be. Each day will involve a certain level of suffering and a certain level of danger. Recognition of that reality is going to be your first step in understanding how to cope and how to survive.

"Marcos will take the boat back to a village a few hours away. If for some reason any of you don't think you're going to be able to make it, this is your last chance to turn back." Max snickered and looked at Katiya. The others remained silent. Zane continued. "It looks like we're all in. Good. We depart in five minutes. No exceptions. Please check to make sure you have everything you need because, absent a medical emergency, we're not coming back until our work is finished or we run out of supplies."

As they began to gather their things, Zane held up a hand. "Let me remind you of one other thing. This is not going to be a democracy. Democracies don't survive in the jungle. It's a dictatorship. If you have questions or need assistance, feel free to ask Jorge or me." He placed a hand on Jorge's shoulder. "He probably knows this place better than you know your own backyard, so we're going to rely on his expertise."

Amanda cleared her throat. "What is our schedule going to be like? It seems like it might be better to travel when it's a little cooler."

"That's a good question," Zane replied. "We will try to avoid the midday heat as much as possible. My plan is to spend most of our time traveling in the early morning and late afternoon."

"So no night travel?" she asked.

Zane shook his head. "You don't travel in the jungle at night. Too many dangerous creatures prowl around after dark. It's the most dangerous time in the jungle, so we'll have no choice but to stop and set up a defensive perimeter."

Brett pointed at something in the distance. "It looks like we may not have to worry about the sun for much longer."

Zane turned and looked across the river. A wall of coal-black clouds was moving in their direction.

Not again.

"You said it's going to be too dangerous to travel at night," Amanda said. "What's to stop us from getting attacked in the middle of the night?"

Jorge looked at her. "If I may, the jungle is never safe, at least not in the way you think of safety. But we will make it as secure as possible under the circumstances. For example, we're going to keep a fire burning every night. No exceptions. It's... how you say... an insurance policy against the biggest predators."

"Not only that," Zane said, "but we're also going to put up a state-of-the-art motion-sensor system. We'll supplement that with nightlong patrols."

Amanda nodded, but the assurances didn't seem to have their intended effect. It was as though she realized that the high level of protective measures indicated the seriousness of the threat.

Zane glanced at his watch and said, "We depart in two minutes."

CHAPTER SEVENTEEN

"YOU FOUND A boot print?" the Oracle asked.

Zane held the satellite phone tightly against the side of his head as he strode down the jungle path. "Yes, at the head of the trail."

There was a moment of silence. Either there was a delay in the signal or the Oracle was digesting the new information. Finally, his reply came through the speaker. "I wouldn't be too concerned, Watson. During the planning phase, Salvador told me the trail was still used occasionally."

"Not this particular stretch."

"I specifically remember Salvador telling me that."

"Ross, we're entering a bit further down than most groups, including the researchers and tourists. They generally want to get off their boat as soon as possible. We went further up the tributary to save time. Once we cross the stream later this morning, we'll be on the main trail. It would be normal to find prints there."

As he waited for the reply, Zane looked ahead. Jorge and

Bennett were about ten yards in front of him, discussing something as they walked. Taking a quick glance back, he saw Katiya and Max about an equal distance behind him.

"Was the print fresh?" the Oracle finally asked.

"It looked that way. Jorge has some tracking experience as well, and he thought it had been there about twelve hours, maybe more."

"Where there any other prints?"

Zane heard the haunting howl of a monkey overhead. He tilted his head back up just in time to see several dark forms swinging through the tops of the trees. They seemed to be moving in the same direction as the team. Zane frowned.

"Watson?"

"Yeah, sorry... no, there weren't any other prints on the path."

"What about the beach?"

"I was the first one off, and I didn't see anything, although I must confess I wasn't looking very closely. Then, by the time we found the other print, everyone had disembarked and was walking all over the sand. At that point, there was zero chance of finding anything."

"Did you tell the group?"

"Negative."

Zane looked up. The monkeys had grown silent, but he could still see their dark forms moving through the canopy.

"You made the right decision. No need to rattle the cage until you have something more solid. For now, I'd say it's best to keep everything under wraps. I still think there is a harmless explanation for the print, but you need to stay alert." After a brief pause, he asked, "Anything else to report?"

"No, nothing out of the ordinary." Thunder grumbled low in the distance. Zane turned and saw a wisp of dark gray through the holes in the canopy. "We've got another storm on the way. We're going to try to get across the stream before it hits. Once we're on the other side, we'll set up camp."

"Copy that. Chris has been able to use your signal to plot the group on a virtual map here, but it's good to get verbal confirmation."

There was another grumble behind them.

"Ross, we may get cut off soon. Before I go, any more information on the crater?"

"I'm glad you mentioned that. Chris noticed something that seemed out of place. We ordered some new images, but it's not likely we'll have them until sometime tomorrow. They're having to reposition the satellite."

Zane frowned. "Something seemed out of place? I don't follow."

"It could be, but we won't know until we get a chance to look at the new pictures. That area hasn't been photographed in a while, likely because it's not considered a region vital to national security. As you probably know, the new cameras can pick up much greater detail than the older ones."

Zane nodded, even though the Oracle couldn't see him. "Right. Like going from standard definition to high definition on your television."

"Precisely."

"Copy that. Before I go, how's my girl?"

"Huh?"

"Keiko."

The Oracle laughed. "She's doing fine. Just a little miffed that she missed you when you were here."

Keiko was the world's most advanced humanoid. Created by Ian Higgs, the father of Amanda Higgs, Keiko incorporated technology that was a generation ahead of its time. She had the appearance of an Asian woman in her thirties and could move, speak, and think in a way that blurred the lines between humans and machines.

Her brief history read like the plot of a thriller novel. After Higgs was murdered on the streets of London, the robot remained in the possession of the deceased man's employer, the Renaissance Group, a multinational conglomerate led by the Russian billionaire Alexander Mironov.

When a Delphi team led by Zane Watson and Carmen Petrosino had begun working against Renaissance, Keiko changed sides, assisting the Americans in thwarting Mironov's plans to commandeer the CERN particle physics laboratory in eastern France. Although difficult to understand, the switch seemed to have been the result of ethics programming by Ian Higgs.

During the events at CERN, Keiko had triggered a self-destruct explosive that took out members of the Renaissance team, including Mironov. After the fighting was over, Delphi took possession of the humanoid's remains, transporting her back to the United States. There, a team led by Brett Foster restored the robot to her former state.

"Please tell her I'm sorry," Zane said, remembering that the humanoid had been taken down for programming when he was there. "It was just bad timing. Tell her she'll be my top priority next time." There was loud clap of thunder, this time closer. "Look, Ross, I've got to go. The storm is right on our heels."

"Copy that."

"I'll be back in touch tonight if anything comes up. Otherwise, let's talk tomorrow morning."

After ending the call, Zane saw that Jorge had stopped to wait for him just ahead. The Brazilian lit the tip of a cigar, puffing until he was shrouded in smoke. "Did I hear you say they have some information about our target?"

"Someone has big ears."

"Those big ears keep me alive in the jungle, senhor," Jorge said with a wink.

"Regarding your question, they don't have anything yet. They picked up something on satellite imagery but won't have any details until tomorrow." Zane pulled a canteen from his pack and took a long swig. "Ross didn't sound overly concerned about the boot print."

Jorge shrugged. "Maybe he's right. No one can say for sure. Then again, who would've been out here with the storms we've had over the last two days? The biologists would likely stay on their boats until the weather clears." He took a draw on his cigar then said, "Something just seems a little unusual about it."

Zane was about to reply when a voice squawked out of his pants. "Sir, are you there?"

Zane pulled the radio out of his pocket. "Go ahead, Bennett."

"I'm at the stream. I think you may want to see this."

"We'll be right there."

As Zane and Jorge quickened their pace, Zane wondered what the Green Beret had found. He sounded concerned, but at the same time, his voice didn't convey that he was in any sort of immediate danger.

A minute later, they rounded a bend and entered a clearing. Bennett was crouched on the far side by the stream, facing the other direction. *Maybe he found some footprints along the bank,* Zane thought.

Bennett looked up at them. "You did say there was supposed to be a bridge here, didn't you?"

Jorge pulled to a stop, a look of shock forming on his face.

Zane knew from their discussions that there was supposed to be a rope-and-wood bridge here. In fact, Jorge had spoken to a man who passed through the area regularly, and he said it had still been in place just a month ago.

"Yes," Jorge whispered.

Zane stepped closer to the bank and looked up and down the stream. Seeing nothing, he turned toward Jorge. "Could we be in the wrong place?"

Jorge shook his head. "There is only one trail, and we are on it. I even saw some landmarks I recognized along the way."

Zane nodded.

Suddenly the Brazilian's eyes narrowed as he gazed at a clump of ferns along the bank. He walked over and pulled some of the fronds back. "Just what I thought."

Zane came and stood next to him. There, on the other side of the plants, were two posts with holes in the top. "I take it that was a part of the bridge?"

Jorge nodded but remained silent. He leaned forward and examined the wood more closely.

Zane looked out across the coffee-colored water of the stream. There was no sign of the bridge. No ropes, no boards. Nothing. As he drew his gaze back to the shore, he fixed his eyes on a slight impression in the soft sand at the water's edge. He frowned. Moving past the posts, he jumped down onto the spit. He bent over and examined the lines closely. They looked like prints of some kind, but the moisture in the sand had already begun to smooth them out.

"You see something?" Bennett asked.

"Who knows?" he replied, standing. For now, he was going to keep the prior discovery of the footprint from the others. "Just looking for something that might tell us what happened."

"One thing I can tell you is that it didn't just fall," Jorge said.

"Even with the storms we just had?"

"No, it was designed to rise with the waters. Some conservation group is responsible for its upkeep."

Zane stepped back up onto the bank. "And you just had a contact verify that it was still in place a few weeks ago."

Jorge nodded.

"Is there another way across?" Bennett asked. "Maybe we could try downstream."

Jorge looked in both directions. "We probably need to cross here. The water shouldn't be too deep."

A voice spoke from behind them. "I think that's a dumb idea."

Zane turned and saw Max and Katiya approaching. The others were spilling out into the clearing just behind them.

"You don't expect us to cross through that filth, do you?" Max asked.

"Max." Katiya shot him a look.

"Fine, knock yourself out," Zane said, removing a hatchet from his belt. He threw it toward the linguist hilt first. Max jumped but was able to catch it.

Max glared at him. "What are you talking about?"

"You want to find another bridge then be my guest." He pointed toward the tangle of vegetation along their side of the stream. "You can start hacking in either direction. Should only take you a day or two to find something better."

"What's going on?" Amanda asked as she neared the group. She stopped when she realized there was no bridge. "Oops."

Zane looked at Jorge. "How deep is it?"

"Not very. Waist high, at most."

Zane nodded. "Not bad."

Artur nodded toward the water. "I've crossed many streams this size. As long as the bottom isn't slippery, we should be able to cross."

Max shook his head and mumbled something.

Zane picked up a small limb, hopped back down to the spit of sand, and plunged the stick into the water. When the tip reached the bottom, he felt a layer of mud. Pressing, he found solid ground about an inch down. "It's not too bad. We're just going to have to take our time." He nodded at Jorge. "The two of us will enter first. Once we're in the water, we'll let you know if there are any issues."

"Let's do it," Brett finally said.

Zane examined the others' faces. With the exception of Max, most seemed to be fine with crossing.

Jorge pointed toward the trees. "You may want to find yourselves walking sticks. Anything to help you balance."

Zane looked at his watch. "I'll give you a couple of minutes to do that."

There was another clap of thunder as everyone headed toward the trees. Zane looked at the surface of the stream. The rain hadn't reached them yet, but it wouldn't be much longer. He guessed they had a half hour to get across and set up camp, maybe less.

Suddenly, Zane heard a noise and caught movement out of the corner of his eye. He turned his head just in time to see a big swirl on the surface of the stream about a hundred yards away.

Probably a carp, he thought.

CHAPTER EIGHTEEN

AMANDA HAD JUST spotted a second tree limb when Zane blew a whistle, calling everyone back. She ran over to the base of a large tree, bent over, and picked it up. One end was gnarled and shaped like a handle. *Perfect.*

She wasn't thrilled about crossing the murky stream, but at least she'd have a couple of sticks to keep her steady.

Slipping them under her arm, she maneuvered through the maze of trunks and reentered the clearing. The others were exiting the forest at the same time.

"Nice," said a voice.

She turned to see Brett walking up behind her.

She held up the one with the knobby end. "You like my cane?"

"I do. That's almost as nice as my granny's."

"I have to confess I'm not big on this whole crossing the river thing," Amanda whispered with a smile.

Brett frowned. "Why not?"

"Maybe it's just me, but I'm not a fan of walking through

water so dark I can't see what's around me. I've been that way ever since seeing *Jaws* as a kid." She held up one of the sticks. "So, in addition to helping me with my balance, I won't hesitate to put these babies to use." She made like she was beating something with one of the sticks.

Brett grabbed her bicep with two fingers. "I feel for any caiman that might be foolish enough to challenge these."

"Brett!" Amanda said, shaking her head.

"I'm joking, I'm joking. There aren't going to be any caiman out there. They were all eaten by the anacondas."

"You jerk!" She slapped his arm playfully. "I'm going to give *you* the end of this stick if you keep this up."

Zane was about to speak when suddenly a clap of thunder boomed in the distance and a strong gust of wind rattled through the nearby trees. Everyone turned and looked skyward at the sound. Even the soldiers lifted their heads nervously. She liked the idea of crossing less with every passing second.

"Okay, make sure you have all of your gear, because we're not making two trips," Zane said.

"You sure this is still a good idea?" Brett asked, nodding in the direction of the last boom.

"It seemed close, but it's still over a mile away," Zane said. "If we move quickly, we'll be across in plenty of time." He nodded at Jorge, who was standing next to him. "My friend also reminded me that this storm could trigger some serious flooding. The stream is already well above its normal level, so another hard rain could make it rise another few feet overnight. And if that happens, there's no telling how long we'd have to wait to get across. A day, perhaps two. Who knows? Unfortunately, we don't have enough supplies to take that risk."

Amanda watched as Max leaned toward Katiya and mumbled, "Does the idiot realize that if the lightning strikes the water—"

"Did I hear a question?" Zane asked, looking in their direction.

"Sorry, Zane," Katiya said. "Please continue."

Zane's eyes lingered on Max for a moment. Amanda could tell that he'd about reached his tipping point with the linguist. Finally, he continued. "Jorge and I are going to cross first. Once we're about halfway across, enter the water one at a time. Leave about ten feet between you and the person in front of you."

"Why is that, Zane?" Katiya asked. "Don't we want to be close together?"

"No. If one person slips, we don't want to have a domino effect. I've seen it happen before. If any of you fall, make sure you get out of your pack and get up on two feet. If you need help, I'll come get you."

Katiya nodded. "That makes sense. Thank you."

"Anyone else?" Zane scanned the faces gathered around. "If not, then let's go."

Zane and Jorge shouldered their packs and entered the water. The Brazilian wasn't using a stick. He'd probably crossed hundreds of streams like this in his life.

As the two made their way across, the rest formed a line. Katiya, Max, and Bennett were ahead of Amanda, while Brett, Artur, Wilson, Tocchet, and Nash brought up the rear. She felt good knowing that she would be right behind Bennett. If forced to make your way through dark jungle water, it was good to have a Green Beret a few feet away.

A few minutes later, Zane reached the halfway point and gave the signal that all was clear. As far as she could tell, he and Jorge seemed fine. No bloodstains on their clothing and no missing limbs. Maybe this wouldn't be as bad as she'd thought.

A few minutes later, Bennett sloshed out into the stream.

Here goes.

Amanda drew in a deep breath and stepped onto the thin strip of sand at the water's edge. She looked at the water, and her pulse quickened. It was even darker than she'd thought. She could just about kill Brett right now for planting all those images in her mind. She suddenly pictured a twenty-foot anaconda slithering along the stream bottom, drawn by the motion in the water.

Pull yourself together.

Before entering, she looked ahead one last time. Bennett was about ten feet out, looking back and forth as he strode confidently through the water. If there was something to be worried about, the soldier sure didn't show it.

Taking a deep breath, she waded out into the water. The bottom was exactly as Zane had described it: a thin layer of mud covering solid ground.

A minute later, Brett spoke from behind her. "How's the water?"

Without turning, she said, "It's not Waikiki, but I think I'm going to be okay."

The bottom sloped downward, and suddenly she was in

water up to her waist.

She stopped to gather herself. *Just keep going. Don't stop and allow your fear to set in.*

After pulling her pack further up her back, she continued on her way. *One foot after another,* she thought. Despite all her efforts to resist, she couldn't help but occasionally glance down into the murky depths. The swirls of mud rolled into odd shapes. One moment they seemed like the slithering coils of a giant serpent, the next they formed the snout of a caiman.

When she was about halfway across, Amanda stepped out, but her right foot failed to touch the bottom. Instead it plunged downward into a hole. The surface of the water came toward her as she fell. Adjusting quickly, she extended her left foot and set it onto solid ground. Amazingly, she was able to maintain her balance.

"You okay?" Brett asked.

"I think so. Be careful, there's a hole right here."

She looked up. Bennett was about twenty or thirty feet away now, still looking back and forth as he moved strongly through the water. Her heart beat faster in her chest. She'd wanted to stay as close to him as possible.

Determined to make up ground, she pushed ahead. A few seconds later, Amanda noticed that Bennett had come to an abrupt halt. She frowned. His body language had changed completely. The rugged soldier was alert and staring at something down the stream to the right.

No, please no. Just keep going!

The soldier held up a pair of binoculars. Something had really drawn his attention.

THE PORTAL

There is nothing there. Please just keep going.

Unable to resist, Amanda turned to see what he was looking at. He seemed to be focused on a small cove on the far bank. As she watched, she thought she saw a slight ripple on the surface of the water.

Fish, Amanda. They're just fish.

She looked toward the far bank. Zane was standing there, watching Bennett. The operative sensed something was wrong and looked ready to return to the water if necessary.

A shout suddenly broke the silence. "Everybody get moving! Now!" It was Bennett.

Amanda instinctively turned her head back toward the cove, and when she did, her blood ran cold.

Something massive swirled beneath the surface, sending ripples out into the stream.

It stayed in place for a moment then left the cove and began moving toward them with speed.

***

Amanda watched in horror as Bennett raised his rifle and squeezed off two shots in quick succession. After firing, he waded toward the swell then fired again.

He's putting himself between us and the predator, she thought.

The animal seemed to sense the movement in the water and surged toward him.

"Amanda, go!" Brett yelled from behind.

Snapping out of her thoughts, she pushed ahead, using the sticks to maintain her balance.

One step at a time.

Bennett continued to fire as she surged past him. Now moving with speed, she felt the urge to look.

Don't do it. Keep moving.

But the urge was too strong. Turning, she stole a quick glance out over the water. And when she did, her heart began to thump wildly in her chest. There were now several swells, and one had broken off and was moving toward her.

Bennett must have realized what was happening, because he turned and began firing at it.

"Go!" Brett shouted.

Amanda suddenly realized she had slowed. This time she ran through the water, bouncing lightly off the bottom with each step. She knew there was a greater chance of toppling over, but it was a risk she had to take. The only way she was going to survive was to make it to shore before the predator made it to her.

Seconds later, she heard the swirling of water to her right. The predator had closed to within twenty feet.

"No!" she said through gritted teeth.

She ran as hard as she could, her feet barely touching the bottom. Her legs burned, but she ignored the pain and pushed her muscles to their limit. She would either win the race or lose her life. It was as simple as that.

About fifteen yards from the shore, the unthinkable happened—her foot caught a root that snaked along the bottom, and she tumbled forward. With no way to adjust this time, she fell face-first into the dark waters of the stream.

She hit the muddy bottom with outstretched hands. The

impact sent a cloud of sediment and bubbles into the water, making it impossible to see in any direction. She pushed up slightly. The water was a bit clearer near the surface, so she looked to her right. When she did, chill bumps spread across her body. She hadn't expected the sight that greeted her.

Hundreds of silver fish swarmed toward her, their scaly bodies thrashing in frenzied anticipation. She froze. The sight was both beautiful and terrifying at the same time. They were now so close that she could see the rows of razor-sharp teeth that lined their protruding lower jaws.

A shout gurgled through the water. Someone was yelling at her to get up.

Using her last ounce of energy, Amanda pushed off the bottom. After breaking the surface, she braced for the impact.

CHAPTER NINETEEN

AFTER HELPING KATIYA and Max out of the water, Zane turned around just in time to see Amanda's blond hair plunge beneath the surface. She'd somehow run off course. Instead of moving directly toward the shore, she'd been moving toward the right. She'd undoubtedly gotten confused in all the excitement.

Zane dove into the stream. After taking a couple of powerful strokes underwater, he surfaced in the area where she'd gone under. He looked in every direction, but the clouds of sediment made it impossible to see anything near the bottom.

There.

Blond hair was rushing toward the surface. A second later, Amanda burst out of the water with a gasp.

Zane grabbed her around the waist, lifting her into the air. As he was about to leave the water, he caught something out of the corner of his eye. Dozens of silver bodies thrashed just feet away.

Piranha.

Fortunately, the fish seemed confused by the clouds of sediment. They swam in circles and snapped their jaws in frustration, angry that their prey had somehow escaped.

Suddenly, one of the fish broke from the group and latched onto Zane's pants, gnawing through the fabric with its razor-sharp teeth. He shook it off momentarily then ran toward the shore with Amanda in his arms. The movement in the water drew the other fish, and seconds later dozens of mouths found his legs.

As he neared shore, one or two piranha broke through the fabric and sunk their needle-sharp teeth into his flesh. Zane gasped in pain and pressed forward.

"Here, give her to me," someone said.

Zane looked up. At great risk to herself, Katiya had waded into the water. She was standing directly in front of him with her hands extended. It was a great thought, but there wasn't time for a hand-off.

"Get back," he said.

After brushing her aside, Zane surged out of the water and fell onto the bank.

He made sure Amanda was okay then looked down at his legs. His pants were shredded and soaked in blood. A couple of piranha had let go and were flopping around on the ground. Two others were still attached to his calf muscle, unwilling to release their hold.

Zane reached down and yanked them off, taking out a hunk of flesh in the process.

"Be careful," Amanda said.

Zane was about to tell her he was fine when he heard sloshing behind him. He turned and saw Brett stagger out of the water. Artur, Wilson, and Tocchet were right behind him. All four immediately collapsed in the sand, their chests heaving with exhaustion.

Amanda suddenly sat up. Zane had almost forgotten about her. She pointed at the stream and tried to speak, but nothing came out.

Bennett and Nash. In all the confusion, Zane had forgotten about the final two soldiers. He stood and joined Jorge at the water's edge.

Bennett was now moving toward shore, but Nash remained where he was, firing rounds at the swell that moved toward him.

"Just go!" Bennett shouted.

Nash said something in return, but Zane couldn't hear him.

Bennett continued toward the shore. Zane entered the water and held out his hands. The piranha immediately swarmed around his legs. Zane kicked at them, but it was like trying to swat away a swarm of bees.

With a shout, Bennett dove toward Zane. The operative grabbed him and heaved him onto land.

As they lay there, Zane heard Katiya scream, "No!"

Nash.

Zane rose up on one elbow. The soldier was still a good twenty yards out. The fish swarmed around him. At this point, there were probably a hundred or more ravaging his legs. Nash had abandoned his gun and was trying to push the fish away with his hands. It was futile. No human being could keep a swarm of piranha off their body.

The soldier let out a scream as some of the teeth finally found his flesh.

Zane stood. Despite the only small chance of saving him, he couldn't just let Nash suffer like that. He had to act, even if it meant he'd die with him.

He ran toward the water, but Jorge grabbed him around the waist. Zane tried to fight him off, but the Brazilian shook his head and nodded at the stream.

When Zane looked, his heart sank. Nash was no longer visible. The water churned where he'd been standing only moments before. Even if he could be pulled out now, there was very little chance he would survive.

Zane tried to shake free, but two more hands grabbed him from behind.

"Zane, no," Bennett whispered. "It's over."

Zane finally shook him off but remained in place. He watched in silence as the thrashing swarm of fish moved downstream.

Bennett stepped up next to him. "We did what we could."

Zane remained silent, unable to turn away from the macabre scene.

Bennett spoke without turning his head. "Right in the middle of the fight, Corporal Nash told me something. He said he was sorry for what happened earlier when we got off the boat. He also said he was determined to make things right."

Zane's brow furrowed. If true, it was an incredible act of

valor. He looked at Bennett. "You think he planned all that?"

Bennett shrugged. "I'm not sure. I just know he was determined to protect everyone." After a long pause, he continued. "What happened back at the river… shooting at those monkeys… that wasn't the Corporal Nash I knew. He's as solid as they come. Something seemed to have changed when we got to Manaus. He became a different person."

"What do you think it was?"

"I don't know." Bennett exhaled. "But whatever it was, I hope it doesn't happen to anyone else."

Zane gave him a nod of understanding. Nothing was worse than losing a soldier under your command. In this case, it was likely made worse by the corporal's strange behavior prior to his death.

"Let's get back to the others," Zane said.

As they rejoined the group, Zane saw Amanda sitting in the sand, weeping softly. Katiya stood next to her, staring at the place where Nash had made his last stand. A tear ran down her cheek.

"Hey, I think he's going to need some help over here," Artur said.

Zane turned. The Brazilian had just finished cutting off one of Brett's pant legs. Zane cringed at the sight underneath. It looked like his leg had taken a close-range shotgun blast. The cuts weren't particularly deep, but they had to be painful.

Katiya moved quickly to Artur's side. She looked at Max, who had come over as well. "Can you bring us some water? Oh, and please get a bottle of disinfectant from one of the first aid kits."

The linguist nodded and walked away.

Zane crouched next to Katiya. "How does it look?"

"Fortunately, the wounds appear to be superficial," she said without looking up. "The main thing we have to worry about is infection. I'm sure there's a lot of bacteria here in the Amazon basin that our bodies aren't used to fighting."

"Wonderful," Brett groaned.

Zane laid a hand on his shoulder.

Max arrived with the items Katiya had requested. She poured the water across Brett's legs, washing away the excess blood. Then she wiped them with a clean towel.

"Okay, this is going to sting a little," she said, squeezing some of the antibacterial ointment into her hand.

"Go for it," he said.

Brett grimaced and let out a loud groan as she spread it over his skin. "A little?"

"Amazing the damage they can do in such little time," Zane said as he examined the wounds.

She looked up at him. "Sometimes the piranha are in such a frenzy that they end up biting each other. That's why you'll often find one with a hunk taken out of its tail or an eye missing."

"Lovely creatures," Zane said.

"Believe it or not, some species are quite docile," Katiya said. "Unfortunately, we happened to cross a stream filled with *Pygocentrus nattereri*."

Zane gave her an odd look. "Pygo what?"

"Red-bellied piranha. Unlike some of its brethren, these boys have a nasty temper." She squeezed out some more antibacterial gel then continued. "You know, even though these particular piranha are known to be aggressive killers, I'm still a bit surprised we were attacked."

Zane's brow furrowed. "Why would that surprise you?"

"Attacks on humans aren't unheard of, but they're usually during the dry season when their usual prey are scarce."

"I guess they couldn't resist my legs," Zane quipped.

Brett shook his head. "Unfortunately, I think they liked mine better than yours."

Zane rose to his feet.

"Speaking of legs," Katiya said, "I need to look at yours next."

Zane glanced at his pants. They were soaked in blood, but he could tell the cuts were superficial. "I need to go help the others set up the tents. I'll be fine."

"Well, as soon as you're done, get back over here," she said.

As Zane walked away, he heard the growl of thunder directly overhead. Steel-gray clouds had moved in, and the first raindrops were hitting the surface of the stream.

A hand touched his arm, causing him to turn. Jorge stood at his side, a cigar dangling from his mouth. The Brazilian nodded toward the woods, indicating Zane should follow him.

"What's up?" Zane whispered as they climbed the bank.

Jorge paused. He gestured back toward the stream with his cigar. "The jungle just delivered a death sentence. From here on out, we need to make sure everyone here gives it the respect it deserves. If they don't, then I fear we may suffer loss again."

Zane nodded but said nothing.

"But that's not why I called you over. I think we have a

problem."

A hard gust of wind blew through the clearing. A few leaves broke from tree branches and bounced across the ground. Zane could tell that the storm was about to unleash its fury. "I know. I was just about to get everyone to set up the tents—"

"No, not that. Something else." The Brazilian motioned for Zane to follow him.

As they continued up the trail, Zane could see that it ended in a T-shaped intersection with another, larger trail that ran north-south along the east side of the stream. Before arriving at the intersection, Jorge stopped at a large grove of ferns on the left. He grabbed several fronds and pulled them back. Zane squatted and looked in the darkness beyond. There, lying hidden just out of sight, was a pile of ropes and boards.

The bridge.

"I found some more footprints and followed them here," Jorge said.

Zane bent over and grabbed one of the ropes. He examined the end carefully, noting the strands had been sliced through cleanly. "I'd say it was cut with a knife, a very sharp one."

Jorge nodded. "It confirms what I had already guessed, that someone took the bridge down on purpose."

Zane tossed the rope back to the ground. "Who do you think did it?"

"That is the million-dollar question."

"And what's the answer?"

Jorge took a draw on his cigar and allowed the smoke to drift slowly out of his mouth. Finally, he said, "Someone who hoped a few of us would die crossing that stream."

CHAPTER TWENTY

AMANDA TOSSED ANOTHER tree limb on the fire, sending a plume of crackling embers into the air. Thankfully, Artur had collected and covered some wood before the storm hit. And now that the fire was going, he had stacked some wet limbs and branches nearby to dry them out. The Brazilians were worth their weight in gold out here in the jungle.

A melancholy atmosphere permeated the camp in the wake of Nash's death. Everyone was still stunned by the scene they'd witnessed only hours before. It was one thing to hear of a horrible death. It was another thing altogether to witness it for yourself. But it wasn't only the shock of watching it; it was the shock of knowing they'd been on land for less than twenty-four hours and already someone had lost their life.

As Amanda had listened to the conversations earlier in the evening, she'd noticed that everyone seemed to be divided on the significance of Nash's death. Some thought the incident was simply nature running its course. Predators had taken prey, and nothing else. But a few held to a more superstitious view. They claimed the jungle had exacted its revenge, clearly insinuating that the soldier had paid for his earlier misdeeds.

Trying to shake off all the negative thoughts, Amanda looked out across the camp. Something glowed red in the distance. Squinting, she saw it was the tip of Jorge's cigar. He and Zane were huddled in a grove of trees just beyond the firelight. Ever since the attack, the two had been inseparable, wandering off to talk at every opportunity. What were they talking about?

Amanda's eyes settled on Zane's silhouette. He hadn't been his usual self ever since they stepped off the boat. He was more quiet and pensive than usual. Perhaps it was just the responsibility of leading a group into a dangerous place. Maybe it was something else. Whatever it was, he was keeping it to himself.

Now that she thought about it, even Jorge had changed. He'd been a lively presence on the boat, telling jokes and doing everything he could to put the team at ease. But now he seemed to be perpetually serious, looking around with a wary eye. On several occasions, Amanda saw him turn his head quickly, his eyes locking on something out in the jungle. She'd tried to see what he was looking at but was always too late.

"A penny for your thoughts," someone asked.

Amanda flinched. Katiya was hovering over her.

"Hey," Amanda said.

Katiya smiled. "Sorry, didn't mean to startle you. Mind if I have a seat?"

"No, not at all." Amanda patted the ground. "Please."

The anthropologist sat down next to her and crossed her

legs. "You looked so thoughtful, I just had to come over and find out what was on your mind."

"Was it that obvious?"

"Yes."

They both laughed.

Amanda wondered if she should share her concerns about Zane and Jorge. At this point, probably not. It was tempting to get someone else's opinion, but there was no sense in getting others stirred up. The group needed to trust the two men to lead them.

"There's just so much to think about," Amanda said truthfully. "For one, I've never seen someone die before, and to be honest, I'm a little shaken up."

"I understand." Katiya squeezed her arm gently.

"And not only was it difficult to see someone die, but it makes me wonder what else is waiting for us out there."

An owl screeched in the distance, its haunting voice echoing through the towering trees. Amanda thought she heard the faint sound of flapping after the screech died away.

Katiya looked at the fire. "You're right. We're in a beautiful world, but a dangerous one. You know, I don't blame you one bit for being concerned. Heck, I've been in the jungle many times, but I've never seen anything that comes close to what I saw this afternoon." She thought for a moment then said, "Even in the best of conditions, the rainforest has a way of overwhelming the uninitiated. It's one of those places where safety is always on the tip of your thoughts. You just don't expect to actually see someone die."

They sat in silence for a moment. Finally, Katiya asked, "So can you tell me more about what happened in Europe?"

Amanda gave her a confused look.

"The operation in Switzerland and France."

Amanda shook her head. "Sorry, my mind isn't functioning too well right now. Is there anything in particular you want to know?"

Katiya threw a stick in the fire and watched as the flames engulfed it. "To be honest, I never felt like I got the entire story of what happened over there."

"They didn't brief you?"

"They did, but it seemed like a sanitized version. I had a very short phone conversation with Dr. Ross. He gave me a quick overview of the events at CERN, but he spent most of the time telling me about the sound NASA picked up. I guess he figured that was what I was most interested in. And he was right.

"But then, toward the end, he seemed to hint that some pretty bizarre things were seen that night. He sounded as though he was going to tell me more, but apparently he had to rush off to a meeting. I'm not sure if that was true or not, but it seemed to come at a convenient time." Katiya chuckled.

"Have you talked to Zane?" Amanda asked.

"Not yet. I thought I'd try you first."

Amanda smiled. "I guess I seemed like an easier target."

Katiya laughed. "You seem very truthful, I'll put it that way."

"Thank you." Amanda's expression grew more serious. "The bizarre things you referred to all happened in the tunnel below CERN. Of the four people who were down there, only two survived."

"And Zane was one of those people?"

"Yes, which is why I think you should talk to him at some point." Amanda glanced toward the woods. He and Jorge were still in the grove. The Brazilian was waving his arms around, clearly emotional about whatever they were discussing. She turned back toward Katiya and continued. "Unfortunately, his mind seems to be on other things, so I don't mind sharing what I know." Amanda crossed her legs, resting her hands in her lap. "First of all, I want to be clear that I didn't witness any of the things I'm about to discuss. I never entered the tunnel, and most of the information I have comes from my friend Philippe. Zane and I haven't talked about it much."

"Philippe?"

"He's a Swiss pastor who helped us."

"Yes, I remember him now."

Amanda glanced around the area to make sure no one was within earshot. She didn't mind sharing the entire narrative with Katiya, but she didn't necessarily want anyone else to hear it. Satisfied they were alone, she said, "This is where it gets murky, and unfortunately I'm probably not going to be able to answer any questions you might have. I'm not even sure the people who were there could answer all of your questions." She lowered her voice and said, "The bottom line is that something *did* happen that night."

Katiya raised an eyebrow. "Meaning?"

"Meaning whatever Mironov and Marrese were trying to do with the collider apparently worked."

Katiya's eyes widened, but she remained silent.

"Zane and Philippe saw things in the tunnel that night," Amanda said. "Creatures… whatever you want to call them."

"Did they provide a description?"

"The only thing Zane said was that they were large. He called them giants. As for Philippe, he only shared a few small details, and I didn't push him for more. He told me the main thing I needed to know was that God protected him that night." She tossed a few leaves on the fire and watched them burn then continued. "But I can share one thing that Philippe told me: whatever creatures he saw down there, he doesn't believe they were aliens. In fact, even before we got to CERN that night, he told me we were dealing with something from the supernatural realm."

"It's very interesting that he chose to use those words," Katiya said. "He didn't give you any indication of who or what that might be?"

"No. I think he's trying to protect me. It's almost like he believes something permanent may have taken place that night."

"What did he mean by that?"

Amanda bit her lower lip. "Like something was released, and now we can't put the genie back in the bottle."

"Have any of these creatures been seen since?"

Amanda shook her head. "Not that I'm aware of. There was a final powerful explosion when the collider was shut down prematurely. Zane and Philippe were able to make it back to the surface alive, just before a fire gutted the tunnel completely. Most are working on the assumption that anyone or anything still down there was incinerated."

Katiya stared at the fire, lost in thought. After a moment, she looked at Amanda. "I think I'm starting to piece this together now."

"Piece what together?"

"Do you remember our conversation on the boat?"

Not only did Amanda remember the entire conversation, but she could probably repeat it verbatim. She had hung on Katiya's every word. She nodded.

Katiya's eyes gleamed in the firelight. "I think I've discovered a link between CERN and the place we're marching toward here in the Amazon. But it doesn't stop there... I think I've been able to find a thread that links places all over the earth, including sites in the United States."

"What?"

Katiya leaned forward and whispered, "In regards to extraterrestrials, you've probably heard the word *disclosure*. People keep waiting for governments to finally admit that alien life exists and that they've been visiting us for decades, if not centuries or longer. Well, if I'm right, then I believe that in the not-too-distant future, they won't have a choice any longer. They'll have to admit it because the flood gates will have opened, and there'll be no turning back."

CHAPTER TWENTY-ONE

"OKAY, YOU'VE BEEN way too cryptic," Amanda said. "Time for some answers."

"I agree," Katiya replied. "Stay right here." The anthropologist rose to her feet, skirted the fire, and entered her tent.

As she waited, Amanda thought back on what Katiya had just said: that she'd discovered a link between CERN and the place they were trying to find deep in the jungle. But other than the audio transmission picked up by NASA, Amanda couldn't imagine what that link might be. She'd conducted her own research on the crater while they were on the boat, and she'd only been able to find out a few insignificant facts. One being that scientists weren't sure whether the crater had been caused by a meteor or whether it had simply formed that way.

Katiya returned with her tablet and sat down once again. "Okay, here we go." She turned on the device as Amanda scooted closer. "I'm sorry it's taken me so long to share this information. Remember, I'm an academic, which means I don't like to share things until I'm certain I'm on solid ground."

"Has Zane seen this?"

"No, but I'm going to show it to him as soon as we're done." Katiya tapped on a folder titled Global Research. Then she opened a subfolder titled Map. "I actually started putting this together a couple of years ago."

An interactive map of the earth appeared, filling most of the screen. Hundreds of red dots were scattered across every continent.

"As you may have already guessed," Katiya continued, "the red markers represent sightings, abductions… any event potentially linked to extraterrestrials." She used a finger to rotate the image of the earth. Some places had only a few dots, while others had clusters so thick the entire region became red. "I thought it might be nice to see if there were any geographic trends."

"Amazing how many sightings there are."

"Keep in mind these only represent the ones we've accepted. Each event has to go through a vetting process. First, we screen each one for fraud. As I told you before, we do that by conducting interviews and performing background checks on the person or persons making the claim. Next, we make sure the sighting couldn't be explained by something mundane. For example, UFO sightings near Air Force bases are often just stealth bombers or other classified aircraft."

Amanda nodded. "I've often wondered about that."

"If an event makes it through each of our hurdles, it becomes official. It's then, and only then, that we place a red marker on the interactive map. As expected, we discovered there are indeed areas of high activity around the world. You can see a UFO anywhere, but they tend to be clustered in areas we call hot zones." Katiya used the touch screen to zoom in on the southwestern US. She traced a finger along a rectangular red blotch that seemed to stretch for hundreds of miles. "This corridor in Arizona and New Mexico is one of the biggest on the planet."

"Amazing," Amanda whispered.

"It is, but you haven't seen anything yet. What I'm about to show you will blow your mind. Take a look at this." Katiya selected an option from a drop-down menu, and suddenly green dots appeared, many of them clustered in the same places as the red ones. "As we plotted all of this out, one of my graduate students noticed something strange. As our map began to take shape, she recognized something immediately. She noticed that the places with the most UFO sightings were also places associated with high levels of paranormal activity: floating orbs, mysterious lights, ghosts, apparitions, strange creatures, animal mutilations... basically things that go bump in the night."

"How did she know that?"

"She had been obsessed with paranormal things her entire life. She watched horror movies and read books on ghosts as a kid... she was even a ghost tour guide at one time."

"So do you think there's some sort of a connection?"

"There is no doubt in my mind there's a connection. To be sure, there are a few places where the correlation isn't precise, but it's the exceptions that confirm the rule. Here, let me give you another example." She moved the map until the eastern United States came into view. She pointed at a spot along the southeast coast that was smothered in red and green. "This is Savannah, Georgia. I always knew it was famous for its resident ghosts, but until we started gathering data, I had no idea it had more than its share of UFO sightings as well. Go fifty miles in any direction, and the sightings seem to dry up."

Amanda nodded slowly. "My parents took me to Savannah when I was a kid. I remember hearing someone say it's the most haunted city in the United States."

"Precisely. Show me a haunted area, and I'll show you lots of UFOs and abduction claims. The two go hand in hand."

Amanda leaned back. "Any theories as to why that might be?"

"The way I see it, there are really only two possibilities. You could take the alien view, which means extraterrestrials are responsible for events that we would classify as paranormal. Or, conversely, there are some who might say that all of these things, including UFOs, have some sort of spiritual explanation."

"I'm confused. How can extraterrestrials be responsible for ghosts?"

Katiya shrugged. "Cloaking devices, for one. We may see them only when they want us to or only when there is a malfunction of their technology. Ghosts could also be some sort of hologram, images projected by the aliens. A lot of this could be experimentation, with Earth as their test tube."

"Okay, so we know we're dealing with either ETs or something from the spirit world," Amanda said. "Whatever the

THE PORTAL

source, why do they congregate in certain areas?"

"*That,* my friend, is what I've been working on night and day. And I think I have the answer." Katiya looked at the map again. "Let's go back to the area of high activity in the southwestern US." She zoomed in on the area. "As you can see, a large corridor of markers stretches across two states, Arizona and New Mexico. The most infamous event in this zone was the crash of the alien craft in Roswell, New Mexico. But that's just the tip of the iceberg." Katiya pointed at the swath of green that also covered the area. "What most people don't realize is that this region is also known to have some of the most haunted pieces of real estate anywhere on earth."

Amanda lifted an eyebrow. "I didn't know that."

"As I said, most don't. The paranormal side of the equation doesn't get as much publicity as do UFO sightings. I think it's because it's easier for people to believe in alien life than it is for them to believe in the supernatural, although that's changing." She turned back to her screen. "Anyway, let's look at a couple of places within this zone, specifically in Arizona. One is a remote mountain range known as the Superstition Mountains. The Apache Indians call it the Devil's Playground."

"That rings a distant bell," Amanda said.

"It's not the kind of place you'd want to take your family on vacation. There are regular reports of shadow figures, spirit faces, and a subterranean world in which reptilian humanoids are said to reside. Sure, a lot of it is hocus and myth, but if there is that much smoke, then there has to be at least a small flame."

Katiya pointed to another place on the map. "Just north of

the Superstition Mountains is Sedona, home of the alleged Sedona Vortex. It's another hot zone for all things paranormal—haunted ranches, unusual animal activity, strange lights, beams, and orbs."

"Is there a punch line in here somewhere?" Amanda smiled.

"Stay with me, I'm about to tie all of this together. At many of these sites, including the ones I just described, we hear reports of objects just appearing in the sky, seemingly out of nowhere." She toggled to another screen and turned the tablet toward Amanda. "Here, I want you to take a look at this. It's a short video that was filmed from the top of one of the Superstition Mountains."

Katiya hit play, and a grainy video began. At first, the camera seemed to be aimed at some short trees and bushes in the foreground, but the person filming soon focused on a dark object in the distance. Amanda thought it looked like a mountain.

Katiya pointed at a place in the middle of the screen. "Look right here, between the two mountains."

Amanda saw what appeared to be a cloud. It was moving and spinning so fast that it looked like a time-lapse video. After a few seconds, it began to morph into a ring. She could hear one of the people filming the video gasp.

Amanda's eyes widened as a disc-shaped object began to come out of the ring. It moved slowly toward the camera before banking into a ninety-degree turn. The camera followed the craft to the left until it finally disappeared behind a row of trees.

Amanda could hear the person shooting the video mumble

THE PORTAL

a few expletives. Then he turned the camera back toward the cloud ring, but it was gone.

Katiya closed the browser and looked at Amanda. "What I believe you just witnessed was the opening of a portal. I could show you a few other videos demonstrating the same thing, but that's the clearest one ever filmed." She set the tablet on the ground. "So, in answer to your question, we believe all of these hot zones are associated with portals."

Amanda sat in silence, trying to digest everything she'd seen and heard. "So, you're telling me this is like a wormhole?"

Katiya nodded. "And lest you think this is some sort of crazy idea, ask any degreed astronomer if he believes in wormholes. They're a scientific reality, Amanda. No one denies their existence." She tossed another limb on the fire. "I believe it's possible that some advanced alien cultures have learned how to either manipulate or create their own portals. Can I prove it? No. But at least the theory can be rooted in science."

"I guess this means you ascribe to the extraterrestrial explanation for the activity in these hot zones?"

"I do lean that way, although I'm still open to other explanations. Those who study the paranormal also believe in portals. They believe spirit beings use portals to pass back and forth between dimensions."

Amanda remembered this theory from studying ancient cultures in college. Many myths and legends supposed spirits came through some opening that connected our world with others.

Suddenly her eyes lit with understanding. "I think I see

now how this relates to the events at CERN. You believe that Moronov and Marrese opened up some sort of portal, don't you?"

"I do," Katiya said without hesitation. "I think the evidence is pretty clear that's what happened. They were somehow able to open up a wormhole."

"You really think a subatomic particle collider can do that?"

"I'm no physicist, so I can't give you the mechanics of it, but how else can you explain what happened?" She looked Amanda in the eye. "Think about what your friends saw in the tunnel that night. How can someone explain that away? Two different men, both imagining the same thing? It defies logic to believe that."

"Well, if all of this is true, then what does it have to do with the crater? What do you think we're going to find there?"

"I believe it's some kind of outpost. And if it's still there, then we may be on the verge of one of the greatest discoveries in the history of mankind."

CHAPTER TWENTY-TWO

ZANE AWAKENED SLOWLY, the pressure on his bladder pulling him rudely out of his dreams. He rubbed his eyes and rolled onto his side, allowing his pupils to adjust to the darkness inside the tent.

He could kick himself for drinking so much water, although the intake had been more inadvertent than intentional. He and Jorge had talked for several hours that evening, and sipping water had merely been a way to occupy his hands.

He sat up and ran his fingers through his long hair. Time to get it over with. Waiting wasn't going to make the trek out into the woods any easier. Rising to his knees, he looked toward the other side of the tent to make sure he hadn't disturbed Jorge. He frowned. The Brazilian wasn't there. Was it his turn to be on patrol? Zane looked at his watch. No, it should be Bennett and Wilson. Jorge must have gone out for a smoke.

Zane slipped on his boots and tucked his Glock into his

waistband. He pushed aside the mosquito netting and stepped outside. The camp was eerily quiet. Some of his team were sleeping in tents, and some hung in hammocks. The fire was still lit, although it had burned down to a pile of glowing embers. *Strange,* he thought. He and Jorge had given explicit instructions that it be kept alive all night. He'd worry about that later. Right now, his bladder felt as though it was going to explode.

Zane strode past the tents to the edge of the woods. After a brief search, he found the two trees that marked the sole opening in their motion-sensor system. After slipping through, he continued down the path until he found the marker for the latrine. As he turned off the trail, Zane realized he hadn't seen Bennett or Wilson, although that wasn't necessarily a concern. They'd set up a large boundary, which meant those two were probably just somewhere else along the perimeter.

Zane skirted the freshly dug hole, preferring instead to use the tree just beyond. He circled to the other side then unzipped his pants and relieved himself against the trunk. The easing of the pressure felt good.

As nature ran its course, he listened to the nighttime symphony cascading down from the canopy. There was the ever-present din of insects as well as the occasional screech of an owl. He even heard a strange cough in the distance, which Katiya had told him was a hunting jaguar.

His bladder empty, Zane zipped up his pants and circled to the other side of the tree. When he arrived at the hole, he stopped as a faint noise reached his ears. Someone was walking down the trail, undoubtedly coming to use the latrine.

THE PORTAL

He was about to warn them that he was coming out, but something stopped him.

As the steps grew louder, Zane backed up and crouched down. Seconds later, he saw the shadow of a man pass along the trail. But instead of stopping, he continued out into the jungle.

Who was it? It was too dark to tell. The man had seemed about six feet tall, which wasn't helpful. That pretty much described every male on the team except for Jorge.

Zane bit his lower lip as he pondered what to do next. He thought about going back to his tent, but his instincts told him to find out where this person was going. At the very least, the whole thing seemed bizarre. After waiting a few more seconds, Zane rose and returned to the trail. Once there, he paused and listened. He could still hear footsteps, but they were fading quickly. Whoever it was, they were in a hurry.

Suddenly, the beam of a flashlight appeared in the distance. Zane's pulse quickened. There could be only one reason the man had waited to turn on his flashlight. Clearly he didn't want to be seen by the others back at camp.

Zane picked up his speed, his senses on high alert. He could see the man better now. Something about him seemed familiar. Perhaps it was his gait. Perhaps it was the way he held his shoulders.

After rounding a bend in the trail, Zane's foot came down squarely on a stick, snapping it loudly. He cringed and looked up. The man stopped and pivoted, swinging his flashlight around in the process. Zane stepped quickly behind a tree, placing his back against the trunk. The flashlight's beam illuminated the section of the trail where Zane had just been standing. If he had waited a second longer, he would've been seen.

Moments later, the sound of footsteps reached his ears. The man was coming back. Zane pressed against the tree and placed a hand on his Glock. Finally, the footsteps came to a halt. The man was so close now that Zane could hear the movement of his arms as he waved the flashlight around. The beam soon shone on both sides of the tree where Zane was hidden. He squeezed his arms in as tightly as possible, fearful that some of his clothes might be showing.

A moment later, the beam swept away and the area was plunged into darkness. Zane counted off thirty seconds then stepped back onto the trail. To his relief, the light was already fading into the distance.

Zane began following the man once again, this time keeping more distance between them. He wouldn't be able to identify him this far back, but the additional space would provide some measure of safety.

"Who are you?" Zane whispered.

Eventually the path began to descend sharply into a ravine. The man slowed his pace, and Zane followed suit. Not only did he want to stay at a distance, but the path was also more slippery here. One bad step might send him hurtling down the slope.

Upon reaching the bottom, the man extinguished his light. Had he reached his destination? Or did he realize he was being followed? Not willing to take any chances, Zane hunched down and crept into a cluster of bushes on the right side of the trail. The thought of stepping on a coiled bushmaster sent a cold chill down his spine, but at this point, he had no choice. He couldn't risk exposing himself if the man doubled back.

Once he was safely hidden, he looked down into the ravine. A loud chorus of croaks and barks greeted him. *Frogs.* There must be a body of water close by. Zane stared intently toward the bottom of the ravine and was eventually able to make out the surface of a small pond.

Suddenly, a light flashed three times on the far shore. It seemed like some sort of signal. Seconds later, another light flashed three times from where the man had been standing. The hairs on Zane's neck stood on end. He could no longer deny the hypothesis that had already formed in his mind minutes earlier: he was witnessing a clandestine rendezvous, and it likely involved someone from his team.

About a minute later, the sound of muffled voices carried up the hill. Despite trying, Zane couldn't make out any individual words. The chorus of frogs was too loud and the distance too great. But what if he were able to get closer? He rose a bit and examined the area below him. Just beyond the cluster of bushes, the ground seemed to be relatively clear. If he could just get down there, he might be able to pick up a few snippets of the conversation.

Slowly, Zane stepped out of the bushes and crept down the slope. He was walking through leaf litter, but the steady drone of noise from the pond cloaked the sound. About ten yards out, he stepped on a thin layer of leaves strewn across a patch of mud. His feet went out from under him, and he tumbled several times before finally coming to a stop.

There could be no doubt the sound had carried to the men below. That was confirmed seconds later when four flashlight beams panned back and forth across the hill. Zane slithered over to some bushes and lay flat against the ground. Several of the beams passed directly overhead but didn't stop. About a minute later, the ravine went dark again.

Zane lay there for a moment to make sure the light didn't return then rose up on one knee. Now that he was clear of the ground, he could hear the men talking again. Their conversation was a bit clearer now, but he still couldn't figure out what they were saying.

At this point, he didn't dare try to get any closer. More noise would undoubtedly bring the men over for a thorough search. He might be able to slip away, but it wasn't worth the risk. He would be outnumbered and outgunned. All he could do now was wait.

After some time had passed, Zane noticed the men had grown silent. The only sound in the ravine came from the raft of frogs sitting along the pond's edge. Apparently the meeting had ended.

Zane rose up on the balls of his feet. It was imperative that he get back to camp and hide somewhere along the path. Once there, it would be easy to identify the mystery man when he returned. The only question would be whether or not to confront him immediately. That would likely depend on who it was.

As Zane stood to leave, he heard footsteps coming up the hill. He'd waited too long. Seconds later, a distant shadow passed by and continued up the hill. When the man neared the top, he turned on his flashlight and disappeared over the crest.

If I can't wait for you, at least I'll follow you back.

Zane had only taken one step when he grunted in pain. Somehow he'd twisted his ankle in the fall. It wasn't a bad sprain, but it was enough to prevent him from moving with speed.

He bent over and grabbed his knees, letting out a long sigh of frustration.

After remaining still for a full minute, he slowly rose and hobbled back toward the path.

As he turned and made his way up the hill, two things weighed heavily on his mind: The group had a mole. And he might never know who it was.

CHAPTER TWENTY-THREE

JORGE PULLED THE cigar out of his mouth. "You're sure it was someone from our team, amigo?"

The group had been marching again since dawn, and Zane had just spent the last few minutes describing everything that had taken place the night before, including his theory that there was a mole in their midst.

"I have zero doubt that it was one of ours," Zane replied.

"What makes you so sure?"

"For starters, he came out through the opening in our motion-sensor perimeter."

Jorge nodded, then his eyes narrowed. "Unless they watched your men setting it up."

"You'd have to get awfully close to know that."

The two men began walking again.

"You said that you couldn't tell who the person was," Jorge said. "Could you tell *anything* about them?"

"Nothing other than it was a man who was about six feet tall," Zane said.

"Which is obviously why you were comfortable coming to me," Jorge said with a laugh.

"You said that, not me." Zane slapped the Brazilian on the back.

"If a certain soldado wasn't already dead, I might have already made a guess," Jorge said.

"Agreed."

As Jorge paused to relight his cigar, Zane looked ahead. Katiya and Max disappeared around a bend in the trail. Zane had kept his eye on the linguist ever since departing Manaus. He was about six feet tall, give or take a couple of inches, so he certainly fit the size and build of the man in the woods. But why on earth would he be meeting with someone in the middle of the jungle? For that matter, why would anyone?

"You said you couldn't hear the conversation that took place?" Jorge asked.

"Nothing. Too far and too much background noise."

"Did the people he was meeting have an accent?"

In the aftermath of the events, Zane thought he'd remembered something about the voices. But no matter how hard he tried to retrieve the little nugget of information, it always seemed just out of reach. Was it a Chinese accent? He couldn't say. "There was something unusual about their voices, but I can't put my finger on what it was. I'm hoping that something will jar my memory over the next day or so."

"How many were there?" The Brazilian's questions were coming quickly now.

"I counted four flashlight beams all together. I'm assuming one of those was from the person I followed."

"So three?"

"At least."

Jorge puffed a few times, obscuring his head in a cloud of smoke. "Do you think they knew they were being watched?"

"Probably not. If they suspected something, I think they would've searched the area where I was hidden."

There was a long pause. Jorge used the opportunity to take another long draw, allowing the smoke to drift slowly out of his mouth. Finally, he asked, "So if you had to guess, who do you think it was?"

"For one of the few times in my life, I don't even have a guess." He sighed loudly. "I certainly can't bring myself to think it was one of the soldiers."

"You shouldn't eliminate anyone until you have more information."

Zane knew the Brazilian was right. He was no detective, but he did know you followed the evidence, regardless of where it led. Finally, he nodded and said, "I haven't scratched them off my list. It's just hard for me to believe that any of those men would be working against us somehow."

"All I'm saying is to keep your eyes wide open, amigo."

"If you eliminate the women, that really only leaves four other suspects."

"Not so fast." Jorge used his cigar to point at the two walking on the trail ahead. "The professor could've had her hair pulled up. She's not close to six feet, but she's not short either. Remember it was dark—"

Zane's head turned quickly toward him. "Surely you're not saying it was Dr. Mills I followed last night?

Jorge shrugged. "Why not? I hold her in high regard. She seems trustworthy. But I also know that our eyes can play tricks on us out here in the jungle."

The two walked in silence for a few minutes. Zane knew it was a man he'd followed. The gait, the way he'd carried himself. And yet, he didn't want to play favorites either. If something popped back into his memory that suggested it might have been a woman, he'd be open to that. But for now, he'd stay focused on the men.

"Have you considered calling this whole thing off and going back?" Jorge asked.

Zane's answer was immediate. "No, I haven't considered that."

"Why not?" Jorge asked after pulling the cigar from his mouth. "You don't think it's dangerous to go deep in the jungle with a traitor in our midst?"

"Wouldn't it be just as dangerous to announce that we have a mole and we're going back? That might trigger this person to act irrationally. There is no telling what they might do. Not to mention whoever it is they're working with. That would be a trigger, not a solution."

Jorge shrugged. "You could always come up with a—"

Suddenly Zane's radio squawked, cutting the Brazilian off. "Sir, are you there?" It was Bennett.

"Go ahead, Sergeant."

"Sir, I think you need to get up here."

Bennett's voice had a tone Zane hadn't heard before. He looked at Jorge then said, "We'll be right there."

CHAPTER TWENTY-FOUR

AFTER ROUNDING A bend in the trail, Amanda came to an abrupt halt. Two of the Green Berets were standing in the middle of the path just ahead. Sergeant Bennett was facing the other way with a radio pressed against his ear. Corporal Wilson, who was standing next to him, turned and held up a hand, indicating she should proceed slowly.

Amanda approached carefully. What were they looking at? Was it a jaguar? An anaconda? She couldn't see anything yet, but she still couldn't help but picture a giant serpent coiled in the middle of the trail.

As she drew within a few feet, Wilson nodded at something just ahead. Amanda stepped closer then stopped. A wave of shock washed over her. She could scarcely believe her own eyes. There, in the trail about fifty yards away, stood an indigenous boy. She figured he was likely a preteen, although it was hard to tell because his muscles seemed developed beyond his years.

Bennett put away his radio and whispered, "He was just

standing there when we came around the turn. Hasn't moved since."

"He doesn't seem dangerous," Wilson said in a low tone.

The corporal was right. The boy's demeanor was one of calm curiosity. As far as she could tell, there was no hint of aggression in his eyes.

"He's well armed though," Bennett said.

The boy held a bow in one hand, and a quiver of arrows was slung over his back. His hair was typical of the indigenous males, an inverted bowl with bangs as straight as a ruler. A sharp piece of wood stuck horizontally through his nose, and black lines were painted across each cheek. From a distance, they looked like whiskers.

"Oh my," Katiya said as she eased up next to them.

Max arrived just behind her, his eyes wide in awe. "Very young, but still probably a seasoned hunter."

"He's beautiful," Katiya whispered.

"He is," Amanda replied. "It's one thing to see them in photographs, but it's another to see one of them in person."

Zane and Jorge came running around the bend in the trail then slowed when they saw everyone gathered in silence.

Jorge pushed up to the front. When he saw the boy, a startled look crossed his face. After staring at him for a while, he said, "I recognize the tribe. Papaqua. The face painting is typical of their hunting males."

Max nodded. "I was thinking the same thing."

"He looks awfully young," Zane said.

"They begin hunting at an early age," Jorge said. "This one has probably been hunting on his own for some time."

Katiya looked at Max. "Can you speak to him?"

"I don't know the Papaqua language well," Max said, "but I know enough to hold a basic conversation."

"Why don't you give it a shot?" Amanda asked. She was dying to know what was on the young boy's mind. How fascinating to think that they might actually be able to talk to him.

"Let's give him a little time to adjust." Max stared at the foliage on both sides of the path. "I'm not so sure he doesn't have more friends waiting out in the bush."

Jorge's gaze had already been fixed on the jungle. "For now, I think he's the only one."

"What's he wearing?" Bennett said, pointing with his rifle. "A puma hide?"

Amanda glanced at the garment he was referring to. At first it appeared to be a cloth tucked into the boy's belt, but she quickly realized it was some sort of animal hide.

"*O gato grande... jaguar,*" Jorge replied. "Likely his first kill. They wear it as a source of pride."

"Amazing that one so young could kill one of those stealthy jungle cats," Zane said.

Katiya looked at Jorge. "And the necklace... is there any meaning to those teeth?"

"Likely another display of his skills as a hunter. I'm not entirely sure, but each tooth may represent a large kill."

"It's just like helmets in college football," Bennett said. "You put a little sticker on the back each time you make a big tackle or a hit."

Jorge nodded. "We may not like to admit it, but we are all

much the same. Somewhere deep within, all men want to be known as warriors."

"The more kills he makes, the higher his standing in the tribe," Max said. "And the higher his standing, the better his choice of wife."

The boy squatted down, his gaze still fixed on all the strange people in front of him. Amanda thought he seemed more relaxed, although it was hard to know for sure.

"I think it's time." Max looked at Amanda and Katiya. "I want the two of you to come with me."

Zane looked at him. "I'm not so sure—"

"He's right," Jorge said. "Many of the tribes are dominated by males, so they don't see females as a threat. I believe the two ladies will have a calming influence on him."

Amanda saw Zane and Bennett exchange a knowing glance. It was obvious Zane was letting him know that they needed to be ready to take action if necessary.

Max looked at Amanda and Katiya then nodded toward the boy. As he stepped forward, they followed close behind. Amanda noticed that he moved slowly, with both hands at his side, palms facing forward. He'd obviously spent enough time with tribesmen to know what put them at ease, so she followed suit.

About halfway there, he turned his head slightly and whispered, "We're going to be fine. Just don't make any sudden moves. And please don't do anything unless I say so."

"I can't get over how beautiful he is," Katiya whispered as they drew closer. "I've been to the rainforest on many occasions, but I've never experienced anything like this."

"He's probably thinking the same thing," Amanda said with a low chuckle.

When they approached within about ten yards, the boy stiffened slightly. Max stopped and got down on one knee. Amanda and Katiya did likewise.

Max smiled at the boy and then spoke in a strange, almost guttural tongue. Amanda marveled that the linguist could even make his mouth and voice box work like that.

The boy's eyes widened at the sound of his own language. A smile spread over his face as he made a quick reply.

Moving slowly, Max reached into a pocket and pulled something out. Amanda shifted slightly, trying to get a look. It was a stick of beef jerky. After removing the wrapper, the linguist held the snack up in the air and said something. The boy nodded, and Max tossed it toward him. Without taking his eyes off them, the boy reached down and picked up the jerky. He lifted it to his nose and sniffed it for a few seconds before taking a bite. After chewing and swallowing, he nodded and smiled.

Max turned his head slightly. "That's good news. He received my gift."

Not to be outdone, the boy reached into an animal skin pouch that was hanging at his side. A few seconds later, he pulled out what appeared to be two nuts and tossed them toward the linguist, who gathered them up and ate them slowly. The two exchanged a few words, then the boy stood once again.

"We can approach now," Max said softly.

Amanda rose and followed. The boy's big brown eyes

watched them closely, but she didn't sense any distrust in his gaze.

When they drew within a few feet, Max stopped, and the two began to speak back and forth. Their exchange lasted for several minutes. At one point, Max gestured toward Amanda and Katiya and said something. Amanda presumed he was making a brief introduction. Katiya smiled and nodded, so Amanda did likewise. The boy spoke and then bowed his head slightly.

"We're quite fortunate," Max said. His face with beaming with excitement. "He's very friendly and very trusting. Perhaps too trusting."

"I see your point," Katiya said. "Not everyone is as friendly as we are. Who did you say we are?"

"I told him that we're a friendly tribe of people who are simply passing through. I told him we respect their boundaries and that we mean his people no harm. I also told him that we'd be happy to help him in any way we could."

"And what did he say?" Amanda asked.

Max looked at her. "Something very exciting… he said that he would be willing to help us as well."

Katiya's face beamed. "Maybe he'd be willing to accompany us. Did you get his name?"

"Osak."

Upon hearing his name, the boy's eyes widened. Amanda smiled at him.

"As I told you before, they are generally much more comfortable around females, which is why I brought the two of you with me. I think they can sense that you're much less prone to aggression. I've seen it time and time again."

"Is he good with that bow?" Amanda asked.

Max nodded. "You wouldn't want to be on the other end of one of those arrows. He could probably impale a lizard on a tree trunk at fifty feet."

Suddenly the boy began to speak and gesture with his hands.

Katiya's brow furrowed. "Uh-oh. What did he say?"

"I'm not completely sure, something about a chieftain."

"Maybe he's asking who our leader is," Katiya said. "Shall we call Zane forward?"

Max first frowned at the mention of the operative's name then shrugged. "I guess it wouldn't hurt."

Katiya turned and waved at Zane while Max continued speaking to the boy.

"You were right," Max said. "He does want to speak to our leader."

Zane approached slowly. When he drew even with the others, he said, "I see you made a new friend."

Osak fixed his gaze on him. After studying the operative for a few seconds, he said a few words that sounded like a short statement of some kind.

Zane patted his own chest. "Zane."

"Zane," Osak repeated.

Osak's expression suddenly changed. Amanda could tell he was upset about something. He pointed at the sky and spoke in an excited tone.

"He doesn't seem happy," Katiya said.

Max listened for a moment then translated what the boy

had said. "He's telling Zane that a bad storm is approaching, and that he should help his people find cover. He mentioned something about fire from the sky."

Zane looked up. "It's been clear all—"

Suddenly there was a clap of thunder in the distance. Amanda looked toward a distant break in the trees. The previously blue sky was now steel gray. Seconds later, the trees began to sway, blown by the approaching winds.

As Zane turned to the others and barked orders for everyone to set up their tents, Katiya turned to Amanda. "Osak needs to come with us. Can you imagine how much help he'd be?"

Amanda had to agree. It was as though the little boy had been sent by God.

CHAPTER TWENTY-FIVE

ZANE STUCK HIS head out from underneath the tarp they'd set up between four trees. The wind had died, and the rain had lightened to a steady drizzle. The worst of the storm appeared to be over, giving him hope that they could be moving again soon.

Hearing a gasp of delight, Zane turned around. Jorge was sitting a few feet away, lighting the tip of a cigar. Osak stared at the flame, his eyes widening with wonder. Then he said something in an excited tone.

Amanda looked at Max. "What did he say?"

"He said he's heard of fire makers, but it's the first time he's ever seen one," Max said.

Jorge held his lighter out in front of the boy. He flicked the thumbwheel, causing the flame to leap out of the steel hood. Unable to control himself, Osak reached out and took the lighter from Jorge. He flicked the thumbwheel a couple of times, to no avail.

Jorge looked at Max. "Tell him to keep his thumb down."

The linguist pointed at the lighter and said something to the boy. Osak tried again, this time keeping his thumb in place. The flame flickered to life, and the boy to jump with excitement. He stared at it for a moment before finally bursting into laughter.

"I could just eat him up," Katiya said. "His reaction is priceless."

Zane bent over and patted Osak on the back. "We can also thank him for dry gear."

"Sometimes I think they understand the jungle better than scientists," Jorge said from a cloud of smoke. "It's one thing to visit this place for a week or two, studying this or that. It's another thing to have to survive out here from the moment you're born."

"There is so much we can learn from them," Katiya said.

"Right now I'd like to know where the nearest bar is," Zane said.

"Three days, and you already have the shakes?" Katiya asked with a wink.

Zane smiled at her then sat down. "On a more serious note, we need to ask him if he knows anything about the crater."

"We do know how to get there, don't we?" Katiya asked.

"I know how to get to the crater rim," Jorge said, "although I've never actually been there." He leaned forward and used the palm of his hand to clear away a few leaves, exposing the soil. Then he picked up a nearby stick and drew a line in the dirt. "This is the trail we're on now. Eventually we'll come to a place where you can either keep going straight or turn off to the right." He drew another line, this one perpendicular to the first. "If you turn right, it will take you in a big loop back to where we crossed the stream yesterday."

"That's the route that everybody takes," Zane said. "Ecotourists, birdwatchers, adrenaline junkies."

"But instead of turning right, we'll keep going straight," Jorge continued. "That's where... how do you say in English... the going gets tough. The trail will be narrower. We may even have to hack our way through in a couple of spots." He used the stick to extend the first line a few more inches then drew a circle at the end. "My contacts tell me that if we continue in that direction, we'll eventually arrive at the crater rim."

"The slope is fairly steep," Zane said as he touched the edge of the circle, "but Jorge was told it shouldn't be too difficult to get to the bottom."

"And after that?" Katiya asked.

"Once we reach the valley floor, we'll officially be inside our target zone. Where we go after that depends on what we find. If there are trails, then obviously we'll use those as much as possible. That's where I was hoping our friend could help us." He nodded at Osak.

Katiya looked at Max. "Can you ask him if he knows anything about the crater?"

Max turned and addressed Osak. On several occasions, the linguist reached out and touched the lines drawn in the dirt. After speaking for a couple of minutes, he stopped and allowed everything to sink in.

At first Osak didn't seem to understand. He simply stared

at the lines without expression. Was he even familiar with the concept of a map? Surely he was.

Suddenly a look of recognition spread across the boy's face. He tapped the circle with a finger, repeating the same phrase over and over.

Max nodded. "He knows about the crater."

Osak spoke again, this time in a lower tone.

"Apparently the Papaqua see it as a forbidden region, a dark place of myth and legend. He seems shocked that we'd even want to go."

Osak tapped the circle and uttered a short phrase.

"He said many have gone in, but only a few have come out," Max said.

"The ones that made it out... what did they say?" Zane asked.

Max posed the question to Osak, who spoke for several minutes. When he was finished, Max said, "He says that he's never spoken to any of them himself, but that his tribe has passed down the stories. Apparently the ones who made it out were reluctant to say much about their time there. In fact, some refused to talk at all. The ones who did share spoke about seeing spirits and strange creatures."

Amanda let out a little gasp.

The last thing Zane wanted was for his group to have an unreasonable fear of their destination. It was imperative that they not give in to irrational fear. "Look, we know the crater is in a dark corner of the jungle. My guess is that some of these legends are true, but the likeliest explanation is that many of the people who entered either got lost or were killed by predators."

"What about the ones who did make it out?" Amanda asked. "They saw spirits and strange creatures. That doesn't sound like jaguars and ocelots."

Zane shrugged. "As I said, it's a dark place... but I believe that's only in a biological sense. I'd guess their imaginations ran wild."

"I'm just not sure it's that simple, Zane," Katiya said.

"Did you ever get lost out in the woods as a kid?" Zane asked. "Well, I did. And once you realized you didn't know the way home, things began to change. All of a sudden the trees got bigger and nothing looked familiar. Panic set in and gave you brain fog. That's a recipe for hallucinations. It's also how legends are started."

"These were probably grown men, that's the difference," Katiya said. "These aren't children wandering around in the woods at dusk."

"He also told me something else. I think it might be helpful." Max grabbed a stick and used it to draw a dot inside the circle. "He says that there's a mountain right in the center of the crater. His people believe that many of the strange creatures come from that mountain."

Zane's eyes narrowed. He wondered if that was the anomaly that Ross and Chris were looking at back in DC.

"Why do they believe that?" Amanda asked.

"He didn't say. Apparently the ones that made it back said the closer you got to the mountain the crazier things got. He didn't use this word, but it's similar to us saying a certain place is haunted."

Katiya bit her lower lip then said, "I wonder if this has anything to do with why we're here. I mean, don't you find it more than a little strange that the very place we're going to search for an alien presence is also a place the indigenous people say is haunted? To me it couldn't be clearer. They saw aliens."

"It's not unreasonable to make that connection," Zane agreed.

"It's interesting they said things got stranger in close proximity to that mountain," Amanda said. "Can you think of a better place from which to transmit a signal?"

Zane nodded then looked at Brett. "Do you remember seeing anything like that on our sat photos?"

"No, but I can't rule out the presence of a mountain, particularly if it's covered by jungle vegetation. Remember, it's very difficult to discern topography from a satellite photo. You're looking straight down at some of the thickest rainforest in the world."

"I agree," Katiya said. "If you're looking straight down, it would likely appear to be one giant swath of green."

Brett's eyes narrowed. "I do remember that something caught my attention when I was reviewing the photos. It was a narrow area devoid of vegetation. I assumed it was a stream of some sort because that's the one place where the canopy was broken. But now that I think about it, the line formed a circle."

"I don't follow you," Katiya said.

"If the bottom slope of the mountain is steep or rocky, you wouldn't see a lot of trees there."

Katiya nodded.

"Where in the crater was it?" Amanda asked.

"If my memory serves me correctly, it was right here." Brett tapped inside the circle. "Dead center."

Zane thought it was significant that Brett's anomaly was in the same general area that Osak had indicated earlier. It seemed clear that there was a mountain there. He also had to admit he was intrigued by the Papaqua legends regarding the area around the peak. If they saw some sort of alien being, wouldn't that qualify as a strange creature?

Brett broke the silence. "I think that settles the question of what we're going to do once we get in there."

"We go straight to the mountain," Amanda said.

Katiya caught Zane's eye. "I also think we need a certain someone to accompany us." Before he could respond, she said, "He's been with us less than an hour and has already provided loads of assistance. Just think how helpful he could be down in that crater."

"I agree," Zane said. "Except we're not in the business of forcing people to do things against their will. It's up to him."

Brett looked at Max. "He said he was familiar with the crater. Has he actually been there?"

"He said he's been to the rim once, but it was at night and he doesn't remember much about it except that it was a long drop to the bottom." Max nodded at the ground. "He believes the map Jorge drew is accurate. When the trail comes to the fork, we'll need to continue straight ahead."

Katiya looked at Zane. Reading her thoughts, he turned to Max. "Ask him if he'd be willing to come with us."

The linguist spoke to the boy. His answers came surprisingly quick. When he finished, Max translated his words. "Good news. He said he'll come with us, but only because he's afraid our lives are in danger and he wants to protect us. He also said he has two days before his tribe will become concerned by his absence."

"That's wonderful." Katiya beamed.

"Does he know how long it will take to get to the rim?" Jorge asked.

After retrieving an answer from Osak, Max said, "If we hurry, we might get there by nightfall."

CHAPTER TWENTY-SIX

COLONEL ZHENG LEE woke at dawn, hunger pangs gnawing at his stomach. He hated the jungle. The never-ending swarms of insects, the suffocating heat, the lack of a toilet, and now the persistent hunger. And if that weren't enough, the frugal General Kong had insisted they get by on an exclusive diet of MREs. The only thing those skimpy meals did was keep the stomach acid at bay for an hour or so. Thankfully, Zheng had stowed away his own private supply of rice and fruits.

The colonel tried to force himself back to sleep, but to no avail. Not only was he hungry, but now his bladder was becoming painful as well.

With a loud grunt, he rose his knees. He flipped open the mosquito guard and crawled outside. He stood and stretched his muscles, jump-starting his circulation. Then he turned and made his way through the circle of tents, nodding at two guards who were coming off patrol.

After leaving camp, he continued over to the edge of the

jungle about fifty yards away. The newly risen sun had not yet penetrated the thick canopy, but there was just enough light to get around without a flashlight. Finding his favorite clump of ferns, Zheng began relieving himself.

As he stood there, Zheng thought back on their meeting the night before. Apparently the Americans still had no idea what they might find, nor did they know anything about the place they were trying to get to.

Zheng cursed his superiors for sending them on this wild-goose chase. There was nothing out there in the middle of the jungle. After suffering for several days, they would discover what he already knew: the whole thing was a farce. Sure, they would be able to destroy the American team when the time came, exacting some measure of revenge for the dead Chinese Special Forces team, but at what cost? How many men would have to die?

Zheng's bladder was mostly empty when he first felt the sensation that he was being watched. It was a sensation that he'd learned to heed. Turning slowly, he examined the tangle of jungle around him. If someone were hiding in the maze of lush vegetation, there was little chance he'd see them.

Seeing movement in his peripheral vision, Zheng looked to his left, down the line of trees. When he did, he flinched, causing a stream of urine to soak his pant legs. Standing twenty feet away was a native, his face decorated with reddish-orange stripes. He wore a skimpy loincloth, and a bow and a quiver of arrows were slung over one shoulder.

Zheng weighed his options. The boy couldn't be old, perhaps late teens or early twenties, but the markings on his face gave him a menacing appearance. The colonel seemed to remember that the brighter the paint, the more deadly the tribe. Or was that poison frogs?

Zheng zipped his pants and turned toward the boy. His expression seemed peaceful, but looks could be deceiving. He was a savage at heart, and savages would kill if provoked.

His pulse quickening, Zheng slid his right hand into the front pocket of his pants. He was careful not to move it quickly, lest he alert the boy to what he was doing. Once inside, he patted his hand around then cursed. He'd left his pistol in his backpack.

What now? Should he run for the tents? That would probably mean certain death. It would take him ten to fifteen seconds to cover the distance, more than ample time for the boy to place several arrows in his back.

What about calling for his guards? It would only take seconds for them to arrive, and should the boy reach for his bow, Zheng could always dive into the bushes.

Pursing his lips, Zheng gave a quick, high-pitched whistle. Hearing nothing in response, he whistled again, this time louder.

Suddenly he heard movement. Turning his head slightly, Zheng saw guards moving out from the tents. They walked casually, unaware that anything was amiss. When they made it halfway to the clearing, the colonel lifted a hand. Once he had their attention, he pointed toward the boy. As soon they saw him, they stopped, startled.

"Cover me, you idiots!" Zheng hissed.

The two men raised their weapons slowly.

The boy suddenly became aware of their presence, and a

THE PORTAL

look of confusion spread over his face. After staring for a moment, he reached into a pouch. Zheng stiffened. What was he doing? Much to his relief, the boy pulled out a piece of fruit. He stepped toward the men and lifted it in the air.

Zheng frowned. It looked like the boy was making some sort of peace offering. Should they accept it? It might be better to keep the natives on their side. Who knew how many were hovering in the trees around the camp. There could be hundreds watching them right now, although Zheng couldn't see any evidence of that.

The guards looked at their commander warily, unsure how to react. Zheng signaled them to lower their weapons.

Zheng was about to start walking toward his men when something moved in the direction of the tents. He turned and saw a massive figure walking toward them. *Ho Chen.* The giant normally slept in but must have been awakened by the commotion.

Zheng turned back toward the boy and saw his eyes widen at the sight of Ho. He'd probably never seen any living creature as large as the one coming toward him. For the first time, a tinge of fear appeared on his countenance.

Ho strode toward the boy without hesitation. What was the idiot going to do?

"Be careful!" Zheng shouted. While Ho could crush any other human being in hand-to-hand combat, it would only take one well-placed arrow in the chest to bring him down. Even a man like Ho was susceptible to weaponry. And if Ho was killed, Beijing would hold Zheng responsible.

As Ho drew near, the boy extended the fruit in the palm of

his hand.

The giant slowed at the sight of the food. Lieutenant General Huang had mentioned that Ho had the mental ability of a small child, so Zheng had no idea what to expect. The giant seemed confused at the boy's offer of kindness.

The boy said something, jabbing the fruit toward Ho.

The giant took a few more steps, stopping several feet away. "Take the fruit!" Zheng shouted. "He wants you to have it."

Zheng watched as Ho flexed his right hand, which was the size of a dinner plate.

The boy smiled and waved the fruit a bit, trying to entice him to take it. Ho's hand shot out like the head of a snake, but instead of seizing the fruit, he grabbed the boy's neck and lifted him in the air. The boy tried to scream but couldn't get any air through his windpipe, which was being mashed flat by the giant's vicelike grip.

The boy reached up and tried to pry Ho's hands away. *He might as well try to rip open a locked car door.*

Zheng turned away. He was a hardened officer and had seen many horrible things in his life, but what he was witnessing now made his stomach churn. He thought about telling Ho to stop, but then he ran the risk of enraging the giant. Better to let him follow his instincts as a killer.

Zheng cringed as he heard the lifeless body hit the ground with a dull thud. He stole a quick glance. Ho bent over and picked something up.

The fruit.

Ho held it in front of his face, examining it for a moment.

Smiling, he took a bite and began to chew.

CHAPTER TWENTY-SEVEN

THE ORACLE'S VOICE crackled out of the satellite phone. "Can you repeat?"

"I said we've made contact with one of the indigenous people," Zane said in a louder voice.

"Did you say indigenous tribe?"

Zane stepped up on a lichen-covered log. After checking the other side for snakes, he hopped off and continued walking. "One person, actually. A young boy."

"You've got the linguist there with you." The signal was better now. Zane could hear the rustling of papers in the background, then the Oracle continued. "Maxwell Cameron. The name escaped me for a moment. Has he been able to communicate with him?"

"He's not completely fluent, but they've been able to talk." After rounding a turn, Zane saw Tocchet, Katiya, and Max walking about forty or fifty yards ahead. "Ross, we've decided to take him with us. He knows this jungle even better than Jorge."

"Watson, I don't think—"

"He's also been able to pass along some information on our crater."

There was a moment of silence before the Oracle spoke again. "I see." Another long pause. "And you trust him?"

"Absolutely."

"He could be leading you into an ambush."

Zane stopped and turned to his right. He could have sworn he'd heard something back in the woods. It sounded like the rustling of leaves. Wilson had spotted an ocelot earlier, so maybe another of the small cats was following them.

Seconds later, he heard the snap of a twig. Once is happenstance, twice is significant. Crouching, Zane stared through the maze of trunks. Nothing moved.

"Watson?"

Zane stood slowly and began walking again. "Sorry. Yes, that's a valid concern. In fact, Jorge and I were just discussing that very thing."

"And?"

"A couple of things. First of all, both of us believe he's reliable. If he's got us snowed, he's one of the best actors I've ever seen."

"You really think you can size up someone you can't even talk to?"

Zane ignored the remark. "Second, I find it hard to believe an indigenous tribe could pull off something that sophisticated. No offense to them, but do you really believe they'd know how to plant someone like that?" Hearing no response, he continued. "Look, I admit I know almost nothing about this boy. And it's certainly difficult to know what his motivation is for helping us. But he put himself at risk by joining us. How did he know we wouldn't kill him on sight? To me, the reward of his help outweighs the slim chance he's going to betray us. Besides, we're keeping a close eye on our surroundings."

Even before placing the call, Zane had known this was going to be the Oracle's reaction. To say the man was cautious didn't even begin to describe his careful nature. Then again, it had served him well over the years.

"I trust you, Watson. You're the one on the ground and the one with the most information. Just remember that you can't completely trust someone you can't communicate with. None of us truly knows how the indigenous people think." After a brief pause, the Oracle said, "You mentioned he knows about the crater. What did he tell you to expect?"

"Apparently the place has a reputation. He says a number of tribesmen have ventured in there over the centuries. Some made it out, and some didn't." Zane cut himself off. The Oracle was already concerned enough as it was.

"Brazil's version of the Bermuda Triangle?"

"I guess you could say that."

"What about the ones who made it out?"

"They were reluctant to talk. Those who did spoke of some pretty bizarre stuff. Too much to go into."

"What do you think about that?"

"Dr. Mills is convinced there may be some connection between those stories and our mission. She believes it's too much of a coincidence that the signal may have been transmitted from the very place where local legends say strange things have happened."

"What do *you* think?"

Zane glanced ahead and noticed the others were out of sight. He quickened his pace. "That's a good question. I'll admit it's a bit odd."

"Did he mention anything else?"

Zane thought for a moment. "He did. He claims there's a mountain in the center of the crater. Apparently it's the focal point of all these tribal tales. Did you ever get the new sat photos?"

Zane could hear fingers tapping on a keyboard. Finally, the Oracle said, "I'm looking at them now. No, I don't see a mountain."

"That was my memory of it as well. But he's convinced it's there."

"I'll have Chris look for a topo map of the area."

Zane wondered if he should share what had happened the night before. The news of Nash's death had already rattled the Oracle, so telling him there was a mole might push him over the edge. In fact, he'd probably send in an extraction team and force everyone to turn over their weapons until they were able to figure out who the infiltrator was. That would essentially shut down the entire operation, something Zane didn't want to do unless absolutely necessary. They'd come too far for that. Instead, he'd watch a bit longer. In fact, he'd already planned on staying up tonight in case the perpetrator tried to leave camp a second time.

"The doctor does have a good point," the Oracle said.

"This whole thing does seem a bit odd. We get a signal from a large patch of jungle, then we find out that's a place where a number of people have been killed. In some ways, it makes me feel better about sending all of you down there."

"Hopefully I'll have something to report twenty-four hours from now."

"Regarding the native, I hope I haven't spoken too harshly of him. He may turn out to be a valuable asset. I guess I'm just trying to help you see both sides. From the outside looking in, it seems too good to be true. An indigenous boy shows up with information that is very helpful. And then he agrees to tag along as your guide. But I trust you, Watson. You've always had a good sense about people." There was a long pause. "Just proceed with caution."

"We will. I think if you were here on the ground, your gut would tell you the same thing mine does."

The Oracle let out a sigh. "Fair enough. Just remember we're responsible for the lives of three civilians, and I want all of you to make it out of there alive."

"Understood. If it will make you feel any better—"

A loud snap caused Zane to stop midsentence. It seemed to come from his left this time. He frowned. Lowering to one knee, he scanned that section of the jungle. The sun was lower now, making it difficult to see through the tangle of foliage.

"Watson?"

"Ross, let me get back to you."

"Is everything okay?"

"Yes. Just need to check something out."

Without waiting for a response, he ended the call. Looking

at the trail ahead, he realized he could no longer see any of the others.

Another shuffling sound caused him to swivel back to the left. Shadows moved, morphing into odd shapes. After tucking his phone away, Zane slowly lifted the Glock and slid his finger over the trigger. He focused on a thick line of bushes with thick flat fronds. Both noises seemed to have come from somewhere in that vicinity.

One of the vines suddenly jiggled slightly. His eyes narrowed. Had it really moved, or were the late afternoon shadows playing tricks on him?

"Zane!" someone shouted from the trail ahead.

Zane ignored the shout and remained still. A minute passed without any further sounds.

"Zane!"

Amanda.

"I'll be right there!" he shouted back.

As he rose, Zane thought he saw a shadow slip back into the dark recess of the jungle.

"Who are you?" he whispered.

Holstering his weapon, he took off down the trail.

CHAPTER TWENTY-EIGHT

"ZANE, IS THAT you?"

Zane looked up as he came around a bend in the trail. Amanda was standing just ahead, barely visible in the dim light. He slowed as he neared her. "Sorry, I was talking to Ross on the sat link and fell behind."

"Just glad you're okay," Amanda said, giving him a funny look. "Anyway, we found the rim."

Zane looked past her and saw that the others were gathered about two hundred yards down the trail. "Is there a way down?"

"We can't tell." She gestured for him to follow her. "You'll see what I mean when we get there."

They arrived at the rim a minute later. The group parted so that Zane could step through and see what was beyond. Jorge, Tocchet, and Osak were kneeling on a rock ledge. Jorge turned upon hearing his approach. He removed a cigar from his mouth and waved him over.

"What do we have?" Zane asked.

"Hard to say," Jorge said.

Zane stepped up to the edge. He immediately saw what the Brazilian meant. Clouds of thick fog billowed up toward them, and visibility was no more than ten feet.

Tocchet looked up at him. "If we go down tonight, we're going to have to go down blind."

Bennett turned on a flashlight and directed the beam down into the crater.

"It's like the beams of a headlight," Jorge said. "Best to simply use our eyes."

The soldier nodded and turned it off.

"Welcome to the haunted forest," Tocchet said. He picked up a rock and launched it out into the fog. About two seconds later, they heard a *knock* as it hit the side of a tree trunk. A second after that, a thud followed as it hit the ground.

"Well, I'd say we've got a pretty good climb down," Zane said.

Bennett pointed at the portion of the crater wall they could see. "Fortunately, it runs down at an angle. Should be relatively easy to rappel down as long as there aren't any surprises."

"Are we going down tonight?" Tocchet asked.

"I think we need to make sure this is the best spot." Zane got Max's attention then nodded at Osak. "Ask him if he knows of a better way down."

Max posed the question to the boy, who replied without hesitation. "He says that it's the same for the next several miles. He says there is a place where you can simply walk down, but it's about a two-day march from here."

THE PORTAL

"We don't have that much time," Zane said.

Osak spoke again, gesturing toward the fog.

"He says we can go down now, but we must stop when we get there."

Zane frowned. "Why's that?"

Seconds later, Max translated the boy's answer. "He said to approach the mountain at night would be certain death."

***

"Okay, everybody, listen up," Zane said, holding up a rope. One end was tied to a nearby tree, and the other end disappeared into the fog. He'd tied knots along it at three-foot intervals. "Sergeant Bennett is going down first. He'll clear the landing area, then the rest of us will go down one by one. I'll bring up the rear."

"What if we slip?" Amanda asked.

"Don't."

"Then we'll have one less mouth to feed," Tocchet said with a chuckle.

"Isn't there going to be a safety line?"

Zane gestured toward Artur, who was standing at the tree. "We're taking care of that right now. That safety will go around your waist.

"As we've already pointed out, the slope doesn't appear to be too steep. We're not talking a ninety-degree drop here. Bennett will give us a report when he gets to the bottom, but my guess is that you're simply going to be able to walk backwards most of the way down."

Max shook his head and mumbled something to Katiya.

"Do you at least have a guess as to how far down it is?" Katiya asked.

"It took the rock a couple of seconds to reach the bottom," Zane said. "I'm no physicist, but we're probably looking at a hundred feet, maybe more."

"Those trees must be massive, then." Brett pointed to the canopy of green that mushroomed out of the crater. Wisps of fog tangled around the crowns of the trees like gray snakes. "If your calculation is correct, then they're well over two hundred feet."

Zane nodded. "We're about to enter a different kind of place. My guess is that everything is going to be bigger and wilder down there. And I mean everything."

"Sorry to be the one wimp in the group, but I wish we would set up camp and go down in the morning," Amanda said.

Ordinarily Zane would've agreed with her. All things being equal, you'd want to descend into a crater during daylight hours. But all things weren't equal. They were being followed, and getting down tonight might allow them to put some distance between them and whoever or whatever was on their tail. But for now, he needed to focus on the practical reasons for going down right away.

"We still have some light now, and who's to say there won't be clouds and fog in the morning? On top of that, I have to be mindful of our supplies. I want us to be well on our way to that mountain by the time the sun comes up tomorrow morning."

Amanda looked at him but remained silent.

THE PORTAL

"Look," Zane continued, "if Sergeant Bennett finds it's too dangerous tonight, then we'll make camp here and get started in the morning. If necessary, we can even send a few people out along the rim to see if there's a better way down. But since there's still some light left, we need to at least make the attempt now."

"He's right," Jorge said. "We absolutely need to get down tonight if we can."

Amanda shrugged. "Okay. I'm game if everyone else is."

Zane surveyed the others. They probably weren't excited about descending through a blanket of fog, but for the most part, they appeared to be willing. "If there are no further questions then, let's get started. We only have another hour or so of light left, if that."

As everyone gathered their things, Zane noticed that Artur had just finished tying off the safety line. He gave the other end to Bennett, who looped it around his waist and tied it off. Each line was thin, but Zane knew they would hold, even under stress.

"You seem awfully determined to go down tonight," someone whispered at Zane's ear.

He turned to find Jorge standing just behind him.

The Brazilian continued. "You made a good choice." He nodded back toward the jungle. "It's going to be good to put some distance between us and whoever is back there."

Zane raised an eyebrow. "You knew we were being followed?"

"Of course. We've been followed from the moment we left the boat. The signs have been obvious if you're looking in the right places."

Zane frowned. "And you didn't tell me?"

Jorge shook his head. "I wasn't sure at first. When we entered the jungle, I thought it was a jaguar. I'd see the occasional flash of darkness across an opening in the woods. I sensed eyes watching us. But as I began to think about it, I realized a big cat would never follow us for this long."

Zane's mind turned to the mole. "Do you think it's the Chinese?"

"No, they're not that good. Soldiers, even good ones, are too noisy."

Zane's frown deepened. "Do you think it's Osak's tribe?"

Jorge shook his head immediately. "No, I've been watching him. He noticed some of the same noises I did. He didn't have the look of someone hearing friends, more the look of someone who was concerned."

"Another tribe then?"

Jorge shrugged his shoulders. "Probably, but at this point, it's hard to say. It's generally been one or two approaching. Now they have to stay far enough away to escape detection."

"They got pretty close to me earlier."

Tocchet approached before Jorge could respond. "Sir, we're ready to go down."

"We'll be right there, Sergeant."

Zane gave Jorge a look indicating they would talk later, then followed the Green Beret over to the crater rim. When they arrived, Bennett was checking his knots one last time. Satisfied that everything was in order, he slid on specialized gloves with goat-leather palms and neoprene cuffs.

"All set?" Tocchet asked.

Bennett lifted a thumb in the air.

"Let us know how things look down there," Zane reminded him.

Bennett saluted and said, "Yes, sir. See you on the other end."

The soldier gripped the rope tightly and began his descent. Seconds later, his head disappeared into the fog. What was he going to find at the bottom? The more Zane thought about it, the more intrigued he became. Even if only a few of Osak's stories were true, they were potentially headed into a kill zone. The only question was who or what was doing the killing. He hoped and prayed they'd all fare better than the others who'd gone before them.

A few minutes later, Bennett's voice crackled out of the radio. "I'm down. There was some incline to the wall, so it wasn't bad at all."

"Copy that," Zane said. "Can you give me a sitrep on conditions at the bottom?"

For a long moment, the only sound coming through the radio was heavy breathing.

Zane lifted the radio again. "Bennett?"

"Sorry. It's dark, very dark." There was a shuffling sound and a click. "It's like it's already night down here."

"Are you able to use your flashlight?"

"Affirmative. The…"

Zane gave him a moment then asked, "Bennett?"

"Sorry, it's just strange."

"What's strange?

"The plants. The trees. They just seem different down here."

Katiya looked at Zane. "Not surprising. Think of an island, where the flora and fauna are unique." Zane gave her a confused look, and she tried again. "Essentially, the crater rim has provided some level of separation from the rest of the jungle. It doesn't seem like much of a buffer, but my guess is we're looking at a very different ecosystem down there."

Bennett spoke again through the radio. "There is something else... we're in luck. The trail seems to pick up again down here."

"See if you can find a place for us to set up."

"Roger that."

Zane turned to the group and said in a loud voice, "Okay, let's line up, everybody. One at a time in the order I gave you. We all need to be down in the next thirty minutes. Let's move it."

CHAPTER TWENTY-NINE

"WELL, IT LOOKS like it's just us," Katiya said as Tocchet's head lowered into the foggy abyss.

"And then there were two," Zane said.

In order to save time, they had decided to use two safety lines. While Tocchet descended using one, Zane pulled up the other one, which had been untied at the bottom. He looped it around Katiya's waist, making sure it was tied off securely. As he double-checked the knot, he realized his body was only an inch or two away from hers. He felt another surge of warmth pass through him. It was starting to become regular now, despite his efforts to ignore it.

After tugging on her line one last time, he said, "I'm really concerned about something though."

"Oh?" she asked with a raised eyebrow.

"Just a little worried about someone from academia trying to rappel down a rock cliff. I've known a few professors, and they tend to be a little soft."

"Is being soft such a bad thing?" She gave him a wink.

"It is when an anaconda sizes you up on the way down. They always look for the easiest catch."

Katiya grinned and stepped closer. *Good grief, she even smells good after two days in the jungle.* "So, tell me"—her face was only about an inch away now—"if something happens on the way down, are you going to come get me?"

He placed a hand on her shoulder. "If I do, do you promise to behave?"

"No."

Their eyes met. It seemed like minutes passed, then a monkey screeched from a nearby tree, giving Zane an excuse to avert his eyes. "Have you climbed before?" He turned Katiya around to examine her pack.

"A little in my gym back home."

"How much is a little?"

"Ummm... twice."

Zane turned her around again. "Well, then... let me give you a little tip that might come in handy. Don't look—"

"Down," she said, finishing the sentence for him. They both laughed. "Yes, I know. That's one thing I do remember from my little trainer."

"Good. I'm expecting big things now. Just remember that there are no thick-padded mats at the bottom."

"Har, har." A moment later, she bit her lower lip and said, "In all seriousness, what do you think we'll find down there? You've been awfully quiet."

"My honest answer? I have no idea. I'll admit I was a bit cynical when this trip first began. I knew the government had good reason to send us out here. After all, you can't ignore what NASA picked up. But did I really expect to find anything? No." He let out a long sigh. "Now, I'm not so sure. Like you, I think there seems to be too much *there* there."

Katiya smiled. "I agree."

Zane pulled out his flashlight and clicked it on. "Sure, it's easy to write off all the stories from the Papaqua tribe. But why would they pass down a lie? And even if the story got embellished a bit, I still believe there are splinters of truth in there. At this point, I think it's safe to say *something* happened."

"What about the signal? Do you really think there's something to it?"

Before Zane could speak, Bennett's voice crackled out of the radio. "Eight has arrived. Please confirm next descent."

Zane reached down and picked up the primary line. "Your turn, professor."

"Don't think you're going to get out of it that easy. We'll talk later."

"And don't think I won't have some questions of my own. After all, you're the expert on these things."

"I look forward to it." Katiya stepped closer to him once again, giving him a hard stare. "See you on the other end?"

"See you on the other end."

Katiya backed up to the precipice, holding on to the first knot. Once her feet were positioned, she looked back at him, smiled, and lifted her thumb.

Zane spoke into the radio. "Nine headed your way."

"Copy that."

Before backing down, Katiya turned her head slightly, as though trying to look down the incline.

"Hey, hey. What did I tell you?"

Katiya looked at him and rolled her eyes. "Okay, okay."

As the anthropologist backed into the fog, Zane couldn't help but notice how cute she was in her formfitting gray leggings and boots. Even without makeup and with her hair in a ponytail, she was the picture of feminine beauty.

His thoughts reverted back to what had taken place just moments before. That should clear up any doubts he'd had before about her level of interest. The positioning of her face only an inch or two away from his. The hard stare. The flirtatious comments. He was just glad Eagle Eye Brett was already down at the bottom.

But one question remained—was *he* truly interested? The first and obvious answer was "yes," although there couldn't be a worse time to embark on a new romance. He was responsible for the mission's success, as well as getting everyone back safe and alive. If there was something between them, it would have to simmer until they got back. And if it didn't continue to simmer, then there likely hadn't been anything there to begin with.

Zane knew that Claire, his last serious relationship, hadn't completely vacated his heart. He'd said many times that when some ships sailed away they never returned to port, but in her case, he never could figure out if that was true. Despite the faulty logistics of their previous relationship, he found it hard to picture a better match for him than his former lover.

Then again, Katiya had everything Claire had, and perhaps even more. He could envision the two of them settling down into something permanent. They hadn't even been out on one date and yet he knew there would be a deep connection.

But Zane did make one promise to himself, and that was to try to keep a lid on the flirtation until the operation was over. Not only did he need to stay focused on their objective, but he also needed everyone else to have faith in his ability to lead. People weren't dumb, and giving them hints that something was between them would be disastrous. All that said, he knew that suppressing the feelings completely would be virtually impossible. He was a man, after all. And when she'd looked into his eyes earlier, it was as though he'd been hit with a jolt of electricity.

Shaking off his thoughts, he looked down. Time to get back to work. The primary line was taut, while the safety line continued to unwind and slither over the edge. Everything appeared to be running smoothly.

Bennett's voice broke the silence a few minutes later. "Nine has arrived safe and sound. Come on down, Ten."

"Roger that."

After pulling the safety line back up, Zane lifted his pack and slung it over his shoulders. He placed the radio in his left pocket and put on his gloves. He had done quite a bit of climbing in the mountains of North Carolina, so easing down a knotted rope should be child's play.

He looped the safety line around his waist, tied it off, then looked around the area one last time to make sure they hadn't left anything behind. Seeing nothing, he backed up to the edge and began his descent.

He had only taken two steps down when he heard shuffling in the forest nearby. Was it an animal? The trees were teeming with monkeys, but this sound seemed too low to the ground. And, unless he was mistaken, had emanated from somewhere around the tree where the lines were tied off. He squinted but saw no movement.

He was about to resume when he heard it again. It was soft, as though someone or something was trying not to be heard.

Zane carefully pulled the Glock from his pocket and waited. A couple of times he thought he saw something move but then realized it was a shadow. Two minutes passed, and the only sound was a family of monkeys making their way through the canopy about a quarter mile away.

Zane knew he couldn't wait forever. In fact, if someone was out there, it would be foolish to remain here, exposed on the rim.

After pocketing his gun, he backed down into the fog.

CHAPTER THIRTY

AFTER DESCENDING ABOUT twenty feet, Zane realized it was going to be even easier than he had expected. The rim face was sloped, meaning all he had to do was hang on tightly and walk backwards. He doubted it would take him more than a few minutes to reach the bottom.

His greater concern was the noise he'd heard at the top. Should he have cleared the area first? In the end, he felt as though he'd done the right thing. There were so many sounds in the jungle that you'd never get anywhere if you followed up on each one. Besides, if anyone tampered with the lines, he already had a backup plan—he'd grab the rocky slope and climb down. It was slippery and would likely take time, but he had no doubt he could do it.

Zane soon began to notice more plants. Mounds of moss covered large patches of rock, and tiny plants seemed to spring out of every millimeter of soil. The downside was that the moist flora made it more difficult to step firmly, so he slowed his pace, making sure his foot was firmly in place with each step before pushing off again.

Suddenly, he felt a twitch in the climb line. Was it just the rope sliding into a new rut somewhere at the rim or had someone touched it? The movement had been subtle but distinct. Continuing to hold the line with his left hand, he reached into his pocket with the other and pulled out his flashlight. Perhaps he was still close enough to see if someone was standing at the rim. He turned it on, but the beam simply bounced off the fog.

What now? If someone was tampering with the rope, then it would be folly to try to make it back up to the top. The farther back up he went, the farther he'd fall if something happened. So far, he'd only felt a slight twitch, not yet reason enough to transition to a manual climb.

After pondering his options, he decided to do the only thing that made sense. Returning the flashlight to his pocket, he backed down with as much speed as possible. He began to move so quickly that he bounced off the rock with each step.

Bennett's voice rose out of the darkness below. "You're almost home."

The safety line grew taut, indicating he'd made it to the point at which it needed to be removed. He was almost there.

Two flashlights clicked on, illuminating Zane from below. Taking advantage of the light, he pulled himself up a bit in order to give the line some slack, then he reached down and untied the line.

It happened just seconds later: Zane felt movement in the climbing rope, but before he could react, it was cut loose. He fell, spinning out of control as he went down. He made impact

THE PORTAL

on his side, his shoulder and head landing flush against a boulder. He rolled several times before finally coming to rest on the crater floor.

Pain shot through his body. His shoulder felt as though someone had hit it with a sledgehammer, and his head hurt so badly that he wondered if he'd cracked his skull.

A flashlight bounced toward him. Then legs appeared at his side. "What happened?" It was Bennett.

"The line... someone cut the line," Zane muttered painfully through clenched teeth.

"Someone *what*?"

Zane pushed himself up into a sitting position. "We need to get back in the trees."

Katiya appeared and knelt down next to him. She reached out and pushed his face gently to one side. "You don't need to go anywhere. You're bruised pretty badly."

"Let's take a look." Bennett knelt and used a finger to press against his jaw.

Zane pushed the soldier's hand away and tried to stand. "I'm telling you, we need to get moving... now!"

"Easy does it." Tocchet pushed him back down. "How do you know the line was cut?"

"Why the heck do you think I'm lying here?"

Tocchet turned. "Someone get me the climb rope."

Lights began to bounce around the area. About thirty seconds later, Brett approached with one of the lines in hand. "He's right. Looks like it was cut about three-quarters of the way through, and the rest ripped."

Zane rose up again. "That's what I was trying to—"

Before he could finish, a series of rapid pops sounded from above.

Gunfire.

Shots rained down around them. Some rounds chewed through the soil, and others sparked off boulders.

Amanda screamed as others sought cover behind rocks and trunks. Bennett knelt down a few feet away and raised his rifle toward the crater's rim. He calmly squeezed the trigger, spraying bullets toward the target. After providing some measure of cover, he turned and shouted, "Move it! Get back into the trees... now!"

Tocchet and Katiya each grabbed one of Zane's arms in an effort to lift him, but he waved them off. With a loud grunt, he rolled over and climbed to his feet.

More gunshots echoed from above. One bullet impacted close by, causing Tocchet to pivot and loose a barrage of return fire. His movements were fluid. *Green Beret fluid,* Zane thought.

After suppressing the gunmen, Tocchet turned back to Zane. "Here." The soldier placed an arm around him. This time Zane didn't stop him.

Katiya did likewise, but a figure appeared and pushed her aside. *Osak.* Zane had almost forgotten about the boy. He must have climbed down on his own. Once everyone was in place, the three moved forward into the trees.

Zane rolled his head toward Katiya. "Please make sure Amanda is okay."

She nodded then ran ahead.

After traveling about a hundred yards, Tocchet and Osak

set Zane up against a tree at the edge of the clearing. Brett, Artur, and Wilson were already fanned out, making sure no other attackers waited in the woods.

"Where's Rod?" Zane asked.

As if on cue, Bennett jogged into view. "We're safe for the time being," he said, kneeling next to Zane. "Have no idea where that came from.".

Now that Bennett had arrived, Tocchet left to join the others walking the perimeter.

Zane leaned his head back against the tree, wincing in pain. "That has to be the Chinese."

"That seems likely," Bennett said.

"I guess we all knew they could be out here," Zane said. "I just didn't expect full engagement this early." He looked at Bennett. "How many do you think there were?"

"A lot," the soldier said. "I counted at least ten muzzle flashes on the rim.

"I didn't want to do this." Zane reached over and pulled his pack closer. "But it's time to get Ross to send in backup. If you saw ten, then that means there could be fifteen or twenty... maybe even more."

Zane fished around in his pack for a moment then pulled the phone out. He frowned as he touched something along the edge. "What the..."

Bennett stepped closer, illuminating the phone with his light. "What is it?"

Zane held the phone at an angle so the Green Beret could see it. The side of the device was crushed, undoubtedly due to the impact with the boulder.

Just to be sure, he pressed the power button. Seconds passed, but the screen remained dark. After letting out a long sigh, he tossed the phone aside and turned toward Bennett. "Looks like we're on our own."

CHAPTER THIRTY-ONE

Joint Base Anacostia-Bolling
Washington, DC

THIRTY-ONE-YEAR-old Defense Intelligence Agency (DIA) officer Russell "Russ" Grimes yawned as he lifted the glass carafe and delivered a stream of coffee into his Washington Nationals mug. A lifelong caffeine addict, Grimes generally made the break-room pilgrimage five times prior to lunch and three times after. He then capped off the day with a can of Red Bull on the Metro.

It therefore came as no surprise that colleagues referred to him as the "Jack Russell" of national intelligence, a man of boundless energy who had the heart rate of a caffeinated hummingbird. In fact, some believed it was the caffeine that enabled him to maintain such long hours in the office. Others said it was his insatiable desire to hunt down the enemy.

"Well, well, if it isn't lover boy. So how was the big date?" Grimes didn't even have to turn around to recognize the speaker as his chubby coworker Sam Howard.

Grimes wasn't the least bit surprised at the question. He knew he'd get the third degree after he and his date, Rachel Wickham, had run into Sam and his buddies at a watering hole near Dupont Circle the night before.

"Unspeakably bad," Grimes said, dumping the usual into his coffee, two packets of sugar and a dash of cream.

"Huh? You gotta be kidding me. That chick was hot. What happened?"

Grimes lifted his hand and rubbed his thumb against his index finger.

Sam nodded slowly. "Gold digger, eh?"

"Of the highest order," Grimes said, running a hand through his mop of brown hair.

"Well, she must be a dumb gold digger, because Renegades isn't exactly pricey."

"Oh, that was only the beginning… the proverbial warm-up." Grimes set the carafe back in the coffeemaker before turning to face Sam. "Take a guess where we wound up for dinner."

Sam thought for a moment then shrugged. "Haven't a clue."

"Victor."

Sam's eyes widened. "Good grief. I need to talk to HR. You must be making a helluva lot more than—"

"I'm not. Trust me." Grimes took a quick sip of coffee then held up a finger. "But that isn't all. After paying my triple-digit bill at Victor, she insisted we catch the end of the Caps game… *lower level.*"

Sam laughed. "This girl knows how to work it."

"She's a professional. Ended up paying some clown outside the Verizon Center a hundred bucks for a period and a half of hockey."

"Well, please tell me she made all that spending worth your—"

Grimes shook his head and raised an eyebrow. "You apparently weren't listening very well. It's all about the money, chief."

"You at least got some nice tonsil hockey at the end of the night, didn't you?"

"You kidding? She might as well have had a chastity belt wrapped around her face." Grimes looked at the ground and shook his head. "She told me she didn't like to kiss on the first date."

Sam burst into laughter. "But of course she likes to consume on the first date. Look, just tell her it's a trip to the Smithsonian on your second date."

"There isn't going to be a second date," Grimes insisted. He walked toward the door and held up his cup. "Anyway, got to run. Time to go catch some bad guys. Gonna be a good way to get the looming financial crisis off my mind."

Sam lifted his cup in return. "Jack Russell is on the prowl! Have fun."

Grimes couldn't help but laugh at what had happened. He should have known better. When the black-haired beauty had approached him at a wedding reception two weeks ago, he'd heard the alarm bells going off as soon as she name-dropped and flashed the expensive jewelry. He had no one to blame but himself.

Then again, could he really blame himself for taking a shot? Rachel was a stunner, and if it had somehow worked out, he'd have been the envy of every red-blooded single man in DC. Besides, his DIA salary could afford one hit like that. Just not two. Next weekend it would be the old standby, cheap beer and a night out with the guys.

After rounding a corner, Grimes entered the cavernous nerve center of the DIA. The room was a maze of cubicles, most of which were already occupied by the early arrivers. Three of the room's walls were adorned with a special soundproof buffer. The fourth was a floor-to-ceiling window overlooking the Potomac. Grimes, a senior officer, was fortunate to occupy a cubicle that looked out over the river.

As he neared his seat, the red-haired girl in the cubicle next to his leaned back and looked at him. "Good morning, Russ!"

"Morning, Claudia," he replied with a nod.

"Sorry I can't talk right now," she said in a raised voice, turning back to her computer. "Too much work."

As usual, her voice was irritatingly loud, the product of her long-standing iPod addiction. Grimes had seriously wondered if she ever turned the thing off. He'd once joked to colleagues that she'd had the buds surgically attached to her ear canal.

Grimes looked across the river before sitting down. A Boeing 777 descended gracefully toward the tarmac at Reagan National, its wings moving gently back and forth. The big bird eventually settled on the runway, its rear wheels hitting with a jolt, followed by the front. Even from this distance, he could see the wing flaps slowing the plane as it cruised toward the terminal.

He smiled. It never got old.

Grimes finally turned, plunked down in his seat, and unlocked his screen saver. As he waited for the system to go through its protocols, he took another sip of coffee and thought about the new task he'd been assigned. It was something he'd never done before, and he was only doing it now because the two people usually responsible for it were both on vacation. He didn't anticipate any problems though. The software would do most of the work for him.

Grimes double-clicked on the program icon. It was called Sweeper, the DIA's newest tool in what Grimes referred to as World War III, the battle for global electronic supremacy. Sweeper was the most powerful etool of its kind, able to scan email and other communications for suspicious keywords or contacts. What separated it from similar software was its ability to find links between literally trillions of pieces of information, unwinding confusing trails that would take thousands of man-hours if attempted manually.

A login screen appeared, and Grimes entered his sixteen-digit password and answered three random security questions. His fingers moved without hesitation, snapping across the keys like a concert pianist.

His task was to search through all communications of individuals associated with hundreds of ongoing operations throughout the US intelligence community. The purpose was two-fold: make sure no one associated with those missions was working for the enemy, and make sure the enemy hadn't somehow penetrated communications networks. The ultimate goal was to ensure the integrity of each mission.

The manual Grimes had read the night before recommended analyzing a half dozen operations at a time, so Grimes checked off the first six that came up and pressed Start. A box appeared, and inside it a series of numbers began to spin, indicating the amount of data being processed. Simultaneously, a green bar filled from left to right.

While Sweeper did its work, Grimes grabbed his Nationals cup and swiveled around in his chair. The early-morning sun reflected off of the blue waters of the Potomac. Several outboards raced by along the near shore, while a tourist cruise boat chugged in the opposite direction.

He took a long sip of coffee and allowed his mind to chew over the events from the night before. How much longer would he be single? A part of him enjoyed the dating game, the excitement of meeting new women, but the years seemed to be passing at hypersonic speed now. And the older he got, the smaller the pool of potential mates. In his midtwenties he'd laughed at his parents' concern that he wasn't involved in a serious relationship. But he wasn't laughing anymore. In fact, while he was reluctant to admit it, he'd truly been hoping that Rachel would turn out to be more than a pretty face.

A loud ding caused Grimes to stiffen. It was too early for Sweeper to have finished. Based on everything he'd read, an analysis of six operations should take anywhere from fifteen to twenty minutes.

He spun his chair around and scooted closer to the monitor. A box had appeared in the center of the screen. Leaning closer, he read the information displayed.

THE PORTAL

Mission Name: Operation Green Beacon
Location: South America
Mission Objective: Classified - Access Denied
Agency: Classified - Access Denied
Contact: Director of the CIA
Comments: *Issues of Concern Detected*

Operation Green Beacon? He wasn't familiar with it, but that wasn't surprising. What *was* surprising was that it had denied him access to any further information. Grimes had the second-highest level of clearance in the government. Theoretically the only missions he didn't have clearance for were ones that could only be seen by fewer than five eyes, including the President and the DNI. Those were the blackest of black ops. Soot black, he called them.

Grimes clicked on *Issues of Concern Detected*. His cursor transitioned to an hourglass as the software retrieved the requested information. Seconds later, an email account was referenced on the screen. He glanced at the details displayed. The account seemed innocuous enough, having been established using a major ISP right here in the US. So far nothing seemed out of the ordinary.

He leaned forward and double-clicked on the account, which he assumed was owned by someone on the Operation Green Beacon team. The name had been blacked out to protect their identity.

Strangely, there were only twenty or so emails in the Inbox. That alone was a red flag. Who kept their Inbox that clean? As he examined the subject lines, he realized that most, if not all, of the messages were spam. An advertisement for cheap sexual performance pills, another peddling a scheme to make a thousand dollars a day working out of your home.

The absence of any meaningful emails did seem a bit suspicious, but was that the only reason it had been flagged? Was there something else? And then it hit him. How could he have forgotten Sweeper's most important feature? Grimes used his cursor to access a drop-down menu at the top of the screen. He looked at the various choices and selected Highlight Suspect Items. A flash of red appeared immediately on the left side of the screen.

The draft folder.

When he opened it up, there was one email. He double-clicked on it. Empty.

Grimes smiled. It was one of the oldest tricks in the book, and still one of the most effective. It was a way of communicating without having to send messages across the Internet, where they could be snatched up by law enforcement or the intelligence community. Instead, two or more parties would establish an email account. All parties would have the login information and could access the account from anywhere in the world. If one member of the group wanted to communicate something, he or she would login and create an email. Then, instead of sending it, they would simply save the email into the draft folder. That allowed others to sign in and read the same message at their convenience. Once the message was read by all parties, it would be deleted.

So Sweeper had found the suspicious email in the draft

folder, but that didn't necessarily mean there was malevolent intent. Every day thousands of people across the planet started emails only to be interrupted before they could actually send the message.

So how should he proceed? Grimes tapped his teeth with a pen, sifting through ideas like a data processor.

Bingo.

Grimes opened the Sweeper drop-down menu again, asking it to search for the IP addresses of those accessing the account. About a minute later, several addresses displayed on the screen. He clicked on the first one and noted the geographic location. It was a medium-sized city in the United States, probably the location of the mission team operative. Nothing unusual about that, at least not on the surface.

Grimes then clicked on the second IP address. As he read the information, he frowned. Why would someone be accessing the account from there? Needing more information about the location, Grimes toggled over to Google Maps and entered the specific address. When the pertinent information came up, the blood rushed from his face. He could scarcely believe what he was reading.

His heart pounding, Grimes snatched up a headset, securing it over both ears. Then he accessed a secure line via his computer.

After two rings, a female voice spoke in his headphones. "Central Intelligence Agency. Secure Line Operator. How may I direct your call?"

CHAPTER THIRTY-TWO

THE ORACLE SENT a text and then leaned back in his chair, letting out a deep sigh. "Keiko, be glad you're not married."

The humanoid looked up from her chair in the corner of the office. "Is there a problem, sir?"

"Unfortunately there is," he said, tossing his phone onto a pile of folders on his desk. "It's Helen's birthday—"

"Her birthday is not until Friday," Keiko said. "She was born in—"

The Oracle held up a hand. "I know, I know, Keiko. That's not what's important here. We were going to celebrate it tonight, and she's not happy about my plans."

"Oh?"

"Apparently the grand opening gala for the new Mars wing of the Air and Space Museum isn't good enough for her."

Keiko tilted her head. "You were going to tour the new wing of the museum on her birthday."

"Look, it's not what you're thinking. It's one of those fancy schmancy gala dinners with champagne, gerbil food, classical music... all those things she *says* she loves. Only apparently now she doesn't!" He lifted his hands in the air.

"Sir, might I suggest—"

"Any other time she would've been elated. It's her kind of thing. I'm telling you, the only time Helen doesn't want to go to one of these events is when I plan it. The woman is insufferable!"

"I think—"

"In fact, I can't tell you how many times she's complained that we don't do the DC social circuit. No cocktail parties, she says. No summer concerts at the art gallery, she says." He glared at the phone, as if somehow Helen were still there on the other end. "I'll never understand women, Keiko."

Keiko blinked twice and said, "Sir, if you're willing, I'd be happy to help you with the arrangements."

"You know, if she had only told me..." He looked up at Keiko. "I'm sorry?"

"I'd love to help you arrange your date with Mrs. Ross. Brett gave me some special programming for this type of thing."

"Foster did *what*?"

"He programmed me with information regarding the psychological motivations of both men and women, and more specifically how they apply to dating in the modern world."

The Oracle lifted an eyebrow. "He asked you to do that, did he?"

"Yes, sir. He also asked me to download a database of restaurants and a calendar of special events in the DC area."

"I'll have to speak to him about this when he gets back." Ross leaned forward and placed his arms on the desk. "So you really think you can help me?"

"I know I can, sir. I can run a diagnostic report on your wife that will help me determine the ideal place for you to take her. Brett had me run the same report on Ms. Amanda Higgs." The Oracle's eyes narrowed. Keiko looked at him for a moment then continued. "I can change a few parameters to correspond with your wife's—"

A loud buzz sounded from a speaker on the Oracle's desk. "Sir?"

The Oracle leaned forward. "Yes, Kristine."

"I have Lieutenant General Charles McFadden on the line, sir. He says it's urgent."

McFadden. What could the Director of the DIA want? Delphi rarely worked with that arm of intelligence. In fact, he only remembered speaking to McFadden on two occasions, both social events. This couldn't be good news.

"Okay, I'll take it," the Oracle said. He mashed a lighted button on his phone. "This is Ross."

A deep voice boomed out of the speaker. "Ross, this is Director McFadden."

"Good morning." Ross leaned back in his chair and clasped his hands behind his head.

"Thank you. It was a good morning… until about ten minutes ago."

The Oracle frowned.

McFadden continued. "I'm afraid we've uncovered something requiring our immediate attention. What can you tell me about Operation Green Beacon?"

Why was he asking about Green Beacon? Ross wasn't concerned that McFadden was aware of their operation in Brazil—after all, the director was one of a few select individuals who knew about the existence of Delphi. But he *was* concerned about why he wanted to know.

The Oracle leaned forward and put his arms on the desk. "We're performing covert due diligence. I can give you more detail if you need it, but in essence, we are following up on a signal that was broadcast from the Amazon basin."

"A signal?" McFadden sounded concerned. "Does this involve the Brazilian military?"

"No. We're attempting to locate the source of a strange audio transmission that was initiated in the Amazon basin," the Oracle said. "The CliffsNotes version is that we feel there could be advanced technology involved." He paused for a moment before continuing. "It's even a little more bizarre than that. But I'm not sure how much information you need."

"Let me tell you what we've discovered, and then we can decide if we need to discuss the operation further." McFadden cleared his throat. "Ross, I don't know any other way to put this, but it appears your operation has a mole."

The blood rushed out of the Oracle's face. "A mole? There must be some mistake." His mind shuffled through the names and faces of those involved, lingering on a couple who jumped out as suspects.

"I wish there were."

"Who is it?"

McFadden gave him the name of the mole and who that

person had been in contact with.

The Oracle's heart pounded. It seemed unthinkable that he could be responsible for this kind of betrayal. The entire mission was now at risk. In fact, unless they could figure something out, it was likely they'd have to abort.

"Who's your man in charge?" McFadden asked.

"Zane Watson." The Oracle put his glasses on the desk and rubbed his temples.

"I'm assuming you have a way of contacting him. I think the three of us should probably discuss how to proceed from here."

The Oracle opened a drawer and retrieved a satellite phone. "I'll conference him in right now, General."

CHAPTER THIRTY-THREE

ZANE AWAKENED SLOWLY. The acetaminophen was wearing off, and his head was throbbing again. He could tell that he was lying in a hammock, and he could hear the crackle of a fire close by. He tried to force himself back to sleep, but the pain wouldn't let him.

Suddenly, he detected the odor of tobacco. "How is the head?"

Jorge.

Zane opened one eye. The Brazilian sat a few feet away, smoking a cigar.

"Not good." Zane groaned and adjusted his position in the hammock. "When did you put me in a hammock?"

"Before going to sleep you complained of nausea. Dr. Mills was scared that if you were on the ground you might roll onto your stomach, vomit in your sleep, and choke. My job is to make sure you stay on your side."

"So I guess you drew the short straw."

Jorge looked at him. "Short straw?"

"It's an expression," Zane said as he adjusted the rolled-up shirt someone had placed under his head. "It means you got picked to sit here until I woke up."

Jorge laughed. "I don't mind watching you." He looked back at the fire. "This is perfect, actually. It's given me time to think."

"Glad your mind is functioning. Not even sure I know my own name."

Realizing sleep was no longer an option, Zane tossed aside the mosquito netting then turned and put his feet on the ground. After easing out of the hammock, he took a few ginger steps and sat down near the fire.

"Easy, amigo," the Brazilian said, watching him with a wary eye.

"I'm fine." Zane eased back against a tree.

"I'll get you some water." The Brazilian stood, walked over to a tent, and ducked inside.

While he was gone, Zane looked around. They had made camp in a natural clearing in the forest. Along the perimeter of the clearing were some of the largest trees he'd ever seen. They reminded him of the redwoods in the Sierra Nevada, only these might be even larger. *The whole scene looks prehistoric,* he thought.

Something moved on the far side of camp. Turning, Zane saw Bennett walking patrol along the perimeter. The soldier gripped his rifle tightly as he stared out into the maze of giant trunks.

Closer in, Zane saw Katiya, Amanda, and Max sitting on a log, discussing something in low whispers. A second fire burned there.

"Here you are," the Brazilian said, offering him a canteen.

Zane took it and unscrewed the cap. "Thank you." He took a swig then said, "I guess we were wrong."

Jorge frowned and pulled the cigar out of his mouth. "Wrong? Wrong about what?"

"You and I both thought there were two groups out there." He took another swig of water. "The Chinese and the one or two men who've been following us through the jungle. I think it's obvious now that they're one and the same."

Jorge's brow furrowed. "Why do you assume that?"

"It's pretty simple, actually. Just before we arrived at the crater rim, I heard someone slipping around through the woods, probably the same person or persons you saw. Then an hour later, we're hit with gunfire from the ridge." Zane looked at Jorge, trying to see if there was understanding in the Brazilian's eyes. "Don't you see? Those were scouts sent out to gather information. They reported that we were in a vulnerable position, and an attack was organized."

"If you say so," Jorge said, taking another draw on his cigar.

Zane frowned. "You don't think that's what happened?"

"No, I don't. First of all, the one following us was a man of the jungle, someone who knows this place as well or better than I do. I've been tracking animals and people for many years, and this man was as good as I've ever seen, assuming there is only one. He was a shadow in the trees, always able to stay just beyond my senses." He looked at Zane. "No offense, but if this were some Chinese soldier slipping around in the woods, even your Green Berets would've known it."

Zane shrugged. "And yet, you and I both knew he was there."

"You're right, he got a little sloppy." Jorge stroked his mustache with two fingers. "At first he watched us from a distance, and I doubt it took him very long to realize that most in our group had no clue what was going on around them. So he came closer and watched some more. At that point, he made a costly mistake. Instead of remaining cautious, he assumed that we were all new to the jungle. He didn't realize that some of us could detect him if he wasn't careful."

"You and me," Zane said.

"And the boy, Osak."

Zane frowned. "But what about this afternoon? I heard him clearly. That doesn't sound like a jungle genius."

"As I said, he became sloppy, arrogant even. He could probably see you'd become separated from the others. My guess is he thought it strange you were talking into something and wanted a closer look." He shrugged. "Even the best make mistakes if they underestimate their prey."

"Then how did the Chinese get called in so fast?"

"They weren't called in. Their source—this mole—probably told them we were headed toward the crater rim, and they simply set up in the woods there. They probably figured they'd wait until we were at the bottom then take us all out at one time."

Zane rubbed the tender place on his head as he sorted through everything he'd just heard. Finally, he asked, "So who was the man in the woods? Surely you have some idea."

There was a long moment of silence. Jorge stared at the fire and took a couple of draws on his cigar before speaking. "I've been trying to push the thought away for some time, but I can't anymore. I believe whoever is following us belongs to a hostile tribe."

Zane sat up straight. "What a minute. You assured us that all of the resident tribes were harmless. That's what I've communicated to our team from day one."

Jorge looked at Zane. "Everything I told you and your people was true. The tribes in this region generally don't pose any threat to outsiders." Jorge stared intensely at the fire, a look of deep concern spreading across his face. It was the first time Zane had seen him display anything approaching fear. Finally, the Brazilian continued. "There is a legend... I've only heard it a few times... that speaks of a band of male Indians. They're almost never seen, but those who have seen them speak of their frightening appearance. Their bodies are said to be painted entirely black, except for white rings around their eyes. Some say that their teeth are carved to points like vampiros."

"Vampires," Zane said with a frown.

"These men are said to sneak into villages like phantoms. They're able to move past sentries and into the tents of women. They have their way with them then slip out again."

"Why don't the women raise the alarm?"

"When they wake up, there is a knife against their throat. Not only that, but when they look into those eyes and see the teeth, they are frozen with fear." The Brazilian picked up a stick and held it into the flames, lighting its tip. "It is said that if the bastard child is a male, the hostile tribe will return later to take him as one of their own."

"And what are these hostiles called?"

"The Dawanis." The Brazilian's gaze moved around the camp as if even the mention of the word might cause one of them to appear.

"Never heard of them."

"If the stories are to be believed, they are also known for randomly killing many of the indigenous people. It doesn't happen often, but it does happen. They are said to have the ability to mimic voices, luring them out into the jungle."

"Sirens," Zane said. "So why random killings?"

"To project fear. They're wanderers, so my guess is it helps them maintain control over the people throughout their range. Sometimes they even place the heads of their victims just outside the village."

Zane's eyes narrowed. "I've always wondered if the stories of headhunters were true."

"While not common, I can assure you they're very much real." Jorge tossed the remainder of his cigar in the fire.

After a long pause, Zane asked, "Why didn't you tell me about this before?"

"Because there are many legends associated with the jungle. Some are just that—legends. But many of the stories are true. And if I told you everything I know, you'd have nightmares of shrunken heads and evil spirits." Jorge gave a little laugh.

He had a point. Zane had heard many jungle legends, and it would have been foolish to try to warn the team of every potential threat. Now that he thought about it, tourist groups traveled safely through this region all the time, and the only threats they faced were from nature—venomous snakes, poisonous frogs, jaguars, electric eels, piranha.

"So you believe we're being followed by one or more men from this tribe?" Zane asked.

"Either the Dawanis or another tribe with hostile intentions, yes. I think the Dawanis are the most likely culprit because they wander across a large territory. One of the secrets of their success is their ability to stay on the move. There are stories of the Dawanis showing up in Peru and Columbia to the west, and in the hilly north near the border with Venezuela. They even raided an indigenous village mere miles from Manaus. It's part of what makes them so frightening. They could show up anywhere, at any time. In fact, they're so unpredictable that many Indians believe they're spirits and not human."

"And I take it they've been seen in this area?"

Jorge nodded. "There have only been a few reports, but they have been seen here on rare occasions. It wouldn't surprise me if our friend Osak has heard of them, although he's still young."

"Maybe we should bring him in... mention your suspicions." Zane leaned back against the tree. "Who knows, he might be able to help us keep an eye on things."

"No," Jorge said firmly. "I don't want to tell anyone until I have more information, not even Osak. At this point, everyone understands that there is danger lurking out in the jungle. For now, that is good enough."

Zane's brow furrowed as he looked around the clearing. "Speaking of Osak, where is he?"

"He left about an hour ago." Jorge nodded toward the other side of camp. "You know, he's seemed different since we arrived in the crater."

"How so?"

"He's a child of the jungle, and yet he doesn't seem comfortable here. He almost looks nervous, which is not like him."

"Do you think he'll be okay on his own?"

"I hope so."

It wasn't the answer Zane had expected. "Should we go look for him?"

"No, he'll be fine. I didn't mean to scare you. I don't think he'll go far. I think he's trying to get a feel for the jungle down here, learn its ways."

Zane hoped he was right. Because if Osak wasn't safe, then neither were they.

CHAPTER THIRTY-FOUR

AFTER USING THE latrine, Corporal Dez Wilson stepped over to a nearby tree and retrieved his rifle. Despite all of the usual irritants, something about nighttime in the jungle was refreshing. It reminded him of moonlit fishing trips as a kid in the lowland swamps of his native South Carolina.

Gun in hand, he paused to enjoy the moment. It was then that he noticed something odd: the jungle had suddenly grown quiet. Just moments before, the forest had resonated with the noisy din of thousands of insects and the bark of dozens of frogs. Now, the silence was deafening.

"Strange," he muttered.

Had some big cat approached? It was possible, but even if something was lurking out there, he'd be back inside the perimeter within a couple of minutes.

Suddenly a noise broke the silence. Wilson stiffened and turned in the direction it seemed to have come from. He couldn't be sure, but it sounded like the soft pad of footsteps.

"Dez!" someone called.

Wilson flinched and lifted his rifle. The voice sounded odd, but they had clearly called his name.

Maybe it was Corporal Tocchet. He was the only other one on patrol right now. And yet the voice had come from farther out in the jungle. The whole thing didn't make sense. Slowly, he reached into his pocket. He moved his hand around, searching for his radio, then cursed when he remembered he'd left it sitting against the tree just inside the motion-sensor system.

He cupped his hands around his mouth. "Landon, is that you?"

Hearing no response, Wilson flipped his night vision visor over his eyes. He scanned the area, looking for any signs of life. About a hundred yards away, high in the trees, he saw several heat signatures. A family of monkeys was hunkered down on a large limb. *Strange,* he thought. *They seem to be frozen in place.*

"Dez, over here!"

Wilson frowned. *Now that sounded like Tocchet.* But there was still something strange about the voice.

"Stay where you are," he barked.

Growling in frustration, he followed an animal trail that led generally in the direction of the voice. The undergrowth was thicker here, making it more difficult to see anything off the path. He gripped his M4 tightly as he brushed past limbs and vines. The hot professor had told them that jaguars were most active at night, and if true, he wanted to be prepared to fire if necessary.

As he continued forward, Wilson tried to reconcile something in his mind. If it really was his partner, then what the heck was he doing out here? Their routine was to circle the perimeter of the camp in a way that put them on opposite sides at all times. It just didn't make any sense.

A few minutes later, Wilson found himself in a clearing. He scanned in each direction, but there were no other ways out. The surrounding foliage was too thick. The trail seemed to have come to an end. What now?

He cupped his hands again. "Landon!"

Silence. The presence of a big cat or snake seemed the only plausible reason for the silence that gripped the forest. He remembered from a biology class in college that animals would instinctively freeze when a predator was close by.

Maybe that's why Landon needs me. He's in some kind of trouble.

"Hey, man, where are you?"

He heard the snap of a twig to his right and swung his rifle in that direction. A tiny limb jiggled, but other than that, he saw nothing move. As he continued to stare in that direction, beads of sweat formed on his forehead. Some of it pooled and streamed into his eyes, forcing him to reach up and wipe under his visor.

Something just didn't feel right. His sense of direction was good, and Tocchet should have been right in this very spot. In fact, if he'd been using the same trail, then he couldn't have gone any farther without making a ruckus.

Suddenly there was a slight rustling directly ahead. It seemed to come from behind a large tree on the far side of the clearing, so he took a few steps toward it. "Landon? If you're pulling my leg… man, I'm gonna kill you."

Something moved in his peripheral vision. Wilson turned and saw a cloud seeping into the clearing. He assumed it was fog, but it had a strange odor, almost like the scent of a flower or herb.

Wilson took a deep breath then exhaled slowly. It was time to get back to camp. If Tocchet really was lost somewhere out there, then he wasn't going to find him alone. He needed to bring back some of the others.

He was about to call out for his partner one last time when he noticed something strange: he couldn't move the muscles of his mouth.

What the...?

Next he tried to lift his rifle. It felt like it weighed two hundred pounds, and he was able to shift it only slightly. Something was happening to him.

There was more shuffling in the undergrowth nearby, but Wilson was unable to turn and look.

The fog. The words echoed in his thoughts. It was the fog that had caused this. It's why he couldn't move.

Seconds later, Wilson fell over. He remained there, unable to move or speak. Paralysis now gripped every inch of his body. The rustling grew louder. Whoever was out there knew he could no longer defend himself.

A pair of black legs suddenly appeared in the mist, moving toward him. They stopped a few feet away. Wilson flinched in fear, his heart beating wildly in his chest.

Now he could hear others entering the clearing as well. He'd been lured into a trap, and there was nothing he could do to save himself.

THE PORTAL

A foot was placed roughly under his body and flipped him over. After settling onto his back, Wilson could see the silhouettes of several men looming over him, their features obscured by the fog.

One of the figures descended toward him. Seconds later, a face appeared out of the mist. It was painted black with white rings around the eyes.

Wilson tried to scream, but the sound died in his throat.

CHAPTER THIRTY-FIVE

"HE'S JUST GONE without a trace?" Katiya asked. "That seems impossible."

The group had assembled around the fire. Zane, Bennett, and Tocchet had just completed a two-hour search for Corporal Wilson, and several brief arguments had broken out since their return. The growing tension was now clearly inscribed on each person's face. Some were angry but couldn't figure out where to direct that anger.

Zane glanced toward the edge of camp to make sure the new measures were being followed. Tocchet and Artur were patrolling a shrunken perimeter and were now in plain sight of the others. He wished he'd done that before. Having such a wide area to cover had been a mistake, and he took full responsibility for any trouble it may have caused.

Bennett looked at Katiya. "As I said, ma'am, we searched as far as we possibly could. We were able to follow his footprints into a grove of saplings, but that's where the trail grew cold." He turned and addressed the others. "The good news is that there was no sign of blood... there weren't even any signs of a scuffle."

"I'm assuming you weren't able to reach him on the radio?" Katiya asked.

Zane and Bennett exchanged glances. Zane nodded at the soldier, giving him permission to answer. "We actually found his radio against a tree just inside the perimeter."

Max threw his hands in the air. "Now you tell us! Of course, you wouldn't have had she not asked."

Zane looked at the linguist. "What difference does it make where his radio was found? He obviously chose to leave it and his canteen behind when he went to the latrine. He probably figured it wouldn't matter since he was only going to be gone for a couple of minutes."

Max shook his head but remained silent.

Zane continued. "We actually believe it's good news that we found no signs of a struggle."

"We've a man missing. I can't wait to hear how that is good news," Max said.

Zane tried to suppress his temper. "I didn't say that it was good news he was missing. If you're not going to listen then shut up. The good news is that he likely just got lost. Don't forget that there's still a lot of fog out there. It seems to have cleared out a bit, but there are still some pretty thick pockets in low-lying areas."

"Maybe he's with Osak," Amanda said. "We haven't seen him in a while."

"A good point," Zane said. He paused for a moment, gathering his thoughts. "Look, I can't put a diamond necklace on this pig and make it look better. We have a highly skilled soldier missing, and that's obviously not good. We told you before that the Amazon is a wild and dangerous place, and this crater appears to be even more dangerous than the rest of it. At least we have a sliver of hope that the corporal is still alive."

Katiya frowned. "What now?"

Zane looked at his watch. "Dawn comes in a couple of hours. At first light, we're going back out to the site and try to pick up his trail. The sun will make our job a little easier. There's only so much you can do with a few flashlights."

Katiya rubbed her face then ran her fingers back through her hair. Zane could tell that something was still bothering her. Finally she looked up and said, "I realize this is more difficult for you than it is for the rest of us. You're responsible for our safety, and it's important that you maintain an air of positivity. Dez is certainly not going to be found if we give up hope.

"But we have to be honest with each other. After all, we're in this together."

"What are you trying to say?" Brett asked.

"I may not have any experience with this kind of thing, but I do know this… something doesn't smell right. This man was a Green Beret, and with all due respect, I'm not buying that a pocket of fog turned him around."

"We didn't say we were certain that's what happened," Bennett said. "We're only saying it's possible."

"Out here almost anything is possible, but that doesn't mean it's likely." She looked at Zane then at Bennett. "We're a team, and a team communicates. Not communicating puts us all in danger."

Max seemed to realize where she was going. "Is there something you're not telling us?"

"I think there is a lot we don't know." She pointed off into the distance. "Just hours ago we were shot at by some men on a ridge. Someone whispered that it was probably one of the local cartels but that they wouldn't follow us into the crater because of its reputation. Then tonight one of our soldiers goes missing. Call me crazy, but I find this all a little strange."

Zane wasn't sure who'd told her it was a cartel, but if he didn't know about the Chinese, he might have thought the same himself. There weren't many in this part of Brazil, but it wouldn't be a shock to run into a small-time group transporting narcotics through the jungle.

He rubbed his beard as he thought about how to respond. Should he tell them about the Dawanis? He had a great deal of respect for Katiya, and he had to admit that she was right about communication. If the group was under immediate threat, then everyone deserved to know that in order to take the necessary precautions to protect themselves.

"First of all, we don't know with any level of certainty who that was up on the ridge. For all I know, maybe we did cross through the turf of some cartel." He looked at the fire for a moment, choosing his words carefully. "But I do want to share something that I haven't up until now. Another government may be aware of this operation. We're not sure how much they know or what they plan on doing with that information, but they have it."

"You knew this, and you didn't tell us?" Max's face was red.

"We didn't tell you because that's *all* we knew. We figured it was possible they might send in their own team to investigate, but that wouldn't necessarily involve violence." Zane knew that he wasn't being completely forthright, but he couldn't mention the attack on Garet Slater's lodge. That was classified information. "And even if they did send a team in, what are the odds that they would come at precisely the same time *and* decide to launch an attack on us?"

Max was about to respond, but Katiya held up a hand. "No, he's right." She looked at Zane. "While I still think you should have told us, I see why you didn't. We knew what we were getting into. We knew that our government was trying to keep this a secret, and we also knew that other countries might want this information. In fact, I think Dr. Ross told me that very thing. Maybe it was his way of giving me a subtle warning."

"Which country is it?" Amanda asked.

Zane told her.

Max muttered something about that being the worst possible answer then shook his head.

Zane looked at Katiya. "But I still can't tell you who shot at us from the rim. Who knows, maybe it *was* a cartel. So far, I don't have any definitive evidence that the Chinese are here. It's all anecdotal."

She nodded slowly. "Is there anything else we should know?"

Zane and Jorge exchanged a brief glance. The Brazilian then cleared his throat and said, "Like Senhor Zane, I can't tell you who was shooting at us, nor can I tell you where the missing soldier is or what happened to him. But I want to remind you that while most tribes are friendly, there are some who aren't."

"Wait, wait," Amanda said. "Back on the boat you told us that all the tribes here are friendly."

Jorge shook his head. "No, that's not what I said. I said that *most* of the tribes here are friendly. Of course, everyone here knows that Brazil has some indigenous people who aren't. You're all fully aware of the documented attacks."

"I'm not aware of any indigenous hostiles in this area," Max said.

"Have you heard of the Dawanis?"

Max shook his head. "The name rings a bell, but I can't say I'm familiar with them."

"That doesn't surprise me," Jorge said. "You won't find this tribe in a textbook or on the Internet, at least not that I'm aware of. Some say they're a legend, but there have been enough victims and sightings over the years to indicate they're very real."

Katiya's eyes narrowed. "I'm like Max. The name sounds vaguely familiar, but that's about it."

Jorge used the next several minutes to give the group a more sanitized version of the description he'd given Zane. He simply told them that the Dawanis wandered through the region, terrorizing other tribes. Truthful but without the disturbing details.

"Good heavens," Katiya said after he'd finished. "They sound horrible. But surely you don't think they were the ones shooting at—"

Jorge gave her a half smile. "No, they don't own guns."

"Then what makes you think they're here?" Brett asked.

"I've seen a few things out in the jungle that led me to believe we were being followed. You may be curious why I didn't mention it before now. Well, that's because I had no proof. The things I saw also could have been some animal of the jungle. Now, to be honest, I didn't think it was an animal, but I wasn't about to create panic without solid evidence that something was out there."

"Do you think it's possible they were responsible for Corporal Wilson's disappearance?" Brett asked.

"I can't say it was the Dawanis, but I do believe it's possible the answer involves some hostile tribe, perhaps one that lives here in this place."

Katiya frowned. "Has this ever happened before?"

"To my knowledge, there are no reports of Dawanis attacking people traveling along the Amazon. Of course, I'm not aware of any official confirmation that they even exist. The few Brazilians who do know the name believe it's a legend."

"You indicated that they were wanderers," Katiya said. "Perhaps this is their home base. Perhaps they conduct their raids from here." She picked up a stick and drew an odd-looking shape in the dirt. "If this is Brazil, then we're somewhere in here." She drew a small circle indicating the approximate location of the crater. "You told us earlier that the attacks have taken place from Peru and Columbia in the west to Manaus in the east." She tapped the circle and said, "This crater is right in the center."

"Yes, I guess it's possible," Jorge said. "Though, again, all we can do at this point is speculate."

"It might also explain all of the strange stories about this place," Amanda said, leaning forward and pointing at the drawn circle. "Maybe that's why so many who came here never made it back out."

Katiya tapped her chin lightly with the stick. "Let's take this a bit further. What are we here for? We're here because we're looking for an alien outpost."

Zane frowned. "Are you trying to say these tribesmen *are* the aliens?"

"No, although we shouldn't rule anything out at this point." She drew a dot in the center of the small circle. "We're trying to find some sort of mountain in the center of the crater, right? What better place for our alien friends to set up shop than right in the center of a place no one dares go? It's like a built-in security system."

Brett's brow furrowed. "So you're saying they might be working together?"

"No, more like some sort of symbiotic relationship. In other words, perhaps the aliens picked this place precisely because no one dared come here. They may have been visiting our planet for centuries, and if so, they likely know the remote areas better than we do."

Zane nodded. There was a strong ring of truth to what she was saying. If you were going to visit Earth and stay hidden, why not here?

Katiya fixed her gaze on Jorge. "You obviously know more about this tribe than we do. How can we protect ourselves?"

The Brazilian was lighting a cigar as she spoke. After taking a few puffs, he put away his lighter and said, "Well, despite the stories of their spiritual powers, one thing we can be sure of is that they are still flesh and blood like you and me."

"Which means they'll go down if we fill them full of bullets." Tocchet patted the M4A1 draped across his chest.

"So, we do the same things we've been doing in order to maintain our safety," Jorge said. "But now we must do them even better."

"Which reminds me," Zane said. "We're going to change things up. From this point forward, nobody, and I mean nobody, travels outside camp alone. I don't care if it's just to use the latrine or pick a flower, you will have someone next to you at all times. Everybody understand that?" After seeing nods, he continued. "As you can see, we've already reduced the perimeter so that we're always within shouting distance of one another."

Jorge let a raft of smoke spill out of his mouth. "And if you see or hear anything out of the ordinary, please come to me immediately. I don't care how small it is. Anything might be important."

Zane surveyed the group. Most were still in shock, and yet there seemed to be a collective resolve to finish their job. "Okay, let's try to get some rest. I'm going to lead a search party out at first light. Once we've done that, we're going to march as fast as we can. Jorge believes we can be at the mountain by nightfall."

CHAPTER THIRTY-SIX

ZANE TOOK A long swig from his canteen, allowing the warm water to moisten his parched throat. They had been marching for most of the day, and even he was beginning to tire in the suffocating heat and humidity. For the last several miles he had simply willed his feet to keep moving, knowing that the quicker they got to the mountain, the quicker they'd all be able to rest.

They had spent several hours searching for Wilson that morning, but despite covering several square miles, they'd found nothing. No footprints, no piece of fabric, no sign that the corporal had ever been there. It was as if the soldier had been plucked out of the jungle by some mysterious hand, leaving no trace behind.

Zane bit his lower lip. He worried about the mental state of his team. There had been shock after Corporal Nash's death, but that had been more sorrow than fear. The piranhas posed no ongoing threat to the group. Wilson's disappearance had changed everything. Now the same eyes that had previously been filled with awe and wonder were flitting nervously from one side of the path to the other. Even the two remaining Green Berets behaved differently. They gripped their rifles a little tighter and turned quickly at the slightest movement in the jungle.

"Any updates on our sat phone?" Zane asked Brett as they walked at the front.

"I spent about an hour working on it this morning," Brett said. "I don't want to give anyone false hope, but I actually think there's a chance I can get this thing up and running. The problem is that it's going to take time, lots of time."

"How much?"

"If I can sit down undisturbed… perhaps five or six hours."

"Unfortunately we don't even have an hour." Zane took a swig from his canteen and held it up. "The water isn't holding out as well as I thought. Nash was carrying about a third of our water supply when he went down. I made a brief survey of the group, and I think we have about a three-day supply left."

Brett patted one of his pockets. "Remember we still have the water purification pills."

"I was hoping we wouldn't have to go there. All of the water down here looks like primordial ooze."

Brett took a long draw from his bottle. "We'll be fine. If we have a three-day supply, then that means we should be on our way back when we run low. We can always boil some river water and treat it with pills."

"All the same, I'd prefer we get that phone up and running. I need to give the Oracle a report on Wilson. He'll want to send in a search team, and we can get resupplied when that happens."

"As I said, it's going to take time. It's not something I can fiddle around with while we're walking."

"I might be able to give you some time once we reach the mountain." Zane squinted at the trail ahead. It seemed to rise a bit. He felt a surge of optimism. Perhaps it was an indication they weren't far away. "But I can't even consider stopping until we get there."

"And what if we don't find the mountain?"

"It's there," Zane said, his eyes still fixed on the trail ahead. "So far this place has lived up to its billing."

Brett suddenly slowed his pace and crept toward something on the right side of the trail. As Zane followed with his eyes, he saw a large scaly tail sticking out of the foliage. It was a dull olive, sprinkled with black spots. "Green anaconda."

Brett crouched. "Just from the size of the tail, I'd say it has to be over twenty feet."

"Easy, cowboy," Zane said, pulling his Glock from its holster.

Brett whacked down with his stick. As soon as the stick made contact, the tail whipped sharply before disappearing into the bushes. Zane saw saplings bend back and forth as the massive reptile slowly made its retreat.

"You trying to get us killed?" Zane asked, putting the pistol away.

"Freaking garter snake, and you're pulling a weapon." Brett said as they began walking again.

"Garter, huh? I noticed you didn't grab the tail." Zane's expression changed to a frown. "From what I've read, they're almost always near water."

Brett shrugged. "I don't see anything. Perhaps all the rain enticed him away from home."

"Maybe."

About a minute later, Zane came to a halt. A shadowy figure was moving toward them with speed.

Zane instinctively unslung his rifle, but Brett grabbed his arm.

Seconds later, the figure came into view. *Osak.*

"I wonder where he's been," Zane said.

"It looks like he's upset about something," Brett said.

The boy stopped a few feet away. He spoke in an excited tone, pointing back in the direction he had come from.

"You want us to follow you?" Brett asked.

Osak pointed again.

"He must've found something," Zane said as he turned around. He and Brett had set a fast pace, so the others were a good hundred yards back. He could see Tocchet walking alongside Katiya and Amanda.

Zane pulled out his radio. "Tocchet, do you read?"

He watched the soldier pull out his radio. "Yes, sir."

"Osak is here. Apparently he's found something ahead. We're going to go check it out. Get everyone moving."

"Roger that."

Zane put his radio away. "Let's go."

As they followed Osak, Zane marveled at how effortlessly the boy ran, his feet always finding every solid patch of ground. And he never seemed to tire. It was as though they were trying to keep up with a deer.

THE PORTAL

A few minutes later, they entered a clearing, and Osak finally slowed to a walk. He turned toward them then pointed at something in the distance. At first all Zane could see was a broad stream snaking along the edge of the woods, but then he noticed that the ground sloped up sharply just beyond the stream. The mountain couldn't be far away.

Osak led them in the direction of the stream. As they walked, he continued to speak. Something was clearly bothering him.

"Sorry, I don't understand a word you're saying, bud," Zane said.

Brett pointed. "I think that's what he's talking about."

Zane looked ahead, and his eyes widened. Just ahead, spanning the stream, was a large stone bridge.

"Talk about being out of place." Zane crossed the remaining distance and stepped onto the bridge. He squatted and examined the individual stones, most of which were covered with pale-green lichen. "I'm no archaeologist, but these are some really old stones."

Brett stood next to him. "Do you think it's Mayan?"

"No, it's not Mayan," someone said from behind them.

Zane turned his head. Amanda was striding toward them, a look of shock written on her face. She approached one of the columns at the head of the bridge. "I can't believe it. This shouldn't be here."

"You sure it's not Mayan?" Brett asked.

"Positive." She ran her hand across the surface of the lichen-covered stone. "I would know this architecture anywhere. Besides, they never lived here."

There were little gasps of surprise as the others arrived and spread out across the bridge.

Brett looked over at Amanda. "I know the Mayans were in modern-day Mexico, but I thought they were also in South America."

"No, never." Amanda shook her head.

"She's right," Katiya said as she bent over to examine the stone. "Besides, this doesn't look anything like Mayan construction."

Zane frowned. "Then who built it?"

Amanda walked farther down and pointed at one of the pylons that wasn't covered by quite as much lichen. "Look at the seam. Notice anything?"

Zane shook his head.

"There's no mortar, as far as I can tell. The Mayans almost always used a special mortar they made from limestone."

"So if this wasn't built with mortar, how has it held up for so long?" Brett asked. "It looks like it's been here for hundreds of years."

Amanda ran her finger along one of the joints. "See how tightly the stones are fit together? They were cut and stacked so precisely that no mortar was necessary."

Zane could see what she meant about the fit. It was so tight he doubted you could even slide a razor blade in there.

"Well, if not the Mayans, then who?" Brett asked.

"It's possible this was built by the same people who built the ancient megaliths in Peru," she said. "The construction looks eerily similar."

"Where those the Incas?" Zane asked.

"That's what most would say."

"You don't sound too convinced."

"It's possible the Incas built this bridge," Amanda said. "But there is another possibility." She patted one of the crowns at the top of one of the pylons. "This construction seems a lot like the citadel at Saksaywaman, as well as a number of other megaliths there."

"What's similar about it?" Brett asked.

"The large stones, the precise cuts, and the lack of mortar."

Katiya raised a finger in the air. "That reminds me of something I read a while back. As you explore archaeological sites in Peru, you often find that the more technologically advanced construction is farther down in the strata. Normally, it's the other way around. Normally, the farther down you dig, the more primitive the buildings."

"She's right," Amanda said with a nod. "In fact, there's a city in central Peru where you can see this for yourself. A number of buildings there were added to over time. One was built right on top of another. The older, lower parts have stones that are cut and fit so precisely that it would be difficult to reproduce, even with modern-day equipment. Then, above that, you see the newer construction that is actually more primitive. It's almost like the stones were just mortared together haphazardly. There's little or no evidence of precision.

"Mainstream archaeologists will tell you the entire building was constructed by the Incas, but anyone who looks at these structures can tell you that is preposterous. If that were true, you'd have to believe the Incas got less proficient at stone masonry as time went on."

"So what are you trying to say?" Zane asked. "How is that possible?"

Amanda looked at him and said, "Take a guess."

"I think I know where you're going," Brett said. "It's the whole ancient-alien theory again. They came to earth many millennia ago and passed along their technology. But one thing still bothers me. Why didn't the subsequent cultures keep using those same methods?"

"We don't really know," Katiya said. "Assuming it's true, we can only guess that at some point the aliens left. And once they left, it's also possible that the culture that received the technology died out. Then, when the Incas came along, it was as though they had to start all over again."

Brett nodded. "I guess it's the same theory that's used to explain mysterious advances in other parts of the ancient world. Egypt, for example."

"Speaking of Peru," Amanda said, "I just remembered something I read in college. It was a footnote in one of my textbooks, and I found it so fascinating that I did some more reading on the Internet." She looked at Katiya. "Aren't there supposed to be some sort of alien airstrips in Peru?"

"Yes," Katiya said. "The Nazca Lines. A series of geoglyphs located about two hundred miles southeast of Lima."

"Geoglyphs?" Zane asked.

"Sorry." Katiya smiled. "Think of geoglyphs as large works of art that are etched into the landscape. Most are so large that you can only tell what they are from a higher elevation, such as a nearby mountain or a plane. There are hundreds of them in southern Peru. Most are simple designs and shapes, but there are also some pretty detailed drawings of animals—spiders, monkeys, lizards."

"I have heard of those," Zane said. "But what does that have to do with an alien airstrip?"

"Good question. As I said, most of the designs are simple objects. Lines, triangles, squares, that kind of thing. Well, some of those lines look a lot like modern-day airstrips. I'm not a fan of this particular theory, but there is some resemblance."

"Why aren't you a fan of the theory?" Zane asked.

Katiya chuckled. "I just can't get past the fact that the same alien ship that can travel across galaxies would also need to coast to a stop like an airplane. Seems nonsensical to me."

"I think the animal drawings debunk the whole thing anyway," Brett said. "Why draw something like—"

Before he could finish, a shout came from the far side of the stream. Osak was standing at a point where the trail disappeared into the jungle, speaking loudly and waving his arms.

Zane frowned. "Maybe it wasn't the bridge he wanted to show us."

"He wants us to follow him," Max said.

"Is something wrong?" Brett asked.

"No," Max said. "I think he's found our mountain."

CHAPTER THIRTY-SEVEN

ARTUR STOOD QUIETLY on the bridge and watched as the others gathered their belongings. Some were already making their way up the trail. Hoping to buy time, he bent down and fiddled with his pack.

Hearing footsteps, he looked up to see the red-haired American, Tocchet, coming toward him. "Everything okay?"

"I'm fine," Artur replied, his eyes moving nervously toward the rucksack. "I was just looking for something." He patted the rifle slung over his shoulder. "I'll watch the rear this time."

"You sure I can't carry something?"

Artur felt a little surge of frustration but pushed it aside and gave the soldier a smile. "Really, I'm fine. I appreciate it."

Tocchet nodded slowly. "Just let me know if you change your mind." The soldier turned and strode off the bridge. A few seconds later, he disappeared into the dense foliage on the hill.

Satisfied that everyone was gone, Artur reached into a pocket on the side of his pack and pulled out a plain flask.

After taking one last glance toward the trees, he unscrewed the cap and took a long swig of Johnnie Walker. He let the whisky linger in his mouth for a moment before tilting his head back and allowing it to slide down his throat. He wiped his mouth with a sleeve as he debated how much he should have.

Normally the Brazilian drank only at night, long after Jorge had retired for the evening. But the events of the last twenty-four hours had shot his nerves. He had sensed the presence of evil the moment they'd descended into the crater. It was the same sensation he'd experienced when he and his grandmother had lived next to a witch doctor in Santarem. Thankfully, he'd been able to convince her to move after strange things had begun to happen around the house.

He looked at the flask. *What the heck.* He took another swig, this one even longer. He felt a little guilty but quickly swept the feeling away. The amber-colored liquor would help him get through the next few days.

Artur glanced up at the trail again. If he didn't get started, the American soldier would likely come back to see what was wrong.

One more, and that's it.

Tilting his head back, the Brazilian took his third and final drink. Then he screwed the cap back on the flask and stowed it away.

As he slung his pack over his back, his gaze fell on a pod of ferns at the edge of the clearing. Some of the fronds waved back and forth as though something was moving underneath. He took a few steps closer, a frown spreading across his face.

Maybe it's the whiskey, he thought.

Suddenly, he saw something in the shadows near the bottom. He took several steps closer and squinted. As the details came into focus, he froze. A black face stared at him from the darkness.

His heart racing, Artur flipped the rifle off his shoulder and raised it with both hands. A second later, he lowered it. The face was gone now, but some of the fronds were moving again.

A twig snapped to his right. Pivoting in that direction, Artur saw a shadow flash across an opening in the trees.

His heart thumping wildly in his chest, he slung his pack over a shoulder and backstepped across the bridge, swinging his gun back and forth. He heard more movement in the jungle, but each time he turned, there was nothing there.

A few steps later, he felt soil under his feet, and relief swept over him. After taking one last look, he turned and raced up the hill.

CHAPTER THIRTY-EIGHT

THE LAST RAYS of afternoon sunlight filtered down through the canopy as the group filed up the hill. Zane wiped sweat out of his eyes and glanced ahead. Osak stood in the middle of the trail about fifty yards away. He said something then waved them on.

"He says we're almost there," Max said.

Bennett looked at Zane. "I'll go up and clear things at the top."

Zane nodded, and the soldier sprinted off.

"I hope we're there." Katiya rubbed her thigh with a hand. "My legs feel like linguine."

"I think we could all use a rest soon," Brett said.

A few minutes later, the path leveled off, and the trees and undergrowth began to thin out.

"All clear, sir," Bennett shouted from just ahead.

Shortly thereafter, the group spilled out of the trees into a clearing. Zane's eyes widened as he took in the view.

"Good heavens," Katiya whispered.

A short mountain rose up in front of them. Its steep slope was covered with a tangled mass of vines, ferns, and bushes. The vegetation was so thick that most of the mountain itself couldn't be seen, save for a few patches of rock here and there.

Brett looked up. "No wonder this didn't show up on any satellite photos. Even though it rises above the canopy, it looks just like the surrounding jungle."

"It's gorgeous," Amanda said, her voice barely above a whisper.

Zane noticed the precipice rose at a sharp angle before transitioning to a flat crown about four hundred feet up. He looked to the right then to the left. The base seemed to cover a large area. What the mountain lacked in height, it made up in circumference.

"It looks like we're standing on some sort of buffer," Bennett said, tapping the ground with his rifle.

Zane looked around. He was right. A barren strip of land seemed to run around the circumference of the mountain, at least as far as he could see.

"I think this is the winding strip you saw in the satellite photos," Zane said.

Brett nodded. "I was just thinking the same thing."

As the group began to fan out, Zane asked the two Green Berets to take up positions along the buffer, one to the east and the other to the west. Now was not the time to let down their guard. If anything, they needed to be more cautious.

Katiya kicked at one of the rocks. "It's almost like someone came through here with a jumbo bottle of Roundup." She squatted and looked at a very lonely-looking weed that had sprouted up through a crack in the hard soil.

Zane looked at her. "Any ideas why nothing seems to grow here?"

Katiya rose, placing her hands on her hips. "It's hard to say. Perhaps the soil quality is poor."

"Why would the soil be fine in the jungle and fine on the mountain but not on this fifty-foot strip?" Brett asked.

Zane walked toward the mountain base. He stopped and tilted his head back. "It's hard to tell from this angle, but it looks like our mountain has a flat top."

Brett and Amanda walked over and looked up. "Obviously that's where I'd want to be if I were going to transmit a signal."

Zane nodded slowly. "We need to find a way up there."

Brett set down his pack then retrieved a pair of binoculars from one of the pockets. He trained them on the slope. "I hope you're not thinking about climbing up." He lowered them and looked at Zane. "That would be pure suicide without the appropriate gear."

"It might not be as hard as you think." Amanda pointed at the vines. "It has its own built-in climbing ropes."

"Yeah, good luck with that," Brett said. "One snap, and you're done."

"She may actually be on to something." Zane squatted and grasped one of the cordons. "These things appear to be pretty strong. I'm thinking they'd hold pretty well." He stood and looked up. "The slope is steep, but it isn't anywhere close to ninety degrees. That means a group of us could probably get to the top if we took our time."

Amanda wandered off to join Katiya, who was examining a flower on one of the vines. Brett turned to Zane. "I'm not sold on attempting a climb. I'd like to find a flatter slope than the one here."

"I agree with you that climbing up is not our best option." He glanced at the jungle. "After seeing that bridge, I'm convinced some ancient culture lived here. I'm also convinced that they either lived in or on that mountain. That being said, we need to—"

Zane was cut off by the sound of Jorge's approach. The Brazilian's brow was furrowed with concern.

"You don't look too happy," Zane said.

Jorge nodded at Max and Osak, who were standing about fifty yards down the buffer. "Take it for what it's worth, but our little friend doesn't like this place at all. He feels we need to turn back."

Zane frowned. "You know that's not an option. Did he say why?"

"He kept talking about bad spirits living on this mountain." He pointed at the ground. "He said it's why nothing will grow here. Even the jungle keeps its distance."

"That's nonsense."

"Perhaps." Jorge pulled a cigar from his shirt pocket. After lighting it, he said, "Like I said, take it for what it's worth. I would simply remind you that he's been pretty reliable so far."

Zane looked down. "I still think Katiya's theory is the right one. The soil just seems bad here."

Jorge nodded toward the mountain. "The boy also said something else… he said that the vines have a voice."

"What's that supposed to mean?"

"I don't know. He didn't say, but he didn't seem to like whatever they were saying."

Zane did have to admit the plants seemed odd, particularly their white flowers the size of dinner plates. He made a mental note to ask Katiya about it later.

"I wonder if Osak knows how to get up the mountain," Brett said.

"He's never been here before, so I doubt it," Jorge said. "But as long as we can convince him to stay, I'm sure he can help us find a way."

Zane turned and looked west. The last tiny sliver of sun sat on the horizon, deepening the shadows along the buffer. "Speaking of which, we need to get moving. We don't have much daylight left."

"Shouldn't we just set up camp here?" Brett asked. "Everyone is exhausted, and it would give me time to work on the sat phone."

He was right. The group *was* exhausted. But Zane knew now was not the time to stop, with one or even two hostile groups pressing them from the rear. If there was something here to find, then they needed to find it first.

"Unfortunately, we don't have the luxury of stopping right now," Zane said. "I want to at least find a way in or up before nightfall. Besides, it will be easier to travel on the buffer."

Brett nodded, although Zane could tell he was disappointed.

Zane glanced at his watch. "We still have an hour or two left. Let's split into two teams. We travel and search in opposite directions along the base." He looked at Jorge. "Sound good?"

The Brazilian was staring out at the jungle through narrowed eyes.

"What's wrong?"

"I think you're right." He broke his stare and looked at Zane. "We need to do as much as we can now. If the night was bad in the crater, then it will be even worse here."

CHAPTER THIRTY-NINE

AFTER CALLING EVERYONE together, Zane divided the group into two teams. He, Jorge, Brett, and Artur would search east along the base of the mountain. Bennett and Tocchet would lead the others to the west. The thought of separating concerned him, but it would allow them to cover more ground. It would be dark soon, and he was determined to find a way up the mountain before stopping to set up camp.

He watched Amanda and Katiya gather their belongings. He wouldn't like them being out of sight but took comfort in the fact that they'd be under the protection of heavily armed Green Berets.

And what about the mole? He still had no idea who it might be, and at this point, he still couldn't rule out either of the remaining soldiers. For that matter, he couldn't rule out Wilson. Maybe he had wandered off and joined the people he'd been working with. Although Zane found that hard to believe, it would certainly explain a lot of what had happened.

He pushed all the concerns aside as he addressed the group.

"Each team will continue searching until we find something."

"And if we don't?" Max asked.

"Assuming this buffer extends around the mountain, we'll meet on the other side."

Amanda lifted her hand. "I'm sorry, but what exactly are we supposed to be looking for?"

"Good question," Zane said. "It's reasonable to assume that the signal was transmitted from this mountain. It matches the location given by NASA, and it would give the sender an elevated and remote position. So what are we looking for? A way up or a way in."

Amanda frowned. "A way in?"

"Mountains are made largely of rock, therefore we need to be looking for tunnel openings, shafts, ravines, or anything that might provide a way to reach the top," Zane said. "We've already seen a stone bridge, so let's also watch for other man-made structures, particularly any that might give us access to the summit."

"Watch the slope as well," Jorge said. "If it flattens enough, we might be able to make the climb."

"So what happens if we don't find anything and we do end up meeting on the other side?" Katiya asked. "What then?"

"Then we'll find a secure place to make camp. That's another benefit of doing it this way—if nothing turns up, then at least we'll be farther away from whoever is coming up behind us."

Katiya nodded.

"Any other questions?" he asked. Several shook their heads.

As Zane bent over to gather his belongings, he felt a hand

on his arm. He looked up to find Katiya standing next to him. "I just want you to know how much I appreciate your leadership." She nodded toward the others. "It can't be easy trying to herd such a large group of opinionated people."

"I appreciate that." Zane stood and slung his pack over a shoulder. "I want you to run point on your team. I'll feel better if you're calling the shots." He squeezed her shoulder. "Let me know the minute you find something."

Zane held her gaze for a moment before shouldering his rifle and turning away.

"Want us to leave you two alone for a while?" Brett asked as the two walked off.

"You're a regular riot," Zane said. "So I guess I'm not supposed to give the other team some last-minute encouragement?"

"If she were any more encouraged, she might have undone her ponytail."

"I didn't realize you were analyzing my every move now. If you spent as much time on that sat phone, we'd probably have an extraction team on the way by now."

Brett smiled and took a swig from his canteen.

They spent the next few minutes walking in silence. Despite the need to find a way up the mountain, Zane found his eyes repeatedly drawn back to the jungle. Who was lurking out there? Were they hiding just out of sight, waiting for the opportunity to spring another attack? He'd seen no sign of their approach, which hopefully meant they were still some distance off.

Brett looked over at the slope. "My fear is that if there is an opening, it will be almost impossible to see underneath the tangle of vines, particularly this late in the day."

"Just keep your eyes open. As Jorge said, perhaps the slope will flatten out at some point."

Brett elbowed Zane then pointed. Jorge and Artur had stopped and were looking at something just down the buffer.

"Got something?" Zane asked as they arrived.

"Artur thinks he saw someone," Jorge replied.

"No, I *know* I saw someone," Artur said.

Zane stopped, a frown spreading over his face. "You saw someone? Where? What did they look like?"

Artur pointed at two boulders in the distance. "There was a little girl, standing next to one of the rocks. When I looked at her... she just disappeared."

Zane's eyes narrowed. That wasn't what he'd expected to hear.

"What did she look like?" Brett asked.

Artur shrugged. "She was an Indian girl... that's all I could tell. Very young. Maybe three or four at most."

"Maybe she lives here on the mountain," Brett said. "And if she does, then it's possible we're near an entrance."

"Possibly," Zane whispered. Something bothered him about the sighting, but for now he tucked it away. He pulled his rifle off his shoulder. "Let's go have a look."

The boulders were about four feet tall, just high enough for someone to crouch behind. Zane approached slowly, not because the little girl posed a threat, but because of who might be with her. Zane lifted his rifle as he came around the rocks. No one was there.

After the others joined him, Jorge squatted and stared at something on the ground. "There was someone here." He pointed at a faint impression in the hard-packed soil. "And the footprint seems to be about the size of a small child's."

Zane scanned the area. The buffer seemed to narrow just ahead, with the jungle a mere thirty feet or so from the escarpment. That was likely the direction she'd fled, although she could have ducked off into the woods too.

"Let's keep going," Brett said. "I believe she may be the key to getting up the mountain."

Zane felt a pinch in his gut. Something still bothered him, although he wasn't sure what. "You may be right, but let's keep our eyes and ears open."

They moved forward in the growing darkness. Not only were the jungle trees closer here, but as they traveled to the northeast, the sun was becoming blocked by the mountain.

Suddenly Jorge stopped and grabbed Zane's arm. "Look!"

Zane stared ahead. At first he couldn't see anything, but as his eyes adjusted, he made out a tiny figure standing about fifty yards ahead. *The girl.*

Brett lifted his binoculars. "She looks scared."

"I think she's lost," Jorge said.

"Maybe," Zane whispered.

"We need to help her," Artur said.

Zane used the scope on his rifle to view the girl. She was clad in the typical garb of an Indian tribe, with animal skin clothing and a clump of necklaces looped around her neck. Brett was right, there was a look of concern on her face. Zane felt another pinch in his gut.

Zane rose to his feet. "Let's see if she'll let us get close."

The four proceeded slowly. In addition to watching the girl, Zane took an occasional glance toward the trees on their right.

"She's moving," Jorge said.

Zane looked up just in time to see her disappear around a bend.

"Let's go," Zane shouted.

They sprinted the remaining distance. After making the turn, they came to an abrupt halt. The buffer had widened again, and they found themselves in a large clearing about the size of a football field. Zane frowned. The girl was nowhere to be seen.

Brett turned in several different directions. "Where is she? There's no way she could've made it to the other end. An Olympic sprinter couldn't have made it that far."

Jorge pointed toward some scattered boulders on the left. "What about over there? That seems like the only place she could've made it to."

Zane led them over to the boulders, but once again they came up empty. Jorge walked over to the base of the mountain and pushed aside some of the vines with his rifle. After looking around for a few seconds, he looked at Zane and shook his head.

Brett stared at the jungle, hands on his hips. "It's like she vanished into thin air."

Jorge got down on one knee and examined the ground behind the boulders. "I see signs that people have been here, but it's hard to tell how recent the prints are."

THE PORTAL

Zane clenched his jaw as they stood in silence. Where had she gone? The only possibility was into the jungle. But if that was true, then why hadn't she simply run there to begin with?

Artur cleared his throat. "I need to tell all of you something."

Jorge stood and stared at him with a frown.

After a long pause, Artur said, "Something happened back at the bridge."

"What are you talking about?" Jorge asked.

"I stayed behind to gather my things… and… and I saw something in the bushes."

Something lurched in the pit of Zane's stomach. He sensed he was about to learn why he'd felt the pinch in his gut.

Jorge nodded that he should continue.

The Brazilian let out a sigh. "As I got ready to leave, I saw something in the shadows. At first I didn't know what it was, but then I realized someone was looking at me."

"Are you sure it wasn't an animal?" Jorge asked.

"I don't think so. I saw the eyes… a man's eyes, just peering at me from the shadows."

Jorge's face reddened. "Why didn't you tell us about that?"

"I'm sorry. I wasn't sure what it was… I mean, I thought it was a man, but I couldn't be sure."

"What did you do?" Brett asked.

"I got my gun, but by the time I looked back, the face was gone. After that, I heard some movement in several places, but I couldn't really see anything."

Jorge said something in Portuguese. From his tone, it sounded like a string of expletives.

Brett looked at Jorge. "Do you think it was the Dawanis?"

"Possibly," he said, stroking his mustache. "Unfortunately we don't have any way of knowing."

Brett looked at Zane. "Do you think it has something to do with what happened here?"

"Yes, I think it does. In fact, I think we'd better—"

Before he could finish, Artur gave a loud grunt. Zane turned in time to see the Brazilian wobble then collapse to the ground. Something was sticking out of his shoulder.

Just as Zane realized what was happening, a long, wailing shriek bellowed out of the jungle behind them.

CHAPTER FORTY

"BEHIND THE ROCKS!" Zane shouted as another arrow hissed overhead.

A third was right behind it, burying into a vine branch behind them.

Zane seized Brett, pulling him down behind the largest boulder. It was a miracle they hadn't been hit. He turned and saw that Jorge had pulled Artur behind another rock a few feet away.

The barrage of arrows intensified over the next few seconds. Zane dropped his pack and brought his rifle around. He crept to his left, setting up in the space between two boulders. It only gave him a limited view of the jungle, but it was all he had.

Zane looked at Brett. "Get your gun out."

"All I have is a pistol. I can't—"

"Just do it. We have to scare them. It's the only way to keep them from making a run. They do that, and we'll be overrun."

War cries and wails echoed out of the jungle, raising the hairs on the back of Zane's neck. The sounds were primordial, beast-like.

Zane rose up on one elbow then unleashed a spray of bullets across the wall of green. The wails and arrows seemed to die in response, at least for the time being.

Brett rose and fired off several rounds. Suddenly, he looked to his right and shouted, "One o'clock!"

Zane pivoted just in time to see one of the attackers dart across a gap in the jungle, only to disappear once again. He projected where the man would come to a stop and fired two shots. He heard a scream. At least one of the bullets had found its mark.

With the lull in action, Zane looked over to check on Artur. Jorge was working on the wound. "How is he?"

Jorge spoke without looking up. "I think he's going to be fine." As Zane watched, Jorge used a knife to saw off part of the arrow about an inch from where it had entered Artur's flesh. "I'm going to have to leave most of it in. I think the bleeding will be worse if I take it out."

Zane hoped it hadn't delivered poison into the Brazilian's bloodstream. He'd read that some indigenous tribes still coated the tips of their arrows with secretions from the skin of the poison dart frog. The dose was so potent that death often came within minutes.

Without warning, the wailing began again, followed by several more arrows. Brett continued to fire random shots into the jungle, which seemed to help, but they needed something else. In a few minutes, the tribe would get used to the strange weapons, and once they did, they might make a full-frontal assault.

What they needed was to actually kill a few of the attackers. Killing them at such a distance might cause general panic.

"Three o'clock!" Brett shouted. Zane turned and saw that two tribesmen had crept toward them using the shadow cast by the mountain. As soon as they were spotted, they sprinted forward, wailing, their spears raised. They were painted in black, their eyes circled in white.

Dawanis.

Before Zane could react, Brett raised his pistol with two hands. He squeezed the trigger, but nothing happened. The gun had jammed.

The attackers seemed to sense their opportunity. They howled with delight and rushed the boulders.

Zane reacted instinctively, lifting his rifle. It would be risky shooting past Brett's head, but he had no choice. Steadying his aim, he squeezing off two successive shots. The tribesmen stiffened, the wails dying in their throats. Both men wobbled for a moment before falling over. They were dead before they hit the ground.

The wailing died immediately. He doubted it would last, but at least it gave them time to regroup. Taking advantage of the opportunity, Zane reached down and removed his radio.

Jorge shook his head. "I've already tried. They don't work here."

"What?" Zane's brow furrowed. "They have a range of several miles."

Jorge nodded toward the slope of the mountain. "The only

thing I can figure is that it's something about the rocks."

He had to try anyway, while there was a lull in the fighting. Lifting the radio, he tried to raise one of the Green Berets. There was only static in response. Zane cursed and slid the radio back in his pocket.

"What are they doing?" Brett hissed. "Things have gotten awfully quiet."

"Hard to say," Zane said. "We might have injected some fear into them, or they could be gearing up for an attack. If they do, we may be in some serious trouble."

"Why do you say that?" Jorge asked.

Zane nodded toward the tree line. "My eyes and ears tell me there are at least several dozen archers back in those trees, which means there could be many more than that. If they decide to rush, we have no chance of bringing them all down, even with our semiautomatics."

"I'm down to two magazines," Brett said.

"They've seen what our weapons can do now, so the fear of the unknown may hold them off for a bit longer," Zane continued. "In the meantime, I have an idea." He moved to his left and lay down between the two boulders.

"What are you doing?" Brett asked.

"Just keep me covered. Make sure they don't try to creep up on us again."

After sorting through several options, Zane kept coming back to one in particular. If he could somehow kill the leader, the head of the snake, that might cause the others to lose the will to fight. They had already witnessed two of their own drop dead, and hopefully seeing the same thing happen to their chieftain would be too much.

Zane placed his rifle against his shoulder and used the scope to examine the jungle on the other side of the clearing. He focused on a large Brazil nut tree with lots of dense foliage. Each time the wailing commenced, it started with a shriek that seemed to come from there. Now it was just a matter of finding his man.

He moved the sights around, examining openings in the foliage, looking for movement or flashes of color.

Suddenly an arrow hissed out of the woods and glanced off the boulder on Zane's left, missing him by about a foot.

"One of them is locked in on you," Brett said.

Jorge scooted closer to him. "Whatever you're doing... it's too risky."

"I need the two of you to watch the jungle," Zane said without moving. "Let me know if it looks like they're about to make a move. If they fire, fire back. I just need some time."

Seconds later, another arrow glanced off the boulder to Zane's right. Jorge and Brett responded immediately by returning fire.

As they kept the attackers occupied, Zane continued looking for his target. As he moved his scope back and forth, the wailing began again, only this time the cries were joined by the beating of drums. Zane's heart thumped loudly in his chest. In all likelihood, they were preparing for an assault.

Just as he was about to move his scope, Zane caught a flash of color on the left side of the tree. He placed the sights on a small opening between two limbs. Something hovered in the shadows there. He moved his body a bit, giving himself a better angle. Suddenly he froze. Staring out of the foliage were two cold eyes rimmed in white.

Boom, boom, boom. Boom, boom, boom. The drums continued, and the wails grew louder. The tribesmen were trying to whip themselves into a frenzy.

As Zane fixed on his target, rivulets of sweat ran down his forehead and into his eyes.

Boomboomboom. Boomboomboom. The beat was faster now.

"I can see a couple of them crouching just inside the trees, preparing for an attack," Brett said, his voice tinged with concern.

Zane spoke without turning his head. "Be prepared to fire if they come out, but not a second before."

Zane realized his scope had shifted slightly, causing him to lose his target. He moved it back to the left. *Where was the opening?*

The booming of the drums was building toward a crescendo, and the tribe seemed to be working itself into a state of delirium.

"They're gathering at the forest edge," Brett said. "I'm going to fire."

"No, don't shoot!" Zane shouted. "I need a few more seconds."

He moved the scope sights around quickly, searching.

Got it!

"They're coming!" Brett shouted.

"I said don't shoot."

The drums were beating so fast that they seemed like a beating heart. The tribesmen were seconds away from launching their attack.

"Zane!"

The loud crack of the gunshot pierced the air. The forest went silent, followed by the sound of a body snapping through the limbs on its way to the ground. A second later, it landed with a loud thud.

A long moment of silence was followed by the distinct sound of movement in the jungle. Were they attacking? Zane raised his rifle then lowered it again when he realized the footsteps were fading into the distance. The tribe was retreating.

As Zane let out a sigh, a voice barked from his radio. "Zane? Do you read?"

He reached down and pulled it out of his pocket. "This is Watson, over."

"What's going on down there?" It was Tocchet.

"We ran into a little trouble, but I think we're all clear now."

"Copy that. We couldn't reach you earlier, so I started heading in your direction. While en route I heard a shot fired."

Zane frowned. "Why were you trying to reach us? Is there a problem?"

"No problem at all." After a brief pause, he said, "In fact, I have good news. We think Osak may have found a way inside the mountain."

CHAPTER FORTY-ONE

ZANE LOOKED OVER at Artur as they moved west down the buffer. Pain was scrawled across his face, but on a positive note, he had been able to keep pace. They still hadn't removed the arrow. Jorge and Zane both thought it would be better to let one of the Green Berets take a look first. Both had extensive medical training, and the decision was better left in their hands.

"Looks like we have two at twelve o'clock," Brett said.

Zane looked up. Tocchet was coming toward them, and someone was walking at his side. The setting sun cast them as silhouettes, so at this point, he couldn't tell more than that it was a woman. "Who is that with him?"

"It looks like Dr. Mills," Brett said.

As they drew closer, the familiar shape of the anthropologist came into view.

"How is our patient?" Katiya asked as she rushed toward them.

"He's hanging in there," Zane said.

"When you told me he was injured, I called down Dr. Mills," Tocchet explained. "She told me before that her father was a doctor."

Zane looked at her. "Anthropologist, biologist, and now general practitioner?"

"And there's a lot more you still don't know." She moved to Artur's side and saw that the makeshift bandage was soaked in blood. "Oh my."

"As you can see, he took an arrow to his upper arm," Jorge said. "I used a shirt to wrap up the wound, but I'm not sure it will last."

Katiya leaned closer. "You did a fine job. I'll take a closer look when we get back." She looked up at Artur. "How do you feel?"

"I'm not going to lie. It's killing me, but I'll be fine."

"I was worried we might have been dealing with poisoned tips," Zane said.

"He wouldn't be walking now if they had been," Katiya said. "The use of poison-tipped arrows isn't particularly widespread anymore, but out here anything is possible." She looked at him. "Who did this?"

"My guess would be the Dawanis."

"Could you tell how many there were?"

"Too many to count," Zane said. "The jungle was crawling with them."

"Glad you all made it out alive."

As Katiya made a couple of quick adjustments to the bandage, Zane glanced over at the slope. His eyes narrowed as he surveyed the vines. They seemed thicker here. A few of the primary branches were the size of tree trunks.

"So what did Osak find, exactly?" Brett asked as Katiya finished up and the group began walking again.

"We're not sure. He somehow got ahead of us, and when he came back, he told us he'd found a way into the mountain."

"So you never saw what he was talking about?" Zane asked.

"Not yet. We followed him to a ravine. There was a trail that ran back through some shrub, but that's as far as I got. We discovered our radios weren't working, so Sergeant Bennett sent Sergeant Tocchet back to establish contact with you guys."

"He didn't describe it at all?" Brett asked.

Katiya shook her head. "Max said he couldn't understand all the details. Apparently Osak kept using a word he wasn't familiar with."

Zane suddenly noticed that Tocchet had begun to slow. Just ahead on the right was a ravine that cut into the mountain. Each side was guarded by a rocky ridge, and the center was filled with what appeared to be an impenetrable mass of shrubs and vines. "Talk about a briar patch," he said.

Tocchet waited for them to catch up then said, "Not sure we could even hack our way through if we had to."

Katiya pointed toward an opening. "Thankfully, we won't need to. There's our trail."

Tocchet led the way in, and the others followed in single file. Zane entered last, right behind Katiya.

Once inside, he realized that the thick vegetation wasn't really a mix of plants. There might be a few small shrubs, but the bulk of the growth was the same vine that seemed to cover the mountain. It was so thick in places that he doubted he could even stick a hand through.

Katiya caught Zane's attention then pointed up. "It's like a tunnel in here."

Zane tilted his head back. She was right. The vines curled overhead, forming a tightly fitted roof, so tight that it blotted out the sky. The whole structure had a bizarre feel. "If this is the entrance, I'm not sure I want to go in," he said, only half joking. "Who do you think cut this out?"

Katiya slowed so that the two could walk together. "I wondered the same thing. At first, I thought it was the animals passing through, but it seems way too smooth for that."

"It reminds me of one of those covered plant tunnels in an arboretum." He pulled out a flashlight and shone it on some of the limbs as they passed by. "The strange thing is that they don't look cut. It's almost as though they grew this way. Only that can't be possible."

After they rounded a turn, Katiya squeezed his arm. "Sorry, I didn't get a chance to speak earlier. I wanted to make sure Artur was okay."

Zane held up a hand. "Don't even think twice. We're all more worried about his health than anything else. How did he look?"

"I think he's going to be fine. I'm ninety percent sure it missed all the arteries in that part of the arm, but I want to have a closer look before I jump to any conclusions."

"Are you going to recommend we take the arrow out?"

Katiya pressed her lips together tightly. "That's part of what I'm going to look at. Again, if it isn't near an artery, it will be better to pull it out and sew him up."

The trail suddenly narrowed ahead, leaving only enough room for one person to pass through at a time, so Zane placed his hand on Katiya's waist and guided her forward. She smiled at him as she continued past.

He followed her through, and as they neared the end of the tight stretch, he saw a vine dangling out into the path. It seemed oddly out of place. It reminded him of well-coiffed men with one rogue strand of hair sticking out.

Unable to resist, Zane reached out to push the vine back into place. Then, as his fingers were about to make contact, a tendril at the end curled away from him. He stopped, a scowl crossing his face. He reached out again, and once again the tendril curled back. He remembered reading about the phenomenon of certain plants moving when stimulated. The Venus flytrap was one the article had mentioned. When an insect touched the trigger bristle, the two giant leaves would slam shut, trapping the unfortunate bug inside.

Only that was movement after contact. How could a plant sense that it was *about* to be touched?

"Something wrong?" Katiya asked.

"No, everything's fine." After taking one last glance, he continued on. "I was just looking at some of the vines. Is it just me or do some of these plants seem a little strange?"

"You know, it's funny you say that," she said, "because I've been thinking the same thing. As I mentioned before, I've studied the flora and fauna of the Amazon for a long time." She gestured toward the plants that encircled the trail. "But I don't recognize this particular species. At first, I thought it was a strangler fig, but now I'm not so sure. It almost looks like a strangler fig on steroids, larger and more powerful than the ones I'm familiar with."

Zane looked at her. "Strangler figs? That's really the name?"

She smiled. "Yes, they're part of the genus Ficus. It's one of the most fascinating plants in the rainforest."

"So they really do strangle?"

"In a sense, yes. If there is such a thing as a malevolent plant, the strangler fig is it." She gave a little laugh. "But the most amazing thing about them is how they start out."

Zane was amazed at her unending fount of knowledge. "Tell me more."

She seemed pleased at his interest. "Okay, it all starts with animal poop."

"Animal poop?"

"Yep, the life history of a strangler fig begins when a canopy-dwelling animal, perhaps a bird or a monkey, releases feces containing a seed. The seed ends up in the crotch of a tree and germinates there. After germination, the plant sends its massive roots all the way down the trunk and into the soil. Over time, those roots begin to suck up all the moisture, robbing the host tree's roots of that same resource. At the same time, the roots cover and squeeze the tree's trunk. And if that weren't enough, the strangler fig sprouts leaves that block out the leaves of its host, sapping up all the nutrients provided by the sun."

"Doesn't sound like this ends well for the tree," Zane said.

"Often it doesn't. Many of the hosts end up dying. What was once a majestic tree morphs into a column of strangler fig vines wrapped around a dead trunk."

"Good grief. A plant that preys on other plants."

"It's not all bad though. The dying tree will often develop holes and crannies, the perfect breeding cavities for various species of birds and mammals."

Zane grabbed one of the vines along the trail and shook it. "And you think these are relatives of the strangler fig?"

"They seem similar, and yet I've never seen stranglers spread over such a large area. Generally they attack one solitary tree and spend their entire life cycle in that one place. These seem to be running everywhere."

Zane was about to ask her another question when he saw lights ahead. A minute later, they entered a large clearing. It was bordered on three sides by the vines; the fourth side, directly ahead, butted up against the rocky base of the mountain. Most of the group was already gathered there.

At the sound of their arrival, Bennett came over to them. The soldier's eyes widened when he saw Artur's blood-soaked bandage. "Let's get him over here." He pointed to a flat boulder where they had piled some of their packs.

"Oh my gosh, what happened?" Amanda asked, rushing over to help lower the Brazilian onto the rock.

"An arrow," Zane said.

Katiya asked Tocchet to retrieve the medical kit. After sitting down, she slowly unraveled the bandage. She pulled out a flashlight, clicked it on, and began to examine the wound.

Bennett pulled Zane to the side. "Who did this?"

"We came under attack by an indigenous tribe," Zane replied. "I'm convinced it was the Dawanis. Fortunately we sent them running, but I have no doubt they'll be back."

Bennett gestured toward the rock face. "Sir, I need to show you something."

After making sure Artur was attended to, Zane followed the Green Beret to the base of the mountain. There was a row of bushes, and just beyond, Zane saw a stone slab partially blocking an opening in the rock face. Max Cameron was down on one knee, shining a flashlight into the gap.

"The indigenous boy entered about ten minutes ago to see what he could find," Bennett said.

Zane looked down at Max. "See anything?"

The linguist spoke without looking up. "Just rock walls." He leaned closer and tilted his head. "But I do hear something. I think he's on his way back."

Seconds later, Osak crawled out of the dark interior and spoke to Max in an excited tone. Zane watched the boy's face carefully. He didn't seem upset, which was a good sign.

After he finished, Max turned to Zane and Bennett. "He says the tunnel goes straight back from here. The floor is flat and smooth, easy to travel on."

"Excellent," Bennett replied.

"One problem though," Max continued. "He eventually came to a body of water and was unable to go any further."

"Water?" Zane asked. "Inside the mountain?"

"That's what he said."

Zane frowned. "Was it a stream? A lake?"

"He couldn't tell. He says one minute he was walking on stone and the next he was up to his knees in water."

Bennett looked at Zane. "Hopefully we can get a better

idea of what we're dealing with once we take some lights in there. I'm assuming you want us to go in tonight?"

"Yes, at least some of us." Zane looked back at Artur, sitting on the boulder. Katiya was cleaning the wound with a wet cloth. "I'll go check on our patient first, and then you and I will take the boy back in to see what we can learn about the body of water he found."

"Yes, sir. Roger that."

As Bennett stooped to gather his things, Zane reached into his pack and pulled out a flashlight. How the rest of the night played out would depend on Artur's condition. If the injury wasn't serious, he preferred to enter the mountain tonight. On the other hand, if the Brazilian was doing poorly, it might be best to give him a night of rest. That might also give Brett enough time to fix the sat phone.

Zane clicked on his flashlight and left Max at the entrance. As he stepped past the bushes, his beam swung across the clearing. He stopped. Something wasn't right. He swung the beam back, this time more slowly. Eventually it illuminated the opening in the plant wall, the one they had just walked out of a few minutes earlier. He frowned and took a few steps in that direction. He held the beam there, his eyes soaking in the details.

What's wrong with this picture?

And then it hit him. The opening was smaller than it had been before. Or was it?

He approached more closely, stopping a few feet away. The opening appeared to be the size of a normal house door, and yet he could have sworn that when he and Katiya had come through earlier they'd been walking side by side with room to spare.

Probably your mind playing tricks on you.

Zane turned to rejoin the others. As his light swept away from the opening, he could have sworn he saw several of the tendrils moving.

CHAPTER FORTY-TWO

ZANE CROSSED TO the flat stone where Katiya and Amanda were working on Artur. Two puncture wounds marred the Brazilian's upper arm. Amanda held him still as Katiya finished stitching him up.

"That's better treatment than I've seen in some hospitals," Zane remarked.

Katiya tied off the stitch and snipped off the excess. "Let's not get carried away. The arrow passed through the side of his deltoid muscle. Thankfully that means it missed his arteries."

"They'll need to bring something better than that to kill me," Artur said with a laugh.

Zane gave him a quick smile then turned toward Katiya. "And the prognosis?"

"Again, I'm no doctor, but I'd say he's going to be fine," Katiya said. "I think infection is going to be the biggest concern. That and he won't be able to lift his arm for a while. As soon as he gets something to eat, I'll give him some oral antibiotics."

Zane frowned. "We have antibiotics?"

Katiya turned red and looked at Jorge. "Not officially."

Zane looked at the Brazilian, who shrugged, smiled, and walked away.

Artur flexed his good arm as though demonstrating his strength. "A few minutes more, and I'll be good to go."

Katiya placed a hand on Artur's leg. "No, you need more rest than that." She looked at Zane. "I know you're eager to keep going, but he needs at least four or five hours of rest. He lost a good amount of blood today."

Zane rubbed his beard. Despite the Brazilian's bravado, Artur's face had paled considerably. No doubt the blood loss had weakened him. If they needed to stay, at least the ravine provided a safe place to make camp. The only way in was down the narrow path, which could easily be guarded. So, unless the Chinese had artillery, they should be safe for now.

"You're right," Zane said to Katiya. "Let's give him a few hours. I'll check back later."

Artur shook his head. "I'm fine… honestly."

"You're not doing as well as you think," Zane said. He placed a hand on the Brazilian's good shoulder. "While you're resting, we'll check out the tunnel. We're going to need you healthy when we all go in."

Artur nodded.

Zane gave him a pat and turned to Katiya. "Let me know if you need anything."

"I will," Katiya said. She then mouthed a silent "thank you" as he turned to leave.

Zane found Bennett in the middle of the clearing, checking

his gear.

"You about ready?"

Bennett looked up. "Yes, sir. How much do you think we'll need?"

"Not much. Our main objective is to learn more about the body of water Osak found. I want to know how big it is and how we can get across."

Bennett nodded. "My guess is that it's an underground stream. We did some light spelunking during our training, and I ran into them all the time. Most are shallow and should be easy to cross. The only things you have to worry about are those little blind fish nibbling your feet."

"Unfortunately, this place is anything but normal," Zane said. "No telling—"

He was cut off by a loud shout of alarm. The voice sounded strangely muffled. He and Bennett turned, sweeping their beams around. Others joined them. Soon cones of light waved in every direction.

"Over here!" Amanda shouted.

Zane swung his beam around, as did the others. His eyes widened. Tocchet was lying on the ground near the edge of the clearing, struggling with something that seemed to be dragging him across the ground.

Zane and Bennett rushed over to him. Bennett was the first to arrive. "What the...?"

Zane pulled up short, horrified at the sight. Tocchet's face was purple, much like someone's whose air had been cut off. Something was coiled around the soldier's neck. At first he thought it was a snake, but now, to his horror, he saw that it was one of the vines. It moved like an animal, tightening and pulling at the same time.

Amanda, who had just arrived, let out a scream.

"Get back!" Zane shouted.

Bennett had already dropped to his knees and was tugging at the plant.

"Please... help me," Tocchet gurgled.

Zane knelt down and wrapped his fingers around the living noose. He was shocked at how strong it was, almost like ribbed steel.

"It's trying to pull him into the thicket," Bennett said.

He was right. Slowly but surely the soldier was being tugged toward the wall of vegetation.

Suddenly Zane heard a startled grunt, and Bennett slid out of view. Figuring he must have lost his grip, Zane continued to work on getting Tocchet loose.

Amanda screamed again, directing her flashlight to Zane's right.

Zane turned then froze. A massive vine, much larger than the first, was wrapped around Bennett's leg. The soldier was trying to shift and grab it with his hands, but the vine prevented it by dragging him more quickly.

Zane hesitated for a moment but knew he had to stay with Tocchet. The soldier was slowly choking to death. He turned toward the others. "Someone help Bennett!"

Jorge and Brett were already rushing to Bennett's aid, allowing Zane to refocus on Tocchet. He straddled Tocchet's chest and jammed his fingers into the crease between the vine and the soldier's throat. If he could find the tip, he might be able to unravel the whole thing. He grunted, shoving his fingers as far into the coils as he could. Unfortunately, the further he got, the more difficult it was for Tocchet to breathe. He guessed the soldier had less than a minute to live.

Seconds later, Zane felt the tip of the vine. But as he closed his fingers around it, the plant pulled away as though it was equipped with its own central nervous system.

"I can't... I can't breathe," Tocchet hissed through clenched teeth.

"Hang in there," Zane said, probing again with his hands.

He glanced up again. The vine was pulling them steadily toward the edge of the clearing. They were only inches away, and now more vines were slithering toward them. The whole grove had now awakened as darkness fell over the ravine.

Just as Zane was about to give up and try something else, a shadow appeared on his left. A figure stood over the vine and lifted an ax with both arms. Seconds later, the blade cut through the air, slicing cleanly through the vine. A plume of dark sap sprayed like a fountain, and the stub whipped back into the wall.

Tocchet coughed and spit, gasping for air. With no time to lose, Zane gathered him up and carried him back toward the center of the clearing. It was only then that he noticed Katiya striding beside him.

As he set the soldier down on the grass, Zane heard continued commotion not far away.

Bennett.

Leaving Katiya to tend to Tocchet, he turned and ran toward the lights at the edge of the clearing. He soon saw Brett and Bennett struggling with a massive vine. It was the largest one Zane had ever seen, probably three or four times the girth of an anaconda.

He rushed forward, but before he could reach them, the sound of a gunshot cracked in the air. Then another. He turned and saw Jorge standing about ten yards away, a rifle pressed against his shoulder. As he continued firing, bullets ripped into the plant, sending plumes of dark sap in every direction.

Seconds later, a shriek rang out from somewhere far off, deep in the tangle of plants, and the vine snapped back into the darkness.

With the immediate threat now suppressed, Zane and Jorge rushed to help Brett and Bennett to their feet. The four then retreated to the mountain face along with the others.

As they arrived, Katiya grabbed Zane's arm and pulled him to the side. "We need to get out of here… now."

"It's gone."

She shook her head and swept the beam of her flashlight across the clearing. Zane flinched. Hundreds of vines were now snaking out of the plant wall, inching toward them from all directions. Some of the vines had been beaten back, but others had taken their place.

Zane stared in stunned silence. The tendrils were moving more slowly now, probably cautious after the blows their brethren had taken, but in a matter of minutes they would likely move in from every direction. And when that happened, no amount of bullets would stop them.

Zane turned to the group. "Everybody, gather your things

quickly. We're entering the tunnel.

Max scowled at Zane. "How do we know you aren't leading us toward something even more dangerous than what's out here? We need to kill this—"

"Good, we have a volunteer who's going to stay behind and fight. The rest of you prepare to leave."

Max muttered something under his breath but reached for his pack. The others wasted no time gathering their belongings and moving toward the rock face.

Zane slung his own pack over a shoulder then turned toward Tocchet. The soldier was sitting up now, breathing deeply. "I know you're weak, but we're going to have to get you over to the tunnel."

Tocchet coughed then spoke in a soft voice. "I'm ready."

Zane lifted him to his feet and looped an arm around his back, holding him up. The two then walked over to where the others were queuing up in front of the opening. Maxwell Cameron was already on his knees, crawling through as quickly as he could. Zane shook his head at the pathetic sight.

After making sure Tocchet could stand on his own, Zane looked at Brett. "Is everyone here?"

"Yes," Brett said with a nod.

"Good, let's—"

"Look!" Amanda shouted.

Zane turned. Amanda had directed her beam back toward the clearing. The vines had closed the distance even more quickly than expected. Some of the shoots were only about fifteen or twenty yards away and closing fast.

"Holy crap," Zane said.

Katiya came over and stood at his side. "I think the plant uses its tendrils to sense movement. Which means when we all ran over here, it was able to track us. It also seems to be coming with greater numbers this time, probably something it's learned to do when it realizes it's up against prey that's able to fight back."

"It's almost like that thing has a brain." Zane looked at her. "You said plant, singular. There are hundreds of those things."

"I've been thinking about it ever since we had our little discussion earlier." She gestured toward the vines. "There are hundreds of vines, but my guess is that if you could trace them all back you'd find there is only one plant."

Amanda's eyes widened. "That's one organism?"

"Yes. I suspected it before, but after watching all the vines move in unison, I no longer have any doubt."

"What the hell is it?" Zane asked.

"A carnivorous plant of the highest order."

"Like a Venus flytrap?" Amanda asked.

Katiya nodded. "Yes, but only in the sense that they're both carnivores." She looked at Zane. "Remember I told you it had some resemblance to the strangler fig? I think we're looking at one of its long-lost relatives, possibly something that dates back to the prehistoric era."

"Why aren't there others?" Zane asked. "If they were all over the planet, we'd know about it."

"Who knows," she replied with a shrug. "Survival of the fittest. As powerful as this plant seems, a microorganism in the soil outside the crater might be able to bring it to its knees. It's hard to say."

Zane's brow furrowed. "Why did it wait to attack?"

"I'd guess it probably gathers energy during the day via photosynthesis then attacks unwitting prey at night."

"I think we'd better get moving." Amanda shone her beam out toward the vines once again. A few were now about ten yards away.

"She's right," Katiya said.

Zane turned back toward the rock face. Everyone except Bennett had entered the tunnel. After helping Amanda and Katiya through the opening, the two men turned and faced the clearing. Some of the vines were perilously close, making Zane wonder if a couple of them might make a quick attack if they turned.

"Let's buy ourselves a little space," Zane said.

He unslung his rifle and sprayed bullets in an arc. Some of the larger vines pulled back with a hiss, but other smaller ones seemed to be drawn by the movement.

"I think it's time to let them know we mean business," Bennett said. The soldier had already pulled a grenade from his sack. After pulling the safety clip, he launched it out into the clearing. Seconds later there was a white flash, followed by an ear-splitting explosion.

A shriek erupted in the distance, causing the hairs on the back of Zane's neck to rise. The vines that had been hit either pulled back or went limp, while others became more aggressive, rising off the ground like cobras.

"Give me one," Zane said.

Bennett reached into his pack and handed the operative a grenade.

THE PORTAL

"Get in the tunnel... I'll be right behind you."

Bennett hesitated. "Are you sure—"

"Get in!"

Bennett quickly retrieved his pack and rifle then took one last look at the vines before ducking through the opening.

After the soldier disappeared, Zane shouldered his pack and rifle. Dropping to his knees, he backed up to the opening. It was dark, but he could tell that about a dozen vines were now only a few feet away, hovering in front of him like snakes.

Zane lifted the grenade, but as he pulled the clip, he felt something like a cold rope slide around his neck. It tightened and yanked him up against the top of the opening.

A vine.

One of them must have slithered across the rock face and approached him from above.

As he reached up to pry the tentacle loose, the live grenade dropped out of his hand, rolling several feet away. Zane grimaced. He knew the explosive's timer would trigger in five seconds, which meant if he didn't get inside, he'd be blown into a hundred pieces.

Straining with everything he had, he thrust his body downward, and in one smooth motion, he grabbed the grenade and flung it as hard as he could.

Just as it detonated, Zane felt something grasp his ankles and pull.

CHAPTER FORTY-THREE

THE GROUP MOVED down the tunnel quietly, their beams slicing through the Stygian darkness. Amanda couldn't figure out whether the silence was due to lingering thoughts of the terror behind them or of what might be lurking ahead.

For her part, she was just thankful that Zane was alive. She had watched the whole event play out from a few feet away. Somehow Sergeant Bennett had realized what was going on and had managed to grab Zane's legs and pull him to safety. Had it happened a second or two later, Zane might have been seriously injured by the blast, or worse.

To everyone's horror, a few vines had appeared at the opening a few minutes later, but they'd refused to cross the threshold. Amanda believed they were safe now, provided the tunnel didn't lead to something even worse.

She shook all the troubling thoughts out of her mind and focused on her dark surroundings. As she panned her light around, she couldn't help but wonder how the passage had come into being. Had it been cut by human hands? Or had it formed through some natural process? Its sheer size suggested the former, but she couldn't rule out the latter.

As they continued walking, she was struck by the intense mustiness that permeated the air. It was as though they were walking through some ancient catacomb in Europe. The smell was so strong that it blotted out almost every other scent.

Amanda looked up and noticed that Katiya had stopped and was playing her beam around on the ceiling.

"See something?" Amanda asked.

Katiya nodded toward the area her light had illuminated. "The tunnel is starting to change."

Amanda aimed her own light at the same place. There, about five feet above them, large flat stones stretched from one side of the tunnel to the other. "That's definitely manmade." She stared intently at the seams. "And they're fitted tightly together just like the bridge. It reminds me a bit of all the tunnels underneath the pyramids in Egypt. Strange."

"It is strange, but then again, perhaps it makes perfect sense," Katiya said as they continued down the passage.

Amanda looked up and saw that the space had widened considerably. Zane and the others were standing in the distance, their flashlights trained on something out of sight. "Looks like they may have found the water."

When they arrived, Amanda's eyes widened. Directly in front of her was an underground lake, its still, dark surface spreading in every direction. How far did it go? Was this the end of their subterranean journey? The thought of going back to the vines made her shudder.

Bennett stood on the shore and looked out over the water.

"I guess I was wrong," he said, looking back at Zane. "It's not some little stream."

"It looks like we're at an intersection of tunnels." Katiya pointed her flashlight to the left and then to the right. The water disappeared into openings in both directions.

"My guess is that it may be a sewer system of some kind," Amanda said, "funneling water out of upper chambers."

Katiya nodded. "Apparently we're at the low point in the network, where the water gathers temporarily after a storm."

"It would be hard for this much water to evaporate," Zane said. "If I had to guess, I'd say this little lake is permanent."

Bennett bent over and rummaged through his pack, eventually pulling out a flashlight that was a full two feet long. Amanda had seen them use it when Corporal Wilson had gone missing.

The soldier waded out into the water and directed the powerful LED beam toward the far shore. A rocky ledge appeared in the cone of light, and beyond the ledge was another opening. "Looks like the tunnel continues on the far side."

"Good," Zane said. "How deep do you think this gets?"

The water was up to Bennett's knees. "Using the tunnels as a gauge, my guess is that it will max out about here." He held a hand just above his waist.

"How about the bottom?" Zane asked.

"No mud or slickness that I can tell," Bennett replied. "Hard pan rock."

"Good." Zane turned toward the others. "We're going across. Take your time. Don't feel like you have to rush.

Sergeant Bennett and I will go first and check for holes, so follow directly behind us."

As everyone prepared to enter, they heard splashing out in the lake, a bit to the right. Several beams turned in that direction, searching for the source. Suddenly a figure appeared, moving in their direction through the water. Tocchet raised his rifle, but Zane held up a hand.

"It's Osak," Katiya said as he came into view.

The boy stopped about twenty yards from shore. He spoke a few quick words, which Max translated. "He says he believes something large is out there, down at one of the crossing tunnels."

Zane frowned. "What is it?"

After another brief exchange with Osak, Max said, "It was hard to understand what he said, but I believe he picked up some vibrations in the water. He said we need to cross now."

Katiya flashed a concerned look at Zane. "Do you really think we should?"

"We have to. The tunnels to the right and left are flooded, and we're certainly not going back outside."

"He's right," Brett said. "We really have no choice."

Katiya nodded reluctantly and adjusted her pack.

"Okay, let's go, everybody," Zane said, wading out into the water.

Amanda slung her pack over her shoulder then walked over to the water's edge. She was concerned about what might be out there under the surface and therefore knew she needed to just go before her fear got the best of her.

Amanda took a deep breath and entered the dark water.

She pointed her flashlight downward, but the beam couldn't penetrate the coffee-colored depths. If something was down there, she wouldn't know until it was too late.

As she continued walking, someone sloshed up behind her. "Thank goodness I haven't bumped up against a plesiosaurus yet." It was Katiya.

"Hush." Amanda smiled at her. "You're worse than Brett."

Katiya laughed. "In all seriousness, I wouldn't worry. Despite what Osak said, I doubt there are any life forms in here. As large as it is, it's not connected to any other bodies of water, so I can't imagine anything living here. I mean, what would it eat?"

"A team of explorers might fill a belly up pretty quick," said Brett, who had suddenly appeared on Amanda's right.

Amanda looked at Katiya then jerked a thumb toward Brett. "See what I mean?"

"Funny guy. The problem with that theory is we're likely the first human beings to pass through here in decades, if not centuries."

Amanda looked down. The water had now risen to her waist. Bennett had said that was about as high as it would go. She hoped he was right.

About a minute later, someone at the front of the line shouted. She turned her flashlight in that direction and saw Osak standing next to Zane and Bennett. The boy was pointing at the tunnel to their left.

"What on earth is he so upset about?" Katiya asked.

Amanda turned and played her beam around in the general direction Osak was pointing. A few seconds later, she saw something, a slight swirl in the water. It was subtle, but clearly something was moving beneath the surface.

"Everybody get going!" Zane shouted from just ahead.

Amanda didn't need to be told twice. Just as she had in the river, she focused on moving her feet one at a time. As she did that, she also kept reminding herself of what Katiya had said. It did make perfect sense. How could something of any appreciable size live down here? What would it eat?

Suddenly a shot rang out. Then another.

So much for that theory.

Amanda didn't bother to look up. She pressed forward, moving as fast as she could. She heard something sloshing close by but didn't dare risk turning to see who or what it was.

Shortly thereafter, Amanda stepped on a slick stone and lost her balance. The surface came toward her as she fell, but just before she plunged into the water, a strong hand grabbed her arm, keeping her up.

Zane.

"Almost there," he said, pulling her toward the shore.

About a minute later, the operative pulled her up onto the rock ledge and set her down. He then turned and waded back into the lake, helping the others out of the water.

Tocchet was bringing up the rear. After stepping out, he turned and fired several shots at a place that swirled about ten yards out.

"What the heck was that?" Brett asked.

Zane's eyes narrowed as he stared at the spot Tocchet had fired at. "We're not sure. Osak said something was coming, but we couldn't figure out what it was. Probably just a cave fish or amphibian of some kind, but we weren't taking any chances."

"If that was a fish, it must have been the size of a tuna," Brett said.

Katiya aimed her flashlight downward. "Check it out."

Amanda looked toward the illumination. Rather than worn rock, they were standing on cut stone.

"And here's where the tunnel picks up again," Bennett said from behind them.

Everyone turned to see the soldier standing at an arched stone doorway.

"Perfect," Zane said. "Let's move out, everybody."

As the group passed through the archway, Amanda noticed that there was a set of stone stairs beyond.

"Looks like I was right," Katiya said. "These lower tunnels are some sort of primitive sewer system." She pointed her beam up the stairs. "That means whatever we're looking for is likely somewhere up there."

Zane and Bennett took the lead as they made the ascent. The musty smell was back again. How long had these stairs been here? And how long had it been since human beings had set foot on them?

A few minutes later, Zane held up a hand, bringing everyone to a halt. He was looking at something on the stairs above.

"Oh my," Katiya said.

Amanda looked and let out a little groan of frustration. A stack of assorted boulders, stones, and rubble stretched from one side of the stairwell to the other. Apparently one of the walls had caved in, perhaps from an earthquake or plate shift.

"Not good," Bennett muttered.

"No, it's not," Zane said, moving his beam up toward the ceiling.

"What's going on?" Max asked as he pushed his way toward the front.

Bennett pointed toward the pile with his rifle.

There was a flash of light, and Amanda turned to see Jorge lighting up a cigar.

Max sneered. "Must you?"

Jorge shrugged. "Why not? It helps me think."

Before Max could respond, Zane said, "Wait a minute." He played his light toward the right side of the passageway.

Amanda let her eyes follow his beam. At first she couldn't figure out what he'd found, but then she saw a narrow opening, perhaps only two feet wide, between the boulders and the wall. Apparently the cave-in hadn't extended across the entire staircase.

Zane took a few steps forward and leaned into the crevice. "It's going to be tight, but I think it goes all the way to the other side. There seem to be a few places where some of us are going to have to suck in some air to get through."

Jorge took a draw on his cigar and patted his stomach. "I think he's talking about me."

Amanda watched as Zane removed his pack. "I'm going to go through first," he said. "I'll radio back once I'm on the other side."

Tocchet nodded. "Copy that."

The operative wiggled sideways into the crevice, his pack in one hand and a flashlight in the other.

Amanda was thankful for her background as an archaeologist. It had prepared her for work in tight spaces, although she couldn't recall anything quite like this.

About five minutes later, Zane's voice crackled over Tocchet's radio. "Made it."

Bennett lifted the radio to his mouth. "Can you see anything?"

"There's a landing just ahead," Zane said. "I think we're about to find out where all of this leads."

CHAPTER FORTY-FOUR

AS SOON AS Zane pocketed the radio, he heard a noise behind him. He extinguished his light and turned around quietly. It seemed to have come from somewhere on the stairs above. It had sounded like a pebble bouncing across stone, but the distance was too great to know for sure.

He remained perfectly still as he continued to listen. Was someone or something waiting up there? It was probably just a rat, but since the others were on their way up, he needed to make sure they weren't walking into a trap.

Turning back to the crevice, Zane peered down the stairs. He saw a tiny point of light moving in his direction. Despite the distance, he could tell it was Katiya. She seemed to be moving slowly, so it would probably take her at least six or eight minutes to get to him. That would allow just enough time to investigate the noise.

Opening his pack, Zane retrieved his night vision visor and secured it over his head. He then set his rifle and backpack against the wall, pulled out his Glock, and took the stairs. As he neared the landing, he could see that the stairwell turned to the left from there, so he hugged that side of the passage as he approached.

Upon arriving at the top, he stopped one step short. Leaning forward, he peered around the corner. The steps rose for about twenty yards before disappearing through a stone archway. Zane stared at the opening for several minutes but saw and heard nothing. Whatever he had heard before must have moved off.

Satisfied it had likely been a small mammal, he returned to the crevice and pulled off his visor. As soon as he stuck his head in the opening, he heard Katiya's voice echo toward him. "Zane?"

"Yes, I'm here."

"Sorry, I think I'm stuck."

He could see she was about three-quarters of the way up, standing in a place he remembered was tight. A triangular rock stuck out into the passage, and the easiest way to get by it was by ducking down.

"Put your things through first, and then—"

"Do you mind helping me?"

"Not at all. I'll be right there."

Zane hated to leave the top unguarded, but how could he refuse that voice?

Sliding into the opening, he moved toward her one step at a time. He was surprised she hadn't been able to figure it out herself. She was relatively thin, so it shouldn't be difficult for her to pass underneath the rock. Then he remembered that some people just didn't function well in tight spaces. Bodies and minds tended to freeze when encountering a phobia.

When Zane neared the light, he looked up then came to an abrupt stop. Katiya was standing on his side of the triangular rock.

So she did make it through.

He tried to look at her face, but her flashlight was aimed down at the steps, shrouding the upper half of her body in darkness.

He stepped closer. "I'm proud of you—"

Before he could finish his sentence, her hand shot out. She grabbed a fistful of his shirt and yanked him toward her. Their bodies were now only a few inches apart, and Zane could see her looking at him, her eyes unblinking and filled with passion.

He reached up to place a hand on her cheek, and she clicked off the light. Their lips found each other in the darkness, pressing together softly at first, then more firmly.

Zane slid an arm around her waist and drew her closer as the kisses became more passionate, even as they were careful not to make any noise. It was the first time he'd felt the warmth of a woman in months, and the feelings he'd developed for Katiya made it all the better.

"Everything okay?" Bennett asked from the radio in Zane's pocket.

The two snickered simultaneously but managed to keep from laughing out loud.

Zane lifted both of his hands and held Katiya's cheeks as he kissed her lightly one last time. As he drew back, she reached up and grabbed his forearms, pulling him back again for another kiss, this one firmer.

"Zane?" Bennett's voice was a bit louder.

As Zane reached for the radio, Katiya playfully pulled on his arms as though she didn't want their embrace to end. Zane smiled at her, and she smiled back, releasing him at the same time.

His body still tingling with warmth, Zane retrieved the radio out of his pocket. "We had a damsel in distress, but I think she's fine now. Go ahead and send the next one on up."

CHAPTER FORTY-FIVE

ZANE'S BODY WAS still glowing as the last of the group emerged from the crevice. But despite the physical and emotional passion, he still had mixed feelings about what had just taken place, at least in terms of the timing. On the one hand, he was glad she had taken the initiative. It had been beyond exhilarating to discover the other side of the woman he already admired for her impressive intellect. It also cleared up any doubts he might have had about the subtle flirtation that had taken place before. On the other hand, the timing couldn't have been worse. Instead of focusing on what lay ahead, he was having flashbacks of the embrace in the tight space.

"Eleven," Brett said.

Zane addressed the group in a low tone of voice, his voice echoing off the stone walls. "Everybody listen up. As you can see, there's a landing just head, followed by another short flight of steps."

After shouldering his pack and rifle, Zane clicked on his

light and took the steps. Bennett was already way out in front, sweeping his beam back and forth. A few minutes later, they stood on the first landing. The soldier was using his powerful light to examine the archway at the top of the next flight.

"It's tough to tell anything from here," the Green Beret said. "But it does look clear."

Zane nodded, and the two climbed the steps. After cautiously passing through the doorway, they realized they were on another landing. A third flight of stairs rose to the left, taking them back toward the exterior of the mountain. At the top was yet another stone archway.

Bennett trained his beam toward the opening. "All clear."

The two climbed the stairs and then stepped out into a stone corridor.

As the others arrived and spilled out into the passage, Zane used his light to get their bearings. The corridor curved out of sight in both directions, apparently following the circumference of the mountain.

"This is incredible," Amanda said, running her hand along one of the walls. "The stone work here is even more precise than what we've seen already."

Katiya directed her light toward the floor, then the walls. "I think this place is occupied."

"Why do you think that?" Jorge asked.

"There're no cobwebs anywhere," she replied. "No dirt or gravel along the floor. I wouldn't say we're in a high-traffic area, but at the same time, you can tell it's been used fairly regularly."

Bennett nudged Zane and pointed at the floor with his

rifle. "Looks like the floor goes upward in that direction."

Zane nodded. "Then that's our route. I want to check the top of the mountain before anything else."

"Roger that."

Zane addressed the group, his voice barely a whisper. "We're going up and are hoping that it will take us to the summit. As before, Sergeant Bennett and I will lead. Sergeant Tocchet will bring up the rear. As Dr. Mills said, this place may be occupied, so keep your eyes and ears open." He paused for a moment then said, "And one other thing: be prepared to kill your lights if I ask you to."

Zane turned and moved down the passage with Bennett. The soldier was using the light mounted on his M4 to clear the area ahead as they rounded each turn. As Zane had guessed, the passage seemed roughly to follow the circumference of the mountain.

After traversing the tunnel for about twenty minutes, Bennett slowed and trained his beam on something directly ahead. When Zane caught up, he realized what had drawn the soldier's attention. Just ahead, the passage narrowed considerably, running between two giant slabs of rock that converged on each side. It was hard to tell if it was another cave-in or a natural formation.

The two approached and aimed their beams into the gap.

"It looks like this section hasn't been used in a while, that's for sure," Bennett said.

More lights illuminated the rock as the others arrived.

"Uh-oh," Brett said. "Not good."

Bennett stepped into the narrow space between the two

boulders. "Well, I think we found what we were looking for."

Zane stood next to him and peered down the gap. There, on the other end, was a wall of vines and leaves.

"What is it?" Katiya said from behind him.

"I think we just reached the summit," Zane replied. He turned to Bennett, who was backing out. "Give me your blade."

The soldier yanked the machete out of the scabbard at his belt and handed it to Zane.

"Let's see where this leads," Zane said, stepping into the gap.

"Wait!" Amanda shouted.

Zane turned and looked at her.

"Those are vines," she said, pointing at the plants. The implication was clear.

Katiya stepped closer and squinted. "You should be fine," she said finally. "That's a different species. The leaves look totally different."

"Guess it doesn't like heights," Brett quipped.

Zane turned back toward Bennett. "Keep me covered just in case."

"Roger that." The soldier gripped his rifle more tightly.

Zane grimaced as he moved down the gap between the rocks. It was even narrower than the crevice they'd encountered below.

After finally reaching the far end, he lifted the machete and began slashing through the curtain of vines. After a few cuts, he paused to see if the plants showed any signs of movement. Seeing nothing, he continued to hack his way through, stepping forward as each layer fell at his feet.

A minute later, he stepped through the remaining vines and found himself under the stars. He drew his Glock and surveyed the area. He heard the sounds of the jungle, but nothing moved.

He retrieved his radio and said, "All clear. Let's keep the lights off from this point forward."

"Roger that," Bennett replied.

As the others started to come through the gap, Zane used the time to look around. The silhouettes of towering trees rose up on all sides. The summit seemed to be covered by the rainforest.

After taking a few steps, Zane suddenly looked toward his feet. He was standing on a slope that ran down toward the center of the summit. That meant the mountaintop was shaped like a bowl, not flat as he'd imagined.

Zane felt a hand on his shoulder. Katiya had come up behind him, but her eyes were trained on the sky. "Absolutely gorgeous. It's been a really long time since I've seen the stars without light pollution."

"I think I could get used to this." He slid a hand around her waist and enjoyed the moment. A few seconds later, he nodded at the trees. "Unfortunately, it looks like our search isn't going to be as easy as I thought it would be."

There was a rustling behind them, so Zane removed his hand and turned. Max was pushing his way through the remaining vines. The linguist gave them both a strange look then averted his eyes.

Had he seen the hand?

Thankfully, Amanda and Brett pushed through right behind him, relieving the awkwardness.

"Wow, not what I expected," Amanda said as she looked up at the trees.

A few minutes later, the entire group stood in the clearing. Tocchet, the last man through, walked down the slope with Bennett to make sure the area was clear.

"This mountain may not have much elevation, but its circumference is unbelievably large," Brett said. "How are we going to handle this? It might take all night to search all this acreage."

"As you may have noticed, the summit is concave." Zane pointed down the slope with his rifle. "If something is up here, my guess is that it's on the valley floor."

Brett nodded. "Sounds reasonable."

"Sir!" came a shout from below.

Zane saw Tocchet standing at the edge of the forest, waving them down. After they arrived, he briefly turned on his light and shone it on a path that wound down through the undergrowth. He clicked the light off again then said, "Looks like an animal trail."

Zane nodded. "Hopefully it will take us all the way to the bottom. Remember, no lights."

Before leaving, Zane stepped over to one of the trees that stood at the head of the trail. He drew his machete and hacked out several large hunks, marking the spot.

"Okay, let's go," he said.

After a quarter mile, Zane brought the group to a stop. The forest thinned just ahead, transitioning to a clearing. He lifted his visor and whispered, "Things open up down there. I'm not sure what that means, but Sergeant Bennett and I will approach first and make sure everything is clear."

Zane flipped his visor down again. He and Bennett crept forward, setting up behind two trees at the edge of the clearing.

Zane couldn't help but notice the sky again. The arc of the Milky Way rose up into the heavens, glittering in shades of gold and lavender. The stars were so vivid that they seemed only a few miles away.

Bennett looked downhill with his binoculars. "It looks like the clearing ends at a ridge."

Zane drew out his own pair. After adjusting the focus, he could see an outcrop of rock about two hundred yards away. "Got it."

Bennett lowered his binoculars. "Any heat signatures?"

Zane looked in every direction. Several thin orange splashes appeared high in the trees to their left, which he guessed was a family of spider monkeys. "I got nothing, you?"

"No, just a few giant rats scurrying across the clearing."

"Let's call the others down and try to make that ridge. It's probably going to give us a good view of the entire summit."

Zane radioed Tocchet, and moments later the others had joined them. The group then made their way down the slope, hugging the right side of the clearing to reduce exposure.

About ten minutes later, they arrived at the ridge. It was exactly what Zane had hoped for. The massive boulders would give them a clear view of the entire valley.

After clearing the area, the team climbed up on the rocks. Zane lowered onto his stomach and scanned the valley floor with binoculars. Despite the limited visibility, he could see that the bottom was mostly covered by jungle growth.

"What the heck is that?" Bennett asked.

"What?" Zane asked.

Everyone crowded around the Green Beret, trying to see what he was looking at.

He pointed directly down the slope. "The trees. Look toward the trees."

Zane lifted his binoculars again then focused on the tree line about a hundred yards away.

Amanda let out a little gasp. "What is that?"

Zane quickly turned the focus wheel back and forth. When the view finally sharpened, the hairs on his neck stood on end. There, floating in and out of the forest, were balls of light that looked like giant fireflies. There must have been hundreds, if not thousands. Some seemed to drift aimlessly, while others appeared to move with purpose.

Katiya let out a gasp. "I can't believe it. I should've known."

Zane looked at her. "You know what they are?"

She continued to stare through her eyepieces. "They're orbs."

"Orbs?" Amanda asked.

"Yes." Katiya's voice quivered with excitement. "They're always present in places like this."

"Places like what?" Brett asked.

Katiya lowered her binoculars and looked at him. "Places with high levels of extraterrestrial activity. Don't you see? We've found what we're looking for!"

CHAPTER FORTY-SIX

AFTER LEAVING FINAL instructions with Tocchet, Zane led Katiya and Bennett down the slope to conduct surveillance of the valley floor. He had originally indicated that it would only be he and Bennett. However, Katiya then reminded him of his promise to consider taking at least one of the anthropologists with him if there was a reasonable chance of alien contact. With dozens of orbs floating through the trees, it had been hard for the operative to argue against her coming.

Once they arrived at the tree line, they were quickly able to locate another trail, this one narrower than the one before. So many limbs and vines hung over the path that Bennett occasionally had to use his machete to clear the way.

As they descended quietly, Zane looked up toward the canopy. He saw the hint of an orb here and there but nothing like the numbers they'd seen from above. For whatever reason, most were impossible to detect with the naked eye. Something about that bothered him.

"Why can't we see most of them down here?" he

whispered.

"It's normal," she said. "Most orbs can only be seen or recorded through a synthetic lens." She pointed at an orb dancing across the opening in the canopy. "So the fact that we can see even a few tells me these are extremely powerful."

"It's a bit unsettling having them hover over us and yet not being able to see them. Who's to say they aren't some sort of warning system for whatever is down there?"

"That's actually one theory regarding their purpose," Katiya admitted.

After a brief pause, Zane asked, "Do you really think they're connected to an alien presence?"

"First of all, there are many different types of orbs. For example, many of the orbs that show up in pictures are simply the result of flash photography. They appear when the light reflects off of dust and water particles floating in the air. I'm sure you've seen those before." She paused to watch an orb float overhead then continued. "I also believe that some are residue from energy sources. It's why they're often seen around transformers, large batteries, and so on."

"Sounds pretty mundane." He pointed toward the canopy. "What about these?"

"That's what's so exciting. We know these aren't the result of flash photography, nor are there any power transformers nearby."

"So where do they come from?"

She gave Zane a little smile. "Think about it. Wouldn't an alien craft be the ultimate energy source?"

"So you think they're simply bundles of energy from—"

Zane was cut off after almost running into Bennett. The soldier raised a hand in the air then pointed to something ahead. Zane saw that the trail was about to cross another clearing, this one smaller than the last.

The soldier quickly raised his binoculars. After studying the scene for a couple of minutes, he whispered, "I'm going to assume the trail resumes on the other side of the clearing. That means we can either cross it in the open, which will leave us exposed for a couple of minutes, or we can try to skirt it through the jungle."

"Leaving the trail to circle the clearing doesn't seem like a good idea," Zane whispered, stroking his beard. "No telling what we'll have to hack our way through. That might draw more attention than a brief scamper out in the open. Let's set up at the upper edge of the clearing first. If everything looks clear, we'll go straight across."

Bennett nodded, and the three continued down the trail, this time more slowly. Once at the bottom, they crept into a row of ferns at the edge of the clearing. The site not only provided concealment, but it also gave them a panoramic view of the area.

After settling down into the plants, Zane reached to his left around Katiya and tapped Bennett. "Check the left for heat signatures," he whispered. "I'll clear the right."

Zane eased forward a bit, regretfully leaving Katiya's warmth. Pulling aside a large frond, he brought the binoculars up to his night vision visor, which was now pulled down over his eyes. Hundreds of orbs sprang into view, their translucent skin shimmering as they floated across the clearing. *Like phantoms dancing across a ballroom floor*, he thought.

As he continued to watch, he noticed that not all of the orbs were white. A few were pink, and several others even appeared to be a strange shade of chartreuse.

"Had no idea there were girlie orbs," Zane whispered. "Looks like there are colors for every taste."

Katiya gave a little chuckle. "Some think the colors are significant."

"How so?"

"Whites are the most common, so they're believed to possess the smallest amount of energy. The colored ones are—"

"Hold on," Bennett said. "Twelve o'clock, coming up the slope."

Zane slowly moved his binoculars back into place and immediately picked up a flash of orange just below the clearing. He tried to focus on it, but it disappeared behind a tree.

"What is it?" Zane whispered.

"I only had it for a few seconds," Bennett said. "It was too large to be a monkey."

"Where is it?" Katiya's voice was barely audible. "I can't see anything."

"It's behind a tree," Zane replied. "Bennett?"

"Negative. I can't see a thing."

Seconds later, Zane saw a hint of orange on one side of the tree. The figure paused there briefly then stepped out into the open.

Zane's pulse quickened when he realized what he was looking at.

"What is it?" Katiya asked.

"It's a person," Zane whispered.

"More specifically, a female," Bennett added.

"Indigenous?" Katiya asked.

"Negative," Bennett answered. "Doesn't appear to be."

Zane squinted. Bennett was right. It seemed to be a young Caucasian female, slight of frame, with long, straight hair. She stopped periodically and glanced behind her, as though afraid that someone or something might be following her.

"I see her now," Katiya said. "She's coming right toward us."

"And she's picking up speed," Bennett whispered. "I'd estimate she'll be here in less than thirty seconds."

Zane got Bennett's attention and raised a finger to his lips.

The girl was only about twenty yards away now, and he projected that if she stayed on course, she would enter the woods just to his right. That presented a dilemma, particularly if she was being followed. If he let her pass, there was a risk she'd see them and cry out. If he attempted to subdue her, he risked putting all three of them in harm's way if she was armed.

Zane rose slowly to one knee. He had to bring the girl down. They were well concealed, but she would only be a few feet away. That meant there was a very high likelihood that she'd see them. And if she were armed, she might be able to inflict some damage if she acted first.

Zane gave Bennett a signal that he was going to act. The soldier nodded then drew a pistol, indicating he'd provide cover.

Soon the girl was so close that Zane could hear her breathing. It was heavy and erratic, suggesting she was both frightened and fatigued. Where was she going? And who did she think was behind her?

Finally, she reached the top of the clearing and paused a few feet to Zane's right, her head turning slightly in his direction. Could she see him?

Zane couldn't risk waiting any longer. He launched out of the ferns like a leopard pouncing on prey. He hit her with the full force of his weight, carrying them both out into the clearing. Despite tumbling several times, he managed to wrap a hand over her mouth, stifling the scream that he knew was coming.

As they came to a stop, Zane rolled on top, pinning the girl to the ground. She screamed again, but it died against the palm of his hand.

Realizing she might be armed, he pinned one of her wrists with a knee and the other with his free hand. She squirmed and thrashed but soon realized it was in vain.

"Easy, easy," he said.

The sound of his voice seemed to calm her.

"Do you speak English?" Zane asked.

She stared at him for a while then nodded slowly.

Bennett appeared at Zane's side. As he knelt down, the girl's eyes widened at the sight of the gun.

Zane waved him off. "Someone may have been following her. Make sure we don't get ambushed."

"Roger that." Bennett stood and set up a short distance down the hill.

Katiya appeared, kneeling next to Zane. The girl looked at her then back at Zane. She was calmer now, but there was still fear in her eyes.

"If I take my hand off of your mouth, are you going to scream?" he asked.

She shook her head immediately. It was a good sign.

"I can be a nice guy, but I may not be so nice if you scream. Is that understood?"

She nodded, so Zane slowly removed his hand. The girl opened her mouth, but only to gulp in breath. After a few seconds, she said, "Please don't hurt me."

Katiya leaned closer. "We're not going to hurt you, honey."

The girl coughed a few times.

"What is your name?" Katiya asked.

The girl paused for a moment, as though unsure whether she should answer or not. "Rebecca," she finally whispered.

Zane studied her face. It was hard to read her expression in the dim light of the moon, but she seemed to be telling the truth. "What are you doing up here, Rebecca?"

Her eyes began to moisten, and seconds later she burst into tears. "Please don't take me back. Please—"

"We're not going to take you back." Katiya reassured her by rubbing her arm. "We don't even know who you are or where you came from."

Rebecca cried a bit longer. Zane couldn't tell if she was still afraid or if she was shedding tears of relief.

A moment later, she stopped, wiped her eyes, and looked up at him. "I told you who I was. Now who are *you*?"

"I'm Zane, and this is Katiya." Zane eased off of her. As he pulled away, he could see that she was dressed in a long white robe, covered with black and green stains. *Strange garb for a girl lost in the jungle,* he thought.

Rebecca sat up, flexing her hands to get back her circulation. She took several deep breaths, as though trying to calm herself.

Katiya laid a hand on the girl's shoulder. "How do you feel?"

Suddenly Rebecca's breathing grew labored, then she reached out and grabbed both of Katiya's arms. "Please, I beg you... please don't take me back to them."

Katiya found the girl's hands and held them. "Honey, take you back to who? Who are you talking about?"

The girl's eyes moistened again, and she visibly trembled. Her mouth opened, but it was several seconds before the words spilled out. "The ones from the craft... the grays."

CHAPTER FORTY-SEVEN

"LET US KNOW when you're ready to talk," Katiya said as she rubbed the girl's leg.

It had taken them twenty minutes to climb back to the ridge. Amanda gave Rebecca a pair of jeans and a T-shirt since they were approximately the same size. They had already been worn but were a welcome improvement over the loose-fitting robe she'd had on before.

Zane could see the girl better now. Her sallow features and gaunt appearance left no doubt that most or all she'd told them was true.

Rebecca took another long swig from the canteen, her throat rippling as though she hadn't had water in weeks. After finishing, she wiped her mouth with a sleeve and said, "I believe they came to get me two nights ago. It's the third time for me."

Zane saw Katiya and Max exchange a knowing glance.

"Where do you live?" Amanda asked.

Rebecca turned and looked at her for a moment, as though

the answer were hard to remember. "Prescott... Prescott, Arizona."

Katiya nodded as though she had somehow expected the answer. At least, it didn't surprise her.

Rebecca took another swig from the canteen then said, "They first came late last year. I'd been having trouble sleeping... which isn't like me. Normally I sleep like a rock. My roommate often stays up late working, and I never hear her. Ever."

Katiya's brow knit together. "So your roommate was or was not in the house on the night you were taken?"

"No, she wasn't. They seem to know when I'm going to be alone." Rebecca stared at the ground for a moment, lost in her thoughts. "Anyway, I tossed and turned that night, and finally—I think it was well after midnight—I began to drift off. Only it wasn't the way I normally go to sleep."

"How so?" Katiya asked with a frown.

"It was strange, almost like I'd been drugged."

Katiya looked at Max and mouthed something that looked like *telepathy*.

"So you went to sleep?" Brett asked.

"Not completely. Right as I was about to, I knew that someone or something was in the room. And then, when I opened my eyes, I saw him... or it... just standing there, watching me with those eyes." She visibly trembled, so Katiya reached over and rubbed her leg again. The small gesture seemed to comfort her. "I know you're going to think I'm crazy, but this person, this creature... it looked almost like the ones in the movies. It had a bulbous head"—she held her hands about a foot apart—"and these large, black eyes like bottomless pits."

"What did their bodies look like?" Katiya asked.

"Thin, but you get the impression they're not weak."

"And did they pull you out by force?"

Rebecca shook her head. "No. I couldn't move, so they didn't have to force me to do anything. I tried to scream, but I couldn't even open my mouth."

"Highly advanced telepathic powers," Katiya whispered.

"So how did they get you out?" Amanda asked.

"I just floated. I know that sounds crazy, but it's true. They had the window open, and about the time I passed through it, I just blacked out." Rebecca's eyes moistened at the memory.

"I know this is difficult, but do you remember anything after that?" Katiya asked.

"A little, but not much. There were times I came to, and when I did, I would soon feel a pinch on my arm, and then I'd pass out again."

Katiya nodded. "It sounds like they were administering something to keep you under."

Rebecca pulled her knees up against her chest and stared out into the jungle. As she rested, Zane wondered how much of what she'd said was true. She seemed like an honest girl, and he doubted she'd purposefully lie, but it was also obvious she'd been heavily sedated. No telling how many drugs were coursing through her veins.

But why else would she be out in the middle of the jungle? The only thing that seemed remotely possible was the sex trade. Maybe she'd been kidnapped at one of the local resorts.

After a long minute of silence, Katiya asked, "So, did you report this first incident to the authorities?"

Rebecca shook her head. "The first two times I thought it was a dream, a really bad nightmare. The three people I shared it with told me I should see a psychologist."

"How did you ever find out it was real?" Max asked.

"A couple of things happened." After taking another sip of water, she said, "After the second abduction, I ran into a neighbor the next day as I got into my car. She asked what was going on the night before, and I asked her what she was talking about. Apparently her dogs had run over to the fence separating our backyards and wouldn't stop barking. She eventually had to go out and pull them back in."

"Did she see anything?" Zane asked.

"Nothing. Not a light. Not anything. She has some pretty thick bushes on her side, and I have a row of trees on mine, so that didn't surprise me. But that's when I started thinking that my dreams might not be dreams after all. I mean, her dogs weren't even the type to bark. And yet, that night they couldn't stop."

Zane ran his fingers though his hair. "You said there were a couple of things. What was the other one?"

"Yes." She trembled briefly but gathered herself. "It was when I got home. I went upstairs to change into something more comfortable, and that's when I saw that my window was shut on my curtain."

Max frowned in confusion. "Why is that so surprising?"

"Because I have allergies and I never open my windows. I'm also big time OCD, so if I ever did, I certainly wouldn't shut it on the curtain." She gave a little chuckle, the first Zane had heard from her.

"So what happened this time?" he asked.

"I was abducted again, and once again they injected me with something. After some period of time, I just woke up."

"Which is what usually happens, right?" Brett asked. "Then they inject you again."

"Normally, yes. But that's the odd thing... this time they didn't. As I lay there, I realized that I was slowly waking up and no one was with me."

Zane sat up straight, his brow furrowed. "Where were you?"

"At the time, I didn't know. All I knew was that I was alone in a room that looked like something out of a science fiction movie. I remember these strange-looking glass panels... and I also remember some instruments on a table a few feet away. They were like nothing I'd ever seen before.

"Anyway, at some point I realized that I could move my limbs. I was still woozy, but I could move. So I got up and made my way out into the corridor. It was dark, with lots of little red lights in the floor. I heard a soft hum, so I figured I was on some kind of ship."

"Then what?" Zane asked.

"I ran down the hall, and before long I entered this room with a high ceiling. That's when I saw a door leading to the outside."

"So you ran out into the jungle?" Katiya asked.

"Before I ran out, I heard voices."

Zane frowned. "Human voices?"

Rebecca shook her head. "Not like any I've ever heard. It was the strangest thing. The language used a lot of clicks and strange sounds that I've never heard before. Even now it gives me the chills."

"I'm surprised you were able to move around so easily," Brett said.

"I felt the same way," Rebecca replied. "It's almost like God was protecting me or something. Those... things... they seemed to be upset about something."

"If you couldn't understand them, how did you know they were upset?" Zane asked.

"Call it gut instinct, sixth sense, whatever. They seemed to be angry, talking over the top of each other. I'd heard snippets before when I came to, and this was different. Very different."

"What then?" Katiya asked.

Rebecca wiped her nose. "This voice inside of me said to run. I'd like to think it was God. So I ran outside and found myself on a ramp. When I got to the bottom, I didn't know what to do."

"Where were you?" Katiya asked.

Rebecca nodded toward the valley floor. "I was in a large clearing. It looked like some sort of airstrip. Once my eyes adjusted, I also saw that I was somewhere in the jungle. At that point, I just froze. Then I heard that inner voice again, telling me to turn left and run. So I ran."

"And that's when you ran into us?" Zane asked.

Rebecca shook her head. "No, sorry... that came later. When I reached the edge of the clearing, I found a path. It's like that voice had led me to it. So I ran down it as fast as I could because I knew it wouldn't be long before they came after me.

"Several minutes later, I came to an opening in the woods, and there in front of me was this huge building."

Katiya and Max visibly stiffened.

"A building?" Brett asked.

Rebecca nodded. "Yes. Not a modern building though. It was an ancient one like you'd see in Greece or something."

Katiya's eyes narrowed. "So, you're saying this building is right down the slope from where we are now?"

Rebecca nodded and pointed down the hill and to the right. "Something about the place scared me, but at the same time, I heard that voice again, telling me to hide there." She took another swig of water then continued. "There were these big steps leading up the front, so I ran up to the top and entered. I knew those creatures would be there soon, so I started frantically looking for a place to hide. Eventually I found some steps leading to a basement, and as I went down, I noticed these large cracks in the stone walls, so I squeezed into one and backed up as far as I could go."

"Did the beings eventually come?" Brett asked.

"They came so fast it scared me. About a minute or two after I settled in, I could hear those clicking sounds, and I knew they were in the main room right above me. One eventually came down the stairs, walking right past the very place where I was hidden. I could see his shadow darken the opening for a second as he crept by. A minute or two later he came back up, apparently satisfied that I wasn't down there."

"So one of them walked right past you?" Amanda asked.

"You *were* being protected."

Katiya looked at Zane. "It may be that the use of technology has dulled their senses over millions of years."

"Maybe," Zane said. "Although the large eyes might be highly developed, almost like some of those animals that live in caverns."

"I think it's to overcompensate for a poor sense of smell and poor sense of hearing."

"And yet they didn't notice me in that crevice," Rebecca pointed out.

"What happened next?" Katiya asked.

"I waited for a few minutes before I moved even an inch. Then, when I went to the opening, I listened for another few minutes before going back up the stairs. I didn't see or hear anything in the building, so I ran down the steps and out into the jungle. Eventually I found myself going up a hill."

Katiya nodded. "And that's when you ran into us."

Rebecca fixed her gaze on Zane. "What about you? I've told you my entire story, and I don't even know who you are." She moved her eyes to Katiya. "Fair is fair."

Zane looked at Katiya first, then Brett. Exhaling audibly, he turned to Rebecca. "We're here to investigate a sound."

"A sound?" Rebecca asked.

"Yes, a sound," Zane said. "One that was picked up by the United States government some time back. They weren't able to classify it and believed it might somehow be related to extraterrestrials."

"Do you think it has something to do with what happened to me?"

Zane nodded. "After listening to your story... it's certainly possible."

"So you work for the government?" she asked.

After a short pause, Zane said, "We all come from different fields and work for different people, but yes, the government asked us to come here to look into the matter."

Rebecca turned and looked down into the valley. "This all seems so surreal."

"You got that right," Brett said.

There was a long moment of silence. Finally, Zane grabbed the girl's arm. "Rebecca, you told us about an airstrip and an old building. Can you point to where those are?"

"They're both at the bottom of the valley. The clearing and the craft were over that way," she said, pointing toward the left. Then she gestured to the right. "But the temple was more that way."

"How far was it from one to the other?" Zane asked.

Rebecca shrugged. "Hard to say." Suddenly she looked back at him. "What a minute... you aren't going down there, are you?"

"Don't worry," Zane said. "I'm going to leave a couple of our people with you."

"No! I don't want to be left alone again."

"You will have someone here with you. I'm afraid we have to finish what we came here to do. We have to find out what's going on."

Rebecca sat up straight. "Then I want to go with you."

"I really don't think—"

"No, I have to go." Her eyes flitted around from one

person to the next. "I think we all know this is no coincidence. We were brought together for a reason. If I'm with you, then I can do a lot more than just point. I can take you exactly where you want to go."

Zane slowly lifted his radio. "How are we looking on the perimeter?"

"All clear, sir." It was Bennett. "No sign of hostiles. A few animals, but that's about it."

"Same here," said Tocchet. "All clear on my side."

As Zane lowered the radio, Katiya said, "I think we'll all be safer if we stick together."

Zane exhaled audibly then nodded in agreement. "I think you're probably right."

CHAPTER FORTY-EIGHT

COLONEL ZHENG LEE could see all the way to the valley floor from his position atop the flat boulder. The Americans had occupied this very spot just twenty minutes earlier, and Zheng could still smell their lingering scent.

Thankfully the mole had been able to send out a message earlier, warning them of the carnivorous plant that guarded the ravine. A few well-placed bombs and a bevy of grenades had cleared a path to the entrance, allowing them to march through. Zheng had lost two men to the plant, but that was the cost of war. He still had a dozen soldiers left, more than enough to finish the job.

Zheng lifted a pair of thermal imaging binoculars and trained them on the slope below. He was still unable to pick up any heat signatures. He lowered the glasses and kicked First Lieutenant Shi, who was lying prone next to him. "What do you see?"

Shi looked up from his high-powered scope. "They're almost at the valley floor."

"Excellent," Zheng said. *That's obviously been their destination all along.*

Suddenly Shi muttered an oath.

Zheng's head swiveled toward him. "What?"

"They just... disappeared."

The giant Ho, who was sitting on Zheng's right, grunted his disapproval.

Zheng kicked Shi again. "What do you mean they disappeared? People don't just disappear."

"It's difficult to tell from this distance. Something must be blocking my view."

Zheng wasn't overly concerned, at least not yet. So far, following the Americans had been child's play. After exiting the mountain tunnel, Zheng's men had donned special suits that prevented the release of body heat, allowing them to approach to within a hundred meters without being detected by thermal imaging equipment. Just an hour earlier, Zheng had watched as two American soldiers stared right at him, completely oblivious to his presence.

But what if the Americans had just put on their own suits? Maybe they were using them to set up a trap? After all, most countries had this technology. After considering the possibility for a moment, Zheng quickly dismissed it. Their mole would have told them of such a plan, assuming he hadn't been playing them the entire time.

Zheng narrowed his eyes. "Do you see them yet?"

"No, not yet."

"What do you think is blocking the view?"

Shi shrugged. "Buildings, rocks, another ridge perhaps."

Zheng wondered what was so special about this mountaintop. The last transmission from the mole had been brief and hadn't contained much information. Only that they had exited the tunnel and were going to check the summit.

Shi made a little noise. Zheng looked down at him. "What is it?"

"I'm getting a few flashes of heat again." He continued to turn the focus wheel. "It's hard to say what's going on. I see walls... it looks like they're walking through some sort of village."

Zheng's pulse quickened. "Get up." He kicked Shi a third time for good measure then turned toward the others spread along the ridge. "Get ready to depart."

Ho stood, his massive frame momentarily blotting out the moon. He looked at Zheng, his face showing the hint of a smile. "We kill them now?"

Zheng nodded. "Yes, we're going to kill them now."

As Zheng turned to walk away, Ho grabbed his shoulder roughly. The colonel cringed. If any other soldier had done that, he would have killed them on the spot. But this was Ho, so he bit his tongue.

"Let me have the long-haired one, the leader," Ho said.

Zheng hesitated. He had wanted to fire that shot himself, but how could he deny Ho the pleasure? It's what the brute had been trained for. "You must promise me one thing."

"Promise you what?" Ho asked.

"If you get the opportunity, make him suffer first."

Ho smiled.

CHAPTER FORTY-NINE

BY THE TIME the group reached the clearing where Rebecca had been found, a thick fog had settled over the jungle. It seemed to have appeared out of nowhere, billowing through the trees like some vaporized serpent intent on slowing their progress.

As they reentered the forest, Katiya used her binoculars to scan the canopy above. She was startled at the sight that met her eyes. Not only were the orbs more numerous than before, but most seemed to have gathered over the group. Was that a coincidence or was there some dark purpose? Thus far they seemed benevolent, so she decided not to raise the alarm.

About twenty minutes later, Zane slowed at a fork in the path. The primary trail continued down the slope, while a narrower branch led off to the left.

As had already been planned, the group divided into two teams. Zane, Bennett, Brett, and Jorge would take the pathway to the left. Rebecca said the alien craft was situated at the north end of the clearing, so they would travel in that direction and approach from above. Tocchet would then lead the others in search of the temple where Rebecca had hidden earlier that evening. For her part, Katiya was happy she was going to be a part of the group examining the building, as she had a feeling it had great significance.

After giving a few final instructions, Zane led his team off into the fog. Once they were out of sight, Tocchet reminded everyone to avoid using their lights then led them straight down the slope.

A few minutes later, the slope leveled off, and they found themselves standing in the large clearing Rebecca had described. But instead of walking on a path of clay and rocks, their feet now rested on short grass. As everyone spilled out, Katiya tried to take in her surroundings. The fog was thicker than ever, but she still sensed that the area they were standing in was quite large, perhaps the size of several football fields.

Tocchet looked at Rebecca. "Can you get us there from here?"

"I believe so."

With a surprising boldness, she led them south along the right side of the clearing. When they arrived at the end, she turned to the left along the southern edge. "The trail should be somewhere along in here," Rebecca whispered as they crept through the fog.

Katiya thought it odd that the clearing had such a distinct shape. It seemed like a perfect rectangle, at least the portion she'd seen so far. Perhaps the girl had been right about it being some sort of airstrip.

"Look," Artur said, pointing to a gap between two trees.

Tocchet turned on his light briefly, illuminating a trail that disappeared into the jungle.

"That's it," Rebecca exclaimed.

As they entered, a knot developed in Katiya's stomach. Was it just a case of nerves? Or was her body trying to warn her that all was not well? She tried to brush it off. They were here, and they certainly weren't going to turn back now. The strange feeling was likely just the jitters that came with being on the verge of something so big, and nothing else.

A few minutes later, Rebecca stopped and pointed. "I recognize that line of trees. The building should be just ahead."

"Remember, no lights just yet," Tocchet whispered.

As they passed underneath the trees, the silhouette of a large building appeared, an eerie sentinel rising out of the fog. Katiya stared in awe. It was much larger than she'd imagined.

"Good grief," Amanda said in a low voice.

A large stone staircase ran up the front. It reminded Katiya of the stairs at the front of a museum. At the top, she could see a line of pillars encircling the structure. Although hard to see, the roof appeared to be a dome.

"Definitely not Mayan or Incan," Amanda whispered.

Tocchet took the steps, and the others followed.

Katiya turned to Max, who was on her right. "What do you think?"

He shook his head in disbelief. "Totally out of place."

"I was just thinking the same thing. I've never seen anything quite like this in Brazil, Peru... anywhere."

Amanda fell in next to them. "You're right. Look at the

dome. It shouldn't be here. Even the columns seem out of place."

When the team arrived at the top, Katiya noticed that the fog was a bit thinner, allowing her to take in more detail. They were standing on a walkway that wrapped around the building.

After making sure the area was clear, Tocchet motioned for them to follow him inside.

Before joining the others, Katiya stole a quick glance back toward the trees. The fog was so thick along the ground that she couldn't see the trail anymore. The knot in her stomach grew tighter.

The building's interior was massive, even larger than it looked from the outside. Several structures lay directly ahead, although Katiya couldn't yet tell what they were.

As the group moved forward into the space, Amanda tilted her head back. Katiya followed her gaze and noted the domed ceiling rising high above them. Something appeared to be painted on its surface.

Tocchet turned on his light, so the others followed suit. Someone let out a little gasp.

As Katiya turned, chill bumps spread across both of her arms. Rows of statues rose up in front of them. As best she could tell, they extended all the way to the back of the room.

"Good heavens," Max said.

Katiya clicked on her flashlight and approached the closest one. The nude figure of a man stood on a square stone base. He was handsome and muscular, and yet something about his face gave her the chills.

Max came and stood at her side. "Go down lower again. I

thought I saw something on the base."

Katiya moved the beam back down until she saw what he was referring to. There, in the center of the base, was a plate set into one of the stones.

Max stepped closer, a frown spreading over his face. "It looks like bronze," he said. "No ancient South American culture used anything like this."

"It looks like there's something written on it," Katiya said. "Can you read it?"

"No, most of it's too worn."

Amanda and Tocchet suddenly appeared at Katiya's side. Amanda stared at the plate. "I don't think those letters are worn. I think they're just covered with dust and dirt."

Max looked back at her. "You sure?"

"Let's find out," Tocchet said. He walked over and set his rifle up against the stone base. Then he cupped his hands and stooped down. "Get on."

Max nodded then gingerly stepped into the soldier's hands.

"Careful," Katiya said as Tocchet lifted him into the air.

"Much better." Max pulled a rag from his pocket and used it to wipe the bronze surface. Decades of dirt and dust floated into the air like flakes in a snow globe. After wiping for a few more seconds, he stopped and leaned closer. "It looks like we have five lines. Each line is written in a different language." Suddenly his eyes narrowed.

"What is it?" Katiya asked.

He shook his head. "Just strange... the top two lines contain characters I've never seen before."

Katiya could scarcely believe what she'd just heard.

Maxwell Cameron was one of the world's foremost linguists. Even if he couldn't read a certain language, he would at least recognize its letters.

"Each line is short," Amanda said. "Maybe it's a name repeated in five languages."

Max ran his finger to the bottom. "I think you're right. The first line uses our alphabet."

"What does it say?" Katiya asked.

"It's a little worn, but looks like Az... Aza... Azaral... or Azarel." After staring for a bit longer, he said, "That fifth letter is an *e* if I'm not mistaken."

"Azarel?" Katiya asked.

"Yes, Azarel."

A confused look spread across Amanda's face. "Azarel... why does that name sound familiar?"

"You recognize it?" Katiya asked.

"I'm pretty sure I've heard it before."

"I also see the same name repeated in Greek and Hebrew," Max said as Tocchet lowered him down again.

Hebrew? The whole thing is growing more bizarre by the minute, Katiya thought.

"Azarel," Amanda whispered as she wandered to the next statue.

Katiya paused to take a couple of flash pictures of the statue and its base. Whoever Azarel was, his face unsettled her. He had a malevolent expression, and his features didn't even remotely resemble the indigenous people of Central and South America.

As the others fanned out to explore on their own, Katiya

walked through the rows, bouncing her beam back and forth. At the foot of each statue were various sculpted objects: swords, knives, necklaces, jewels, and sometimes food. She guessed that the items were somehow related to each figure.

Suddenly, something at the back of the room drew her attention, bringing her to a stop.

What is that?

It was a statue, but it stood at least twenty or thirty feet taller than the others. The towering effigy was likely someone of great importance. A political or military leader, perhaps.

When she arrived, she found a squat stone structure in front of the statue. As best she could tell, it was some form of altar. Adding weight to her supposition, there were dark splotches sprinkled across its surface. *Blood,* she thought.

Who are you and why would people sacrifice to you?

Stepping past, Katiya directed her beam at the statue. It was a soot-black effigy of a man. She moved the light up to his head. His demeanor was chilling. Bushy eyebrows sloped downward toward the top of the nose, producing a menacing stare. His nose was long and pointed, almost like a beak. It was one of the most evil-looking faces she'd ever seen.

"Good grief, that's creepy," she muttered.

"I'll say," replied a deep voice behind her.

Katiya jumped and let out a little gasp. "Max, don't do that!"

"I saw you running back here and knew it had to be something important."

"Please don't do that again… especially not in here."

Max looked up at the statue. "You're right, that is one

nasty-looking dude."

"It has another one of those plates," Katiya said with a frown.

"And once again there are five lines. Unfortunately, it's even higher up than the first one." Max moved over to the base. "Let's try something. Keep your beam on it for a sec." Tucking his flashlight into his belt, he lifted his binoculars and focused them on the script high above. "There, got it. No dust and dirt this time."

Katiya wondered if that was significant.

"What does it say?"

"I'm going to look at the bottom line again." Katiya could see him turning the focus wheel. Finally, he said, "Looks like this one is Sem... Semyaza."

The name sounded oddly familiar to her. Where had she heard it? Amanda had recognized the first name, and now she recognized this one. That likely meant the statues represented important historical figures. But who were they and what era were they from?

Max turned and seemed to notice the altar for the first time. He approached and used a fingernail to scratch at a dark blotch on one of the stones. "I think we both know what went on here." He lifted his finger and smelled it.

"Sorry, but I think after hundreds of years it's probably lost its smell."

He shrugged. "Thought I'd give it a try. Wouldn't surprise me if the indigenous still come here and use this place for something, even though they didn't build it."

"I doubt it. I think they're frightened of this mountain."

"So frightened they attacked one of our teams at its base? We know at least one tribe lives in the crater. And based on what we know about them, it wouldn't surprise me at all if they used this temple."

"Then what is the connection to these guys?" Katiya turned and looked at the statue again. "Who are they?"

Someone spoke from behind them. "I think I know."

Katiya and Max turned to find Amanda walking toward them. She directed her light toward the statue's face. "Let me guess, that's Semyaza?"

Max's eyes widened. "How did you know that?"

"Because I finally figured out who they are... *all* of them."

Max gave her a skeptical frown. "So, who are they? Tell us."

"Fallen angels," Amanda said.

Katiya snapped her fingers. "Of course, the watchers... the fallen ones."

Max frowned. "Who?"

"The fallen angels from the sixth chapter of Genesis."

Max tilted his head slightly. "I'm familiar with the biblical account, but I don't recall any names being assigned to the fallen angels."

"That's because the names aren't given in the Bible," Amanda said. "They're given in the Book of Enoch. Genesis gives us an overview of what happened, but it's the Book of Enoch that fills in all the details. For example, it tells us that when the angels first fell, they descended upon Mount Hermon."

Katiya nodded. "There's the mountains and portals

connection again."

Max folded his arms and leaned back against the altar. "So we know the names from the Book of Enoch. All right, fine. But why are they here? How would an ancient tribe of northern Brazil even know of their existence? Something doesn't make sense."

"That's a good question, and I think I have the answer." Amanda paced for a moment then looked up at him. "Let's back up for a second. When the bad angels fell to earth, the Bible says they found the women attractive and had relations with them. Those unions produced offspring known as the Nephilim."

"The giants," Katiya said.

"Yes, that was the first incursion of giants," Amanda said. "In fact, the polluting of the gene pool was one of the reasons God sent the flood."

Katiya nodded. "That reminds me of something. Both the Mayans and the Aztecs have legends that speak of giants roaming the earth in what they call the first age, or the First Sun. Those legends also say that they were all killed by a massive flood. Don't you find it interesting that their story mirrors the biblical account?"

Max looked at Amanda. "So all of the Nephilim were destroyed by the flood?"

"Yes, but unfortunately the angels continued their dark work after the flood, which led to further incursions of Nephilim. Eventually there were thousands, if not tens of thousands, roaming that part of the world."

Max's brow furrowed with skepticism. "Thousands?"

"At least," Amanda said. "Think about all the mentions throughout the Torah and the rest of the Old Testament. People seem to read all the pertinent passages and yet still don't make the connection. Remember what some of the spies said to Moses when they returned from the land of Canaan? They said they found Nephilim there, giants so large that they made the spies feel like grasshoppers. That was after the flood."

Katiya nodded. "And their description takes away any possibility that they were just referring to a few abnormally large men."

"Exactly," Amanda said. "And who doesn't know Goliath? He was a Nephilim, as was Og, king of Bashan."

Max shook his head. "Assuming one believes all these fanciful stories, you still haven't explained why there would be statues of them here in northern Brazil. The whole thing just doesn't add up."

"I'm getting there. God commanded the Israelites to exterminate the Nephilim still in the land after the flood, but most scholars see evidence that many of them escaped, some by land and others by boat. In fact, the historical record confirms that there was a diaspora of giants."

"I find that hard to believe," Max said.

"I can show you the evidence, even though much of it has been covered up," Amanda said. "Giant skeletons, some over fifteen feet tall, have been found across the globe, including many in North America. And all of them seem to date to the diaspora."

Max paced away from the altar, lost in thought. Finally, he looked up and asked, "So you think they came here?"

"Yes, I do," Amanda said. "I believe the Nephilim built this temple to worship the fallen angels." She looked around. "They've long since died off, but clearly something is still going on here."

"I'm not sure I'm completely on board with your fallen angel theory," Katiya said, "but I do see linkage between what happened at Mount Hermon and what happened here.

"I'm going to need to see more evidence before I draw any conclusions," Max said. He looked up at the statue again. "Although I must say it's hard to explain away the names."

Amanda was about to respond, when Katiya held up a hand. "Sorry to interrupt… but where is everybody else? There were lights bouncing around just a few minutes ago. Now the whole place is dark."

Amanda turned toward the front of the room. "Oh, I think Rebecca took them downstairs to that place where she hid before."

"Okay, good," Katiya said. "I was hoping they hadn't wandered outside in that—"

Suddenly a blood-curdling scream cut her off.

It was muffled by stone, but Katiya knew immediately who it was.

CHAPTER FIFTY

"SEE SOMETHING?" ZANE asked.

Bennett had come to a stop and was staring through his binoculars. "I thought it was an outcrop of boulders or rocks, but some of the angles seem too sharp."

"Let's have a look then," Zane said.

As the four moved out from under the cover of the trees, Zane saw what he was referring to, an assortment of stone structures overgrown with bushes and vines. "It looks like the remains of a village."

"It doesn't look like anyone is home," Jorge added.

Bennett looked at Zane as they continued forward. "Should we go down to the clearing or check the village?"

"I say we check the ruins first," Brett said. "Who knows, there may even be a way to get up on one of the structures. If we can, that might give us a view of everything down in the valley."

Bennett looked around as they walked. "The fog has gotten pretty thick. Even if we get a good angle down into the valley,

I doubt we'd be able to see anything."

He was right, the fog was getting thicker by the minute. Then again, why not explore the ruins while they were here? What was left of the ancient town seemed deserted, but it still might yield some useful information. Nothing seemed insignificant on this mountain.

Zane brought them to a stop near the outskirts. "I think Brett's right. If that craft was as big as Rebecca said it was, then we might be able to see it, even through the fog. Besides, I want to have a look around. Who knows what we might find."

"And if it turns out to be a dud, we'll just head down," Brett said.

As they crept forward, Zane realized they were entering the lower end of the village. Most of it spread up the slope to their left. The vast majority of structures were little more than crumbling walls overrun with vines, small trees, and shrubs.

Brett approached one of the walls, pulling aside some of the vines that covered it. He pointed at the stones underneath. "The same construction we saw at the bridge and in the tunnels."

Zane nodded.

"What now?" Jorge asked after pulling an unlit cigar from his mouth.

Zane tapped the ground with the butt of his rifle. "I think this used to be a street." He pointed to the north. "You and Brett follow it through town. Keep your eyes open for anything strange, and see if you can find a building that will give you a good view down the slope." He turned to Bennett. "You and I will do the same on this end."

"Even though it's a long shot, we also need to be looking for any sign of habitation," Brett said.

Zane looked around. "I can't help but think that all of this is somehow connected. The airstrip, these ruins, the temple. If Rebecca's story is true, and I have no reason to doubt it, then why bring her and the other victims here, of all places?"

"It's remote, for one," Brett said.

"True, but there has to be more to it than that." Zane looked at his watch. "Anyway, let's move out. We'll stay in touch by radio. If we get another signal loss, then we'll all meet back here in an hour. No exceptions."

After Brett and Jorge disappeared into the fog, Zane pointed to another road that ran up the slope. "Why don't you head up from here? I'll go down a bit further and do the same."

"Roger that," Bennett said.

As the soldier turned to leave, Zane grabbed his shoulder. "We're going to be spread thin, so please don't take any chances. If you see anything, call me immediately."

Bennett gave him a thumbs-up then moved off.

Zane continued north. After traveling for about a hundred yards, he turned left on a cross street. This part of the village seemed more overgrown than the section before. Trees rose out of the gaps in the ruins, their branches spreading overhead like a giant green awning.

After traveling a short distance up the hill, Zane heard a noise that sounded like a pebble bouncing across stone. Acting instinctively, he moved to the right side of the street, crouching underneath a few limbs overhanging a crumbling wall. He remained perfectly still, his senses on full alert.

The place is probably overrun with animals, he thought.

Hearing no further sounds, he stood and walked on. When he arrived at the next cross street, he turned north but stopped short at the sight of a largely intact two-story building on the right. If he could get to the second story, it might afford him a view of the entire area.

He got down on one knee, looking for any sign of activity. Seeing none, he rose and sprinted the remaining distance. As he drew near, he saw a doorway on the side of the building facing an alley and crouched outside it. He heard a noise in the street. It sounded like it came from where he had just been, but the fog was too thick to see.

Zane waited a full two minutes. Hearing nothing further, he ducked inside and found himself standing in a hallway that ran parallel to the street. The walls were made of stone, with rooms opening on either side. Lifting his rifle, Zane walked down the corridor, clearing each room as he went. When he arrived at the other end, he discovered a stairwell on the left.

Just where I thought you'd be.

His radio crackled in his pocket.

He pulled it out just as Bennett spoke. "Zane?"

"I'm here. Over."

"Do you see what I see?"

"Negative. I'm inside a building right now."

"Can you get up off the ground?"

"There's a second story, yes."

"Get as high as you can and look east."

"Copy that. Give me a minute."

Zane moved up the stairs cautiously, pausing twice to listen for any further sounds. Seconds later, he emerged onto what was left of the second floor. There was no roof, and the night sky opened up above him. Most of the walls still remained, although many had crumbled to a fraction of their original height.

Lifting his weapon, Zane made his way down the central corridor, eventually turning left into the second room facing east. Once inside, he crossed to the window.

He lifted his radio again. "Okay, I'm here."

There was a brief pause before Bennett's voice came through the speaker. "Are you facing east?"

"Yes, I've got a nice view down into the valley."

"No, look up," Bennett said. "Ten or eleven o'clock."

It took Zane only a moment to see what the soldier was referring to. A set of lights shone in the distance, moving toward the summit.

"Is that a plane?" Zane whispered.

"Don't think so. Too low. No noise."

He was right. The large craft was now only a few miles away. At that distance, he should already hear the whine of the engines.

The operative raised his binoculars, propping his elbows on the sill. It took him a moment to locate the craft again, but when he did, the only thing he could see was a thin line of oddly colored lights. A moment later, the craft banked to its left as it crossed over the summit. As it did, Zane caught a glimpse of its body. It was dark and triangular, like a stealth fighter and yet much more massive.

Zane's pulse quickened. He'd seen almost everything in the combat fleet of the US Air Force, including all classified aircraft, but he'd never seen anything like this.

The craft reduced speed as it continued south over the clearing. When it reached the midpoint of the strip, it slowed even further, so slow that it appeared to be hovering. "I guess we can dismiss any idea of this being a stealth fighter," he said. "We don't have anything that can do that."

"Not unless they've been hiding something from us," Bennett said.

"I don't think so. I've seen just about everything they have, including everything currently under development. We have stealth fighters that can fly in relative silence, but we don't have anything that can fly in complete silence. Nor can any of them hover." Zane suddenly remembered who might know more about that technology than him. "Brett, can you hear us?"

After a long pause, Brett spoke, but his voice was distorted. "Yes... hear..."

"What's your position? Can you see the craft?"

"Yes... trees along strip... move out into the open... better look."

Zane frowned. Had they already moved down into the clearing? "Are you at the valley floor?"

He thought he heard a "no," but couldn't be sure.

"Stay put."

"What is that?" Bennett asked.

Zane looked up and saw that the craft was now entering a patch of fog. When it came out on the other side, the hairs on his neck stood on end. A slender blue beam of light shone from the craft, panning back and forth. "Good grief. I have no idea."

"The beam is too thin to provide much illumination, so I'm thinking it's some sort of probe. Maybe it's gathering data."

As Zane watched, the craft and the blue light suddenly disappeared. He raised his binoculars, but nothing was there. "Can you still see it?"

"Negative. Right before it went dark, the probe seemed to extend toward the south, like it was looking for something."

"Its last position bothers me," Zane said. He made an adjustment to the radio's settings and spoke again. "Tocchet, do you read? Over."

Silence. Zane tried again, but still, no response.

"Try a different channel," Bennett said. "They're a ways off."

"I did, but I'll try another." Zane adjusted the setting again. "Tocchet, do you read? Over."

This time a long burst of heavy static issued from the radio. Strangely, it sounded like a female voice, but it was too garbled to understand.

"Katiya, is that you?" He listened intently, but this time it was even harder to hear. *Maybe she can hear me even though I can't hear her.* Zane pressed the mic against his mouth. "Katiya, this is Zane. I can't hear you, but if you can hear me, then listen closely. Hold your position, and we will come to you. I repeat, hold your position, and we will come to you. Do you understand?"

There was a long moment of silence, followed by a brief crackle he thought might have been a "yes."

As Zane was about to speak again, he heard a noise behind him. He retrieved his rifle and heard it again. Someone was moving up the stairs.

CHAPTER FIFTY-ONE

"DID YOU SEE where they went down?" Katiya asked as the three ran toward the front of the temple.

Amanda turned left down one of the rows. "I think they were over here."

Seconds later, they arrived at the wall. The three sucked in breath as they played their beams around the area.

"Rebecca!" Amanda shouted.

"Down here," said a muffled voice.

"Over there!" Max pointed to a half-wall of stone block.

Katiya arrived first. There was a set of stairs behind the half-wall. She aimed her flashlight down into the darkness. "Rebecca, are you there?"

"Yes." This time it was a male voice that sounded like Artur's. "Get down here, quick."

Katiya scrambled down the stairs, followed by Amanda and Max. When she arrived at the bottom, she stepped out into a dark room. Two silhouettes stood a short distance away, holding flashlights. One of them turned toward her and said,

"Watch your step." It was Artur.

Katiya played her beam toward something on the floor then froze at the sight that met her eyes. Piles of bones were strewn across the floor. Rib cages, skulls, femurs, tibias, fibulas.

Amanda let out a little gasp when she saw what was littered at her feet.

"Sorry, I didn't mean to scare you," Rebecca said. "I'm just a bit fragile right now."

"Don't apologize," Katiya said as she walked farther out into the room. "Most people wouldn't even have the guts to come back here."

"It looks like some sort of burial chamber," Artur said.

Katiya frowned as her eyes caught something a few feet away. She walked toward it and crouched. A chill swept over her body as she realized she was looking at the largest human skull she'd ever seen. But what made it even stranger was its elongated shape. She picked it up then stood.

"Oh my!" Amanda walked over for a closer look. "It... it looks like..."

"An alien?" Katiya asked as she turned it back and forth in the light. "Certainly looks like the Hollywood version, doesn't it?"

Max shook his head. "As exciting as that would be, I'm afraid that's a simple case of cradle boarding."

"Cradle boarding?" Rebecca asked.

"Many of the ancient tribes of Central and South America practiced cranial deformation with the use of boards," he explained.

"He's right, it was a common practice," Katiya said, "but

I'm not so sure that's what this is."

Max gave her a scowl. "What do you mean? Of course it is."

"To me, it just seems too large. Cradle boarding flattens the skull, but it doesn't increase the surface area." She tapped the top with a finger. "Take a look at this."

Max stepped closer. After examining it, he shrugged. "What?"

"It has only one parietal bone. Usually there are two, divided by a suture."

"Probably just an anomaly," Max said.

As the linguist walked away to look at another bone, Amanda turned to Katiya and whispered, "What do you think it is?"

"Obviously I can't be dogmatic about this," Katiya admitted, "but I can't help but think about what happened to Rebecca not far from here."

Amanda's brow furrowed immediately. "I'm not sure I follow."

Katiya glanced around to make sure no one was close by. "Based on my experience, these abductions usually relate to reproductive experimentation." She held up the skull again. "I think we could be looking at genetic manipulation."

Amanda's eyes widened. "That would certainly explain the odd shape."

"I think it's possible. But I also think something else is going on." Katiya squatted and panned her beam around. "I saw something just a moment ago. Ah, there it is." She grasped another skull and stood up. "Now look at this one."

Amanda frowned. "What on earth is that?"

"I'm not sure, but I think it's a goat."

"And what does that have to do with anything?

"Did you see the altar upstairs?"

Amanda nodded.

"One of the floor stones in front of it caught my eye. It was square, and a gap ran around all four sides. I'd be willing to bet that if you pried it up, you'd find a chute that connects to this chamber. This could very well be—"

Suddenly she was cut off by the sound of static.

"Your radio," Amanda said.

Katiya reached into her pocket and pulled it out. A scratchy voice was already speaking. "Tocchet, do you read? Over."

"Zane," Amanda said.

Katiya held the radio up to her mouth. "Zane? Zane, can you hear me?"

The operative's voice came through in broken pieces. "Katiya, this is Zane... hear you... come... understand?"

"Zane?"

There was another burst of loud static, then the radio went silent.

Max walked over. "Sergeant Tocchet has a radio. Maybe he was able to hear what he said."

"Wait a minute." Katiya frowned as she directed her flashlight around the room. "Where is he?"

"Where is who?" Amanda asked.

"Sergeant Tocchet. He's not here."

"Isn't he still upstairs?" Artur asked.

Amanda frowned. "I thought I saw him entering the

stairwell with you and Rebecca."

"Not that I remember," Artur said.

"Strange," Katiya whispered. "Maybe he is still upstairs."

"Zane seemed to be telling us something was wrong," Amanda said. "We need to find a way to get in touch with them."

"I didn't hear him say anything was wrong," Max said. "What makes you think that?"

"It wasn't what he said, it was how he said it. There was urgency in his voice. Something is definitely wrong."

"I think she's right," Katiya said. "And now we don't know where Sergeant Tocchet is either. As much as I'd like to stay and sort through some of these bones, we need to get out of here and figure out what's going on."

"Let's go," Artur said. "If we make contact and find out everything is okay, then we'll come back."

As the group moved toward the stairs, Katiya hesitated. Something bothered her. She was forgetting something.

The skull.

She had wanted to take the skull with her. At some point, they could perform DNA analysis and determine what it was. It might hold the key to whatever was going on in this place.

Panning her light around, she finally spotted it near her feet, leaning against a rib cage. Squatting, she set down her radio and her light. Then she rearranged a few items in her pack and stuffed the skull inside.

"Katiya, let's go!" Amanda said from the steps.

"Coming."

She wasn't able to zip the pack completely shut, but it

would have to do. After slinging it over her shoulder, she grabbed the light and ran over to the stairs. Amanda was waiting for her, and the two went up together.

The others were already looking for Tocchet when they reached the top. Artur shouted his name several times, but there was no response. Katiya sensed something was wrong. Why would a trained Green Beret just disappear? Maybe he was investigating something on his own.

She turned to the others. "Let's check outside."

Amanda looked at her. "Shouldn't we keep looking up here first?"

"He's not here," Katiya said firmly. "He must have gotten the message to go back."

"So he just left us?" Amanda asked.

"I don't think he knew we were downstairs. He probably thinks we're already on our way."

"She's right," Max said. "If he were here, he would've heard us shouting."

"I'm certain he's out on the trail waiting for us," Katiya said.

Amanda nodded reluctantly as Katiya led them outside. As they took the stairs down, Katiya noticed that the fog was even thicker now. She frowned. Would they even be able to find the trail?

After reaching the bottom, Max looked at her. "Why don't you try him on the radio? The signal may have been blocked in the basement."

Katiya reached into her pocket, then a frown spread across her face. She shook her head and placed a palm on her forehead.

"What?" Max asked.

"I set my radio down when I picked up the skull. It's still inside." She looked back toward the temple, frustration written on her face. "I'll go back in and get it. The rest of you find the trail and get going."

Max shook his head. "You can't just go back in there by yourself."

"I can, and I am," Katiya said. "Look, we have to have a way to communicate with them once we get back to the clearing. Besides, you're probably going to find Landon waiting on the trail."

"I'll go with you," he said.

Katiya shook her head. "This is going to take five minutes, tops. I need you to find the trail."

Max glared at her but said nothing.

"I'll catch up with you at the airstrip," she said, turning back toward the temple. "Promise."

Without waiting for an answer, she sprinted up the steps. After arriving at the top, she took a quick glance behind her. All she could see now was fog.

Good.

As she walked toward the entrance, Katiya's thoughts turned to Tocchet. Where had he gone? She'd expected him to be outside, within earshot. Despite what she'd told the others, it didn't make sense that he'd just leave after getting a message from Zane to come back, assuming that's even what Zane said. A Green Beret would never abandon his team.

Katiya slowed her pace as she entered the room of statues.

It seemed darker, more foreboding than before. It was one thing to be in such a creepy place with other people all around you. It was another thing altogether to come by yourself. Maybe she should have taken Max up on his offer. Artur and Amanda could have found the trail just fine without him. But it was too late now.

After finding the stairs, Katiya returned to the basement. She waded out into the bones, shining her light across the room, now murky from the dust they'd stirred up before.

Where was I standing?

Her beam found an open space about ten feet away. She walked over then stopped and moved her light in a circle.

Thump.

Katiya stiffened at the noise. It seemed to have come from somewhere above. Had Max come back to help her?

"Hello?" As the sound of her voice dissipated, she thought she heard a distant shuffling.

"Max?"

This time there was only silence.

Her heart thumping, Katiya turned her attention back to her search. Job number one was to find the radio. Once she had it, she could worry about who might be upstairs. If it was Tocchet, she was going to let him have it.

She swept her light around again, this time in a closer arc. A few seconds later, she saw the radio, nestled up against a femur a few feet away.

"Thank you, thank you," she muttered to herself.

She picked the radio up and slipped it in her pocket. She needed to make contact with the others, but that would have to wait. Right now she just needed to get out of this creepy place.

After returning to the stairs, Katiya turned off her flashlight. No sense in drawing attention to herself.

A minute later, she emerged from the temple and raced down the front steps. She stood still for a moment, trying to get her bearings. Amazingly, the fog was even denser than before. Visibility was at most ten feet.

Suddenly, Katiya felt as though someone were watching her. She turned slowly back toward the temple. Her eyes ran up the steps then stopped as they fell on something dark near one of the columns. A shadow? Or was someone standing there? As she tried to determine which, the shadow moved toward the steps then disappeared in the fog.

It's coming.

Her heart pounding, Katiya turned and sprinted to the edge of the clearing. She didn't see the trail, so she moved quickly to the right. She wanted to use her flashlight but realized it would only make things worse in the fog.

There!

Just ahead was an opening in the jungle. The trail seemed narrower than she remembered, but that was probably because she was stressed.

Without looking back, she darted down the path. She wanted to stop and radio the others but needed to put some distance between her and the temple first. She wasn't sure who or what she'd seen at the top of the stairs, but it wasn't Tocchet.

Suddenly, small tree limbs began to whip across her face,

forcing her to come to a stop. Katiya gulped in air as she looked around. Nothing about her surroundings looked familiar. Too many trees pressed in on all sides.

Then the truth hit her like a bucket of cold water: *she had taken the wrong trail.*

Overwhelmed with exhaustion, she crumpled to the ground. She'd done the best she could, but it was time to call for help. She'd have Max or Artur come back and meet her at the clearing in front of the temple. They were going to lose a lot of valuable time, but at least she'd be safe.

Reaching into her pocket, she removed the radio and turned it on. Seconds later, the LED screen lit up.

Thank goodness.

She lifted it to her face then stopped as a distinct shuffling reached her ears. Something had moved behind her. She turned slowly, facing back toward the temple. She couldn't see anything, and yet she knew something was there, watching her.

Suddenly the radio darkened.

What the...?

She pressed the power button and shook it, but the screen remained dark.

After setting it down, she heard another noise, this time closer. Something was moving toward her.

"Max?"

Her heart thumping wildly in her chest, Katiya removed her backpack and pulled a pistol from the side pocket. Zane had given it to her after Corporal Wilson had gone missing. It was just like him. Always taking care of her.

She tried to lift it but suddenly felt resistance in her own mind. She tried again but couldn't move the muscles in her arm. Whatever had turned off the radio now seemed to be controlling her thoughts.

Seconds later, a shadow appeared a few feet away, obscured by the fog. It moved toward her, its form beginning to take shape.

Katiya's vision turned cloudy, and she swooned. Her mind and body were shutting down.

A cloud of fog swirled across the path, and in its wake a pair of black, menacing eyes materialized in front of her.

She tried to cry out, but the scream died in her throat.

The last thing she remembered was spindly, gray hands reaching out for her.

CHAPTER FIFTY-TWO

PRIVATE LIN JIANG smiled from his hiding place behind the crumbled wall. He'd just watched as the long-haired American slipped into the building across the street. Lin had been trailing him for the last two blocks, staying just far enough behind to avoid being seen.

He had purposely not alerted Colonel Zheng. If he'd done that, then Ho would've been dispatched to finish the job. Instead, it would now be Lin who killed the leader of the American team, giving them some measure of revenge for the deaths of the Chinese soldiers on American soil. He could already imagine the accolades that would come his way when they returned to Beijing. Ho be damned.

Suddenly there was movement across the street. The American had made it to the second floor.

As Lin rose, a sharp voice crackled through his headset. "Lin, give me a report."

It was Zheng. Lin cringed, then a response formed quickly in his mind. "I thought I heard a noise inside an old building.

Probably an animal, but I'm going in to check it out."

There was a long pause, and Lin's pulse quickened as he waited for Zheng's response. Had the colonel realized he was lying? The man was notoriously suspicious.

Finally, Zheng said, "Be careful. Contact me immediately if you find something."

Lin exhaled in relief. "Yes, sir."

The only thing left to do now was to kill the American. The dumb brute Ho wouldn't be happy, but Lin already had a plan to cover his tracks. He'd say the American had ambushed him, forcing him to defend himself. No one would criticize him for that. Not even Zheng.

After checking both ways, he sprinted across the street and paused outside the door. Hearing nothing, he entered slowly, his weapon raised. He was standing in a corridor running down the center of the building. He knew from where the American had come out on the second floor that the stairs must be on the other end, so he began moving in that direction.

After finding the stairwell, Lin ascended one step at a time. When he neared the top, his foot crunched down on a piece of gravel. He stopped, listening for any sounds that might indicate he'd been heard. As he waited, the only thing that reached his ears was the faint voice of someone talking on a radio.

He smiled. Fate was delivering the American right into his hands.

After waiting for a couple of minutes, Lin stepped out onto the second floor then paused to get his bearings. Everything was in tatters. It reminded him of the pictures he'd seen of the bombed-out German buildings at the end of the Second World War.

This floor was arranged like the first, with a central corridor and rooms on either side. The voice had seemed to come from one of the rooms on the left, so he moved to that side of the hall.

Lin stopped at the first door. After waiting a few seconds, he leaned forward and peered inside. *Empty.*

A soft sound reached his ears from the next room down. Static from a radio. His pulse quickened. The American was there.

Lin took two more steps and eased up to the door. Sliding his finger over the trigger, he stepped into the gap. The American was huddled on the other side of the room, his rifle pointed out of the window. Lin congratulated himself. This was too easy.

Despite having the element of surprise, the soldier decided to proceed cautiously. Their mole had warned them that this particular American was not someone to be played with. There would be no taunting, no game of cat and mouse. Lin would kill him then call Zheng. Simple as that.

As Lin began to lift his rifle, he stopped. Something about the man huddled on the other side of the room was odd. His shape seemed off somehow.

Stop second-guessing yourself. Kill him before he kills you.

Lin took a step forward and lifted his rifle, settling his head on top of the stock. Then his blood froze. At the other end of his sights was not a man but a backpack with a rifle balanced on top.

The whole thing had been a setup.

Something moved behind him. Lin turned, but it was too late.

A hard object crashed down on his head, plunging his world into darkness.

CHAPTER FIFTY-THREE

AFTER BINDING THE attacker's wrists and ankles, Zane dragged him into the room where he'd set up the dummy. He then sat him up against the interior wall and clicked on his flashlight. The man had Asian features and was young, probably in his early twenties.

They're here.

While Zane had held out hope that they'd lost the Chinese by entering through the tunnel, he certainly wasn't shocked that they had arrived. He assumed the mole had been able to get a message through to them. That was the only way they could have caught up so quickly, unless there was another way up to the summit. The only silver lining was that it ruled out Corporal Wilson as a suspect.

Zane cursed himself for not doing more to uncover the mole's identity. He'd tried to justify his inaction by emphasizing the importance of carrying out the mission, but now it had placed the whole group in danger. He should have demanded to see everyone's electronic devices or at least held things up until Brett could get the satellite phone working again. Now his only choice was to try to get everyone off the mountain as quickly as possible.

He looked down at the soldier again. He was wearing a black body suit. The outer material superficially resembled neoprene, and yet the texture seemed a bit different. Now curious, he unzipped the man's suit, pulled one flap aside, and shone his flashlight on the lining. It looked like some sort of reflective foil. *Of course.* A suit made to camouflage body heat. The Americans had the same technology, although Zane had never used it himself.

Zane clenched his jaw. That explained why they could never see anyone trailing them, despite all the signs that it was happening.

Recognizing the need to move quickly, Zane removed the man's boots and flung them out the window. He did the same with the rifle. He then removed one of the man's socks and stuffed it into his mouth.

Satisfied that he was now completely disabled, Zane retrieved his radio and spoke in a whisper. "Bennett, do you read?"

A few seconds later, Bennett replied softly, "I'm here."

Zane had previously asked the others to go radio silent while he investigated the noise. "The Chinese. They're here."

There was a long pause. "Copy that. How many?"

Zane crept over to the door and looked in the direction of the stairwell. "Don't know. I just put one down but haven't seen any others."

"Copy that. What do you want us to do?"

Zane thought for a moment then asked, "Brett, are you there?"

Brett checked in, although his voice was still somewhat distorted.

"Let's all meet at the place where we separated on the edge of town. Then we'll go down to the clearing and try to establish contact with the others."

"Roger that," Bennett said.

"Artur and I can be there in fifteen minutes," Brett said.

Zane lifted the radio to his mouth. "My guess is that the village is now crawling with Chinese. Make sure you stick to the shadows and watch your back. See you in fifteen."

Zane turned off the radio without waiting for an answer. After retrieving his pack and rifle, he moved cautiously down the stairwell. Despite being concerned about a possible ambush, he found no one waiting on the first floor. The attacker had obviously been operating alone.

He paused at the exit. Everything seemed clear, so he sprinted across the street. Once on the other side, he crab walked down to a crumbled wall and squatted in its shadow.

As he waited, he thought he heard shuffling a block or two away. He thought of turning around and trying to find another way down to the main street but then realized that would take too long. He needed to take the shortest route possible, even if it meant putting himself in further danger. Besides, the Chinese had likely fanned out, meaning it might be impossible to find a safe route.

While he continued to listen, Zane slung his rifle over his shoulder and pulled out his Glock. He preferred a pistol in close quarters, particularly with the fog limiting visibility.

Hearing nothing, Zane stood and walked carefully down the side of the street. Soon a low-lying wall appeared on his right. He didn't remember seeing it on the way in. *I wonder if that's where the noise came from.* He peered over the top. It looked like some sort of ancient walled garden or park that was now being retaken by the jungle.

His senses on high alert, Zane continued down the wall and entered an area darkened by overhanging limbs. He paused, scanning the heavy fog for any signs of movement. As far as he could see, the street was empty. Whoever had made the noise must be gone now.

As he stood, he heard something directly overhead. Someone was on top of the wall.

He turned just in time to see a shadow coming toward him. He was hit with a force so strong that it knocked him out into the street. As he tumbled, the Glock flew out of his hand and clattered across the ground.

As Zane rose to his knees, he saw a shadow moving toward him. He turned his head slightly then froze. The silhouette of a massive man towered overhead. He had to be well over seven feet, with the girth of a body builder. It might have been the largest man Zane had ever seen.

Before he could react, the giant grabbed his hair and lifted him into the air. The man then used his other hand to punch Zane in the abdomen, knocking him back on the ground. Zane rolled into the fetal position, groaning in pain from the powerful blow.

The man picked him up again, this time grabbing his neck

with a meaty paw. Zane was close enough to see the attacker now. He had Asian features, and his squarish face was the size of a cinder block. In fact, it was so wide that it pulled his features apart, giving him a frightening appearance. He looked more cyborg than human.

The man gave Zane a cunning smile then slung him violently back toward the side of the street. Zane flew through an opening in the wall, tumbling across a tangle of tree limbs and vines in the old garden beyond. He rolled to a stop then slowly rose to one knee. Despite the pain, he realized this might be the opportunity he'd been looking for. If the giant had continued to pummel him in the street, it might already be over. The toss had knocked the wind out of him, but it also gave him the chance to regroup.

Heavy footsteps approached through the gap in the wall. As Zane waited for the man to arrive, he thought of how he might turn the tables.

Think, Zane. Think.

The giant's shadow appeared, coming toward him through the fog.

Suddenly he remembered something the Oracle had told him years ago. *Some fights require unconventional weapons. When your life is in danger, you win using whatever means necessary.*

Zane extended his right hand and patted around in the dark. It soon brushed over a rock. He closed his fingers around it. It was time for Goliath to go down. As the giant neared, Zane launched the rock at his head then bull-rushed him. The projectile glanced off the giant's skull with a sickening thud, causing him to reach up reflexively. That exposed his midriff, which bore the full brunt of Zane's charge.

The two went to the ground with Zane on top. He pulled back and began punching the man's midsection as hard as he could. It didn't take long for him to realize the futility of hitting the equivalent of a cement block.

Ignoring the punches, the giant reached up and grabbed Zane's neck. His grip was like that of a hydraulic vice, and Zane coughed as his breath was pinched off. He tried to pry the man's hands free, to no avail.

Zane's vision began to swim. If he didn't get out of the man's grip, he would pass out soon. He probably had less than a minute. And if that happened, he was as good as dead.

As Zane turned to look for something to use as a weapon, he noticed a dark-red spot at the upper edge of the man's massive forehead, where the rock had made impact. Zane knew what he needed to do. With only a few more seconds of consciousness, he pulled his head back, using his strong neck muscles to draw the man's hands and arms outward. When he reached the point where he could pull no more, Zane whipped his head forward, surprising his opponent.

Zane's head made direct contact on the wound. Screaming in pain, the giant reached for his head, giving Zane the opportunity to roll away.

He searched around until he found another rock. It was small, but it would have to do. He lifted it in the air then brought it down toward the man's head. This time the giant got an arm up, causing the rock to strike a glancing blow on his jaw.

THE PORTAL

The monster of a man growled and rose to his feet, much more quickly than a man his size should be able to. As he stood, Zane could see that he was frothing at the mouth. There would be no more playing around. Now there was murder in his eyes.

As the giant lunged toward him, Zane stepped to the side and launched a right uppercut at the wounded jaw. The man seemed to expect the move, reaching out quickly and grabbing Zane's arm. His speed was shocking. With a grunt of anger, the man flung Zane against a nearby tree. His head struck the trunk cleanly, nearly knocking him out. Sparks splashed across his retina as he tried to maintain consciousness.

The giant appeared a few seconds later, looming above him. Despite the swirling fog, Zane could see that he was now clutching a large stone about the size of a basketball, but he was handling it as though it were a piece of Styrofoam.

"Now you die," the giant said.

Zane knew it would be senseless to put up an arm. A rock that size would pulverize any body part that got in its way. At this point, his only hope was to try to move at the last minute.

With a sneer, the giant lifted the rock into the air. As Zane watched, he noticed movement in the foliage past the man's head. Something, perhaps an animal, was moving around on one of the limbs.

The giant growled and started his arm forward. As he did, the figure leaped out of the tree, landing on the man's shoulders. The giant teetered, a look of confusion spreading over his face. Suddenly an arm wrapped around the giant's head, pulling it back and exposing his neck. A knife flashed in the darkness, and there was a loud grunt as the giant swayed slightly then fell to the ground.

The man with the knife moved toward Zane, the blade flashing at his side.

Zane waited. If this one was also an enemy, then he was likely going to die.

Soon a face appeared out of the darkness, and it was one that Zane knew well.

CHAPTER FIFTY-FOUR

ROD BENNETT SCANNED the area from his perch high in the tree. Other than a few rats scurrying amongst the stones, his thermal imaging visor showed no signs of life. The Chinese might be somewhere in the village, but they weren't here.

Grabbing the limb he was sitting on, he dropped to the next one below. After gaining his balance, he looked around one last time. From here on down, he'd no longer be protected by the tree's dense foliage. Look twice, move once.

As his eyes panned the slope above, he caught a brief flash of orange about fifty yards away. He moved his eyes back quickly, but it had already disappeared. The heat signature had been a mere sliver, which confused him.

Careful to maintain his balance, he brought the binoculars up once again, training them on the area of the flash. He turned the focus wheel slowly then stopped. A man was crouching there, hiding behind a pile of rocks. He rotated left and saw another man crouched a few feet away.

He frowned and lowered the binoculars. Why didn't they

show up on thermal imaging? The only thing he could figure was that they were wearing some sort of protective outerwear.

But could they see him? Since they were facing in his direction, he assumed the answer was "yes."

His heart racing, Bennett looked down. Unfortunately, his rifle was leaning against the crumbling wall near the base of the tree. He had a pistol, but that wasn't going to help with long-range targets.

As he weighed his options, Bennett heard soft footfalls on his left. Another attacker was moving toward him.

The soldier grunted in frustration. He'd stayed in the tree too long. If he'd left immediately after getting orders from Zane, he'd be back at the rendezvous point by now. Instead he'd taken a couple of minutes to look for the craft, time enough for the Chinese to lock in on him.

So what now? There was really only one option. He needed to get down to his rifle as quickly as possible. After taking a deep breath, he grabbed the limb under his feet and swung down to the next limb below. He heard the spit of two rounds coming from the left. One round ripped through the limb he'd just been standing on, while the other sizzled past his ear.

Bennett jumped. The drop was longer than he'd remembered. When he hit the ground, he tumbled backwards before rolling into a crouch. As more shots were fired, the Green Beret retrieved his rifle and placed it on top of the wall.

A shadow moved in the distance, dropping behind a cluster of plants. Bennett took aim and fired. The bushes shook, and there was a faint cry of pain. Bennett squeezed off two more shots, silencing the attacker permanently.

There was more movement along a line of small trees to his left. Seconds later, an attacker broke free, rushing toward him. In one smooth motion, Bennett brought his rifle around and fired two shots. The man spun, his gun misfiring into the air as he crumpled to the ground.

Two down. If his count was right, that meant there were only two left. Assuming no more had arrived.

Suddenly the sound of footsteps reached his ears. They seemed only a few feet away.

A voice spoke in heavily accented English. "Drop gun."

Bennett thought of turning and firing, but now he could hear others approaching as well. He'd been trapped. He'd been so focused on the slope above him that he hadn't paid attention to who might be approaching from behind.

"Drop gun!" the man shouted.

Bennett tossed his rifle to the ground and lifted his hands.

"Now turn... slow!"

Bennett stood then turned and faced his captors. One of them clicked on a flashlight and directed the beam into his eyes. Despite the glare, Bennett was able to count three men standing in front of him.

Two of the soldiers stepped forward. One stopped a few feet away and raised his weapon. The other kicked Bennett's rifle away then approached and removed the pistol from his belt. Bennett could see that this one was older, probably the commanding officer.

"Where the other ones?" the old man asked, tossing the pistol out into the darkness.

Bennett gave him a confused look. "What other ones?"

The old man kicked Bennett's knee from the side. Bennett cried out in pain as he tumbled to the ground. He knew immediately a ligament had been torn, effectively crippling him.

"You lie."

Bennett rose up slightly, pain still searing up his leg. He debated whether to answer truthfully. But it would be silly to try to convince them that he was acting alone.

Finally, he wobbled to his feet and said, "We spread out to search the village, so I don't know precisely where the others are."

The commander looked back at one of the other men, apparently confused. The soldier uttered something that was likely a translation of what Bennet had said.

"That is the honest truth," Bennett said.

The commander suddenly lowered his head and lifted a finger to his ear, apparently hearing something in his headset. He spoke for a couple of minutes then turned and barked an order at one of the other soldiers. The soldier turned off the light, plunging the area into darkness.

Seconds later, Bennett heard the sound of footsteps. He looked up to see three men approaching. Once they arrived, the flashlight was turned on again.

Someone spoke in American English. "What the...?"

Bennett stiffened at the sound of the voice. It was familiar, but yet the fog of the moment prevented him from recognizing who it was.

The commander turned toward the American speaker and said, "He not know where the others are. You kill him."

"Look, that was not a part of our deal."

Bennett's blood froze. He realized who was speaking now. It couldn't be true.

The Chinese commander grabbed the man by the shoulder and shoved him forward. A wave of shock passed through Bennett as he saw the face of his fellow soldier, confirming what his ears had already told him.

After a long moment of silence, Bennett asked, "What the heck is going on, Landon?"

Tocchet's mouth trembled slightly as he spoke. "It wasn't supposed to work like this, bro. I swear, I—"

"*What* wasn't supposed to work like this?" Bennett shouted.

Tocchet's eyes darted toward the Chinese commander. "They... they just wanted access to whatever it was we found down here. I—"

"Shut up," Bennett said. "You disgust me."

"I had no idea they were going to attack. I just figured... if there are aliens here, then why shouldn't the world have access to that knowledge? It's not like I was giving away state secrets."

Bennett felt his own face flush with anger. "How much did they pay you? How much money are they giving you to betray your uniform?"

"It wasn't just about the money!" Tocchet shouted. "I got cold feet, and then they threatened to harm Kate. That's the honest—"

"Enough!" shouted the Chinese commander. He pointed a pistol at Tocchet. "I told you to shoot. If you don't, then I shoot you."

"Go ahead... do it, Landon," Bennett hissed. After a long moment of silence, he continued. "I'll die with pride, knowing I served my great country with distinction."

Tocchet approached to within a few feet, his eyes moist with emotion. "Didn't you hear me? They said they'd kill Kate. At that point I wanted out, but I couldn't let my own wife die. It was Kate for some information... you would've done the same thing."

"We could've helped you. No way they could've gotten to her had you sought help."

Tocchet's lip quivered slightly. "By that time I wasn't thinking straight."

"Shut up!" the Chinese commander screamed. "You have three seconds, or I kill you!"

Tocchet turned his head slightly and fixed his gaze on the commander. Bennett thought he saw a flicker of something in the soldier's eyes.

"Do it," Bennett said.

Finally, Tocchet took a couple of steps back. A tear ran down his cheek.

The commander waved his pistol at Tocchet. "One..."

Tocchet raised his gun. Bennett noticed the barrel was shaking slightly.

"Kill," the commander said.

Tocchet looked at Bennett. It was a blank stare, devoid of any emotion.

"Okay," Tocchet said, sliding his finger over the trigger.

Bennett closed his eyes and waited. His thought only of his boxer, Ava.

"Two!" the commander screamed.

The cough of several suppressed shots rang out. Bennett grit his teeth, but the pain never came. He heard bodies falling and a few grunts.

There were two more shots, then silence.

Bennett opened his eyes slowly. Tocchet stood a few feet away, a curl of smoke twisting out of the barrel of his gun. The Chinese soldiers were sprawled out on the ground around him.

After a long pause, Tocchet spoke without moving. "I... I was having financial problems. I never thought I could..."

"We all have our own demons," Bennett said. "You don't have to explain."

Tocchet turned and faced Bennett. "Please tell Kate I did it for her."

Bennett frowned.

Tocchet dropped the rifle then pulled a pistol out of his pocket, turning it at an odd angle.

"No!" Bennett shouted, lunging toward him.

But it was too late. Tocchet shoved the barrel in his mouth and pulled the trigger.

CHAPTER FIFTY-FIVE

OSAK SLID THE knife back into his loincloth then extended his hand.

Zane smiled at him.

The boy helped Zane rise to his feet. He staggered for a moment, still woozy from the blow to his head. Osak grabbed his arm to steady him.

"Good grief." Zane looked over at the Chinese soldier, who was lying a few feet away. Even though he'd known the man was large, the distraction of the fight had prevented him from seeing how truly massive he was.

Osak pointed and said something Zane didn't understand.

"I agree," he replied facetiously. "He's the biggest man I've ever seen too."

Osak stepped over and pushed at the body with his foot, as if making sure he was truly dead.

Zane walked over to the boy and laid a hand on his shoulder. "Thank you."

Osak met his gaze, and there seemed to be understanding

in the boy's eyes.

Zane looked at his watch then frowned. He was running late. Looking around, he realized he'd lost almost everything during the fight. His visor, his gun, his pack.

"Come." Zane gestured for the boy to follow him.

Zane passed through the gate and returned to the street. He turned in every direction, but the fog and rock piles would make it almost impossible to find any of his belongings. As he started to walk off, his foot struck something, sending it skittering across the ground. He moved in the direction of the sound then crouched and patted the ground. Soon his fingers closed around the barrel of a pistol.

"At least I'll have something."

He stood. He could probably find his pack and rifle if he took the time, but time was the very thing he didn't have.

He turned to Osak. "Follow me."

Osak's brow furrowed in confusion, but he fell in behind the operative.

Several minutes later, they arrived at the rendezvous point. Zane motioned for Osak to join him under the cover of a tree with low, overhanging branches. He didn't want to take the chance of getting ambushed again.

Once they were hidden, Zane looked at Osak. "We wait for Brett, Bennett, and Jorge."

"Jorge," Osak said with a smile.

Zane turned back toward the street. Nothing moved. The only noise came from the jungle about a hundred yards away. It concerned him that none of the other three were here yet. Had they misunderstood his instructions? That didn't seem possible. The radios had been functioning well when he'd given them, and they'd all agreed to meet back here in fifteen minutes.

He glanced at his watch. It had been about half an hour since their last conversation. Bennett had been positioned just uphill, so he should have been the first to arrive. Brett said that it would take him and Artur fifteen minutes, which meant they should be here as well.

Zane ran a hand through his long locks. He had no choice. He needed to find the other team. The women and civilians had to be his top priority.

Turning his head slightly, he whispered, "We go down."

Hearing nothing in response, Zane turned completely around. Osak was no longer there.

He let out a groan of frustration. Apparently the independence bug had bitten his indigenous friend again. At least he knew the boy would be safe. He was probably better equipped to survive out here than anyone, even someone carrying a gun.

After checking for movement one last time, Zane stole across the intersection. Once on the other side, he found a trail that led downhill. He'd seen it when they'd arrived earlier. This one was steeper than the others they'd traveled, forcing him to slow his pace considerably.

About ten minutes later, he came to a halt not far from the valley floor. He thought he heard something just ahead, so he ducked behind a tree on the right side of the path.

As he waited, his eyes caught something about twenty yards away. The movement was slight, a shifting shadow behind a bush.

Suddenly a familiar voice carried up the slope. "Zane?"

Brett.

Zane stepped from behind the tree and moved quickly down the slope. Soon Brett came into view, standing in the middle of the trail. As Zane drew near, another figured appeared out of the shadows. *Jorge.*

"That's a good way to get yourself killed," Zane said. "I thought you were a jungle cat."

"Couldn't be sure it was you. The fog is too thick to see much of anything right now." Brett looked Zane over. "What happened?"

"Long story. I had a run-in with another one of our Chinese friends. It's why I was late."

Brett nodded. "We even tried to raise both of you on the radio."

"I lost mine in the fight. I'm assuming Bennett never responded?"

"No," Brett replied. "In fact, the radio isn't functioning at all now. The signal is dead. Nothing."

Zane's eyes narrowed. "Strange."

"Anyway, after waiting for a while, we realized that the others might need help, so we—"

"No, you did the right thing. The safety of the civilians trumps everything."

"So you got jumped by another soldier?"

Zane nodded. "He looked like some sort of bizarre scientific experiment gone wrong. I'm still not sure if he was even a man."

"That's two notches for Watson tonight," Brett said.

"Had our indigenous friend not come along, I wouldn't have survived the second one."

Brett frowned. "Osak? Where is he?"

"Gone. He took off again to who knows where."

Brett looked back toward the village. "What do you think happened to Bennett?"

"I have no idea. He should've been the first one back. I'm hoping he's just holed up somewhere, hiding from the Chinese." He turned and looked down the path. "Who knows, maybe he had the same idea we did."

"We need to get moving," Jorge said.

Zane nodded. He was right. They'd talked long enough. "Where are we exactly?"

"The valley floor is about thirty or forty yards ahead," Brett said.

"There's a large clearing down there," Jorge added, "just like the girl said."

"Let's go," Zane said.

Several minutes later, they arrived at the clearing. Zane had never seen fog so thick in his life. It was like trying to move through a burning house.

Jorge looked around, clearly uncomfortable. "We could run into someone and not know until it's too late."

"If anyone else is down here, then they're dealing with the same issues we are," Zane said. "And my guess is that the Chinese are still up in the village." He looked down the line of trees. "Speaking of which, let's get moving."

Using Rebecca's directions, he led them south along the

edge of the clearing. The fog limited visibility to anywhere from ten feet to fifty yards. Zane wished he still had his visor, although he realized it wouldn't be able to detect the Chinese.

Jorge suddenly stopped. "What's that noise?"

Zane paused and looked at him. "What noise?"

The Brazilian pointed toward the trees on their right. "You don't hear that buzzing?"

Brett looked up. "He's right."

Zane suddenly realized what they were referring to. A steady hum was coming from the rainforest. He'd been so focused on threats inside the clearing that he hadn't noticed it before.

"It sounds like cicadas, only more intense," Brett said. "Reminds me of standing under one of those transformers in the summer as a kid."

As he moved his eyes across the canopy, Zane noticed an orb bouncing in and out of the foliage. Is that what was making the sound? Was it some form of communication? "I wish we had time to figure it out, but we don't." He gave them the signal to move out.

After a few more minutes of walking, the jungle rose up in front of them, marking the end of the clearing.

"We're here," Jorge said.

Zane pointed to their left. "Rebecca said the trail to the temple was on this end. Let's see what we can find."

The three continued along the edge of the woods, looking for any breaks in the dense foliage. Jorge took the lead, followed by Zane and Brett.

Two minutes later, the Brazilian gave a low whistle and

pointed to something just ahead. When Zane arrived, Jorge turned his flashlight on briefly, illuminating a path that ran south through the trees.

"Bingo," Brett said.

Jorge turned off the light. "This has to be it."

Zane nodded. "I agree. Let's..." His eyes locked on something just down the line of trees.

"What's wrong?" Brett asked.

Zane continued to stare. When the fog had swirled away moments earlier, he could have sworn he'd seen a figure moving north away from the jungle.

"Zane, what's wrong?" Brett asked again.

"I'm not sure," he whispered.

"Was it someone from the other team?" Brett asked.

"I don't think so. I think it was a person, but it might have been an animal."

Brett removed his pistol. "Let's go have a look."

Zane looked at him. "No, I want both of you to head to the temple. I'll catch up in just a sec."

"We're not going to just let you run out there on your own."

Zane held up a hand. "It was probably nothing, but I need to go check it out."

"He's right, we don't need to split up again," Jorge said.

"It won't take long," Zane replied. "I'll figure out what it was, and if it was nothing, I'll catch up with you guys in a couple of minutes."

Brett was about to say something, but Zane nodded at the trail. "Go! Two minutes... I promise."

And with that, Zane turned and sprinted off into the fog. He didn't like separating either, but he had no choice. He needed them to continue in the search for the other team, but unless he was going crazy, he knew he'd just seen someone walking.

He'd noted the direction the figure was moving and tried to put himself on the same general path. But without having the jungle as a landmark, he realized it was going to be almost impossible to stay on a straight line.

As he continued north, Zane's thoughts turned back to the shadowy figure. He'd originally thought it was a man, but now he couldn't be so sure. It looked small and thin, almost like a primate. *No self-respecting monkey should be running around out here,* he thought.

A few minutes later, he came to a halt. He should have caught up with the figure by now. He pivoted in several directions, squinting into the fog. Making matters worse, the humming seemed louder now, making it impossible to hear footsteps.

Where are you? Show yourself.

As Zane looked north, he saw movement about thirty or forty yards away. It was the same figure, and from this angle it appeared to be carrying something. Seconds later, it disappeared into a swirling cloud of gray.

Marking the spot, Zane sprinted forward. A minute later, he saw a dark shadow walking just ahead. The figure stopped and spun around. Zane crouched, reducing his profile.

A blanket of fog swirled in front of him. After passing, the figure was gone again.

Zane stood and began to walk, removing his Glock and chambering a round.

Suddenly his surroundings seemed strange. This part of the clearing was darker, much darker. Finally, he stopped and looked up. To his surprise, the sky was no longer visible. All he could see above him was opaque black. No stars, no moon, nothing.

He shifted his gaze slightly to the right, then to the left. The black ceiling extended in every direction.

And then it hit him…

He was standing underneath a giant craft.

CHAPTER FIFTY-SIX

"SHOULD WE TURN on our lights?" Jorge asked as he and Brett moved slowly down the path.

"No, let's keep them off," Brett said.

"What or who do you think he saw back there?"

"Zane?" Brett looked over at the Brazilian. "I think it was someone from the other team. I mean, who else would be out here?"

Jorge shrugged. "Chinese maybe."

As the two continued walking in silence, Brett's mind turned back to Zane. He wished the operative hadn't gone off on his own. Separating the team never seemed to be a good idea. Each time they did that, trouble arose. If it was only going to take him a couple of minutes, then why not do it together?

"Did you hear that?" Jorge asked.

"Hear what?"

The Brazilian stopped, a frown spreading over his face. Brett remained perfectly still, trying to figure out what he was referring to. A few seconds later, he heard it, the soft sound of voices. There was a group of people just around the next bend in the trail.

"You hear it now?" Jorge asked.

Brett nodded, pulling out his pistol. "Let's try to get closer."

As they neared the bend, the voices grew louder. Whoever was speaking wasn't very far ahead.

Finally, Brett was able to hear what one of them was saying. "We've waited long enough. I'm going back to look for her."

Max.

Brett started walking and gave a low whistle. "Hey, it's me, Brett."

The voices grew quiet, then a flashlight clicked on. The beam bounced around before finally coming to rest on Brett's face. He lifted a hand to shield his eyes from the light.

"Brett?" It was Amanda. "Thank goodness it's you."

Brett and Jorge clicked on their flashlights as the two groups walked toward each other.

"You guys were making enough noise to be heard in Sao Paulo," Jorge said to Artur.

As the others drew near, Brett only counted four people: Amanda, Rebecca, Max, and Artur. Where were Tocchet and Katiya?

Amanda ran up to Brett and gave him a hug then pulled back. "Please tell me you've seen Katiya."

"Katiya?" Brett frowned. "No, why?"

"She went back to the temple to get her radio," Max explained. "We've been waiting here for her. She should've been back by now. We were hoping she'd somehow gotten past us."

"She'd have been better off just leaving it," Brett said, holding up his radio. "They're not working anymore."

Max shook his head.

"So tell me... what's going on?" Amanda asked. "What was Zane trying to tell us earlier?"

After exchanging a glance with Jorge, Brett said, "We saw a craft over the summit."

Rebecca visibly stiffened. "What did it look like?"

"It was hard to tell. Lights ran along each side. It flew south over the clearing, sweeping the area with some sort of blue beam."

"Which way did it go?" Rebecca asked.

"The last we saw, it was moving in this direction."

Artur frowned. "Did it land?"

"We don't know," Brett said. "One minute it was there, and the next it just disappeared."

Max exhaled loudly. "Just like Katiya. Look, this is all very interesting, but I'm going back to look for her. The rest of you can stay here—"

"Wait," Brett said, laying a hand on his shoulder. "I think I may know where she is."

"I thought you just told us you *hadn't* seen her," Max said in a raised voice.

"I meant we never saw her pass us on the trail." Brett nodded back the way they'd come. "Just a few minutes ago, Zane thought he saw someone out in the clearing."

"Did it look like Katiya?" Max asked.

"It was hard to tell who it was because of the fog. He went to check it out and told us to keep going."

"That has to be her," Max said.

"I'd say that's a good guess, but at this point—"

"Guys." Amanda suddenly pointed at something in the distance. "I think we have something coming our way."

Rebecca looked up and let out a little gasp.

Brett turned around. At first he looked back down the trail, then his eyes were drawn upward to something in the sky. It was several miles away but seemed to be growing larger.

As he watched, chill bumps spread across his body.

Another craft was on its way.

CHAPTER FIFTY-SEVEN

ZANE GAZED IN wonder at the imposing size of the craft. No matter which direction he looked, he could only see its dark metal underside. It dwarfed anything he'd ever seen, including military transport planes.

Suddenly he heard a hiss, followed by the sound of hydraulics.

He turned in the direction of the sound. Something moved through the fog. He crept closer. Someone was climbing a ramp, and they appeared to be carrying someone in their arms. And then they were gone.

Zane stood in place, confused by what he had just seen. Was it really a man? It seemed so at the time, and yet there was something odd about his shape.

What if it was someone from the other team? Zane dismissed the thought immediately. The person had left the jungle and made a beeline for the craft, which had been cloaked by the fog. Only someone with an intimate knowledge of the craft's location could've done that.

He clenched his jaw as he considered what to do next. He'd promised Brett and Jorge that he'd return, but only if it turned out to be nothing. This was something. He had also seen someone in the man's arms. The question of who it might be disturbed him.

Throwing caution to the wind, Zane sprinted forward. Soon the ramp came into view. It was wider than he'd expected. He looked toward the top, but the view was obscured by swirling fog.

He placed a foot on its surface then stopped. A distant sound reached his ears, causing him to turn his head slightly. It sounded like the drone of an engine. The noise grew louder, indicating it was moving in the direction of the summit. *Was it another craft?* If so, then he needed to move quickly. He turned and mounted the ramp. He drew his gun, mindful that someone might be waiting for him above. Who knew, perhaps the whole thing had been staged to draw him here.

He paused near the top. Just a few yards ahead, the ramp entered the craft through something that looked like a pane of glass, and yet he could tell it wasn't glass. He frowned. The substance didn't seem real. It was like opaque glass that shimmered, sparkled, and moved.

Zane extended his hand. Just as his fingers neared the strange material, he paused. Would touching it set off an alarm? There was only one way to find out, so he thrust his hand forward. To his utter shock, his hand slipped through easily. It felt like water was sliding down his fingers, then his wrist, and finally his forearm. It was a membrane, some sort of futuristic entry panel.

Sensing it was safe, Zane stepped all the way through and found himself standing in a room that seemed like a bay. It was dimly lit, the only luminescence coming from several circular lights sunken into the floor.

Zane cast his eyes around. The space was not large, but it rose high into the air, perhaps the equivalent of several stories.

Suddenly he sensed movement above. Zane looked up, wondering if he should raise his weapon. A moment later, something descended out of the darkness, sliding down the wall. It had the appearance of a futuristic elevator car. Seconds later, it reached the floor and stopped. Zane raised his pistol, but nothing emerged.

He moved toward it slowly. The capsule was constructed mostly of metal, save for a door facing him that seemed to be made of the same strange substance he had walked through only moments before.

"Let's see where this baby goes," Zane said softly, stepping through the pane.

As he'd expected, the interior was empty. As he looked around, a panel slowly lit on the opposite wall. He stepped closer and examined the long, vertical screen. On it were a series of strange characters that ran from top to bottom. The one at the bottom was blinking.

He touched the second button from the bottom, and the capsule moved upward. It took off so fast that Zane almost toppled over. Moments later, it stopped, and the door facing the wall slid open. A dark corridor loomed beyond. Zane leaned forward, but he couldn't see or hear anything in either direction.

Remembering the car had originally come from one of the upper levels, Zane pulled back inside and hit the fourth character from the bottom. The capsule took off again then stopped a few seconds later. This time Zane stepped out when the door opened.

The corridor he found himself in was mostly dark. Just like the bay, it was dimly lit with small red lights sunken into the floor. For reasons he couldn't explain, he turned right and began walking. He soon saw a corridor branching off to the left. After glancing down it briefly, he continued straight ahead.

The hallway seemed to go on forever. *This thing is the size of a battleship.*

About a minute later, a doorway appeared just ahead. Hearing no sounds, Zane stepped through and stopped. After his eyes adjusted, he could see he was standing at the top of a flight of stairs leading down into a cavernous chamber. At first he saw nothing in the dark interior, then his eyes picked up a faint flicker of light in the distance.

Zane descended the stairs cautiously. When he reached the bottom, he stepped out into the room. Soon more details emerged. He quickly saw that the far wall was not a wall at all; it was a V-shaped pane of dark glass.

A windshield.

Just below it were two strangely contoured seats. A long console ran between them, and just above that was the light he'd seen from above. Strangely, it seemed to hover in midair. Intrigued, he crossed the room and approached the glow. As he drew within a few feet, he realized it was a floating hologram. He also saw that the light was actually an intricate design on the globe's surface. Zane leaned forward then stopped. His pulse quickened as he found himself staring at a 3D representation of the earth. It was so realistic that it gave the appearance of a real-time video.

Zane bent closer and marveled at the amazing technology. The oceans seemed to shimmer, and a few of the scattered clouds seemed to move ever so slightly. *It must be some sort of navigation system,* he thought. As he reached out to touch it, Zane heard a noise behind him. He turned, and at the same time, he backed away from the light of the hologram. He lifted his Glock and stared toward the back of the bridge, watching for movement. For the first time, he noticed that a doorway stood just behind the base of the stairs. The sound had seemed to come from there.

He slowly crossed over to the entryway. Just beyond was a corridor that looked like the one he'd come down earlier. He wanted to go back and examine the globe, but he knew he needed to investigate the sound. Someone might be in danger.

After passing through the door, Zane walked slowly down the hall. About a minute later, he saw a long window running down the right-hand wall. He stepped up to the edge then eased forward. A large room slid into view beyond the glass. Like the rest of the ship, it was mostly dark, but he could see that it was filled with rows of linen-covered gurneys. Situated next to each one was an instrument tower with a number of futuristic-looking knobs and screens. The whole scene reminded him of a hospital ward.

One of the instrument towers on the far end of the room

was giving off ambient light. As Zane turned that way, chill bumps spread over both of his arms. Two figures were moving in and out of the light. They seemed oddly familiar, but the distance was too great to discern any details.

Desiring a better look, Zane squatted and crab-walked down the hall, keeping his head just under the bottom edge of the glass. Moments later, a doorway appeared ahead. Not surprisingly, it was covered by another membrane panel.

Should he enter? Zane knew he had little choice but to go in. It was obvious the creatures were working on someone, likely the same person he'd seen being carried on board. It was also obvious that person had been brought there against their will.

After taking a deep breath, Zane carefully eased through the panel. Once inside, he quickly crawled over to one of the gurneys. As he settled into place, he heard a strange series of monotone clicks, almost like radio static that had been slowed down to the point where the individual bursts of noise could be heard.

Zane bent lower and stared through the tangle of metal legs and wheels. The creatures were to the left in the far corner of the room. Somehow he needed to get closer.

Careful not to make any noise, he turned and crawled down the nearest row. When he got to the end, he situated himself behind a gurney next to the wall. He remained perfectly still, trying to make sure he hadn't been heard. The strange clicks continued unabated, so he rose until his eyes cleared the gurney. He could scarcely believe the sight that greeted him. Two creatures hovered over their patient, their spindly arms moving around as they continued their work.

They had bulbous heads perched on pencil-thin necks, and their bodies were covered with a dull, lifeless gray skin that looked more reptilian than human. But it was their eyes that gave him chills. Looking into the lidless black ovals was like looking into hell itself.

As Zane watched, he noticed that the two occasionally turned toward each other as they worked. They seemed to communicate through the clicks, although strangely, their tiny mouths never moved.

What now? Should he attack? He had a full magazine in the Glock and another in his pocket. He also held the element of surprise. On the other hand, he didn't know what weapons they possessed. Nor did he know anything about their physical capabilities. In fact, other than their appearance, he knew nothing about them at all.

As he weighed his options, Zane rested his arm on the gurney's rail, causing it to creak. The clicking ceased immediately. Zane froze in place. A moment later, the creatures exchanged a few soft clicks. Zane turned his head and watched as they walked toward the other side of the room. They paused for a moment at the door then passed through the membrane.

Zane was stunned that they had been unable to determine the direction of the sound. That likely indicated that their hearing was poorly developed. That, or they had lost any aural acuity over time. Now that he thought about it, he couldn't even remember seeing any ears.

After waiting a full minute, Zane rose and made his way

over to where the two had been working. As he drew near, he could see a thin female arm dangling off one side of the gurney. A splash of long brown hair spread across the pillow and sheets.

Zane paused and looked over at the door. He couldn't see any movement inside the room or in the hall beyond. The aurally challenged creatures were apparently still searching the ship, trying to determine the source of the sound.

Zane turned and approached the gurney. When he arrived, he froze in shock.

There, lying on crisp white sheets, was Dr. Katiya Mills.

Zane was suddenly filled with rage and malice when he saw her condition. Her face was sallow, and she seemed to be barely breathing. There was no telling what the grays were going to do to her.

Fearing they would return soon, he slid his hands carefully under her body. As he began to lift her, her eyes opened and a scream formed on her lips.

CHAPTER FIFTY-EIGHT

ACTING INSTINCTIVELY, ZANE clamped his hand over Katiya's mouth before she could scream. She grabbed his wrists and thrashed around in the bed, trying to shake him loose.

"Katiya, stop." He pressed her into the bed and leaned closer. "Katiya."

She looked into his eyes as though seeing him for the first time. She held his gaze for a moment, then her body relaxed slightly.

"There you go, nice and easy," he said, slowly removing his hand from her mouth.

She gulped in air then grabbed his arms. "Please, we have to leave!"

"Easy, easy. We're going to." He glanced at the door. Still no movement in the room or the hall.

She nodded slowly then looked into his eyes. "I knew you'd come for me."

Her eyes twitched and her voice slurred, likely the result of a tranquilizing agent.

"I'll always come for you," he replied.

"They… they were going to drug me again before you came."

Zane squeezed her arm. "I know. Try not to talk. You're still weak."

"Okay."

He lifted her gently then turned toward the door.

"I love you, Zane Watson," she said in a slurred voice.

Zane smiled as he realized he was dealing with the equivalent of a drunk. He wondered if the drugs were like a truth serum.

"No, I really do."

Zane held a finger to his lips, reminding her not to talk. She nodded dramatically in return.

He carried her over to the door then peered through the glass. As far as he could tell, there was no movement in the corridor. He should have felt relief, but instead, the grays' absence concerned him.

"Hold on," he whispered, leaning through the membrane.

"Wow, that felt good," Katiya said after they'd passed through.

"Quiet," he whispered.

"You're no fun," she moaned.

Zane returned to the bridge. The hologram of Earth seemed to glow more brightly now.

Strange.

Suddenly, Zane had an idea. It involved some element of risk, but there might not be another opportunity. He had to do it, and he had to do it now.

He carried Katiya over to the base of the stairs and propped her up against the rail. He reminded her to remain quiet, and she gave him a mock salute, a silly grin spreading across her face.

After glancing back down the hall, Zane turned and crossed to the globe. It had been stationary before, but now it rotated slowly. He pulled out his smartphone and pressed the power button. He was going to use the camera to document the hologram and some of the ship's instrumentation. There was no telling how much helpful information they might be able to get from just a few images.

He looked at the phone's screen, but it was still dark. He cursed. Either his battery was dead or the grays had somehow disabled it.

As he pressed the power button again, Zane heard shuffling behind him.

Katiya.

He looked back at her then frowned. She hadn't moved. She was still leaning back against the metal rail, her eyes shut tightly.

Zane turned back to his phone and bit his lower lip.

Suddenly, he heard more shuffling, this time closer. He turned his head slightly. A gray figure hovered in the shadows behind him. As Zane reached for his Glock, the creature hissed and charged, knocking him to the floor. It was surprisingly strong and nimble. Before he could react, it grabbed his throat, pinching his windpipe. Zane grabbed its cold arms and tried to pull them away, but the creature was too strong.

Remembering his gun, Zane reached into his pocket. As his

fingers closed around the metal grip, he heard a voice speak clearly in his mind. *Look at me.*

Although he tried to fight it, Zane couldn't resist the command. He looked up slowly, his eyes resting on the shiny black ovals staring back at him. They seemed devoid of life, and yet he couldn't turn away.

Release the gun.

Zane knew the creature was using some form of telepathy, but that knowledge didn't help him fight back. He obediently released the gun.

As Zane struggled to regain control of his will, he suddenly felt as though his internal organs were being squeezed. Was it controlling his body too? Then he remembered reading about people who could bend spoons with their minds. If that were true, anything was possible.

Zane heard a noise coming from the stairs.

Katiya? Please, don't let her come over here.

Surprisingly, the creature released its hold and turned. Zane could see the dark silhouette of a person coming toward them. The size was wrong for Katiya, which was a relief. But if not her, then who was it?

Stop, Zane heard the creature command the intruder.

But the person continued toward them, apparently immune to the telepathic manipulation.

Stop!

The gray backed up, hissing like a cat.

Zane heard something like the whine of hydraulics, and two hands reached out with startling speed, grabbing the creature by the neck. It thrashed and hissed wildly before finally slipping free and darting toward the doorway next to the stairs.

Instead of giving chase, the newcomer turned toward Zane and stepped closer. Zane slowly reached into his pocket for his gun.

The shadow spoke. "I see you've gotten yourself into trouble once again, Zane Watson."

Zane frowned. It couldn't possibly be her, and yet there was no mistaking that voice.

She leaned forward, her face now appearing in the ambient light of the nearby globe.

Zane gave a sigh of relief. "What took you so long, Keiko?"

CHAPTER FIFTY-NINE

"I TAKE IT you are surprised to see me, sir?" Keiko asked.

Zane rose up on one elbow. "I'm still thinking this is a dream."

"I can assure you it is not a dream."

Zane rubbed his neck. "What are you doing here?"

"We discovered that someone close to you had been recruited by Chinese intelligence. We tried to make you aware of the breach but were unable to contact you. Dr. Ross then ordered the formation of an extraction team. We knew you were headed toward this mountain, and we arrived minutes ago."

Zane nodded. "The sat phone got crushed." He rose up on one knee. "I knew there was a mole, but I haven't been able to determine who it is." He looked at her, his expression conveying a question.

Keiko blinked several times. "Sergeant Landon Tocchet was your mole, sir."

Zane felt the life drain out of him. He could scarcely

believe what he'd just heard. Tocchet might have been the *last* person he'd suspected.

Keiko reached out with her powerful arms and pulled Zane to his feet. "We need to get you and Dr. Mills out of here."

Hit with a thought, Zane held up a hand. "Wait. Do you have photographic capability?"

"Of course."

He turned and pointed at the globe. "Then I need you to…" He froze. The holographic image of Earth was gone. In its place, a series of strange letters floated in the air. They looked like runes or symbols. Every second or so some of the letters changed.

Keiko stepped closer. "What's wrong?"

"There was a holographic image here before. It was some sort of navigation technology… and now it's gone… replaced by whatever this is."

Keiko leaned forward. "Very interesting."

Zane turned toward her. "Do you know what it means?"

"Yes, it's an ancient form of Hebrew. Paleo-Hebrew, I think."

Zane gave her a confused look. "Ancient Hebrew? Are you sure?"

"I am certain that is what it is. I do not have a large database to draw on, but most of the characters are a match."

Zane frowned. It didn't make sense. "What does it say?"

Keiko stared at the hologram. "They're numbers. Descending numbers. As you can see, some are changing." She straightened and looked at Zane. "If I had to guess, I would say that it represents time."

"Did you say the numbers were descending?" Zane frowned.

"Yes."

After thinking for a few seconds, Zane's eyes widened. "We need to get out of here. This thing is getting ready to blow."

Keiko paused in confusion then nodded. "Yes, sir."

As they turned to leave, Zane grabbed Keiko's arm. "What time is displayed right now?"

She stared at the floating image. Zane could see her artificial pupils adjusting for the distance. "It's seven followed by—"

Zane shook her arm. "Seven minutes. That's good enough. Set your timer for seven minutes. Let's go."

"It is done," she said.

Zane crossed over to Katiya. He checked her pulse then placed a palm on her forehead. "I think she's fine." He lifted her gently and nodded toward the stairs, indicating Keiko should lead.

It took them a little over a minute to make their way out of the ship. On their way out, they saw no sign of life. No grays. No humans. Nothing.

When they reached the bottom of the ramp, Zane could hear the *thump thump* of helicopter rotors in the distance.

"Hey! They're over here!" someone shouted.

Three silhouettes appeared, running toward them out of the fog. One of the three sprinted ahead of the other two as they drew near. Zane saw that it was a woman clothed in military garb. She had long, raven-black hair and was clutching a semiautomatic rifle. He smiled. He should have known the

Oracle would send Carmen Petrosino.

The Italian came to a halt, with two Special Forces soldiers just behind her. She was about to address Zane when she saw the giant craft looming overhead. "What the...?"

"I'm doing fine, thanks," Zane said.

She looked at him. "Sorry, I—"

"No problem." He jerked a thumb toward the ship. "I'll explain that later. We need to get out of here." He then told her that a timed explosive had likely been set.

She nodded.

Zane looked at Keiko. "How much time do we have?"

"A little over five minutes, sir."

Zane turned to Carmen. "Sounds like you came here on a bird."

"We did."

"Take us there."

Carmen gestured for them to follow her. She then led them north through the fog. One of the soldiers offered to carry Katiya, but Zane waved him off. He wasn't about to let her out of his grasp.

As the *thump thump* of the bird's rotors grew louder, Zane saw running lights appear, then the dark outline of a Sikorsky UH-60 Black Hawk helicopter. Thankfully, it appeared ready for takeoff.

"They're here!" someone shouted.

Zane looked up and saw a group of people gathered near the sliding door at the rear, including Amanda, Brett, Artur, and Jorge.

"Everybody in!" Zane commanded.

Zane ducked under the blades then handed Katiya to one of the soldiers and asked him to put her in the chopper.

"Glad you're okay," Brett said.

Zane looked at him. "Is everybody back?"

"If my count is right, we're still missing Bennett and Tocchet."

Zane cursed under his breath.

"We were just about to form another team to go out—"

"We can't!" Zane yelled. "This place is about to blow."

"What are you talking about?" Jorge asked.

"No time to explain, just trust me." He gave Keiko a questioning look.

"Two minutes, forty-nine seconds."

Zane took a deep breath, trying to calm himself as he sorted through their options. He thought of sending the others up in the chopper while he remained behind, but that would be suicidal. It wouldn't do the soldiers any good if his body were blown into a hundred pieces. He really had only one option.

He looked at Brett. "I need everyone to get inside."

Amanda stepped forward. "Zane, we can't leave Rod and Landon behind."

"We have no choice. I have good reason to believe that this place will be a blackened pancake in a little over two minutes. And if we're here when that happens, *none* of us will get out of here alive." He sighed deeply. "Look, we'll retreat to a safe distance, and if somehow I was wrong, we'll come back. That's the best I can do."

Her eyes were moist with emotion, but she seemed to

understand.

"Okay, people, let's go!" Zane shouted.

Now aware of the urgency, everyone climbed into the chopper. Amanda and Max joined the soldier who was treating Katiya. Zane noticed that the anthropologist's eyes were now open. Once everyone was inside and secure, Carmen barked orders to the pilot. Seconds later, the engine roared and the rotors began to oscillate with more speed.

Zane sat at the open door, his legs dangling outside the bird. He was unable to move or speak. He couldn't stop thinking about the two soldiers who were still out there on the mountain. He wanted both back, even Tocchet. In all likelihood he was guilty, but Zane still held out hope that it was all a big misunderstanding.

One of the pilots turned and got Zane's attention. "Sir, we're ready for takeoff."

Zane signaled his approval.

The bird rocked slightly as it lifted off of the ground.

"Wait!" Amanda shouted. "What's that?"

Zane lifted a palm toward the cockpit. "Stop!"

The pilot kept the chopper in place while Zane looked in the direction Amanda was pointing. A shadowy figure was moving toward them through the fog. Zane reached back and removed his Glock, and two of the soldiers lifted their rifles.

The figure continued toward them with speed. Zane slid his finger off the trigger and squinted, trying to figure out who it was.

"Osak!" Brett shouted.

Zane could hardly believe his eyes. The boy ran toward

them. As he drew closer, Zane could see that Bennett was draped over his back.

Amanda cried out with delight.

Osak stopped just beyond the rotors, afraid to go any farther. Zane hopped off the bird then ran out and took Bennett from the boy. The soldier patted his knee, indicating he couldn't walk.

As they ran back, Zane carrying Bennett, he asked, "Have you seen Tocchet?"

The soldier's eyes said everything. Zane wanted more information but knew there wasn't time to listen to an explanation. After handing the Green Beret to another soldier, he turned back toward Osak. He gestured for him to come, but the boy shook his head and backed away.

"We have less than a minute, sir," Keiko shouted.

Suddenly someone hopped to the ground and ran out to the boy. *Max.* The linguist spoke to him in a loud voice then pointed back at the chopper. At first the boy seemed confused, but finally a look of understanding spread across his face. Apparently Max had been able to convince him that his life depended on getting inside the strange metal bird.

The two ran toward the chopper. Amanda stepped out, helping the boy into the bay.

After everyone was inside, Zane looked at the pilot and said, "Get us out of here."

The pilot nodded, and the chopper rose straight into the air. Everyone stiffened as it rose through the fog. Zane looked over at Osak. His eyes were the size of saucers, and his arms and shoulders trembled with fear.

THE PORTAL

Zane was about to get an update on the time from Keiko then decided against it. What did it matter? Either they would make it or they wouldn't. The time she was keeping wasn't precise anyway.

Seconds later, the chopper broke out of the fog and into the night sky. Hundreds of stars appeared in every direction, and the edge of the Milky Way sparkled on the horizon.

As the chopper began to move horizontally, Zane pulled his legs back inside and slid the door shut.

"*What is that?*" Brett asked, pointing at something in the distance.

Everyone crowded up against the window.

Zane looked out over the horizon. Finally, he saw what Brett was referring to. A thin sliver of brightness appeared in the distance. It slowly grew wider, as though a door to another dimension were being opened.

"Good grief," Amanda whispered.

"What is it?" Brett asked.

"It looks like some kind of portal," Amanda said.

"Look... down there," Jorge said.

Zane lowered his eyes. The dark triangular form of the alien ship rose toward the light. It was moving so quickly that it seemed like it was being sucked upwards by some celestial vacuum. Moments later, it slid into the light and the portal closed, transitioning the night sky back to darkness.

Suddenly Zane caught a flash on the summit below. It began as a point of light then expanded into a towering fireball.

They must have left an explosive device behind, he thought.

They knew their outpost was breached, and they wanted to destroy any remaining evidence of their presence.

Zane turned and shouted for everyone to hold on.

Seconds later, the chopper was rocked violently by the blast wave. The big bird tilted on its side, shaking from the impact. There were yells and screams as everyone rolled toward the bay door.

After rocking dangerously, the bird finally righted itself and continued on, shooting out over the dark jungle below.

CHAPTER SIXTY

One Week Later
Key Largo, Florida

ZANE WATSON PLACED the last of the four drinks on the tray then left the kitchen and exited the house through the sliding glass door. The sun had almost sunk below the horizon as he stepped out onto the deck and closed the screen panel behind him.

The sound of soft conversation greeted him as he made his way over to the semicircle of chairs. He approached the one on the far left first. A brown-haired woman was seated there, her beautiful features flickering in the light of a nearby tiki torch. He extended a pineapple martini. "Dr. Mills."

"Why thank you, Dr. Watson," she said.

He moved two chairs down and handed Brett Foster a bottled beer.

"Thank you, sir," he replied.

Zane then approached the last chair and lifted a glass off

the tray. "And finally, a non-alcoholic watermelon and kiwifruit splash for our nondrinking resident Christian."

"Thank you," Amanda said, taking the glass from him. "Hey, I did have two glasses of wine. I just have my limits. Any more and I might start dancing."

Brett snapped his fingers and pointed at the house. "Zane, another glass of chard for the lady, please."

Amanda popped his arm playfully.

After setting the tray down on the table, Zane took his beer and sank into the seat next to Katiya. She reached over and gave his hand a little squeeze out of the sight of the others.

"I still can't get over this view," Amanda said.

Zane nodded in agreement as he looked out at the private cove behind the home. It was encircled by palm trees, their limbs swaying gently in the evening breeze. In the distance, the last sliver of sun sat on the ocean, casting a few final rays of orange and lavender across the water.

"It must be nice to have rich friends," Brett said. "So how did you swing this place again?"

"Let's just say we've developed a bartering system," Zane said. "I maintain his planes. I clean them, service the engines... I do whatever's necessary to keep them purring like kittens." He waved his hand toward the cove. "In return, he lets me enjoy this little slice of heaven. Oh, and I also get to use his condo in Breckenridge if I'm in the mood for a change in climate."

Brett shook his head. "The southern tip of Florida or the mountains of Colorado? It must be horribly stressful trying to make up your mind."

"I think you're getting the better end of that barter," Katiya said.

Zane smiled and took another sip. The four sat for a few minutes in silence, enjoying the view. Suddenly Zane heard the sound of flapping wings. He looked up and saw several white ibis soaring across the cove before disappearing into a grove of palms.

Brett looked at Katiya. "So, you really believe the grays were fallen angels? Considering your profession, I might have expected a different answer."

Katiya kept her eyes fixed on the sunset. "I only said it was possible, which is a big move for me. I have to follow the facts where they lead. As you know, I'm not a particularly religious person." She took a sip of her martini and set the glass down on the table. "But through my years of research, I have come to believe in the supernatural. The evidence for another realm of existence is overwhelming, and I accepted that long before our little trip into the jungle." She looked at Brett. "As for the grays, I can't rule out the possibility that they were some sort of alien species either. But everything we discovered, particularly what was in that temple, points to the biblical narrative."

Brett's eyes narrowed. "So you're saying they built that temple?"

Amanda addressed him. "Katiya and I have discussed this over the last few days. We believe the Nephilim built all of the stone structures we encountered. The bridge, the mountain tunnels, and the temple."

"Remember the Nephilim were incredibly large," Katiya

added. "Both the ancient texts and the historical record indicate many were in excess of fifteen feet tall. It would've taken immensely large beings to transport some of those stones to the mountain summit."

Amanda nodded in agreement.

Brett looked at Amanda. "You mentioned that the fallen angels descended on Mount Hermon. Let's assume for argument's sake that story is true. How did their offspring, the giants, end up in South America?"

"That's a good question," Amanda said. "Many believe there was a global diaspora of Nephilim after the Israelites conquered the Levant. I'm sure you remember God instructing them to wipe out the tribes living there." After Brett nodded, she continued. "You may also remember that the Israelites weren't completely successful in carrying that out. Some of the Nephilim fled on foot to places like Egypt. Others boarded boats that took them to points as far away as North and South America."

Brett gave her a skeptical look.

Amanda continued. "As Katiya said, the presence of massive skeletons across the globe has been confirmed time and time again."

"Assuming they were there, why did the Nephilim build that temple?" Brett asked.

"The statues clearly show there was fallen angel worship at the site," Katiya said. "My guess is they probably led the local tribes in fallen angel worship. In fact, it looks as though that temple might still be in use… or was in use, I should say." She took another sip of her martini then set the glass down.

"Who knows," Zane added. "That might somehow explain how the Dawanis became so evil."

Katiya looked at him. "I told Amanda that very thing on our way down here."

"You know, I saw something interesting on that hologram on board the ship," Zane said. "There were red dots scattered across the earth. I wonder what that meant?"

Katiya's brow furrowed. "Did you notice where they were located?"

"No. Actually, wait, that's not true. I do remember seeing a large pulsating one over northern Brazil, which I assumed showed the location of the craft."

"I'm still in the alien camp," Brett said. "And what you're describing sounds like some sort of navigation system."

As the group fell silent, Zane looked out over the water. The sun had dipped below the horizon.

Finally, Amanda cleared her throat and said, "We all saw that portal open up. I think the red dots indicated portals. I would love to have seen where they were."

"That's a good point," Brett said.

Amanda scooted her chair around so that she was facing the others. "As a Christian, I believe we're living in the last days. Jesus said in Luke that there would be signs in the sun, moons, and stars. It makes me wonder if he was speaking of portals being opened. He said things would be so bad that men would faint from terror, afraid of what would come upon the world."

Zane was about to respond when he felt his cell vibrating against his thigh. A second later, the sound of classical music filled the air. He reached into his pocket for his phone.

Brett laughed. "That's your ring tone?"

"You know, that's *really* old school, Zane," Amanda said.

"That's because I'm an old guy, Amanda." He looked at the name of the incoming number and engaged the call. "Well, if it isn't Miss Carmen Petrosino." He put the phone on speaker so everyone could hear.

"Hey!"

"What's up?" Zane asked.

"Just a little pissed and needed to vent."

Zane frowned. "Really? What's wrong?"

"It's Ross. He—"

"Wait, I thought you were down at the beach."

"I was. I went down to Ocean City with some friends. That is until Ross called."

Zane lifted his eyebrows. "Uh-oh."

"Yeah, he manages to reach me, and the next thing I know I'm having to cut my vacation short."

"Why?"

"I had to fly to Romania on a wild-goose chase."

"What?" Zane frowned. "So you have to get right back on another plane?"

Carmen gave a long sigh. "I'm so tired, I feel like I could sleep for days."

"So, what was going on in Romania?"

"Nothing. Absolutely nothing. And that's the whole point. Some farmers were hearing strange noises in a few remote mountain valleys, so Skinner and I were handpicked to go hike around out in the middle of nowhere. I told Ross it was just the movement of tectonic plates, but he wouldn't believe me.

He was convinced the sounds were somehow connected to what was going on in Brazil. He kept referring to it as a European portal."

"So let me guess, it *was* tectonic plates?"

"Of course!"

Zane gave a chuckle. "Well, at least Romania is a neat place. Been there several times."

"Speaking of which, where are you? I was surprised you didn't come with us."

Zane felt his face flush. "I'm... I'm taking a little break."

"So was I. Ross didn't call you?"

Zane hesitated for a moment. "To be honest, I told him I was going to be in an area without cell reception. I gave him the address so he could send someone out if he absolutely had to get in touch."

There was a long pause. Finally, Carmen asked, "I'm sorry... if you don't have reception there, then how am I speaking to you?"

Zane cringed. "Okay, the part about the reception is true... but it's only true some of the time. You wouldn't believe how bad—"

"You know what?" Carmen asked.

"What?"

"You're a certified jerk."

Zane laughed and blew on the phone's mic. "I'm sorry, Carmen. I can't hear you. We're having signal problems again."

"You're the king of jerks!" she screamed.

Zane ended the call and dropped the phone onto a towel at

his feet.

Turning toward the others, he lifted his empty bottle and asked, "Can I get anyone another drink?"

Did you enjoy *The Portal*? Be among the first to learn about John's future releases and special discounts by signing up for his newsletter at:

www.johnsneeden.com/?page_id=108

The process is quick and simple. Your email address will not be sold to anyone else, and the newsletter will only be used to inform readers of new releases or special discounts.

AUTHOR'S NOTE

Dear Reader,

Thank you so much for purchasing *The Portal*. I know there are a lot of ways you can spend your entertainment dollars, so I'm grateful you decided to spend yours on one of my novels. I'm currently working on the third book in the series, which will be released soon.

I sincerely hope you found *The Portal* entertaining. If you did, I'd like to ask you to do something: please go online and post an honest review. The reviews of satisfied readers are vital to the success of every author, and please know that your effort will be greatly appreciated.

Please also let me know your thoughts by emailing me at johnsneedenauthor@gmail.com. I love hearing from my readers.

Thanks again and I hope to hear from you soon!

John Sneeden

ABOUT THE AUTHOR

John was born on the coast of North Carolina, and thanks to his mother, a voracious reader, he began discovering books at a very early age. If not outside playing basketball or fishing with friends, he could be found curled up in a living room chair with an Edgar Rice Burroughs novel. In fact, it was Burroughs who first kindled his love for escapist fiction.

After a twenty-five year career in banking, John decided to turn his life-long passion for reading into a career as an author. He still lives in the southern United States, and when not writing he loves to travel and follow NHL hockey.

You can be among the first to learn about John's future releases and special discounts by signing up for his newsletter at:

www.johnsneeden.com/?page_id=108

The process is quick and simple. Your email address will not be sold to anyone else, and the newsletter will only be used to inform readers of new releases or special discounts.

You can also visit John's website at www.johnsneeden.com, like John's author page on Facebook (www.facebook.com/JohnSneedenAuthor), follow him on Twitter (@JohnSneeden), or email him at johnsneedenauthor@gmail.com. He loves to hear from his readers.

Made in the USA
Middletown, DE
01 April 2022